For my mother, I

Acknowledgements ʃ

I would like to thank Claire Harrigan for patiently letting me pick her brains for veterinary details, Michael Tyrrell for giving me a glimpse into the hazards of an architect's life, and Janet Grant for providing my Italian with a Florentine flourish. Special thanks also to Carolyn Caughey, my editor, and to Sarah Molloy, my agent, for their continued encouragement and support.

The girl's knees buckled.

It was as the forceps were thrust into the dog's stomach cavity that her slight frame slid in loose-limbed slow motion to the surgery floor. The unpleasant sound of her blonde head colliding with antiseptic tiles distracted Alexandra Flynn's attention for a moment as she dabbed expertly around the open wound with a cotton wool swab. A professional glance at the crumpled body on the floor reassured her that the girl was, as usual, breathing smoothly, in no danger of choking on her tongue. This was not the first time.

'She's at it again, Maddy,' Alex remarked to her head nurse standing at the opposite side of the operating table. At least she knew she could rely on the oak construction of Maddy Carne's legs.

'Silly girl, she is,' Maddy snapped without sympathy.

The nurse's stout rectangular frame was encased in a green gown and mask, short bristly grey hair clamped down in an efficient hair-grip, green eyes younger than her fifty-five-plus years. Witch's eyes, Alex always thought with affection. Not even heavy spectacles dimmed the effect.

'And she hopes to become a vet!' Maddy snorted in disgust as her foot stepped over the inert body on the floor.

'Here's the culprit.' As Alex bent her head over the black labrador that was stretched supine along the table, she did not allow the swan-dive of her weak-kneed young assistant to break her concentration. Carefully she withdrew the triumphant forceps. In their jaws perched a slimy rubber squash ball. She dropped it into the metal kidney basin that Maddy held out and as her latex fingers began the process of inserting the needle with seamstress skill, she nodded in the direction of the girl on the floor.

'Maddy, you had better check on Lizzie. She's still out for the count. I can manage here.'

She took her usual pride in the precision of the neat, double row of vicryl sutures.

'She can wait,' Maddy grunted dismissively.

The nurse's firm mouth softened into a benign crescent as she adjusted the tube that fed a mixture of oxygen, nitrous oxide and halothane into the labrador's throat. With legs spread wide in undignified display, the animal lay on its back in a plastic cradle that exposed its soft, vulnerable stomach to Alex's surgical skill. Its dark lips had twisted loosely into an imitation snarl but this sham of ferocity only sharpened Maddy Carne's protective juices.

'Silly girl,' she repeated her earlier words, this time with marshmallow indulgence. 'You shouldn't go swallowing rubber balls.'

'Last time it was a stone and before that a metal keyring. Obviously takes the concept of extra minerals in her diet a little too seriously,' Alex laughed, as she sprayed the two-inch mid-line incision with antibiotic solution. 'I've told the owners to put a muzzle on her outdoors and to keep small household objects out of her reach until she's grown out of the habit. But do they bother?'

'Shouldn't be allowed,' Maddy grunted. Her ideas on pet ownership would have done credit to a Stalin manifesto on state control. 'Some people have no sense.' Another grunt for emphasis.

An echo rose from the floor in the form of a mild groan. The blonde ponytail on the tiles was starting to stir.

'Maddy, you had better see to Lizzie. I'll finish up here.'

The operating theatre was long, narrow and strictly utilitarian. Metal dominated the room. The black padded table stood centre-stage with a back-up chorus of neatly stacked shelves, a trolley of elderly gas cylinders, a chrome steriliser holding what looked like instruments of torture and in the corner the inevitable and essential steel sink for scrubbing up. All angular, uncompromising and battleship grey. But to Alex Flynn it was as familiar and comfortable as her favourite armchair.

She had been a part of this practice for nearly five years. Was it really that long? She still remembered vividly arriving straight from Bristol veterinary school, all green and sticky nerves. No trace of that now. Five years of peering down cats' throats and up dogs' rears, pursuing bashful cows across muddy fields and horses round stables soon rubbed off the dewy green down. An old-timer now. With the scars to show for it. Her shin still ached from an argument with a wilful horse's metal-clad hoof the day before. She smiled forgivingly.

Alex drew together the edges of shaven skin and accepted the nylon thread from Maddy. 'She'll probably have quite a headache after that bump. Let's hope today will finally persuade her she's not cut out for surgery.'

'Not much chance of that. Like I said, some people have no sense.'

But the hands that eased the animal-loving young hopeful into a sitting position were gentle, the voice a notch less gruff. Lizzie Baker stumbled to her feet, supported by Maddy's strong arm.

'I'm sorry, Alex,' wailed the eighteen-year-old. 'Ever so sorry. It won't happen again, I promise. I did last a bit longer than last time, didn't I?'

Alex glanced up at the waxy, pallid face and decided to keep her comments for later. 'Yes, you did. Go and sit down in the office now. A cup of tea will make you feel better. How's the head?'

'Not too bad.' The small, delicate mouth was twisted in a grimace that belied the words and the blue eyes still looked mildly out of focus.

'Go on, Lizzie, go and sit down. Maddy will cast her unforgiving eye over your latest collection of bruises, won't you, Maddy?'

Maddy grunted.

The girl turned self-consciously to her support. 'I'm terribly sorry, Maddy. I was sure it wouldn't happen this time. I did lots of deep breathing like you told me but . . .'

'Shut up, Lizzie,' Alex interrupted. 'Let me get on with this poor animal in peace.'

Maddy marched her charge out through the surgery door and down the corridor towards the restroom. Alex automatically checked the halothane dial and registered the sturdy rise and fall of the dog's black drum of a chest. Humming under her breath, she resumed the stitching.

A dental extraction, an abscess to lance and a cat castration followed next. All went smoothly, though the tom cat, a big battered bruiser who bore a striking resemblance to a ginger Boris Karloff, proved as reluctant to yield to the anaesthetic as he was to his hapless rival suitors.

When they were all reclining docilely in recovery cages, Alex went to check on the black labrador. Her whiffling snores were rustling the paper on the floor of her cage. She slipped open the catch and ran her hand over the shoulder and along the muscular back. The skin rippled with pleasure. Another satisfied customer. She rumpled the sleepy ear, fingers unconsciously seeking out the sweet scratchy spot, checked her temperature and heart rate, then with a final pat wished her rabbity dreams.

She wanted a word with Gordon.

Gordon Tamworth was the head of the veterinary practice. He had set it up thirty-five years earlier in Marlborough in a tiny red brick house perched jauntily on the steep hill climbing up to the common. It had not taken the inhabitants long to discover that his skilful ministrations made the Himalayan trek up to his base camp well worth the effort. The practice had flourished and his patients, animals and owners alike, had breathed a collective sigh of relief when he finally acknowledged that his surgery was bursting at the seams and moved to a rambling early Victorian sprawl just off the broad High Street. Its graceless proportions offered scope for a free-flowing expansion into an abundance of high-ceilinged nooks and crannies.

Alex marched down one of its flagstoned corridors to the back of the house where Gordon was in the habit of tucking himself away. She had a juicy bone to pick with him. His office had been selected with care. It was away from the business end of the house, next to the big old kitchen and cannily arranged to be back to back with the feline-strewn Aga. Gordon Tamworth's long, lean bones felt the cold despite, or maybe because of, a snowbound childhood spent in the grip of the Highlands of Scotland.

The door was open. As always. Alex tapped it lightly to gain his attention and went in.

'Alex, my dear. Exquisite timing. I've just made myself a pot of tea.' The Scottish burr had not deserted his tongue despite nearly half a century in Sassenach heartland. He leaned back in his desk chair and removed a cup from an upturned row of them on the windowsill behind him. Bone china molehills on a wide white runway. 'How did this afternoon go? No trouble from that grouchy old tom?'

'It was a bloodbath. Only Maddy emerged unscathed. His claws were everywhere.'

Gordon chuckled delightedly. The older and more crochety the patients, the more he seemed to care about their welfare. In his early sixties himself, he clearly identified with their bad-tempered antics. Not that Gordon would ever indulge in such displays himself. His claws remained sheathed in gentlemanly velvet. Any agitation could only be counted by the number of pots of tea he made himself each day. Alex watched him pour the treacly brew into the cup, his hair fine and white as spiderwebs floating round his angular cheekboned features; eyebrows like snowy caterpillars drawn together in concentration.

It was difficult to be stern with him.

'Gordon, it won't work. She's putting herself through hell to please you.'

'Who is?'

'Lizzie, of course.'

Alex accepted the tea and added a good slug of milk to temper its ferocity. Gordon inhaled the black fumes with a sigh of pleasure and ignored the milk.

'Lizzie? She loves it here. Everything to do with animals.'

'No, Gordon. She loves the animals. Give her a sick dog, cat, parrot or even snake to care for and she's in her element. But she doesn't love everything. Not when that everything includes surgery.'

Gordon's grey eyes hovered for a moment, then lowered to the scarred surface of his desk. 'She fainted again?'

'Yes.'

'Hurt herself?'

'The usual collection of bruises.'

'Poor lass. Ambition isn't enough, it seems, when you have a constitution that wilts at the sight of blood.'

But they both knew why.

Lizzie Bridges was Gordon's great-niece, on his wife's side. Ten years earlier Lizzie's mother was driving her daughter and Gordon's wife to the Bath & West Show, an annual family expedition down the A4. A caravan jack-knifed in front of them. Only Lizzie survived. And there had been a lot of blood.

Alex sipped her tea to fill the momentary silence. For the hundredth time she wondered if its bitterness was intended by Gordon to be a self-inflicted penance for failing to drive his wife to the agricultural show himself.

'She's so eager to please you, Gordon.' She could not bring herself to explain that it was Lizzie's own guilt trip. To make up for her mother killing his wife. 'But you have to accept that it's your ambition, not hers. It's not fair on her.' After a pause she added, 'Or us.'

His grey eyes lifted heavily to hers.

'Of course, you're right,' he said softly, the Scottish lilt more pronounced now. A sure sign of emotion in Gordon. 'It's not fair. And not professional.' Unexpectedly he smiled, a mischievous tilt of the mouth. 'Thank you, Alex. I rely on you to keep me on the professional straight and narrow, to stop me wandering into senile chaos and confusion.'

She grinned, relieved to see him back in control. 'Don't worry, you old reprobate, I won't tell anyone who really does all the work round here.'

He laughed, a boisterous sound which awoke the sleeping mongrel that was sprawled across his feet under the desk. It wandered out, yawned and stretched noisily, scratched a few fleas for good measure and ambled over to say hello to Alex. It plonked its head on her lap and waved a plumed tail at her.

'Hi, Bruno. Did we wake you up?' She tickled his chocolate ears.

'I'll speak to her.'

'Tell her she can give operations a miss?'

'Yes. But she'll be disappointed.'

Alex shook her head. 'No, I think you'll find she will be relieved to be just a veterinary nurse, but with no operations. It's unusual, I know, but let her spend her days caring and fussing over the animals and she'll be happy. She's not like me. Desperate to be a vet ever since I was knee-high to an iguana.'

Gordon Tamworth looked across at his highly qualified and highly motivated young colleague and felt an unflattering tug of envy. She cared so much. The way he had been what seemed like aeons ago. He felt a certain proprietary pride in her, a sort of surrogate satisfaction. Probably unwarranted, he admitted to himself. She may have come to him five years earlier wet behind the ears, brown eyes unnervingly bright with anticipation, but she would have made a success of it whatever practice she had joined. Even without his guiding hand. But it pleased him to think he had helped along the way. Contributed. Since losing his wife, that seemed important. To contribute. But clearly the time had come to stop over-contributing to that skinny wee lass, Lizzie.

'All right, her surgery stints can come to an end, if that is what she'd prefer.'

He stood up, his lean frame looking more like that of a solicitor than a vet. A lifetime of training by his wife still kept his suits smart and his shirt collars clean. Unfortunately it did not extend as far as his office. All around him in splendid disarray galloped a haphazard jumble. Books and papers wrestled with methodically misplaced claw clippers, plastic specimen bottles, woolly scarves and dog biscuits.

'I'm sure she will be grateful, Gordon.'

He nodded, conscious for the first time of how much he actually did rely on Alex Flynn. It made him feel like Methuselah. He attempted to study her face objectively but failed. It was too familiar. Too veiled by fond images. Her large brown eyes set wide apart, full capable mouth above a deceptively gentle chin. Don't underestimate that chin. The cloud of wavy, coppery hair usually tamed into an obedient fox's brush behind her head by a scarf. A favourite green one today. And the ubiquitous, practical trousers. Cords, jeans or summer slacks. But always trousers.

He draped a long, comfortable arm around her shoulder. 'Come on, let's go give Lizzie the good news.'

The red Fiesta missed Alex by at least an inch. And only then because she stood on the brakes. The teenager grinned through his side window at her as he blared past in the middle of the road and raced on down the hill. Machismo intact.

Alex waited a beat for her heart to climb back into her chest, then persuaded her quivering Clio to resume its steep climb out of Marlborough. It took the alpine bend cautiously, giving her ample time for a glance down over the edge to the studious, red brick portals of the college below where it lay dusted with evening sunlight. Deserted now, as the summer holidays had set in.

So many facts in so many heads. A mild shudder crept through her at the memory of her own experience of all those hours spent slogging over dutiful textbooks. Years of it, centuries it felt at the time. Biochemistry had been her pet hate. Grindingly heartless. Biology heartless? A contradiction in terms. She laughed at herself and slipped into fourth gear as the car crested the climb. The engine purred with relief and bounded downhill through the woods towards Pewsey.

She knew just how it felt. Eager to get home, to put its engine in neutral and switch off. It had been a long day. She felt hot and clammy. Needed a shower. She glanced at the clock. Nearly seven o'clock and the heat of the day was only just beginning to fade. At least with the windows down, there was a breeze. Optimistically she wondered if Rory had thought to put something in the oven.

A juicy, meaty aroma greeted her at the door. It reminded her stomach it was starving. In the kitchen she found Rory up to his elbows in onions and mushrooms.

'Smells great,' she said, planted a kiss on his cheek and dipped a finger in the cheese sauce bubbling on the stove.

At the welcome sight of his wife, Rory Flynn abandoned his intention to drop his nugget of good news casually into the conversation at the end of the meal.

'We won the contract,' he announced with accompanying fanfare and theatrical flourish of a wooden spoon. Globules of cheese sauce flicked unheeded to the floor.

'The redevelopment contract?'

He grinned like a cat that has swallowed not only the cream, but the dish as well. 'Got it in one.'

'Rory, you're a genius.'

'I know,' he laughed modestly.

He made an unlikely chef in his pale grey pinstripe. The formality of his office suit was softened by the tie draped loosely round his neck and the length of his bushy black curls. The high forehead and dark, interested eyes were those of a Russian pianist on a good day. Rory Flynn was in fact a qualified architect. Three years earlier he had launched a company in Swindon with his partner, Gary Saunders. They had scrabbled and hustled like terriers for the first twelve months. Gradually their hard work had paid off and the contracts started trickling in. House extensions and shop refits grew into housing developments, small factories and a chain of petrol stations. But this was their first really big contract. A multi-million town centre redevelopment.

'You beat that London firm with their Prince Charles-type designs?'

'Wiped the floor with them.'

Alex draped her arms round his neck and bestowed a long, slow, seductive kiss. 'Brilliance is very tasty,' she murmured.

Rory responded instantly. 'Who needs food?' he asked, tossing the wooden spoon into the sink and wrapping his arms around her.

'I do,' Alex squealed and disentangled herself from his grasp. 'I'm ravenous.'

Rory groaned. 'It was meant to be a rhetorical question.'

'I stink of pig sties. Ben Larcher's old sow put me on my back this evening.'

'Lucky old sow,' Rory laughed unsympathetically.

'You crabby bastard,' Alex whacked him robustly on the chest.

In self defence Rory seized her hand to pull her to him and

suddenly noticed the set of deep diagonal scratches that dragged across the back of her wrist.

'I didn't know sows had claws.'

'It was a grouchy old ginger tom that didn't want to lose his balls.'

'Ouch,' Rory winced, 'I don't blame him.' Nevertheless he kissed the offending hand but pulled a face. 'A bit pongy.'

She laughed. 'I warned you. I had a wash at the farm but I'm still disgusting.'

Reluctantly Rory abandoned his wife to rescue the cheese sauce which was already showing signs of burning. 'Go and have a shower. Dinner will be ready by then. After that, we can resume where we left off.'

'You've got yourself a deal, genius.'

As Alex walked out of the kitchen, Rory called after her, 'I nearly forgot, there's a postcard for you on the hall table. From your sister.'

The tree was very tall. It arched over the upturned heads of the two young children like branches of the sky. One tugged at her fringe nervously.

'Why me?'

The other turned pleading eyes on her. 'Go on, you have to do it.'

'Why does it have to be me?' The tree looked taller by the minute, the branch higher.

'Because you're better at climbing than me.' Then the trump card. 'And you're older.'

The taller child looked down at her sister. Being older was something like eating candyfloss at the fair. It tasted scrummy at first, but too much of it could make you sick.

'But Tinker is your kitten.'

As if the sound of his name prompted hope, a faint pink-mouthed mew drifted down to them. Both pairs of eyes stared up at the black-and-white rigid ball of fluff clutching to a branch with needle claws.

'Poor Tinky,' the younger sister called, her voice choking with tears.

'We could call a fireman.' The idea brought relief.

'No, Ali, no.' The voice rose to a shriek. 'Tinky will fall.'

'Firemen always rescue cats, Zena.' Alex took two steps backwards, eyes riveted to the branch. She risked a glance across the stubbly field to where she knew the hole was in their back garden hedge. The sight did not reassure her. It was a long way for eight-year-old legs to run. And they were supposed to be playing inside the garden, not in the field. Daddy's orders.

The hole was Zena's. The door to unpermitted freedom. Deaf to her older sister's pleas, Zena had flouted the rules yet again and set off blithely with the kitten purring in her arms. She had got as far as the middle of the field when the dog bounded up from nowhere and Tinker evaporated in a flurry of hisses and claws. In the direction of the woods. It looked like the hundred metre sprint. Cat in the lead by a whisker, dog ecstatic in pursuit and in their wake the puffing, pumping six-year-old. Not even breath to scream at the marauder.

Alex had watched the scene unfold within the circle of the hole in the hedge and knew with a child's prescient certainty that she was the one who would be punished for this. Nevertheless she squeezed through the hedge like a criminal and chased across the stubble. The dog had treed the cat and lost interest after a few token barks. Tinker fled to a higher bough at each one of them. Zena was frantic at the base.

'Ali, get Tinky down, Ali, quickly, Ali, he'll fall.'

Alex now faced the inevitable. She abandoned hope of friendly firemen with extending ladders and attempted to climb. After several failed attempts, she managed to grasp the lowest branch by balancing on the wobbly platform of her sister's back. Her fingers clung precariously for a second and the hard ground beckoned invitingly, but with a determined heave, she jerked herself up on to the first rung. The climb from then on was not difficult, the tree's arms comfortingly broad and numerous.

But it did not take long for the height to crash into her mind. It made her sight blur, turned her limbs to lead. The ground was soon a nightmare away and Zena just a smudge.

'Ali, hurry, Ali, Tinky's scared. Hurry.'

Scared? Tinker was a cat. Cats were not afraid of heights. Her father had told her that. High up in the canopy, she twisted the aching muscles of her neck and looked up at the nervous animal. He was just above her, to her left. His yellow eyes looked distinctly disturbed by her approach, even annoyed. But not scared.

'Hurry, Ali.'

The voice made her glance down. A mistake. The tree swayed, the sky lurched and her stomach catapulted into her mouth. Sunday roast and blackberry crumble rained down the tree and splashed over her new white tee-shirt. Her foothold vanished and she slithered down the trunk, clinging in panic to the grating bark. The fall came to a jarring halt as she crunched into a lower branch. Her teeth snapped shut on her tongue and she tasted blood.

'Yuk, Ali, that's disgusting.'

'Shut up, Zena, shut up.'

Desperation took over. Ignoring all alarm bells, she flung herself up the tree and out along the branch where the cat was crouching. He spat at her.

'Come on, Tinky. I'll take you down.' Her voice was quavering so much, the words of comfort came out like a threat.

Tinker backed off another metre.

Alex followed him. The branch grew alarmingly narrow. Even Zena stared, mouth open, no sound.

'Tinky, good Tinky,' Alex croaked soothingly. She held out her hand to him.

Claws raked across the back of it. A flash of black and white and the cat was gone.

Alex screamed at the image of his lifeless body broken on the ground at her sister's feet. Her cheek rested against the warmth of the mottled branch and her eyes fought for a glimpse of him beneath the waves of foliage. A scrabbling, scurrying noise penetrated her fear and she turned her head to catch a glimpse of Tinker backing down the trunk of the tree at top feline speed. A final death-defying leap landed him smugly on the ground where he was instantly scooped up by his mistress.

'Tinky, Tinky, you clever boy. You did it yourself.'

From her eyrie Alex watched Zena bury her face in her pet's fur and smother him with kisses. He took exception to this undignified treatment, leapt out of her arms and made a dash for home.

'Tinky,' Zena squealed and raced after him across the field as fast as her stringy legs could scramble over the stubble.

A tight bubble of misery seemed to burst inside Alex and the tears came. Now Zena was not there, she could let herself cry. Alone, deserted, suspended twenty feet above the earth, she wanted to die. If she just let go of the branch, she could fall effortlessly to her death. Then no one would be angry with her. They would be too busy being sorry. Particularly Zena.

Having made up her mind to die, she released her grip on the branch. But instead of toppling off, she eased her foot to a new position and clutched at another handhold. Very very carefully she backed along her perch. Once in reassuring contact with the trunk again, she made the decision to postpone dying this time, but the nightmare journey to the ground took her ten hour-long minutes. When she finally dropped the last few feet, her clothes were contoured to her body by sweat and redesigned with smears of green and brown, as well as the more colourful hues of her lunch. Knees and hands were shaking and one shin was stripped of skin.

Somehow she reached the hole in the hedge.

Zena was sitting in the middle of the lawn, softly stroking Tinker who was lapping neatly at a saucer of milk. In front of the hole towered her mother. The usually gentle mouth was stern.

'Alex, how dare you sneak away? Leaving your little sister like that and setting her a bad example. I expect better from you. And look at the state of your clothes! What will your father think?'

Zena looked up with wide innocent eyes and smiled sweetly.

The hot water made the scratches and the memories sting. Alex sank lower beneath the bubbles. A steamy bath instead of a shower gave her more time to think. To unblock the storm drains.

Zena was coming to stay.

She rubbed the back of her hand and pushed Tinker from her mind.

Tinker. Her mother and father. All long since dead and buried in neat, well-tended graves.

Only Zena and herself.

The postcard was from Wichita, Kansas. Why Wichita for heaven's sake? Last Alex heard, she was happily married in Denver. Her sister had been living in America for the last eight years, ever since the day after her eighteenth birthday. She had packed a skimpy bag and left. No word for over a year. By the time a card eventually arrived, of a massive Californian sequoia, her father had succumbed to the last of his three heart attacks and her mother was eaten up by cancer. Zena missed both funerals.

Postcards had trickled in erratically. A summer in New England, a winter in Aspen or Florida. Addresses changed almost before Alex could reply. Twice had come an unexpected phone call, both times requesting money. Both times Alex had obliged. What Zena did for a living over there was never divulged but two years ago a letter from Denver had announced that she was now married. Even enclosed a photograph of a big-fisted, rugged outdoor type who apparently owned a lumber business and did very nicely thank you. Postcards followed at intervals from Barbados, Tahiti, Lake Placid and even the Arctic Circle. Nice holidays, nice life.

So why was she coming over here?

Rory was annoyed but decided not to let it show.

By the time Alex had emerged from the bathroom, the meal was past its consume-by date and the planned celebration was as flat as the champagne. He had to admit she did make an effort to be both contrite and convivial, but her heart was not in it. Nevertheless, over coffee in the sitting-room she sat back in her armchair, a feathery white ball of cat on her lap and smiled encouragingly.

'Let me see the completed designs. I want to lay eyes on the stunning masterpiece that is going to put Flynn & Saunders on the architectural map.' Her enthusiasm was almost convincing.

'You saw them develop step by step as I drew them up.'

'But I haven't seen the finished product. Go on, give me the slick presentation.'

'If you've got it, flaunt it?'

'Exactly,' she laughed.

At first, as Rory displayed the outline proposals he remained calmly professional, but as he started explaining the more intricate drawings of the scheme designs, his involvement got the better of him. Spatial arrangements of shopping precincts, roof pitch and window line swept him along at a pace that required no more than comprehending noises from her. When he had finished, she raised her glass to him.

'Positively lyrical. No wonder you won the contract. I congratulate you.' She sipped the lukewarm champagne. 'You deserve it.'

'And Gary. He did his share.'

'Of course. I bet he's whooping it up tonight.'

'Probably dancing naked in some Swindon park, surrounded by vestal virgins and howling at the moon.'

Gary Saunders was three years younger than his thirty-year-old partner and had not quite outgrown the student lifestyle.

'What about you?' Rory asked. 'Feel up to dancing naked?'

Alex grimaced. 'More like the howling part.'

Rory studied her for a moment, then rose and fetched the postcard from the hall table. He propped it up on the mantelpiece where its sunset view of the River Arkansas spread an instant pall of gloom.

'Come on, Alex, it won't be that bad. She has a husband in Denver, so she can't camp on us too long.'

Alex swirled her glass to stimulate the sagging bubbles. 'What if the husband is no longer on the scene?'

Rory poured himself another coffee and thought about that one. 'In that case, she'll stay for a while, then find herself a place of her own. She's quite old enough to look after herself.'

He had only met Zena Chiverton once: at Alex's twenty-first birthday party. He remembered her as being pretty, but not strikingly so. Her auburn hair had been styled into a glossy jaw-length bob and her pale skin warmed with a light dusting of freckles. Not a bad figure but not as shapely as Alex's. No, her attraction had lain elsewhere. It was in the eyes and the way she moved. A tawny young lioness on the prowl. Rory still recalled the anxious, proprietorial concern in her father's eyes as he stood stiff and unwelcome in the shadows of the doorway, tracking both daughters' every move. It had been a relief to whisk Alex away once more to college in Bristol where normal service could be resumed. Memories of the passionate, self-centred intensity of those days provoked a fond smile.

'What are you grinning at?' Alex asked and the cat on her lap opened one curious eye as though interested in the answer. 'You're wearing your that-was-a-bloody-good-bonk leer.'

Rory chuckled, amused that she could read him so accurately. 'Not far off. Just remembering the good old days.'

'Meaning these are the bad new days?' she teased.

'As if I'd dare!'

'You'd better not. Though with Zena lying in wait for us, I'm not so sure.'

Rory picked up the postcard, flipped it over and read out loud the bold, rounded handwriting. '"In England soon. Just me. Beg a bed. Your only Zena." Not exactly informative.'

'That's typical.'

'And what does she mean by "Your only Zena"?'

'Who knows? Maybe emphasising that she is the only blood-relation I have left. Therefore entitled to "beg a bed".'

Rory walked over to where his wife was sitting and placed the postcard in her hand. She accepted it but did not quite manage to hide from him her reluctance. Ignoring the groan from the wooden frame, he sat himself on the chintzy arm of her chair and lightly rumpled the loose folds of her hair, still damp from the bath.

'What is it, Alex? What is it that worries you about Zena?'

A shrug. 'Nothing.'

'She's your sister. You should be pleased to see her after all these years.'

'I am, I really am.' She looked up earnestly, brown eyes eager to reassure him. Seeing his quizzical eyebrow, a self-deprecating huff escaped her. 'Maybe it doesn't look that way, but I am. I was always extremely fond of her.' She smiled. 'Everyone was.'

'So what's the problem?'

Another shrug, more relaxed this time. 'Just nervous, I suppose.'

'Nervous of what?'

'That after all these years, we will have changed. You can't ever go back.'

'Would you want to?'

Alex leant her head against his arm. 'No. No, I wouldn't.'

Rory stared down at the closed eyelids and wondered what pictures lay behind them.

'You're tired. A good night's rest and you'll take Zena and all her problems in your stride. Just like you do with Farmer Larcher's rampant sow.'

'You hope,' she said and they both laughed. A faint purr escaped from her lap and joined in.

Not long after, they made their way upstairs. Alex rooted out another furball that was curled up on the bed, a skinny Siamese. She fed them both in the kitchen in the vain hope of persuading them to spend the night anywhere but on the duvet. When she returned to the bedroom, Rory was waiting for her. They made love and fell asleep draped round each other's familiar curves. Alex was grateful to slip away from everything, down a hole of dream-lined sleep.

2 ∫

Rory woke to the warmth of soft fur against his cheek and the vibration of what sounded like a rackety diesel engine. He recognised the motor as that of the big, white cat purring rustily in the back of its throat. Opening his eyes a generous slit, he drew in a deep breath, content to lie there for the moment with a bar of sunlight slanting across his legs. Dustmotes danced in the spotlight. The summer showed every sign of going on for ever.

Eventually it dawned on his somnolent brain that there was only one set of blue leg bumps in the duvet. And then he remembered. Alex had been called out to a foaling over at Wilton in the early hours. There was always a sense of loss when he awoke without her.

'All right, Horatio, breakfast time.'

It was at least a comfort to have someone to talk to in bed, even if it was only a scrappy pair of feline ears. The purrs grew more staccato and Horatio rose from Alex's pillow to start kneading his great talons into Rory's chest. The furry warmth at his cheek remained.

Two beats and the penny dropped.

Rory leapt from the bed with a howl of distaste, spilling the cat on to the floor.

'You mongrel,' he yelled at it, 'you mangy critter.'

On his pillow lay the warm corpse of a mole, still sleek and glossy black.

Rory grabbed a yard of toilet-roll from the bathroom, picked up the offending body and marched it downstairs into the garden. The cat retreated before him, mewling proudly, reluctant to abandon his trophy. After a thorough shower and change of pillowcases, Rory managed to devour some toast, feed the feline hordes, leave a note for Alex and still be out of the house on the stroke of eight. The sun was already up and bouncing on its toes, bruising the begonias in the hanging baskets. Not a puff of cloud in sight. As he stepped out on to the crazy-paved path heading for the garage, a bicycle bell tinkled at him from the road.

'Hello there, Rory.'

It was Maddy Carne on her way to the surgery. Above the hedge her head travelled disembodied as she pedalled in the direction of her sick and wounded, always early.

'Hi, Maddy,' Rory called with his usual wave. 'Going to be a scorcher for cycling.'

Maddy laughed her witch's cackle without breaking rhythm. Her head sailed smoothly out of sight. She lived in a tiny labourer's cottage on the far side of Pewsey, about two miles south of the Flynns' village. Rory had never actually seen her house himself, but Alex had been there on the occasions when she had arranged to pick Maddy up or drop her off if the weather was particularly rough. The reports were grim. Basic was the word Alex used, to say the least. And brick-red ugly with it. But Maddy was blithely indifferent and continued to pack it full of waifs and strays of every animal persuasion. An emaciated goat abandoned at her gate was the latest acquisition for her garden shed.

It was five years since Rory and Alex had taken the plunge and bought their own home in a similar state of disrepair. Window frames and floors had disintegrated at a tentative touch, ceilings sagged and the stonework did a convincing imitation of a grey sieve. Gruelling weekends of DIY, punctuated with head-shaking electricians and council inspectors had at times exacerbated frayed tempers. But the aching backs had been gratefully oiled with Alex's half of her inheritance after her parents' deaths and eventually their combined efforts had transformed their home into a chocolate-box stone cottage with mullioned gables, roses and honeysuckle rampant round the central porch. It was small, just three up two down, but to them it was ideal. It sat in the middle of a neat and colourful garden, long-stemmed marguerites trying to elbow aside the gossamer cosmos, and borders edged with Oxford blue lobelia. The neatness came from

Alex, but Rory liked to flatter himself that the colourfulness was his contribution. Purposefully he avoided looking at the reproachful length of the grass. It would have to wait until the weekend.

As he backed his pet MGF out of the garage, his head began to fill with appointments for the day. He had on-site meetings at a school in Chippenham this morning and at the new factory unit in Swindon. Then there were the bills of quantity on the nursing home job to prepare, the report for the planning committee and the affidavit to submit for the court case against the cowboy builder. Just before the day's business swamped him completely, a final domestic thought flickered through his mind.

What had Zena done with her share of the inheritance?

It happened as she was driving home. The dog ran out into the road.

Alex was tired. Bone weary and then some. It had been a difficult foaling. The mare was young and the foal had a leg determinedly back. A narrow pelvic canal hadn't helped. Fetlock ropes, an epidural injection and sheer brute force had triumphed after hours of struggle, but then Alex thought she was going to lose the mare. The farmer had become irate and taken his panic out on her, as he watched several thousand pounds worth of point-to-point horseflesh slipping from his grasp. Artery forceps and an intravenous drip later, the mare had rallied and finally managed to stay on her feet to suckle her offspring.

The drive home was proving an effort and Alex had to fight for concentration. The heat didn't help. It blurred the road and stabbed at her co-ordination, while the brilliant blue sky grated on her eyes like sand. Her clothes clung like soggy blotting paper. The winding lanes were narrow with more blind corners than she remembered and at midday were hazardous with shoppers heading home or to favourite watering-holes.

The dog was a black and white sheepdog. It leapt through the bars of a farm gate with the disregard of long years of habit. A milli-second later on the brakes and Alex would have hit it. The Citroën coming the other way was not as fast. Its tyres squealed rubber.

A dull crump and the dog lay on the road.

Through the windscreen Alex saw the woman driver's face crumple into a mask of horror. Paralysed in frozen disbelief. The child in the back seat started to cry. Alex climbed quickly out of her car, seized her case off the passenger seat and hurried over to the animal. It was still alive, whimpering. She knelt down beside it on the tacky tarmac, murmuring reassurance as she ran a professional hand over the piebald head, then down along its back and ribs. No problems there. The only visible injury appeared to be the left back leg. An open fracture, bone and blood on view. The bumper bore signs of matching colours. She snapped open her case, filled a syringe and injected Finadyne into the scruff of the dog's neck. That would help the shock and pain. Its mucous membranes were too pale. Her calm voice was soothing its distressed whining when the driver and the owner arrived simultaneously. Their voices were raised.

'It wasn't my fault,' the young woman kept repeating. 'He ran out in front of me. I wasn't going fast. I couldn't stop in time.' At the sight of the blood she turned away.

The owner proved to be a belligerent farmer, accustomed to the occasional suffering of livestock, but it came as no surprise to Alex that as he cradled his dog's head, tears crept on to his cheeks. He showed no interest in her independent account of the accident, corroborating the driver's panicky statement.

'I'll take him to the surgery in my car,' Alex suggested. 'Try not to worry too much. If it's just the leg, we can pin or plate it.' She offered a smile. 'He won't be performing acrobatics through gates for a while though.'

Relief made the farmer nod too many times.

From the boot of her car Alex brought out a plastic splint and snapped it to a suitable length. Carefully she dressed the wound. No arteries severed. As she bent over the fractured tibia to bind the leg to the splint, she was acutely aware of the sun grilling the back of her head. Abruptly the limb in her hands was no longer covered with fur. It was smooth, freckled and pink, except where the blood painted it red. But the bone was the same. Jutting through the skin like a sharpened spear.

Alex recoiled. Dropped the bandage. Bile caught at her throat. She blinked hard and only felt her lungs restart when her eyes shouted that the leg was once more a canine leg. Furry. Not Zena's.

It was the heat. The lack of sleep.

She had to get a grip on herself. She snatched a glance at the farmer. He was preoccupied with the dog. Only the driver was staring at her with a slightly odd expression.

Covering her lapse with professional briskness, she completed her task quickly and gave the dog a shot of antibiotic. Together they placed the animal on a sheet on the back seat of her car and the farmer, hardly remembering to be grateful, climbed in beside it. After names and addresses were exchanged, Alex turned the car in a driveway and followed the familiar route to Marlborough. As the sun-baked hedges trooped past, the farmer devoted all his attention to his dog, so she permitted her mind to examine what had happened back there.

Zena's leg. Why Zena's leg after all these years? She had lost count of the number of dogs' limbs she had tended since qualifying as a vet, but not one of them had mutated into her sister's. Not until today.

It was obvious. The postcard was the trigger. Zena was returning to her both from the future and from the past. A double responsibility.

'You're supposed to be the responsible one.' Her father's voice, gruff with disappointment, was so loud in her head that for a confused second she glanced at the empty seat beside her. 'If you hadn't shown off to her that you could climb the tree, she would not have attempted it.' An indulgent smile softened his features. Not directed at her. It was aimed at the white plaster cast on Zena's leg. 'You know how reckless your little sister can be.'

Yes, Alex knew. That's why she didn't want that responsibility again. Nor the disruption. She liked her life just the way it was.

Gordon Tamworth performed the operation. Alex was too tired and too shaken. Maddy had eyed her with mild surprise when asked to fetch Gordon to take over the treatment of the accident victim, but passed no comment. It was as Alex was just crawling out of the door that Maddy's voice dragged her back. The apologetic tone told Alex there was more to come.

'Bobby's ill.'

'Oh no,' Alex groaned. 'What is it this time?'

Bobby Bristow was the third vet in the practice, comfortably middle-aged, conscientious and a natural with horses. But accident-prone was not only his middle name, it was his first and last name as well. He was meant to be taking afternoon surgery.

'A bee sting. Allergic reaction. In bed.' Maddy's abrupt speech indicated disapproval.

Gordon was still in the operating theatre.

'So it's me?'

''Fraid so.' Maddy was aware of the weary smudges under Alex's eyes. 'I'll bring you a cup of tea. Would you like a sandwich?'

'No thanks.' She was too exhausted to eat. 'Tea would be nice though.' She sank into a chair.

Maddy patted her head as if she were an obedient puppy and disappeared with, 'I've got to check that Rachel is doing her job with Gordon.'

Rachel was a perfectly able and efficient nurse who resented Maddy's supervision. A moment later young Lizzie arrived with a steaming mug of tea and two digestive biscuits on a plate. Idly she helped herself to one, offering the other to Alex who shook her head. She needed sleep, not food. But the tea helped. Lizzie's chatter about how much more she was enjoying the job now that she wasn't obliged to assist during operations was pleasantly banal. Normality was creeping back into place.

After ten minutes she thanked Lizzie for the tea, made herself down the last digestive, collected Maddy from under Rachel's feet and a clean white overall from the peg, then headed for the surgery.

By the end of the afternoon the High Street was airless, as if the sun had breathed in every scrap of oxygen and left only hot soup in its place. Marlborough was an attractive town, which unfortunately meant attractive to tourists, the bane of the inhabitants' existence. They swelled the cash tills handsomely and filled the hotel beds and bars, but they stole all the parking places and their unhurried queues made every transaction take for ever. Winter suddenly seemed appealing.

After five minutes panting in line, Alex fed her card into the bank cash machine before it melted. For a split second her mind went blank, wiped of its pin number, as clean as the video tape the other night that was supposed to have been recording a documentary on Fangio. Rory had foamed into his Kenyan coffee next morning when he realised, but the blame rested firmly on his own button-pushing fingers. A glance behind her at the impatient pair of shorts shifting pointedly from foot to foot and the numbers leapt in the correct sequence back into the gap. The machine obediently presented her with crisp new notes. She thanked it politely, nodded to the shorts and made her way down the High Street. Her car beckoned with all the charm of a charcoal-grilled sardine tin.

Alex took advantage of the shade offered by the colonnades in front of the shops she was passing and blessed the Georgian architects who had come up with the bright idea. The High Street was broad and gently sloping, letting the sun in with open arms to bake its stylish houses and gracious bay windows, peering down from tile-hung facades. The abundance of sun-burned tee-shirts and shorts dodging along the pavements did not quite meld with the Georgian elegance exhaled by the buildings. Only a flower-sprigged Jane Austen frock staring in at the bookshop window bucked the trend.

Alex smiled. It could only be Joanna.

Joanna Donelli was feminine. There was no other word for her. Her petite figure, tiny feet, heart-shaped face and curly blonde hair made her a dainty miniature poodle to Alex's greyhound. Sticky exhaustion was briefly forgotten as Alex approached her.

'Hello, Joanna. Still with us, I see.'

Joanna turned and the bulge at her stomach ruined the line of her dress.

'Oh Alex, don't say it. I'm late, I know. But then I was overdue with these two rascals as well.'

Beside her heavily pregnant figure, two identical dark-eyed boys with big toothy grins beamed up at Alex from a double pushchair. The twins were nearly three and took after their

Italian father, Marco, who had come over to England some years before with Alfa Romeo. Marco Donelli and Rory Flynn had what they liked to call a hobby, a mutual interest. Alex and Joanna called it an obsession. Big toys for big boys. Formula One Grand Prix racing. Throughout the season Marco and Rory regularly banded together to be transformed into bellowing, yelling, hair-tearing, self-appointed experts as Ferrari fought it out with Williams and McLaren. Nationalist war was declared in the peace of Sunday afternoons in front of the television.

Italian flowed like blood. Tactics, pit times and overtaking manoeuvres were passionately disputed, recorded, replayed in slow motion and then replayed again just for the hell of it because neither could ever see enough of the suicidal bullets that screamed round the tracks. And once each year during a mutually agreed truce, they took themselves off to one of the European races to soak up the decibels and carbon fibre in the flesh. This year it had been the turn of San Marino. Marco had been uncontrollable – along with the other fifty million Italians for whom Formula One was a religion.

'Not getting too tired in this heat?' Alex asked.

'No, I just use it as an excuse not to do anything. I stretch out on the swing seat in the garden and let the twins get on with it. What about you?'

'Been a long day.'

The relaxed blue eyes took in her friend's weary tension and stained olive green slacks and tee-shirt. The sheepdog's blood was swabbed to a muddy smear.

'You should take it easy, Alex. Especially in these temperatures. You're too thin.'

'I'm fine.'

'You're driving yourself too hard. Always did.' She twirled a clean dainty finger through a stray curl. 'You don't catch me with that hair-shirt any more. I must have been mad to flog myself to death for that local rag.'

'But you loved working on the newspaper. You never talked about anything else. For years.'

Joanna chuckled happily. 'That's before I learnt better.'

Joanna had been a dedicated newshound for the local paper,

chasing stories and investigating tasty rumours with her butter-wouldn't-melt-in-my-mouth smile firmly in place. People really believed she was as sweet and harmless as she looked and poured out their hearts to her. The paper still missed her touch. Eventually, under pressure from Marco, she had abandoned her job and dedicated herself to child-rearing with equal fervour.

'You can't be married to an Italian and not have armfuls of bambinos. It's not natural,' Joanna said and patted her swollen stomach. 'I just hope this one's a girl.'

'If it is, Marco will be putty in her hands.'

'You're right. Poor fellow, he won't stand a chance, especially if she's blonde.'

'Poor fellow my arse,' Alex laughed. 'He's in clover.'

'And so am I,' Joanna grinned with such obvious contentment that Alex was mildly bemused.

Where had the hard-nosed, power-dressing, ball-crunching professional gone? Was she hiding under the floating flowered dresses, just waiting to leap out with a microphone the moment the children were in bed? Alex had a feeling the answer was a resounding no.

'By the way, how's Gary?' Joanna asked.

'Rory's partner in crime? On top form, as far as I gather. Why?' Alex bent and picked up the toy car that one of the twins dropped out of the pushchair on to the pavement. He smiled his father's smile at her.

'I bumped into him in Swindon yesterday after I'd been for my check-up at Princess Margaret's. Distinctly furtive he was.'

'Furtive?' Alex respected Joanna's nose for a story. 'In what way?'

'He had a Swedish-type blonde in tow and kept trying to hide her from me in a shop doorway.'

'Doesn't sound like him. He usually parades his conquests.' Alex retrieved the other twin's matching model car from the pavement.

'That's what I thought.'

'Odd. But you know what Gary is like. He's always up to something. Not happy unless he's got some convoluted scheme or scam on the go, juggling his girlfriends about.'

Alex again scooped up the first car and was again rewarded

with the Marco smile. The second car was just on its way down once more when Joanna called a halt.

'That's enough, boys. Alex may be green enough to fall for your games, but don't wear her out.'

Alex looked down in surprise at the pair of knowing grins. She had not realised it was a game. Strapped into their pushchair, they must have been bored out of their miniature skulls by their static view of adult kneecaps. Yet they hadn't whined; they had invented a game. She squatted down in front of them and returned the grin.

'You cheeky chaps! Teasing me, were you?'

The two dark heads collapsed into infectious giggles. She gave them a quick tickle which only heightened the uproar.

'Come on, you horrors. Bath-time for us all,' Joanna announced and after an affectionate kiss from Alex, she waddled off behind the pushchair.

Alex watched them for a moment, squinting against the sun. Even the waddle was dainty.

Another three days and the sun turned up the thermostat another three degrees. In shirt-sleeves and open neck, Rory Flynn arrived at Meadow Green. The neat shiny roofs and virgin gardens gave him immense pleasure. They sheltered homes for couples to build lives in, to make love in and fight in, for children to grow up in. And escape from. The first phase of the housing development on the eastern outskirts of Swindon was nearing completion and Rory was well satisfied with his handiwork. The hard graft over the drawing board and for the constant maintenance of standards in the face of cost cutting had been well worth every drop of blood. A modest phoenix risen out of the mud.

Not that he was talking long-term posterity here, he was under no illusions about that. Long term meant big bucks. And big bucks gave estates of sixty comfortable but unpretentious dwellings the cold shoulder. But to him each one deserved attention. He did not begrudge a morning spent inspecting the contractor's standard of work, quality of materials and compliance with regulations. A mother hen with her chicks.

'Want a look at the show-home?' the foreman asked.

'If I have to.'

Rory found show-homes oddly depressing. Skeletons without souls. An empty, unoccupied house was one thing, but a sham of a home with curtains and sofas, bedside tables and reading lamps, but no books to read nor eyes to read them, a pretence of a home. That grated like fingernails on a blackboard. He followed the foreman past the rows of low garden walls, each with its inset islands of bare earth crying out for aubretia and its little towers of gateposts that he had fought hard to retain.

'When's the inspector due, Reg?'

Reg was a stocky, monosyllabic man in his mid forties who hid his acne behind a beard and his bald pate under a hard hat all day.

'Friday.'

'If it's old Mannings, he's bound to find something to nit-pick about.'

'Cavity ties.'

'Exactly. But I was right. The cavity ties in the first block of houses had faulty spacing. You should have spotted that.'

'All sorted out. Water under the bridge.'

'Money under the bridge, you mean.'

The growl of a tarmac machine greeted them as they rounded a corner. The estate still bustled with workmen, laying kerb stones, planting shrubs and wielding spanners, copper pipes and paint brushes. All sweating in the mid-day heat. Rory didn't fancy getting too close to some of them. The hard hats maintained a steady boiling-point temperature and the contract gardeners were fighting a losing battle against the unrelenting blue of the sky.

'Hi, Rory. Cold enough for you?'

'Hello, Dave. How's the wall going this time?'

Dave Price was a bricklayer who liked his tipple. Highly skilled, unless under the influence. On his last visit Rory had ordered a garden party-wall to be dismantled because of defective workmanship. One of Dave's off-days.

'Take a look. Firm as the iron in your philistine soul.' In good humour Dave waved a trowel to indicate the knee-high and still growing result of his endeavours.

'Immaculate. Good enough for the Tate Gallery.'

'It's all right for some, floating around doing sweet fuck all every day in best bib and tucker.'

'Get on with it, you lazy sod, or the building inspector will play hard to get. Nothing he likes better than wielding his big stick.'

'Power goes to some guys' heads.' Dave cast a dark look in the direction of the foreman.

'More power to your elbow is what you need,' Rory urged with a laugh and continued up the front path of the show-home. Show tomb, more like it. The interior designer's idea of taste proved to be as depressingly predictable as Rory had anticipated: all matching beige walls and carpets, flounces and chintz. Neat and dead as a laboratory specimen.

Half an hour later he was climbing into his silver sports and wondering if it was worth swapping for an air-conditioned model if this global warming really got its skates on, when a grey Volvo drew up beside him. A tall, dapper suit and energetic dark eyes approached, no sign of steam above the imprisoning tie. An estate agent smile announced his arrival.

'It's looking good, Rory. Seen our splendid brochure yet?' Alan Beecroft did not believe in hiding his light under a bushel.

'Yes, nice and glossy. I like the photography.'

'I'm getting buyer interest already. I'm convinced these houses will sell like hot cakes even in the present market. Thought I'd check out the show-home myself though.'

'Help yourself. I'm off for an ice-cold beer.'

'Hang on a tick and I'll join you. Heard of a job that might interest you.'

Duty got the better of inclination. Rory sweated out the wait in his car, watching a fat lazy blue-bottle choose his windscreen for a landing stage and then lack the energy to get its engine whirring again. The air was growing heavier.

The job turned out to be a foreign client looking for an architect to design a luxury detached house on a sizeable chunk of land he had just bought not far from Wootton Bassett. It made the warm beer and the half hour of housing market conversation almost bearable. But a half hour was all Rory was willing to take

of it. Back at the office he telephoned the contact number and
set up a meeting. Perhaps estate agents weren't actually good
for nothing after all. Just as he replaced the receiver, it beeped
at him. He picked it up again.

'Hello?'

'Your wife is on the line,' he was informed by the calm voice
of his receptionist.

'Thanks, Jan. I'll take it.'

A click. 'Rory?'

'What's the matter? Run out of anal passages to examine?'

Alex laughed. 'I'll come and put a thermometer up yours if
you make remarks like that.'

'Promises you never keep.'

'Sounds as if you've had a good day.'

'If you can call inspecting walls and listening to dorks bending
my ear over an absolutely revolting pint a good day, then yes,
I'm having one.'

'Don't give me that sob stuff. I've been playing nursemaid to
Maddy's orphan Squirrel Nutkin so I haven't even had lunch
yet. It's a new contract, isn't it?'

'Early days, but yes, it could be.'

'I knew it. Only the prospect of doodling more masterpieces
puts that note of Flynn perkiness into your voice.'

'Wrong. I can think of something else that induces what you
call Flynn perkiness.'

'Down, boy,' Alex laughed. 'I've got tablets for pests like you.'

'Talking of pests, to what do I owe this interruption to my
daily grind?'

'I thought you'd like to know, Joanna has got a move on at
last. She rang me from the hospital. The deed is done. Early
hours of this morning.'

'Good for her. Boy or girl?'

'A girl. Seven pounds. Apparently, hair as dark and curly as
the poodle puppies I inoculated today.'

'Mother doing well?'

'On cloud nine and eager to show off her momentous achieve-
ment.'

A moment's pause, then Rory got the message. 'I suppose I
could call in on my way home.'

'It's only round the corner from your office.'

'So is the pub.' Hospitals were always hot. Maternity wards even hotter. And they didn't sell cold beer.

'Give her my love and say I'll be in to see her tomorrow after morning surgery. And Rory, if Marco is there, invite him for dinner.'

'If you think I am inviting to my house that Italian madman, who is incapable of admitting that Williams and McLaren can race the wheels off Ferrari any day, any track, you're out of your mind. Anyway, he takes too many handsome lessons.'

'I hear he speaks well of you too.'

Rory indulged in some inarticulate grumblings that she took as a yes.

'Rory, don't forget the flowers.'

'He doesn't deserve any.'

Alex laughed and hung up.

When Marco arrived at eight o'clock, it was with a bottle of champagne under one arm and a Ferrari victory, in the form of a video of the 1994 Hockenheim Grand Prix, under the other. After two seconds' obligatory praise for mother and baby, the evening was spent glued to the sight of the frail machines that roared like jet engines, hurling themselves round and round the four-mile combination of straights and chicanes at speeds of up to two hundred miles an hour. For two hundred miles. It did not take long to raise both the temperature and the decibels in the room.

'Just look at Damon Hill shutting the door at that corner. Slam. No chance. There's no Italian driver to touch him,' Rory enthused.

'Pick any Italian off the street and he has more driving flair in his little finger than your Hill has in his whole British body.' He pronounced it 'leetle' and 'Heel'.

'Then why does Ferrari use foreign drivers?'

The temperature shot to boiling point and Alex played her usual role of referee and stern policewoman. The blood-letting was kept to a minimum. As the grandfather clock chimed twelve, she poured a last glass of wet-the-baby's-head into

Marco, toasted his mother-in-law for baby-sitting the twins and tucked him into the back seat of a taxi where he promptly keeled over and went to sleep. She fed the cats while Rory locked up and turned out the lights, then led her husband up to bed. Despite the champagne, he proved he could still be an efficient pest without too much prompting and when afterwards they were lying in classic spoon-to-spoon cosiness, he felt her slip easily into sleep. Her breath was light and regular on his arm. It was then that he allowed himself to think of Marco returning to a house full of children. An hour passed before he managed to find sleep.

3

The drive back from the hospital seemed to take forever. Alex
wound down the windows to let the hot air at least move about
a bit. Not long after she joined the Marlborough road, she met a
tractor lumbering ahead with a tailback of impatient cars. Then
just before Ogbourne St George a group of frisky cows, being
moved to fresh pasture, clattered on to the road and ambled
curiously from one grass verge to the other and back again,
ignoring the efforts of the cowman. Dog-power eventually did
the trick when a blur of Black Bob sheepdog set them strolling
in the right direction. Alex trailed behind at hoof-pace, watching
the heatwaves in the distance make the cars shimmer on the
tarmac.

She had time to think.

She thought about Angelica. That was the name Joanna and
Marco had settled on for their new baby. Angelica had wrinkled
tiny fingers that gripped like Araldite and a very pink tongue that
seemed always on the move. Her serious dark eyes had stared
intently, though probably myopically, at her mother through
the transparent sides of the hospital crib and her flattened ears
appeared to prick up at every sound of her mother's voice.

I've seen too many puppies, Alex told herself with a smile.
Babies' ears don't prick up. Or do they? She realised she knew
absolutely nothing about babies. Not the human variety anyway.
And was quite happy to keep it that way. She didn't even like
holding them.

'Go on, Alex, give her a cuddle. She's absolutely irresistible,
isn't she?' Joanna had cooed.

'No, I'd better not. I might be carting some animal bugs around with me. I've Hibiscrubbed thoroughly, but you never know. She's so tiny.'

Joanna had believed it. 'Don't breathe over her then, for heaven's sake. I don't want her catching cat flu or distemper.'

The words had been said as a joke but at the same time the instinctively protective mother bundled her newborn out of the crib and into the safety of her own arms. Alex left the rosebud mouth snuffling for an early lunch.

Babies take over. They disrupt the order of your life. Of your mind. Their demanding little fists seize control of the reins.

Like Zena did. Stole her father's love.

The thought leapt out at her and she swerved the steering wheel as if to avoid hitting it. She was lucky. The road was clear.

That's ludicrous, she told herself. Of course he loved her. He loved them both. She still remembered how proud he'd been when the letter came from Bristol offering her a place at the veterinary college.

Of course he'd loved her.

As a vet himself with his own practice, he knew only too well how hard his elder daughter was going to have to work. But he already recognised she was capable of that. Half her childhood had been spent cleaning out cages, swabbing antiseptic on to every available surface and bottle feeding orphan kittens every two or three hours for twenty-four hours at a stretch. As a reward she was allowed to watch her father in the operating theatre, his large capable hands demonstrating a sensitive skill she admired even more now that she had to do it herself. Just for a pat on the back or a satisfied smile from her father, she had declined many a trip to the cinema or disco. Whereas Zena . . .

She was driving too fast. A bend loomed up and she almost lost it. A narrow band of pain kicked into life across her forehead like a headband squeezed too tight. She kept her speed down and concentrated on each twitch of the wheel in her hand.

There was no 'whereas Zena'. Zena had led a perfectly normal childhood: enjoying herself with a permanent cluster of friends, scraping by as an average student at school and getting into occasional hot water, as all teenagers should.

And twisting her father round her little finger.

No, that wasn't fair. Of course Zena took advantage of times when her father was inclined to be indulgent. Who wouldn't?

I wouldn't.

More fool you then.

For heaven's sake, that's enough. Alex shook her head as if to toss the thoughts out of her mind and out of the car's open window. She pushed a Louis Armstrong tape into the slot and let the air flood with spine-shivering sound. It wrapped around her and loosened the band on her forehead.

Her father had disliked jazz. A cacophony, he had called it.

She switched it up louder, picked up speed and felt better. It was early afternoon and the sun was bouncing off the huge yellow monsters that were stripping the landscape of its harvest. Shorn fields flicked past on either side of the road showing her their spiky stubble, like teeth that nibbled at her memory.

It came as a surprise to see Rory's MGF in the garage. He was supposed to be at work. Perhaps he'd had a meeting near home and decided to take the rest of the afternoon off instead of traipsing back up to Swindon. In this heat, she didn't blame him. She backed the Clio in beside the sports car and as she turned off the engine, for a moment she let herself stop. As if the key to her own engine had been switched off. Her head dropped back against the headrest and her eyes closed. The old stone garage was cool and gloomy, peaceful after the glare outside. She had learned how to let her mind empty completely and steal these islands of rest. She knew she was tired. Working too many hours.

Like her father.

Where had that thought crept in from? She dismissed it sternly and wallowed for another couple of minutes in total nothingness before reluctantly opening her eyes and setting herself in motion once more. She would have to have a word with Gordon about taking on another vet to help with the workload. The practice already had one trainee but one just wasn't enough. As she walked down the front path she automatically dead-headed a couple of geraniums en route and stopped to admire a whole family of blue tits clinging precariously to the wire tube of peanuts suspended from the bird table. A second later they disappeared in a feathery puff of wings as the Siamese yowling of Hamilton came trotting on slender legs to greet her.

'Hello, Hammy, chased any more foxes today?'

The previous evening when Alex was drawing the bedroom curtains, she had been treated to the sight of a big dog fox striding boldly across the lawn in the moonlight. A whirling dervish of fur and claws that was Hamilton screaming a battle cry fit to strike terror into even the boldest vulpine heart, had driven it from the territory. Blocking any further progress down the path, the cat's china blue eyes gazed possessively up at Alex and she twined her sleek body around her ankles, fur like gossamer against bare skin. It was safer to pick her up than try to step round her.

Alex stroked the narrow head and tugged an ear affectionately. 'Let's go and see what excuse Rory's offering for skiving off work, shall we?'

'Mauw,' the cat answered and started to drool over a particularly tasty smell emanating from the shoulder of Alex's tee-shirt. A parrot had earlier taken refuge there when she had been trying to examine a deep gash in its breast. She walked into the house, crossed the cool, flagstoned hall and pushed open the sitting-room door.

Rory was seated on the sofa, upright and uncomfortable. Opposite him in Alex's armchair lounged an attractive blonde. Both pairs of eyes turned and looked at Alex expectantly.

It took her five long seconds to recognise her own sister.

'Zena!'

'Hi, Alex. Here I am.' The voice had acquired a faint American drawl. 'I arrived at Heathrow this morning.'

Zena rose to her feet, slim and elegant in a silky, sleeveless dress, blonde hair brushing her shoulders, tawny eyes bright with anticipation. She came over to Alex, who was standing rooted to the spot. The cat leapt warily out of her arms. There was a split second's awkward hesitation, then the sisters embraced. Zena's cheek felt enviably cool and a light springtime perfume enfolded her. Alex became uncomfortably aware of the fact that her own hands reeked of antiseptic scrub and God only knew what farmyard smells her grubby trousers were wafting around. This morning she had called in to check a ram with an

infected foot and the farmer's muddy dog had showered her with
enthusiastic paw prints.

'Zena.' Alex felt as if her tongue was stuck in a groove.

'That's me! All the way from America to see my big sister.' It
was said with the easy teasing laugh that Alex remembered and
disliked.

'You look wonderful, Zena. I hardly recognised you.'

'I noticed.'

'You've changed. More than just the hair.'

The freckled nose that had been slightly heavy was now long
and slender. The lips fuller. And something about the eyes was
different. Alex couldn't put her finger on it.

'That's America for you, Ali. Dreams can come true.'

'Did yours? Come true, I mean.'

The wide smile slipped a fraction. Dense waves of blonde hair
rippled from side to side as Zena shook her head. 'No, I can't say
they did. No such luck. But I had a great time looking for them!'
She resumed her seat, pulled a pack of cigarettes from her bag and
raised a manicured eyebrow at them. 'Don't mind if I smoke, do
you? People are so oddly defensive about it now, I have to ask.'
The cigarette was already in her mouth.

'Actually we do mind.'

Zena removed the cigarette, shrugged good naturedly and
dropped the offending article back into her bag. 'Each to our
own vices,' she laughed. 'What are yours?'

Alex stared at her, deaf to the question. This elegant, sophisticated, controlled face was no one she knew. Where was Zena?
Where was the impetuous, happy-go-lucky, trouble-seeking sister who romped through life with unshakeable self-indulgence.
Only the veneer of charm rang a bell.

'Zena turned up at my office,' Rory spoke for the first time.
At a glance Alex could tell the Zena charm had met a brick
wall there.

'Yes, poor Rory. I caught the train to Swindon, found his firm's
address in Yellow Pages and poof,' she waved a magician's
imaginary wand in the air, 'I materialised on his doorstep. He
looked quite shocked.' Zena's somehow different eyes rested
on Rory with amusement, then on Alex. 'So do you, for that
matter.'

'Of course we are,' Rory responded. 'We were expecting another of your postcards or a phone call. Advance warning of some sort.'

'Warning? Am I a danger that has to be announced? Like hurricanes.' It was said with a laugh that did not reach the eyes.

Alex suddenly felt protective. The familiarity of the feeling was reassuring. Like old times.

'Of course not,' she said firmly, strode over to Zena's chair and gave her a hug. A warm affectionate welcome this time. 'You just took us by surprise. The blonde hair and everything. Not the Zena I remembered. But it's lovely to see you again.' Another hug.

Zena responded, but only for a moment. Clinging to her older sister the way Alex remembered so well, when she had landed herself in trouble. Then Zena pushed her away with a laugh. 'You smell of dog-shit.'

It was meant to hurt.

Rory stood up. 'It comes from working hard.' He put his arm round his wife and sniffed her cheek. 'She smells just great to me.' He kissed the cheek and checked her eyes for damage. If it was there, it was well hidden.

'Don't be silly, Rory. I didn't mean it nastily. Alex knows that. It was always a joke between us as kids that she went around in a blue haze of animal aromas. We always knew she'd become a vet. Doctor Ali I used to call her.'

Alex had forgotten that.

Doc.

'Look, Doc, look. Cutie is tickling my leg,' Zena would squeal as she perched cross-legged on Alex's bed. A white rat in her lap, pink-eyed mice performing a balancing act on her knees and Bluey, the budgerigar, chirruping on her finger.

Alex's bedroom had been a menagerie, walls stacked with fish tanks, cages of rats, mice, hamsters and even a stick insect called Twiggy. She had sworn never to own a caged bird but relented when a friend wanted to abandon an elderly budgerigar with a broken wing – the result of a mauling by the family cat. Alex had given it refuge and every Sunday morning when she played her zoo keeper role of cleaning out all the cages, Bluey loved to squawk its guttural approval from the crow's nest of Zena's finger. When it hopped on to Zena's head for a better vantage point, she would shriek with laughter.

'Look, Doc, look.'

Only Tarzan, Alex's chunky tabby cat, had struck a discordant note with his scratching at the door to join the party.

There had been so much laughter. The silences had come later.

Alex sat down on the sofa, memories softening her smile. 'Yes, that's right. I was Doc and you were Titania, the fairy queen.'

'That's what Daddy used to call me. You didn't.'

Rory decided to leave the sisters together. 'I'll go and put the kettle on.'

'Thanks,' Alex said.

'A nice English cup of tea, the panacea for all problems,' Zena teased and relaxed back in her chair. The pale peach dress shifted its hold and for the first time Alex noticed the larger breasts. A pang of concern twitched at her.

As the door closed, she asked gently, 'What about your husband, Zena? Is he still part of the picture?'

'No, not at all. Completely erased.' Zena's bold golden-brown eyes gave no clues. 'Chet is history.' Abruptly she reached for her handbag in search of a cigarette, seemed to recall the smokeless zone and abandoned the manoeuvre. 'It wasn't even fun while it lasted.'

'I'm sorry.'

'Don't be. It's better this way.'

'Was that his name? Chet?'

'Yes, you know what peculiar names Americans burden their children with. His is Chetwyn Taylor.'

'You're not involved with anyone else?'

'No. As our mother's beloved Fred Astaire used to croon, "I'm fancy free and free for anything fancy".' It was said with a confident laugh and a wide sweep of open arms, as if embracing a benign future.

Alex watched her sister and was impressed. Attractive, groomed, articulate. Why shouldn't her future be benign? Eight years ago when she took off for the States, Zena had been a gauche, rebellious teenager, eighteen years old and just about to sit her final school exams. No trace of that Zena was visible now. Alex was having difficulty adjusting to calling this new self-assured woman of the world sister.

When Rory returned with a tray of tea and biscuits, Horatio, the white one-eyed mole-killer, barged into the room in pursuit of the plate of shortbread.

'What a creature!' Zena exclaimed. 'Talk of battle-scarred! How many animals do you have now?'

The cat, as if aware that he was the object of her comments, scowled balefully at the guest with his one green eye, then leapt on to the arm of Rory's chair in the hope of an offering. Rory scratched its ragged ear sympathetically, shedding copious white fur over his navy sleeve.

'I admit Horatio may not be exactly Mr Handsome, but he's a great character. As well as a useful mouser. And we only have two cats. The other is the Siamese.' He gestured to Hamilton who was casting a suspicious blue eye on Zena from the safety of the broad windowsill.

Zena smiled her approval. 'That one's much cuter. Most Americans wouldn't give the white monstrosity house room.'

'In England, Zena,' Rory said, 'you may have forgotten, we like things to be natural. The way they're meant to be. Horatio Nelson here may be offensive to American sensibilities, but on this side of the Atlantic we're not so obsessed with the shallows of physical appearance.'

There was no mistaking the implication.

The faintest of blushes crept into Zena's cheeks. 'I like the way I look now, brother-in-law.'

'Zena, I was talking about the cats. I didn't mention your appearance.'

'Like hell you didn't.'

'No, you are misinterpreting me. I think your looks are very attractive. Of course they are. It's just that they're not the Zena you were.'

'That's the whole point. To improve on what you've got. In the States, everyone does it all the time. Why not?'

'Because it's important to accept yourself as you are. Like we accept Horatio here, warts and all.' He tweaked the cat's crooked tail.

'Tell that to the perfectionist.'

Rory frowned. 'What do you mean by that?'

'Tell that to the perfectionist.' Zena waved her painted nails in Alex's direction. 'Your wife. She was bottle-fed on the doctrine that if something is not right, work at it until it is perfect. Surely you've noticed her tendency to want to improve things.'

Rory turned to his wife and said loyally, 'Yes, she sets herself high standards.'

Alex smiled her thanks.

'So what's the difference?' Zena pushed her point. 'I set myself higher physical standards, that's all.'

Alex intervened. 'That's not quite the same, Zena. But let's not argue on your first day back. As Rory said, you certainly look very attractive.'

Zena ran a satisfied tongue over her fuller lips. 'I had a great surgeon. He's a real miracle worker. And I see no difference really in spending my inheritance on him, or, as you have done,' she gestured round the room with its smattering of antiques and silver, 'on a comfortable home and pretty toy car. They're both a matter of promoting the desired self-image.'

Rory was about to wade in, when he caught his wife's eye and pulled himself up short. Her eyes pleaded for a truce. There was a pool of uncomfortable silence into which Zena tossed her light cultivated laugh.

Alex drank her tea on the sofa beside Rory, acutely aware of his raised hackles, and felt like pushing Zena out of the door. Start again from scratch. But Zena was here. Contentedly draped in their chair, sinking her perfect teeth into their biscuit and sipping their tea through her redesigned lips.

An afternoon meeting with a client in Avebury enabled Rory to desert the ship with honour. Alex took Zena on a conducted tour of the house and left her to unpack her single suitcase in the spare bedroom. Alex snatched a quick shower and change of clothes. She was due to take five o'clock surgery. When she popped her head round the door to announce that she was leaving, Zena was stretched out on the bed in just bra and panties flicking through an American magazine. An irritating fly was pestering her, as if attracted to a honey pot, and she clouted it with the magazine. The glamorous face on the cover was stained.

'I'll see you later,' Alex said. 'I'm sorry we have to dash off. If I'd known you were coming, I'd have shifted my hours around. Get some rest to recover from the jet-lag.' Automatically she picked up her sister's crumpled peach dress and hung it on a hanger.

Zena yawned a goodbye and closed her eyes. The brown eye-shadow and heavy mascara made dark smudges on a tight pale canvas. Her body was taut and smooth to match. Alex shut the door quietly, glad to avert her eyes from the heap of clothes spilling haphazardly out of the suitcase. The floor was not the place for Versace.

The surgery was busy but not frantic and Alex was grateful for the breathing space. As she cleaned out the mite-ridden ears of a scrawny stray cat, she let her mind drift back to the initial moment of impact. How could she have not recognised her own sister? Had she blanked Zena from her mind so completely? Yet she was genuinely pleased to see her again even though disconcerted by the changes and tensions. As each day passed, would she be able to peel away some of the glossy layers of veneer and find the old Zena underneath? Did she still exist?

Alex gave the cat a worming tablet and an inoculation jab for safe measure. It rewarded her with a ferocious hiss.

The thought of days passing only increased her unease. It was obvious that Rory was not going to find Zena agreeable company. For that matter, would she?

A few snips and the cat's claws were done.

It made no difference whether she found Zena agreeable company or not. No difference at all. She would house her, feed her and pick up clothes for her. Maybe even love her. She was her sister.

The end of the day was spent in polite conversation. To break up the evening they went out to dinner at the Castle & Ball in Marlborough, but jet-lag seemed to be catching up on Zena for she became increasingly silent. When they returned home at nine thirty, she excused herself immediately and went upstairs to bed. No thank-you for the meal.

'Bloody hell, Alex, how long do we have to put up with her spoiling our evenings?'

'I don't know. We didn't get much out of her, did we?'

'An understatement. Her future plans, as well as her past antics, were all shrouded behind sibylline answers.'

'She was tired. Probably felt we were prying.'

'Of course we were prying. We have every right to pry, if she's staying under our roof. What I want to know is when is she leaving?'

'Don't, Rory. She has only just arrived.' To Alex's surprise, she heard her own voice break and felt tears prickle at her lids.

'Damn the woman,' Rory muttered and put an arm around Alex's shoulders. 'Don't let her get to you. She's a mess. I don't want her dragging you into that mess for company. Or me, for that matter.'

Alex sniffed the tears away and gave him a hug. 'No chance.'

'Come on, let's get a breath of fresh air in the garden. Her perfume still stinks this room out.'

It was not quite dark. Twilight enveloped everything, like a soft misty glove that robbed the garden of colour. It stole in through the shadows with gentle persistence and wrapped the figures of Alex and Rory in its shifting folds of grey. Outside the porch, the spidery honeysuckle still trailed its scent in the air and an exuberant lavender bush reached out as they ambled past. Rory plucked a sprig of it, inhaled its old fashioned fragrance and tucked it into the buttonhole of Alex's tee-shirt. She dipped her nose to its spiky flower and breathed deeply.

'Wonderful. Reminds me of childhood. My mother always kept lavender bags in our drawers.'

'Maybe that's why your sister drenches herself in perfume now.'

Alex shook her head. 'Hardly the same.'

Arm still around his wife, Rory led her without purpose across the lawn, behind the dog-rose hedge to the vegetable garden. Even in the dusk its immaculate neatness was evident; lettuces, carrots, peas and onions all in military weedless ranks. A dense regiment of runner beans guarded the far end. Alex's handiwork.

'Tell me,' she asked, 'what went on between you and Zena before I arrived?'

'Nothing really. It was just that I didn't appreciate the way she flounced unannounced into the office and expected me to drop everything to bring her here. As if the world was hers for the asking. I almost dumped her in a taxi instead.'

'Why didn't you?'

Rory gave her a wry smile. 'I thought you might not approve. Not the way to greet your one and only long-lost sister.'

Alex laughed, 'Quite right. Inconsiderate she may be, but she is my sister. So thanks for making the effort.' She snapped a bean off its stalk and held it out to him. 'A peace offering.'

'Accepted.' The noise of his teeth crunching into the crisp flesh of the vegetable was startlingly loud in the silent garden. Rory had a penchant for raw runner beans. Not many escaped as far as a saucepan. 'We'll give her a maximum of a few weeks and then she'll have to fend for herself.'

'What if she hasn't any money?'

'Then she can find herself a job. Or resort to the DSS. She can't possibly expect us to keep her indefinitely.'

'Of course not.' Alex looked up at the darkening sky and sought for the first winking of the stars. 'I'll find out more from her tomorrow when she's had a chance to rest.'

As they wandered back past the hedge, Rory picked a small pink dog-rose and added it to the lavender in Alex's buttonhole.

'That's enough about that sister of yours. Let's forget about her and enjoy what's left of this balmy evening.'

Alex teased, 'You're the barmy one.'

He pulled her closer to him, kissed her lightly on the lips and, arms entwined, they continued their walk.

A faint waft of night air carried the sound of their laughter, soft and intimate. Zena leant unseen against the open window and gazed down on the two figures fused into one as they crossed the lawn. Behind them, two small black shadows trailed in silent four-legged procession. Alex and her husband. Alex and her animals. Alex and her home. Alex and her neatness. All Alex.

4

'It will stop by lunchtime.'

'Typical English weather. I expected no less.' Zena sipped her coffee and stared moodily out at the rainstorm that had announced the end of the drought.

'We've not seen a drop of rain for weeks,' Alex said as she tidied away the breakfast dishes. 'It's a relief from the muggy heat we've been having.' But in fact she had grown so used to being greeted each morning by the sun that its absence was disconcerting. 'Anyway the garden needs it.'

'The garden's welcome to it.'

It was five days since Zena's arrival and a vague sort of routine had emerged. As soon as the front door banged shut behind Rory at eight every morning, a tousled bare-faced Zena appeared in the kitchen, loosely wrapped in a pink and black kimono. She joined Alex for an uncommunicative coffee and orange juice, declining offers of toast, egg or cereal. Today for the first time she had picked up a nectarine from the fruit bowl and was half-heartedly slicing it into pieces. Alex poured herself another coffee and sat down again, her gaze tracing the grain of the surface of the table. Its mellow pine tones were gentler on the eye than her sister's kimono.

'I don't have to leave until ten o'clock this morning. I'm TB testing a dairy herd over near Barbury Castle.'

'How nice for you.' Zena continued to stare out at the rain.

It was the same every day. As if she donned her personality along with the make-up and clothes. Until then, she hardly spoke. Alex found it unsettling.

'Any plans for today?'

A faint shake of the head, nothing more. The honey-blonde hair hung in an unbrushed curtain round her face, the eyes smaller without kohl or mascara. A white inch-long scar above one eyebrow. During the day the mark was hidden under make-up but on the first morning when Alex had noticed it and queried its origin, Zena had just muttered, 'Boating accident.' Alex had left it at that.

The evenings were trickier. Zena and Rory were observing a polite, if hostile, truce.

'What about coming with me out to Barbury Castle? It's pretty round there. You could help with the cows or, if the rain stems up, take a walk across . . .' The suggestion petered out as Alex was treated to horrified raised eyebrows by her sister.

'Not exactly my scene.' The American drawl was exaggerated for effect.

'It would give you some idea of what the area is like. You haven't even been out of the house since you came here, except for the meal in Marlborough.'

Zena shrugged and returned to her black coffee and the rain.

'Aren't you bored?' Alex asked.

'I like being bored.'

That ended the conversation. Neither spoke, each pursuing her own thoughts in the curling steam that rose from the coffee. Alex felt frustrated by Zena's clam-like act. What had led her to her present situation? Any enquiries about her life in America – the marriage, jobs or finances – were brushed aside with an indifferent 'I don't want to even think about that. I told you, it's history.' When Rory had pushed harder to discover the state of her current financial position, Zena had snapped, 'If you mean you want bed and board money from me, then say so.' She had banged five twenty-pound notes on the table and walked out of the room. Rory had looked at Alex and groaned, 'God preserve us!' Before going to bed he had returned the money to her; she had accepted it and beamed at him sweetly. 'Money's not worth squabbling over, is it?'

So they were no further forward.

The silence was broken by the doorbell. At that early hour Alex assumed it was the postman, but when she opened the door, the unmistakable green eyes of Maddy Carne peered out at her from inside the hood of a bright yellow cowl of oilskins. The rain slid down their slick surface with boisterous energy, flooded her spectacles and sky-dived off her chin.

'Maddy, you're drenched.'

'Hello, Alex, I'm on my way to the surgery. I've just stopped to ask a favour of you.'

Alex backed into the hall, retreating from the gusts of rain. 'Come on in.'

'It's Josephine. She needs attention.' Maddy's bulky water-proofed form lumbered into the hallway, leaving a broad swathe of lakes in her wake.

Alex was grateful for the impervious flagstones and led her into the kitchen, where the quarry tiles could stand the strain. 'Come and have a coffee and tell me what's the matter.'

Maddy's forward motion ground to a halt when she saw Zena seated at the table. Zena stared at the yellow apparition in surprise, then burst out laughing. 'What have we here? Lordy, Lordy, I do believe it is the mustard monster from the swamp-lands come to get me at last.'

Maddy glared.

Alex introduced them and told Zena to behave herself. 'Maddy is the one who keeps our surgery going. An intrepid feat in this weather. If you want to leave your bike here, Maddy, I'll run you into Marlborough in the car.'

'No, not necessary. I've got legs, haven't I?' Zena's teasing had succeeded in drawing down the shutters on Maddy's ami-ability.

Alex poured her a coffee. 'Here, this will warm you up.'

Maddy flicked back her hood, wiped the mist from her glasses and accepted the proffered cup with a grunt. Zena watched her every move with the fascination of a scientist discovering a new form of life.

'So what is the problem?' Alex asked.

'I told you.'

'Tell me again.'

'It's Josephine.'

'The goat?'

'Yes.'

'What's the matter with her?'

'I've been up all night with her. She's hot, is drinking gallons of water but won't eat. Gut infection I would guess.'

'Poor Josephine. I'll go over and have a look at her before I do the TB testing.'

Maddy grunted what could have been a thank-you and downed the coffee. Puffing out steamy dragon's breath, she shook herself like a dog after a bath sending a fine shower in Zena's direction, donned her hood and stomped out.

'Give my regards to Swampland,' Zena called after her and turned laughing to Alex. 'What on earth was that?'

'She is our head nurse. She's wonderful with animals.'

'Leaves a little to be desired in the human department, to say the least. How do you manage to work with her? She's so extraordinary.'

Alex wanted to shake her. To shake some good sense and good manners into her. 'Zena, you are a very bad, as well as very rude, judge of character.' She walked out of the kitchen, shutting the door with a satisfying thud behind her.

Zena stared at the blank door and longed for a cigarette. She twitched a hand through her unkempt hair and tugged it hard. The scar over her eyebrow throbbed. 'To hell with them all!'

Rory was glad to be out of the house. The office, even with its frantic activity, offered a haven of relaxation compared to the tension he felt when at home. He disguised it as much as possible from Alex, but he was certain she was under no illusion. The temperature plummeted the moment Zena walked into a room. Polite but icily distant was the best they could manage. He had tried. Despite the shaky start, he had made an effort. For Alex's sake. On his return from Swindon on the day after Zena's invasion, he had presented her with flowers, kissed her cheek and generously welcomed her into his home. But she had been determined to bait him.

'How sweet of you, brother-in-law. A real charmer when you try.' The eyes that looked out at him from the smiling mask offered no friendship. 'I assume little wifey won't let you get a leg over until you and I have kissed and made up. All one big happy family.'

Her intention was clear. She had trampled on his olive branch and come out fighting. Bare knuckled, at that. Zena was not interested in a draw.

He set his mind to concentrate on the work in hand. His desk was threatening to disappear under a mountain of paper. He was in the process of checking over an outline plan of a bus station extension that had been drawn up by his young draftsman Colin Stanley. Flynn & Saunders Chartered Architects employed three draftsmen – Rory politically-corrected his thought to draftspeople: one of them was a woman. Paula Marshall. Alex always referred to her as the spaniel and Rory had to admit she was the spitting image of a Cavalier pooch with very round dark brown eyes, little pug nose and hair that King Charles would have been proud of. Her work was thorough, if uninspired, and at twenty-one she still had a lot to learn. But one thing she had learnt fast: to keep Gary Saunders at arm's length. Rory's partner's wide-eyed sincerity didn't even get him to first base in her game plan. Admirably level-headed and always reliable.

The bus station outline was looking good. No problems there. He remembered designing a bus station himself light years ago in his first position as a qualified architect. In Warwickshire that had been. He glanced up at the proudly framed qualifications that adorned one wall and was as always relieved that examinations were a thing of the past. At thirty he was still close enough to remember the cold sweat of panic that they engendered. His office was not large but was light and airy with framed displays of some of his work on the walls. Designed to impress clients. To one side of his desk, an array of shelves was cluttered with a mixture of architectural reference books and heavily thumbed Formula One racing biographies. Fangio, Clark, Lauda and Stewart, all offered the fire of inspiration when ideas were lacking. A token potted plant was gently expiring on top of Nigel Mansell's determined grin. Beside the telephone an oasis of space was reserved for a framed photograph of Alex, smiling her intimate smile at him. It still turned him on. But he kept its back carefully turned towards the shelves so that she wouldn't see the mess.

The buzz of the telephone broke through his thoughts and he picked up the receiver.

'Hello?'

'Adam Forke on the line for you. Sounds upset.'

'Thanks, Jan. Put him through.'

Adam Forke was the director of Swedish Kitchens, a Lincoln-shire company that imported Scandinavian fitted kitchens and was expanding into southern England. They were just in the process of clinching a deal with Flynn & Saunders to design their new showroom in Swindon. Expected to be the first of several.

A click. Rory got in first.

'Hello, Adam, what can I do for you?'

'Good morning, Rory. I won't beat about the bush. I am calling to say I have decided not to go ahead with your design for our showroom.'

Rory felt that in his solar plexus.

'I'm very sorry to hear you've changed your mind. You said you liked the preliminary drawings.'

'I do.'

'Then why the change?'

'Astrid Lindstrom and I have agreed to look elsewhere.'

Astrid Lindstrom was the daughter of the kitchens' designer and manufacturer. A family business.

'May I remind you, Adam, that we shook hands on the deal.'

'That's true, but nothing has been signed yet. And I'm telling you it's off. We will of course cover your costs for the design.'

'If you want to see some other ideas, I can draw up a few more outlines for you. Why don't I come up and we can discuss whatever the problem is?'

'No, I am already looking elsewhere.' It was said quickly. The man was embarrassed.

Rory's brain started thinking on its feet. 'Listen, Adam, there's obviously some kind of problem or you wouldn't be making this call. We have to get together and thrash it out. I'll book us a London hotel room for tomorrow to give us peace and quiet away from telephones, so that we can take it step by step. Perhaps we could take in a West End show in the evening,' he added as if an afterthought.

The man was tempted.

Rory stepped into the hesitation. 'I hear the new musical at the Piccadilly is worth seeing.'

'Er . . .' then a definite, 'No. But thank you. Goodbye.' The fish wriggled free.

'Damn,' Rory exploded as he banged down the receiver. 'What the hell caused that?' He strode into his partner's office to impart the bad news. 'Gary, the kitchen showroom is cancelled. Adam Forke just dropped that little grenade into my lap.'

A blond head, designer shaggy, looked up from a computer screen. Computer generated extensions of repetitive design work saved literally hundreds of pen-pushing hours and Gary Saunders was the expert. Though not exactly attractive, with eyes too close and nose too large, he had what Alex assured Rory was an endearing and engaging manner. Rory, who had known Gary since they were both teenagers, was willing to take his wife's word for it knowing how effective he was with the opposite sex.

'What?' Gary swung his chair round. 'I thought it was all agreed.'

'Well it is now all un-agreed. We can forget it.'

'I hope you told old Forke to Forke off. The time waster!'

Rory shook his head. 'I don't understand what happened. He was all for my design one day, and the next, wham! All over.'

'Didn't he explain?'

'No, not at all. Maybe another firm has tempted them with a tasty backhander. He gave no clue. Made a passing reference to Astrid, that's all.'

'Wankers the lot of them,' Gary snorted.

It was the way he quickly ducked his head down to the keyboard that caught Rory's attention. Guilty vibrations. Shaggy hair hiding his face, fingers fiddling.

'Gary,' Rory said sharply enough to make his partner look round. 'What do you know about Forke and this . . . ?' He ground to a halt as enlightenment crashed down on him. 'It's Astrid. Astrid Lindstrom, isn't it? What have you been up to with her?'

'You're off your trolley.'

'Like hell I am. The Scandinavian-type girl in Swindon. Alex told me you had been seen with a Scandinavian girl. Furtive was the word she used. You were dating our client, weren't you? And now you've split. Of all the stupid, short-sighted . . .'

'Joanna bloody Ginelli or Dolcelatte or whatever her name is.

She's the nosy little tell-tale, isn't she? I knew when I bumped into her at the Brunel Centre that day that she was going to be trouble.'

'It's Donelli.'

'Once a professional busybody, always a bloody busybody.'

'You must be out of your mind to get involved with a client. First rule of business.'

Gary pulled an apologetic smile and offered himself up to the slaughter with good grace. 'Sorry, partner, you're right. I should have known better. I humbly apologise, even if it is a bit late. Deduct compensation out of my weekly pittance. It's just that she was so . . .'

'Swedish?'

'Utterly.' A blissful smile of remembrance spread over his face.

Rory abandoned his irritation as a lost cause. His partner was not always as reliable as he was talented. 'I don't know what a gorgeous creature like Astrid saw in an ugly bastard like you anyway. Obviously she came to her senses in the end.'

Gary sighed with melodramatic despair. 'Found herself a muscle-bound Rugby Union player, would you believe?'

Rory laughed heartlessly. 'Shows she has taste. But what a waste of the chance of a contract.'

Much more seriously Gary said, 'I am sorry, old pard. Bloody stupid I admit. Not to be repeated, I promise.'

'Damn well better not be,' Rory warned and left it at that. On his way back through reception, he stopped for a word with Jan, the secretary-cum-receptionist who held the strings of the company together with silken control. 'I haven't heard any response from Parker & Crane. I was expecting their tender on the restaurant job by today. Give them a call, will you, Jan and chase it up.'

'Certainly.' The usual efficient nod from Jan Hodge, a woman comfortably in her fifties with nothing to prove. 'And I have a call for you from Marco Donelli.'

'I'll take it in my office. Ask Paula to come in afterwards, will you, with the new statistics on the town centre redevelopment. Thanks.'

He returned to his desk, ever ready to make time for a fiery argument over Ferrari's chances in next Sunday's Belgian Grand Prix.

'*Ciao*, you misguided Mediterranean maniac. Calling to chicken out of Sunday, are you?'

A stream of Italian, in which 'stupido' seemed to figure more than once, shattered his eardrum.

'Didn't quite catch that, Marco.'

'No more than Williams or McLaren will catch Ferrari. You have as much judgement as a piece of your English cabbage. Wet and tasteless.'

Rory grinned. He liked that one.

'Tell Joanna to have the Kleenex piled high. You'll be crying into your chianti and lamenting into your lasagne by the time Sunday's race is over.'

Another burst of Italian, then, '*Domenega*, Sunday, that's what I'm ringing about.'

'I knew it. Defeat looms too large for you to face it.'

'No, no, no, you are blinded by all that warm beer and Yorkshire pudding. I am suggesting that instead of you coming over to Ramsbury on Sunday as arranged, I am prepared to give you the pleasure of seeing Ferrari triumph in your own home. That way your brilliant Alex,' Rory smiled at the 'breeleeant', 'can stand by with her very clever syringes to restore your heart to life after it breaks.'

'What's the matter? Joanna banned Ferrari from the house?'

A deep throaty chuckle crackled down the line. 'No, she values her marriage.'

'Just as well to get the priorities right.'

'*Esatto*!'

'So what's the problem at your place on Sunday?'

During the Grand Prix season Rory and Marco alternated between each other's houses for the ritual race of the multi-cylinder chariots. This Sunday Marco's had been granted the honour.

'*Bambini. Moltissimi bambini.*'

'Too many children?'

'*Si*. The twins' birthday party.'

'Are you telling me that your children's birthday party takes precedence over the Belgian Grand Prix? What kind of Italian are you, for heaven's sake?'

He almost heard Marco's Florentine shrug. 'A married one.'

'Well we certainly cannot permit the sacrilege of infant shrieks to defile the music of a Renault V10. As one devotee to another, I offer you sanctuary.'

'The Ferrari V12 roar will drown out that squawking V10 at Spa.'

'Don't push your luck, Donelli.'

'It's the British cars that will need pushing. And need the luck.'

'A bottle of scotch says it will be a British driver in pole on the starting grid.' Rory's attention was distracted by Paula appearing in the doorway with an armful of papers. 'Ciao, Marco, until Sunday. Don't forget to bring your ice cream.'

It was the smell that hit her. As Alex carried an armful of fresh towels upstairs to the bathroom, a cocktail of bath oils, shampoo, gels and other expensively scented ingredients, drifted down in a fragrant mist. Surely she was out of the bath by now.

It was Sunday morning and Rory was already out waging war against the lawns. Through the open window she could hear the irritated buzz of the mower as it flicked up a migrant stone from the grass. Though the sky overhead was a repetitive blue, the air was muggy and heavy clouds huddled on the horizon. It was an hour earlier that Alex had heard Zena run a bath and she was surprised to see a perfumed vapour still seeping from under the door. She tried the handle and it turned readily. Zena must have finished. Alex walked in, but two strides were enough to show she was mistaken. Inside, the steam hung in a damp haze from the ceiling but swirling into it from below was an unmistakable grey snake of smoke. Cigarette smoke.

'Caught me at it, have you?' Zena laughed unrepentantly as she lay in the bath, chin-deep in bubbles. One hand was raised above the froth, a cigarette firmly in place. The dusty smell of its ash was only just discernible in the onslaught of heavy perfumes that drenched the room.

'Oh, come on, Zena. You know the house rules. It's not much to ask. No smoking indoors.'

Since arriving, Zena had seemed to be complying and had blithely agreed to poison the garden with her nicotine rather than the house. As the weather had been mainly fine, this was no real hardship.

'Like old times, isn't it?' Snatching a final drag, Zena dipped the glowing tip into the bath water. A faint hiss ruffled the bubbles. She added it to the two butts already growing soggy on the side of the bath.

Alex was trying to look annoyed, but a creeping smile spoiled the effect. Old times? Yes, they echoed up from a deep, disused well. Yes, Zena in the bath on a Sunday morning, door carelessly unlocked. Parents at church. Alex had walked in and found her thirteen-year-old sister trying sophisticated on for size. Hair swept up on top of her head, eyes black with kohl and mascara that the steam, smoke and inexperience had smeared to blotchy smudges, one hand elegantly poised wafting a cigarette around as she tried to croon in unconvincing imitation of Cher, her idol. Suppressed coughing sent ripples through the water.

Old, old times. How could she have forgotten?

Panic had only set in when the grandfather clock in the hall struck eleven. Final prayers would be winging their way through the newly restored church roof. Zena had leapt from the bath with undignified haste, her pubescent curves dribbling rivulets of bath water on to the carpet as she raced to the window and yanked it open. Her hands flapped at the air ineffectually, voice rising to a high-pitched wail.

'Ali, Daddy will be furious. Quickly, help me. Get the smoke out of the window. Ali, stop laughing. Just stop it.'

Alex couldn't help it. The sight of her skinny little sister, naked, wet and black-eyed had sent her into a fit of giggles. She had collapsed on to the wicker linen basket, rocking with laughter, legs clamped together against accidents.

Zena had shrieked at her, 'Don't be silly, Ali, stop it, stop it.' She had seized Alex's arm and tugged her off the basket, but the laughter had robbed Alex's legs of strength. She crumpled in a heap of uncontrollable giggles on to the floor, dragging Zena down with her.

That had set Zena off. Now they were both laughing hysterically in a tangle of teenage limbs and auburn hair, whooping for breath and clutching each other weakly. The sound of the car in the drive was like a bucket of cold water. Zena froze and stared at her sister like a deer caught in approaching headlights. Her teeth started to chatter.

Control came swooping back to Alex. She disentangled herself immediately, closed and bolted the bathroom door, then removed every bottle and aerosol from the bathroom cabinet. She tipped a good splash of absolutely everything into the bath water and sprayed the air with a prolonged barrage of deodorant, cologne and furniture polish. The polish was intended by her mother for the windowsill and pine shelving, but it had added a sweet stickiness to the other perfumes that seemed to enhance their effectiveness.

With heaving lungs, Alex sniffed experimentally. 'I can't smell smoke any more. Can you?'

'My nose is on overload,' Zena gasped and began to giggle again.

'Get rid of that thing.' Alex pointed at the incriminating object on the floor. The cigarette butt was squashed but still intact.

Obediently Zena picked it up, dropped it down the loo and flushed the handle. She took a deep, steadying breath of relief as she watched the water drown the evidence under a swirling whirlpool of bubbles.

'Mummy will go mad when she smells all this, Ali. You know we're not supposed to touch her stuff.'

'Which would you prefer? Mummy mad at you? Or Daddy?'

Zena got the point.

She pulled the plug out of the bath, wrapped herself in a towel and from the luxury of brand new safety, grinned at her older sister. 'Bet you haven't smoked yet! I've got the rest of the packet under my bed. I'll show you how. In the woods though.' Hearing her mother's footsteps on the stairs, she unlocked the door and scuttled back to her room.

Alex was just about to follow her example when she decided to check on the loo first. Her heart dropped faster than a bomb.

The filter tip floated in its lake like a buoyant cork island.

Her mother's footsteps were almost at the bathroom door. Already Alex could hear the voice raised in protest. 'Has someone been using my perfume? It smells like a brothel out here. Which of you . . . ?'

Shutting her eyes tight, Alex plunged her hand into the tainted lake and wrapped her fingers round the cigarette end.

Old times. A cat's whisker away from forgotten.

What else was buried down in that well?

Alex opened the window, then sat down on the edge of the bath. 'Those cigarettes in the woods put me off smoking for life.' She smiled at the naked face floating above the water. Equally unwilling to be flushed away. 'I have to thank you for that.'

'Too bad it didn't work like that on me.'

'Remember when Daddy eventually caught you smoking in the surgery. You were drenching the room with antiseptic spray in one hand and cigarette smoke in the other when he walked in. You thought we were still out on an emergency call.'

'Yes, but I was sixteen by then. He couldn't stop me.'

'He didn't see it quite that way.'

Zena gave a hoot of laughter. 'You're telling me. He exploded higher than the stratosphere. I couldn't decide which he was trying to protect most. His beloved surgery or my lungs.'

It had never occurred to Alex that Zena might see it that way. 'You, of course. He was always trying to protect you.'

'From what?'

'From you.'

'What rot! He just wanted control.'

Alex scooped up a handful of bubbles and let them trickle like whipped egg-white through her fingers. 'That was the only way he knew how to show love. To show he cared.'

'Bollocks to the bastard.' Zena sat up, seized the Imperial Leather and started to soap her leg.

Alex watched with interest the movement of the pert new breasts, full yet designer youthful. They jiggled almost naturally. Unexpectedly soft and pliant. But Alex felt again the twinge of concern and tried to separate it from the twinge of envy.

'He just liked to make people march to his tune,' Zena added. 'Especially me.'

But Alex remembered a time when it hadn't been like that. When all Zena had to do was bat her tawny young eyes at him and he would laugh and scoop her up in his arms, happy to let her lead him quite literally by the nose wherever she chose.

'He wasn't like that in the early days, Zena. Not with you.'

As her sister lathered her arms, Alex noticed the pronounced triceps, clearly defined against the slim limbs, as if Zena must have worked out at one time. Another American obsession. 'He let you get away with murder.'

Zena chuckled delightedly. 'Yes, he did, didn't he? Not like you. Always wanting more from you, he was.'

Alex nodded, to the memories rather than to Zena. Yes, always she'd had to produce better and better. The goal posts had kept moving, inch by inch, yard by confusing yard. Nothing she did was ever quite enough. From him she had learnt about striving for what you want in life. Setting yourself aims and working single-mindedly towards them. A perfectionist Zena had called her to Rory. There was nothing wrong with that. It was what produced results. But perfectionism was a harsh and unforgiving taskmaster.

She swirled her hand in the water, washing away the bubbles and the memories. Zena was humming 'The Schoop Schoop Song' and drawing spiralling circles of soap around her nipples. She glanced up and caught the direction of her older sister's gaze.

'Like them?'

'There was nothing wrong with your old ones.'

Zena dunked herself back under the water. 'Don't be stupid, Alex. They were too flat.'

'Too flat for what?'

'Too flat for my liking. And don't give me a lecture on the dangers of silicon. I've already heard it.'

It was too late anyway.

Alex stood up. 'Zena, no more smoking in the house. Got it?'

Zena pulled out her sweetly acquiescent smile and offered it convincingly. 'Of course not.'

Alex had seen the same act for her father. It made her acutely uncomfortable. She left her sister to her bath and Cher walking in Memphis.

5

'Is she up yet?' Rory was scrubbing dirt off his hands over the sink. The throttle cable on the mower had caught and bent on a branch, and it had taken him longer to fix than he had anticipated. His mood was not good. 'Or is she spending the whole morning in bed again?'

'No, she's finished her bath.' Alex was mixing pastry, unaware that she had decorated her cheek with a streak of flour when she brushed a strand of hair away. 'While she dressed, we had quite a chat.'

'Oh? What about?'

'We had been talking about old times together when she was in the bath. It seemed to make her open up a bit because when I took her my hairdrier, she told me she's flat broke.'

Rory looked round sharply. 'I thought as much.' His frown changed to a smile as he noticed his wife's white warpaint but he didn't mention it. 'What has she done with it all?'

'When times were good, she and Chet lived the high life and spent extravagantly – holidays, yachts . . .'

'Plastic surgeons.'

'Yes, plastic surgeons. And jewellery.'

'What happened?'

'The usual. Chet invested badly and the more he lost, the more he borrowed to pour in after it. Eventually there were only debts. Her inheritance from our parents and her jewellery all went. Down the tubes with his business.'

'People are too greedy. I assume when the pot of gold was gone, she walked out on him?'

Alex thumped the dough on to the work surface a little

61 •

harder than was strictly necessary. She shrugged. 'It looks like it.'

Rory glanced at her uneasily. 'That means she could be here forever.'

'No, I'll speak to her.'

'Soon?'

'Soon.'

'She is well dug in. Might take some shifting.'

'She needed time. To recover. We're giving her that without stress. Heaven knows, she does nothing all day, not even prepare a meal or dust a shelf.'

'Or mow a lawn.'

'Exactly. We've put no pressure on her at all. So any day now, I will point her in the direction of the Job Centre and DSS and tell her it's time she started to fend for herself.' The rolling pin squashed the ball of dough flat and promptly stuck to it. 'She takes it all for granted.' Thump, thump on the pastry.

Rory put down the towel and came over to his wife. 'Would you like me to have a word with her?'

A shake of her head.

'I would keep it calm. But firm.' He trailed a finger in the soft white dust, outlining a crude racing car.

'No. It's my job.'

'Sure?'

A nod. 'Thanks anyway.' The pastry received another hefty thump.

Rory turned her towards him. 'Don't get stirred up over this, Alex. If it's really what you want, let her stay longer.' He offered a reassuring grin, 'I'll behave myself, I promise. Not a curt remark will pass my lips.'

The smile was slow coming, but it got there. 'That Prozac I've been hiding in your coffee all summer is working at last then, you old grouch.' But she leant her head against his and added softly, 'Thank you.'

He kissed her twice on the lips, stroked her unmarked cheek with his white finger and said, 'You're welcome.'

*　　*　　*

When Alex heard Zena come downstairs, she gave her five minutes and then went in search of her. As teenagers they had often spent Sunday mornings huddled competitively over that week's crossword puzzle and she anticipated a nostalgic rerun. But when she found Zena draped over the length of the sofa in the sitting-room, feet propped up on the armrest as if she had done a hard day's work, there was no sign that old habits had been maintained. She was skimming with desultory interest through the *Sunday Times* magazine.

'Fancy a go at the crossword?' Alex asked. 'For old times' sake?'

'No thanks.' Zena did not even bother to look up.

Frustrated, Alex wandered round the room, straightening the books on the shelf, resetting the Victorian marble clock that had once belonged to her parents and still insisted on gaining five minutes each day. At the window she stared out across the sun-parched lawn and caught sight of a bushy grey tail scurrying up the dappled sycamore trunk, ducking under a branch and tightroping it into thin air. A quick glance around reassured her that the cats were nowhere in sight. Squirrel-chasing was one of their favourite pastimes. She noticed that two flies had crash-landed on the windowsill during the night and now lay legs aloft in final immobility.

'There seems to be a plague of flies this summer,' she commented out loud. 'It must be the hot weather. Their dead bodies turn up everywhere.'

'Find yourself a cleaning lady to deal with them.'

'I already have one. Had her for years. She's useless. Every Monday morning I make a list of what I want done and by Friday, she's never got through half of it. She drives me up the wall.'

Zena stared around the dust-free zone, searching in vain for a mote of dirt. 'Looks fine to me. But if you're not happy, get rid of her.' Losing interest, Zena returned to her magazine.

'I can't.'

'Why not?' She flicked a page.

'She's me.'

Caught by surprise, Zena looked up, an appreciative smile banishing the bland lethargy. 'Nice one, Ali. You had me going then.' She snuggled deeper into the sofa's lap.

'While we're on the subject, why don't you give a hand around the house while you're here? Rory and I are both working all day. You're not. So how about pulling your weight?'

Slowly Zena lifted her gaze from an article on liposuction. Her stare rested like a ton weight on Alex. 'Don't pull a Daddy act on me. That was his mind-curdling anthem throughout my teens. "Pull your weight around here." No chance!'

Alex did not want to force it. Not yet. It was too early. Using a tissue from her pocket, she picked up the fly corpses and left her sister to her liposuction.

The telephone rang just as Alex was putting the apple pie in the oven. She let it ring while she rinsed her hands. Perhaps it would give up. It didn't oblige.

'Hello?'

'Hi, it's Joanna. Not the warmest of welcomes I've had on the phone. What's up?'

Alex made more of an effort. 'Nothing, just preoccupied. Has anyone ever told you it's rude to ask so many questions all the time?'

'Hundreds of times. Thousands probably. It always means they've something to hide.'

Alex laughed and immediately felt her neck muscles loosen a notch. 'How are the birthday boys?'

'The twins? Ecstatic. Driving me crazy.'

'And Angelica?'

'Living up to her name. An angel.' Joanna's voice had turned to mush. 'Such a happy, easy baby and feeds like a trooper. Can't get enough of her big brothers either, so they maul her like one of their Action men. I wouldn't be surprised to find her riding in their new pedal cars today.'

'Trust Marco. What sort of pedal cars?'

'Guess. Need I say more?'

'Bright red racing ones?'

'Of course. It's bedlam.'

'I was going to pop over later with the twins' birthday presents from us. What time does their party start?'

'That's what I was ringing about. While the big boys are playing with their cars at your house, why don't you come over and join my little boys for their jelly and ice cream? There will be swarms of kids steam-rollering the garden but you can hold my angel for me while I extract jelly from their hair and Lego from the little darlings' mouths. How about it?'

Alex didn't much like the angel idea but was happy to lend a hand with the jelly. 'Sounds too exciting to miss. What time?'

'About two-ish.'

'See you then.'

'Alex?'

'What?'

'Do make sure you hide the duelling pistols before you leave home.'

Marco arrived punctually at a quarter to one. Alex opened the door to him, was kissed enthusiastically on both now clean cheeks and presented with a single pink rose from his garden.

Behind her, Rory groaned. 'You Italians make me sick.'

'Take no notice of him, Marco. He's just jealous because Englishmen have no idea how to treat a lady.' Alex inhaled the seductive perfume of the rose, tantalisingly elusive. 'It's beautiful. Thank you.' She kissed him again.

'That's enough of that. It's cars you've come to drool over, not my wife.'

Marco laughed. 'In Italy we say, go ahead, handle my wife but don't touch my car.'

'Well, perhaps you have a point there.'

'You ruffians,' Alex scolded. 'Go and play your big-boy games in front of the television.'

She headed towards the kitchen. 'I'll put my beautiful, romantic rose in a vase before it wilts. It will have to last me until you come again, Marco.' A mock frown at Rory was meant to make him feel guilty but failed miserably. She expected no less. 'Coffee?'

'*Grazie.*'

'He owes me another bottle of scotch.'

'No, I'm betting it all on Schumacher to beat your Britishmen out of the sight today.'

The mythical bottles of whisky were always being passed from one to the other when the dead-certs failed to finish. Rory owned fourteen of them already.

In the kitchen Alex placed her solitary rose in a vase and smiled to herself at the gift. Charm came to Marco as readily as breathing.

'The Cheshire cat got into you?' It was Zena coming in through the back door. Earlier she had declined lunch and retreated into the garden with her cigarettes and lighter in hand. Today her hair was fastened back in a complicated honey plait and she was wearing pale linen shorts and shirt, light tan leather slingbacks and a gold chain at her neck. The casual elegance of it all was impressively stylish for a stay-at-home Sunday. Alex was hoping it was a good omen, the indicator of a desire to get back out into the big world beyond their four cottage walls. The Siamese cat scuttled out through the open door.

'I was just admiring my rose.'

Zena inspected it, unimpressed. 'It's not from a florist.'

'Of course not,' Alex laughed. 'It's from Marco, not my lover.'

Zena studied her sister closely. 'Do you have one?'

'One what?'

'Lover.'

'Seven actually. One for each day of the week.'

Zena smiled slowly. 'You wouldn't tell me anyway.'

'No, Zena, I assure you I don't have a lover. Nor do I want one.' Alex poured out coffee and placed the cups on a tray. 'Rory is the only lover I want.'

'Husbands make acutely boring lovers.'

'Is that the voice of experience?'

Zena nodded solemnly. 'Sure is.'

'Well you're wrong. It depends on how good the relationship is.'

Zena flashed a superior smile. 'Dream on, big sister. Dream on.'

Alex added sugar and a milk jug to the tray and tried not to get annoyed. 'Coffee?'

'Mmm. Yes.' Zena accepted the cup but was not ready to drop the subject in exchange. 'Had any other lovers? For comparison. And I mean ever?'

'No.'

'No one?'

'No. Rory and I have been together since I was eighteen. There was nobody serious before him.'

Zena reached over, placed her cup beside the milk jug and picked up the tray. 'Point proven.'

'No, Zena. It's not quantity that counts.'

Her sister raised a suggestive eyebrow. 'When it comes to sex, I think you'll find it does.' She waited at the door for Alex to open it for her. 'By the way, what's this Italian like?'

'Tall, dark and impeccably handsome.' Alex said it with bad grace, annoyed with herself for allowing her younger sister to rattle her so easily. She opened the door. 'Don't expect any conversation from them except about slicks, racing lines and down-force effects.' Her invitation to Zena to accompany her to the birthday party had been given scant consideration. 'They won't even notice you're on the same planet.'

Zena smiled with a small snort that sounded almost like a purr. 'Don't bet on it.'

Alex kicked the door shut behind her. It explained the dressy clothes and the willingness to carry trays. If she didn't know Marco better, it might have spoiled the birthday party for her.

Alex was in charge of the paddling pool. Joanna and the other mothers were busy carrying out the Happy Birthday plates for tea on the lawn and Alex had been handed Angelica.

'Just for a minute,' Joanna had assured her and breezed away.

At first, Alex had stared stiffly down at the soft bundle in her arms and been frightened to move. It might cry. Or worse, be sick and choke. The Italian-brown eyes gazed up at her expectantly until Alex tried a smile. The mouth twitched in reply. So far so good. Her grip softened a fraction. A gurgling noise bubbled out of the tiny pursed lips. She had known a puppy make a similar noise when it was well fed and contented, so took it as a good sign. She relaxed enough to turn her attention back to the child in the paddling pool, a girl with rampant freckles and hair scraped back into skinny blonde bunches. She was preparing to empty a plastic bucket full of water over her own head, eyes screwed up as tight as a kitten's at birth. Her shrill shriek of delighted horror as the water descended over her sent a shockwave through Angelica. The baby's face started to pucker. Alex was tempted to panic.

Louis rescued her. He was the quieter of the twins and his dark head popped up in front of her like a saving grace.

'Angelly, Angelly,' he chirped and thrust a finger into Angelica's jerky starfish hand, followed by a bath of kisses on her crumpled face and even a spot of nose rubbing for dessert. The contented bubbles started up again. He grinned up at Alex proudly, 'She's my little sister.'

'Louis, you are a genius.'

'It's tea, Lucy,' Louis informed his young guest succinctly and she whooped off across the garden, abandoning the pool.

'Thank you, Louis.'

He slipped his hot sticky palm into hers and together they trotted over to where a trestle table had been set up in the shade of a cherry tree. The flimsy boards were bowed under the weight of platters of crustless sandwiches, sausages and sausage rolls, crisps, cheese straws, biscuits, cakes, jellies, strawberries, yogurts, ice-cream and . . . Alex stopped counting. She gave Louis's stubby fingers a grateful squeeze and released him to take pride of place at the head of the table with his brother. It was the signal for twenty pairs of hands to start grabbing.

Still cradling the baby, Alex was just about to sink thankfully, but very carefully, to the grass, when Joanna's voice pre-empted her intention.

'Alex, come and help pour the drinks for this horde. Dump Angelica on Connie.'

Connie was sprawled very pregnantly on a lounger. She held out her arms obligingly.

Alex didn't want to dump Angelica. The thought jumped out at her unexpectedly. She realised she was just getting used to carting around the warm extra weight on her arm like an extension of herself. It fitted into the curves like the matching piece of a jigsaw. The dark attentive eyes followed her every move, mouth and limbs wriggling fiercely at intervals. Alex touched the downy cheek with her lips, careful not to poke an eye out with her nose. It was as smooth as . . . Alex smiled. As smooth as a baby's cheek, and the dusky curls smelt oddly of warm lemon.

'Hurry up, Alex, Jamie wants some apple juice.'

Alex looked across at them. Joanna and the other mothers were waltzing round the table, hands passing plates, mopping spills and accepting rejects with practised ease. The sun filtered through the umbrella of leaves and reflected up off the shiny red tablecloth, wrapping the children in a rose-coloured haze. Lucy of the paddling pool emptied the remains of her lemonade over the sandwich on the plate of the boy next to her. 'Apple juice for me too.'

'Come on, Alex, get a move on.'

Alex relinquished Angelica into the waiting arms and replaced her with the jug of apple juice.

Once the candle-blowing ritual was over, it was the turn of the Punch and Judy show. The antics in the striped cubicle on the lawn may not have kept the revellers quiet, but at least it kept them still. The debris of melting ice cream and fizzless lemonade was ferried indoors, quarter-eaten sandwiches and cake dumped on the bird-table.

'Half time,' Joanna announced as she emerged with a hefty pot of tea and the mothers welcomed the excuse to call it a day for the moment. They sat around the table in the dappled sunshine and picked at the remains in front of them, one eye on who was doing what to whom among both the puppets and the audience.

'Great success,' Connie congratulated her hostess. Angelica had been deposited safely in her pram to sleep off the excitement. 'You must be exhausted.'

'Worn out,' Joanna beamed, looking the picture of health.

The conversation ebbed and flowed round the table, in a short time covering a variety of infant illnesses, the relative merits of the nursery schools and playgroups in the area, the amount of weight lost by the vicar's wife and speculation about the reason for it. One mother described in detail the horrors of her previous week at the office during her company's takeover bid, just to

prove that women could now be as boring as men about their
careers.

Alex listened with half an ear. She munched into a tiny
triangular sandwich, discovered its Marmite centre and didn't
even notice that her hand took another. Her attention was
riveted to the round eyes and frantic squeals of the group on
the grass.

'Mr Punch, Mr Punch.'

'He's got the sausages.'

'Behind you, behind you.'

For one particularly young child it was too much to bear. She
buried her face behind her fingers and squeezed her eyes tight
shut on the demons until the show was over. Alex found herself
watching Louis. His twin, Georgie, displayed a macho bravado,
but Louis's eyes grew enormous, black pupils huge caverns of
primal fear, as the crocodile snapped its plastic dentures. She
almost went and rescued him the way he had rescued her. At
the end of twenty minutes all the children emerged from the
traumas of Punch's domestic crises with renewed stamina for
games and races; the birthday pedal cars were put through their
fibreglass paces and the parcel was passed with due deference
to tradition. At six-fifteen on the dot, grubby hands waved
farewell and over-excited faces recited the obligatory 'Thank
you for having me' without too much obvious prompting.

Alex was exhausted.

As the last car backed out of the drive, Joanna sighed with
satisfaction. 'Come on, let's go and have a glass of wine. We
deserve it. Angelica will be due for her feed soon.' The baby
was a lightweight bundle on her shoulder.

Alex stepped over an abandoned tractor and followed her
indoors. The sitting-room floor was covered in colourful pieces
of chunky Lego and trampled balloons, and an African primrose
lay on its side, trailing roots and earth across the windowsill.

'How do you cope with all this, Joanna? You're not even
getting a proper night's sleep and this is non-stop.'

Joanna gave an easy, contented laugh and produced wine and
a glass from a cabinet. 'Of course it is, that's what makes it fun.'
She plonked herself down on the sofa, unfastened her blouse
and bra front and let the nuzzling angel help herself.

Alex cleared up the Lego and plant, then poured herself a drink. Joanna declined on the grounds that she was doing her milk-bar impression. Just when Alex was raising the wine to her lips, Louis and Georgie bounded in and begged her to show them how to fill up their new and highly prized water-pistols. As she allowed herself to be tugged from the room, she cast a glance back at Joanna.

'You must have the emotional stamina of Mother Theresa. Give me a day of hard graft in the surgery and a night in a freezing barn with my arm up a cow – any time. It's a walk in the park compared to this.'

Joanna chuckled from the warmth of her snuggling child. 'But cows don't make you laugh.'

6 ʃ

Not often had Rory been alone with his sister-in-law. Her usual
habit was to retreat to her room when Alex was not around but
this time there was no hint that she might vacate Alex's chair. She
was comfortably entrenched in it, unlit cigarette twirling between
her fingers. It had been performing its acrobatics for more than five
minutes. Intended to irritate, Rory felt certain. And succeeding.

'Why don't you go and smoke that thing in the garden if you
feel like a cigarette?'

She treated him to a cool stare. 'You don't get rid of me that
easily, brother-in-law.'

He had got used to the bluntness now. It had the virtue of
avoiding any misunderstandings between them.

'You can't blame me for trying, sister-in-law.'

'I don't.'

He was mildly amused by the change in her. Gone was the
afternoon's fluttering 'What is the point of the warm-up lap,
Marco?', 'Why don't they carry enough fuel for the whole race,
Marco?' and 'Oh Marco, is that allowed? It's so dangerous.' Bare
legs crossing and uncrossing. And Marco had been dope enough
to fall for it. He had delighted in explaining in detail about weight
ratios, tyre change, slipstreaming and stealing a driver's air,
believing he had found a new convert to his religion. It was
only when she had received his double-cheeked *arriverderci*
kiss and waved farewell to the Alfa Romeo's tail-lights, that
she bestowed on Rory a triumphant smirk and took possession
of her sister's chair.

He watched the clock tick away another three minutes of
silence.

'Zena, what are you planning to do with the rest of your life? You must have some idea about your future.'

'None at all.' More cigarette fiddling.

'Then for heaven's sake let us help you sort something out. It's no good ignoring the situation you're in. You can't stay here indefinitely doing nothing.'

The faintest of smiles. 'I know.'

'Alex tells me you're broke.'

'Sure am. I have exactly one hundred and eighty-five pounds, plus you and dearest sister, between me and starvation.'

Rory was not going to have her sitting in Alex's chair, indifferent to the disruption she caused, assuming it could go on forever.

'Zena, that is melodramatic and completely false, as you well know. Tomorrow morning I will take you down to the DSS and Job Centre and they will start the process of fixing you up with Income Support and some job interviews. So don't give me that helpless and destitute garbage. There's a whole system out there ready to help and to show you how to stand on your own feet, not on somebody else's.'

Zena put the cigarette in her mouth, took a long empty drag and tipping her head back, puffed out imaginary smoke. 'You sound like Alex,' she said to the ceiling.

'Good. We both want to help you, but you must see that you have to help yourself as well.'

'I am helping myself.' She dropped her gaze to look at him directly. 'To your hospitality.'

Rory had to admire the effrontery, if not the sentiment.

'Your life before you came here is your own business, Zena. But right now, by making use of my hospitality you have dumped your present existence in my lap. Made it my business. Therefore I repeat, tomorrow you and I will take a trip, like it or not, to start finding you an income of some sort.'

She removed the cigarette from her lips and dislike hardened her eyes to a muddy amber. 'Another male bully-boy. The world is full of them.'

He resisted the urge to throw her and her suitcase out on to the front lawn, but only just. And only for Alex's sake. From that moment, he started counting the minutes to her departure. Yesterday would not be too soon.

Alex was late back. By the time she arrived home, the heavy clouds that had been piling up on the horizon had joined forces and were marching forward with ominous intent. The air hung in a breathless stupor and when Rory opened yet another window to create a hint of a draught, he felt the first speck of rain.

The meal was a quiet affair. Zena was, as usual, unwilling to contribute and her silent presence cramped any normal flow of table conversation.

'Party go well?' Rory asked Alex.

'Yes.'

'Did Louis and Georgie enjoy the Punch and Judy show?'

'Yes.'

'What about you? Have a good time?'

A nod.

It dawned on Rory that his wife had grown almost as uncommunicative as her sister. To fill the gap he started to tell her about the afternoon's race, intending his enthusiasm for Coulthard's masterly handling of his car to light the usual responding spark in her. He even admitted that Schumacher and Ferrari seemed to be getting it right this season, in the hope of raising a smile. But not a flicker.

Eventually it was Zena who jabbed at him with, 'For God's sake, can't you men ever talk about anything else? Cars are not the be-all and end-all of life and never will be. Only men would want to chase each other round in circles for hours on end. It's completely pointless.'

'Not quite the opinion I heard you express to Marco this afternoon, Zena.'

That irritated her. 'Don't try to be so smart. Marco did attempt to make it vaguely interesting, which is more than I can say for you and your Coulthard.'

'Coming from someone who doesn't bother to make any effort at conversation unless a tempting new pair of trousers walks into the room, that is . . .'

'To hell with you and your insinuations.' Zena's voice was raised, losing its soft American drawl.

Alex threw her fork at the table. It clattered against a glass and ricocheted on to the floor. 'Shut up. Shut up, both of you. Like a pair of squabbling alley cats, you are. I'm sick of it.'

They both stared at her in surprise.

She pushed herself to her feet. 'I have a headache. I'm going to bed.' She slammed out of the room.

Zena's eyes, bright with interest now, held Rory's. 'A headache, eh?'

Her slow smile was infuriating.

When Rory came up to bed, Alex seemed to be already asleep. He had checked on her earlier, bearing a peace offering of two aspirin but she had been subdued and uncommunicative. He had blamed it on the headache but as he slid under the duvet, he noticed that the aspirin still formed a squat Tower of Pisa on the bedside table. The warmth that flowed from his wife's body drew him to her, but he was careful not to disturb her and contented himself with just resting an arm across her naked hip. She was lying on her side, face turned away towards the dark square of window, but as soon as he touched her, he realised she was not asleep. He knew her body even better than his own and it was too rigid, muscles too tight. Only her breathing sounded convincing. He waited for a movement that might indicate she wanted to talk, but none came. Gently he brushed her shoulder with his lips and left her to the privacy of whatever thoughts were tangling up her head.

It was some time later that the window buffeted him awake from a hectic dream about collapsing roof timbers and as he waited for his heartbeat to settle down to a comfortable trot, he listened to the rain battering the glass into submission. He turned to look at the clock and his somnolent brain gradually succeeded in interpreting the arrangement of luminous pinpricks as twenty-five to four. Too early to wake up and too late to go back to sleep. He rolled over and tucked himself around Alex in the hope of catching some of her sleep waves. As he lay in the dark, listening to the wind tearing through the trees outside and a dull rumble of thunder in the distance, the week's major business problem crept into his head and before he could stop it, his mind had cranked up on all cylinders.

The borough council had asked him to adapt his town centre redevelopment scheme to accommodate three hundred and fifty cars instead of the two hundred and fifty that had been in the original brief. That meant something would have to go. He straightened a leg abruptly as if to kick the quandary out of his head but his foot bumped against an immovable object that gave an answering snore. Horatio, curled on the bed in a seamless ball, nose tucked firmly under his tail.

Rory returned to gnawing at the dilemma of whether the outline car park could be expanded to replace a clutch of small shop units without too much disruption to the overall concept. He was loath to lose those units as they were an important element in keeping some of the retail outlets small-scale and friendly, in harmony with the character of the town. Total domination by the large multiples could ruin a High Street and he was determined to keep a good mix of units in the project.

'Rory.'

Alex's voice dropped into the stillness of his thoughts. He had not realised she was awake but now felt her turn towards him.

'Storm wake you too?' he asked.

'No, I wasn't asleep.' Her voice was very low.

Uptight-low or just tired-low? Rory had been married enough years to recognise the signs. He dumped his business problems back into their compartment and asked, 'What's the matter? Not still stewing over my exchange of blows with Zena, are you?'

He felt, rather than saw, the shake of her head.

'No.'

He waited for more but none came. His hand reached out and found the soft hollow of her waist, creating a bridge for the words.

'It was the party today,' she said in the low voice. 'It got to me.'

Rory wanted her to stop. Right there.

But Alex continued, 'Seeing them all laughing and playing, tumbling over each other. Like kittens.'

'Don't, Alex.'

'Don't what? Don't admit it's what I want? What we both want?'

Rory stroked the warm skin of her stomach down to where it ridged faintly in an ancient scar. 'This won't get us anywhere, Alex.' There was no point going on. It had all been said before. Pick at the scab and it would bleed again.

'So we just carry on pretending, is that it? Pretending that just the two of us is enough. Oh God, I'm pretending so hard I even believe it at times.'

Rory pulled her to him and kissed her hair, to comfort himself as much as her. 'There's no harm in believing it. We are enough, just the two of us. A child would have been nice but . . .'

'Nice? Nice? What the hell is nice?'

'Alex, don't put us through this again.'

'I want to talk about it. I have to talk about it or I'll scream.'

'All right, we'll talk about it. If that's what you really want. But we've done this before, and before, and God knows how many times before that. We end up twisting our guts into knots, that's all.'

Alex rubbed her cheek hard against the bone of his shoulder, her version of head-banging. 'I don't want that.'

Then stop now, he almost shouted. Stop now. Please.

It had been over three years since they had decided not to talk about it again. The subject had been locked down in the dungeon and the key tossed away. Childlessness need not be a problem. They both had their work. Both derived enormous satisfaction from it and that was enough. For him, creativity in design was a kind of fatherhood in itself and Alex gave the gift of life to some animal every day of the week, ten times a day even. Wasn't it all enough?

Depends on how hard you pretend.

Even harder for her than for him.

Gently he stroked the coppery head on his shoulder, the fiery mane that had died to black in the darkness, easing out the tangles with familiar fingers. 'Alex,' he kissed the telltale furrows of misery on her forehead, 'I know how much it hurts. If you really need to talk about it again, then go ahead, talk. Or scream. I'm listening.'

A groan from deep inside her shuddered to the surface, but no words came.

'It's not the end of the world, Alex. Nor even the end of the line.' He knew she didn't want to hear it, but now that they had come this far, he wasn't going to leave it unsaid. 'There is always adoption.'

She jerked away from him and sat up, the covers falling away from her bare breasts, breasts that could never perform their natural function. 'I don't want someone else's child, Rory. Can't you understand that?'

'Of course I understand that. I feel much the same, but we both know that it's not possible to have one of our own. So there is no point yearning for it. It is impossible, Alex, so give it up. Accept the truth. The only option is adoption, we both know that.'

Alex jumped angrily out of bed and, outlined against the paler darkness of the window, her black silhouette leant towards him.

'No, no. No adoption. We agreed.'

He took a deep breath. 'Yes, I know we agreed. You made it clear how you felt and at the time I thought the same. But now I'm not so sure.'

'No adoption.' The words were shouted at him.

'No adoption means no child. It's closing the door forever. Is that what you want?'

Alex seized her pillow from the bed. In the darkness he did not realise what she was doing until the pillow hit him in the face. He yanked it from her and dumped it on the floor.

'For heaven's sake, Alex, stop that.'

A drumroll of thunder rattled the windows and the cat shot off the bed.

'I have stopped. Stopped pretending.' She was really yelling now, tearing the wound wide open. 'I'm sick of telling myself that Horatio and Hammy aren't any different from children. We feed and cuddle them and in return they give us their version of love. But it's not the same, Rory. It's not real.'

The unexpected glare of sheet lightning flashed round the room as if to demonstrate reality. Alex was crying. Not just a salty trickle, but the flood released by a breached dam engulfing her cheeks. That split second sight of his wife standing naked except for her tears sent shock waves through Rory.

Alex was losing control.

Alex never lost control. Not ever. Even during sexual abandon, she never quite let go. Not completely. Control was what got her through life.

Keeping his movements very calm, Rory slid out of bed and got as far as two steps towards her. 'Come on, darling, I know cats are no adequate child-replacement. We can . . .'

Thunder exploded overhead, slamming his words into the darkness. Rain blasted the window like shrapnel. The roar of sound pinned them in immobility for the few seconds it took the thunder to empty its cannon across the hills. Rory moved first. He had just reached her, felt her chilled limbs trembling under his fingers, when the lightning came again. Right overhead. A white flare that stripped the night bare. Alex shied like one of her nerve-taut mares and took off.

She was out of the room before he could stop her, her high-pitched wail of despair filtering through the next eruption of thunder. Rory reached for the landing light switch, flicked it down but nothing happened. He tried it again. Still nothing. The storm had taken out the electricity. The blackness was blanket thick.

'Alex,' he called.

He could hear her movements downstairs bumping into furniture, her sobs struggling against the screech of the wind.

'Alex,' he called more urgently and using the walls like braille, felt his way downstairs. Three steps before the bottom, his foot landed on something soft and a terrified yowl announced where Hamilton had been cowering, followed by the scamper of paws as the cat fled past him up the stairs. Rory lost his footing and the inevitable thud into the newel post jarred ribs and hip bone, but he silenced his grunt of pain in an effort to listen for Alex.

Not a sound in the house.

Another flash of lightning gave him a glimpse of an empty hall and an imprint to carry him through the returning darkness to the kitchen. The wind and rain were louder there. Too loud. Blind in the blackness, he stumbled towards the sound and reached it with the crunch of a bare toe. The back door was flapping wide open. Naked was not the best way to confront a storm but he stepped out into the garden heedlessly and bellowed, 'Alex, Alex.'

The wind snatched his words and the rain pummelled his skin.

'Alex, where are you? Alex.'

Nothing.

'Alex.'

Thunder for answer.

He waited for more lightning to illuminate the garden, but now that he wanted it, none came. The darkness was as absolute as sin. With a curse, Rory hurried back indoors, slammed the door on the rain and working by memory, felt his way to the dresser drawer. His fingers found the torch and pressed the switch. Puny it might be next to the storm's pyrotechnics, but its beam had the advantage of obedience to command. Its narrow yellow path of light led him to the cloakroom where coats and wellingtons were stored. He thrust his sodden and muddy feet into the boots, ignoring the mush oozing from his damaged toe, and grabbed his Barbour from a peg.

Alex's was missing. So were her boots.

He felt a trickle of relief.

But once outside again, he knew it was hopeless. She could be anywhere.

'Damn the bloody party.' And the blasted kids, wide-eyed and seductive, stealing under Alex's carefully-constructed defences.

But he did not give up until he had scoured every bush and shed in the garden, then trawled through the downpour in his car along every lane in a half-mile radius but the only sign of life he came across was a skinny rabbit and even that fled through the hedge into the woods. The rain bombarded the windscreen making it difficult to see out along the halogen beam, as it cut a murky swathe between the woods and fields that offered too many hiding places. At least he had the car heater. Alex had nothing.

Except the demons in her head.

When he finally returned home, he did a repeat performance on the garden and every room in the house. Unless she was hiding in a drawer, there was no sign of her.

There remained only Zena's room.

Still in the dripping Barbour, Rory did not hesitate. The need to find his wife drove out any concerns over his sister-in-law. He tapped the door sharply. It opened instantly, as if Zena had been standing on the other side. The torch picked out that she was wearing only a skimpy sleeveless tee-shirt that just about covered the essentials.

'Is Alex with you?'

'No, she's not.'

'Have you seen her tonight?'

'Walked out on you, has she?'

'Have you seen her, Zena?'

'No.'

'Are you sure?'

She stepped back for him to see for himself. 'I'm not hiding her, I assure you.'

Rory walked into her darkened room, flicked the torch over the bed, open wardrobe and rumpled suitcase on the floor, then withdrew.

'Sounds like there's more than one storm raging round this house,' Zena said to his back. 'Maybe she thinks she's better off out there in the rain than in here.'

Rory turned. 'What the hell do you mean by that?'

The beam of torchlight painted dark, mask-like shadows on her face.

'God only knows what you've done to distress her so much, brother-in-law, but it's obvious that she needs to be away from you.'

Rory stared at the face that even in the shadows held so many echoes of his wife's. But in the eyes swirled a barely suppressed panic, so intense that for a moment it even penetrated his own shroud of gloom.

'Go back to bed, Zena,' he said, shut the door on her and returned downstairs to sit out the remaining hour of darkness till dawn.

Zena stared rigidly at the square of black that was the door. Footsteps on the landing walking away. A shudder ran through her and she felt her diaphragm tighten in spasm, shortening her breath.

Careful now.

Air stuttered back into her lungs as the band of muscle loosened its grip.

Alex was gone.

She thrust aside the curtain of tousled hair that was cob-webbing her face, but the darkness did not change. She closed her eyes to shut it out. A sharp crack on the window as the storm snatched a branch from a tree and dashed it against the house made her jump, but did not manage to prise open her eyelids. She wrapped her bare arms around herself and squeezed tight, holding herself together.

Come back, Alex. Come back.

Lightning skidded across the sky in front of Alex's bolt hole, painting the trees silver, turning their leaves to tinsel and the rain to snow. A second later and the woods returned to the dense darkness that cloaked the incessant activity of its nocturnal world. The storm had daunted some of the more timid hearts but now that the first promise of dawn approached, a dash to find berries, worms, beetles and the occasional field-mouse prompted a flurry of movement all around her.

It had been her own fault. The accident. Alex had never blamed it on her father. Not even all those years ago.

Not like her mother. The accusing tones and whispered rows had exploded round her father behind closed doors. They had gone on and on.

'How could you let it happen to her? Your own daughter. How could you, Edward? You should have kept her safe.'

Alex felt foolish.

What was she doing here, a supposedly responsible adult, crouched on the sodden ground of an ancient charcoal-burner chimney in what felt like the middle of the night? What had it achieved?

Nothing. She had not been able to outrun the pain.

She hardly remembered the initial flight from the house, but had started to regain some shaky kind of control when she stumbled into a shallow ditch, finding herself in the nearby woods. Drenched and chilled to the bone, she had retained enough sense to seek shelter, and even in the slithering darkness had managed to follow the familiar path to the charcoal-burner cave. The wide chimney had been built into the hillside in the heart of the wood, an inverted cone of blackened brick, sliced vertically through the middle to form a cave eight foot deep. Years before, the local timber had been burnt there to create charcoal but now it had been reclaimed by the ivy and woodlice.

A sudden blast of rain gusted through the open mouth of the chimney catching Alex with its raw knife and she huddled deeper against the rear wall. Her hair dribbled icy rivulets down her neck. She tucked her naked knees up to her chin inside her Barbour and chafed her frozen fingers against numb cheeks. But neither seemed of any benefit.

Oh God, each year that she grew older it hurt worse. Far, far worse than the physical damage when it had first happened. At that time she had not understood her mother's distress. Nor her anger.

'You never care enough about anything except those damn animals of yours, do you, Edward? Day or night, they come first. You didn't look after her, didn't take care of her. She's your daughter. She was helping you. And you drag her out in the rain to deal with a vicious horse. What decent father would do that? You should have put her first, damn you, damn you.' Tears had always eventually choked the flow of accusations.

Alex had lain in bed, swathed in bandages. Listening.

Stop, for God's sake, stop. You're not being fair. It wasn't his fault. It was mine, my own fault. I let go of the rope. Don't blame him. Leave him alone.

Brief, low tones of her father's voice. Then her mother starting again. 'That's no excuse. She shouldn't have been anywhere near that damn horse.' On and on.

But the thirteen-year-old Alex knew she had let him down. Only just a teenager but shoulders already broadened by the responsibilities her father had laid on them. The horse had been a big dun stallion, black eyes rolling wildly and hooves striking out at the walls of his stall. Her father had calmed him.

The inexplicable magic touch, the soothing voice that somehow connected inside an animal's head. After a last jab that sent the water bucket skittering across the floor, the horse had quietened and allowed her father to run intelligent hands over his neck and shoulder, down to the deep infected gash above the fetlock. All Alex had to do was control the head, keep a tight hold on the rope to the head-collar.

But she had been watching her father instead of the horse. Not expecting retaliation. It took her totally by surprise. The huge head reared up above her, snatching the rope from her hand and rocketing her against the wall with a blow from a foreleg. Screaming its pain at her, the horse had whirled on a sixpence in the narrow stall and let loose with the power of its hindquarters, unleashing the iron-tipped sledgehammers that smashed her pelvis and shredded her innards. Her father had saved her life by seizing the maddened animal's head-collar and never letting go. He had risked his own. How could her mother berate him so unforgivingly?

In the hospital her bones had been pinned together piece by piece. Youth had been on her side and they had healed well. The remains of her uterus and a section of her intestines had been removed but at the time she had not really missed them. She had been much more concerned about getting on her feet again as quickly as possible. When her mother had wrapped her arms around her daughter to offer comfort, the teenager had not really understood.

'I'm okay, don't fuss. The doctors say my pelvis is going to be as good as new.'

Her mother's tears had embarrassed her. 'But my poor darling, you've lost your womb. That means no children.'

Alex had shrugged it off with a genuine lack of concern. 'So what? I'll have animals instead.'

She still remembered the dart of an expression she could not interpret in her mother's pale eyes and the odd, nerve-grating crunch of clenched teeth.

'So what?'

Only a teenager's obsession with present existence to the exclusion of all else could have uttered such careless words.

So what? So everything changes.

For me. For Rory.

Alex sank her head on her knees and groaned. The sound sent a shrew that had crept up beside her for warmth scurrying under the ivy and back out into the rain.

Rory did not deserve this.

No children. No grandchildren. No biological immortality. Was that why she shied away from adoption? Because the genes were not her own. Could she be that selfish?

Thunder rattled over her dank shelter with a resounding affirmative. Yes, she could. Despite the lack of a womb, the biological urge was so great that adoption could not even begin to fulfil it.

The ache just got worse.

Rory stood staring out through the sitting-room window at where he knew the front gate must be. It was shrouded in a winding-sheet of rain and pre-dawn darkness that concealed it from his sight, but his ears strained to catch the telltale clunk that always announced its use. The storm had exhausted its energy and left behind only a tired drizzle that was making a half-hearted effort to keep up the damage of the night. In the amber smudge of light from the window, he could see the nemesia and tagetes flat on their backs in the nearest flowerbed, and the geraniums did not look as if they had fared much better. Alex would grieve for them.

If she had any grieving left in her.

He creaked his neck from side to side in an attempt to ease the rigid muscles but it only made them worse. He kept telling himself she was all right. No way would Alex do anything stupid. No way.

She's all right. Just sheltering somewhere.

But visions of cars on the prowl or mild-looking men armed with flick-knives kept rearing their sordid heads. He turned away from them and made himself pace slowly up and down to the door and back five times. Maybe she would be home by then.

But she wasn't.

He resumed his vigil at the window, waiting for the first whisper of dawn.

*   *   *

All Alex wanted was a hot bath. As she trudged wet and muddy up the road from the woods, that thought kept her going. Her shin was stinging and her right knee griped at every step, both victims of the argument with an unseen tree stump when she had stumbled into the ditch in the dark. At least out on the road the ash-grey veil of dawn was no longer blanked by the canopy of trees and she made faster progress.

Poor Rory. It was unfair to dump this on him.

As if he didn't have enough on his plate already. With that blasted council shifting around the ground rules on the town centre redevelopment. And Zena looking as if she was entrenched in his home.

And now this.

It wasn't kind. But then, she wasn't feeling kind right now.

Self-consciously she pushed open the gate and limped down the path. Instantly the front door swung open and her husband was striding towards her. She stopped and watched him approach, his usually bushy hair flattened by the rain, altering his face. She saw the anger in it a split second before it was swept aside by relief and he opened his arms to her.

She collapsed into them and started to cry.

7

'Good Lord, what's up with you?' Maddy Calne asked as she shifted her attention for a brief moment from the psychedelic macaw in her hands.

Alex tried to ignore the greeting as she walked into the animal recovery room, but Maddy was stubbornly waiting for an answer.

'Nothing's the matter with me.'

'Don't give me that.' Maddy dribbled a final drop of antibiotic into the parrot's inflamed eye, ignored the irritated nip it delivered to her knuckle and soothed its ruffled feathers with greater sensitivity than she granted to Alex's. 'You look like something the cat dragged in.'

Alex unpinned her list of morning calls from the notice-board. 'Don't beat about the bush, Maddy, tell it to me straight. It's just what I need right now.'

'No need for sarcasm. You know what they say. It's the lowest form of wit.'

Alex repented a fraction. 'I didn't get much sleep.'

'You weren't on call last night.'

'I know that.'

'Gordon was on duty.'

'That's right.'

'So what's up with you?'

Alex knew she looked exhausted this morning, dull shadows round her eyes. Cheekbones taut under greyish skin. A case of doctor heal thyself. Maddy's gruff enquiries might be meant kindly, but Alex did not want them. Not today.

'Nothing's up with me.'

'Who are you kidding? You look fit to drop.'

'I'm fine, Maddy.' Alex glanced at the list in her hand. Oh hell, another morning of TB testing at Ramsbury.

'You don't look fine.'

'For God's sake, Maddy, leave it, will you? I said I'm fine. Now leave it alone.'

Maddy said nothing. Just stared at her. Behind the glasses, the green eyes glowed intently but her mouth remained firmly shut.

'I'm tired, Maddy,' Alex offered by way of excuse. 'That's all.'

Maddy nodded curtly. 'That's obvious.' The white overall seemed to tighten across the ledge of her bosom and she moved over to the bank of cages along one wall where she shooed the parrot through the open door of one. He squawked rowdily and took another spiteful swipe at her knuckle. She cooed forgivingly.

But Alex looked at the straight broad back and the straight grey hair, both aimed rigidly in her direction and knew she had offended. She just did not have the strength even to be sorry. No words of apology to dredge up.

'I'll be over at Ramsbury,' she said and walked out of the room.

The next few days passed without Alex remembering them. She went through the motions. That was all. If pushed, she could recall a sheep with scrapie tottering pathetically and a velvety-beige puppy born with a deformed leg, put to sleep because it was a greyhound. But not much else. She was functioning on autopilot and if anybody noticed, they didn't say anything. For that, she was grateful. To Rory most of all. He talked to her, both gently and sternly, kept Zena off her back and when he found her scrubbing behind the fridge one evening, he stripped off her rubber gloves and took her for a brisk walk through Pewsey woods.

Alex worked long hours. Anything to lock out the thoughts. She undertook extra night duty so that she would not have to lie awake in bed hour after hour, counting the grandfather clock chimes striking in unison with her biological clock. At the surgery she was aware of bemused looks from the nurses and the continued silence from Maddy, though Alex found her head nurse dogging her heels, a wary eye watching her every mood. As head of the practice, Gordon Tamworth felt he was working his favourite colleague too hard. He worried about her, his gentle grey eyes saying all the things his Scottish tongue could not. By the end of the week he called her into his hideaway office.

'I've made you a wee dash of tea.' He indicated the bone china cup and saucer that he had placed in a minor oasis of calm amid the chaos that was his desk. The brew looked even more lethal than usual. 'It'll buck you up a mite, lassie.'

'Thank you, Gordon.' She sat down but did not touch the tea.

He eyed her with concern, wings of white hair pushed back in a gesture of frustration. If only his wife were still alive, he thought, as he did in every crisis. Abigail would have known the words to open a path through the thorny barricade. Young Alex was as efficient at defence as she was at everything else. But something was eating her up inside, as sure as haggis is made of sheep's heart. He missed that laugh of hers and her bonnie looks had suffered. No roses in her cheeks. A good strong cup of tea would help put them back.

'Drink up, lassie. Been overdoing it, I fancy.'

'I'm fine, Gordon.' But she sipped the tea and did not even grimace when the bitter tang scoured the roof of her mouth.

'Rory all right?'

'Yes, he's fine.'

'Your sister?'

'She's fine. Gordon, stop fussing. Everything is under control.'

Gordon tugged at his ear-lobe to stop himself muttering, 'Too much under control.' Instead he poured himself a dose of the sticky black brew, resumed his fond old leather seat that, from prolonged contact, mirrored the exact curves and angles of his body with comforting familiarity, and rummaged through the papers on his desk for a biscuit for Bruno, who lay curled up at his feet. The mongrel huffed his canine appreciation and dropped his broad head to rest on his master's knee. Every pair of Gordon's trousers displayed worn, shiny patches at that precise spot, courtesy of Bruno.

'Well, I still think you're overdoing it. But not for much longer. I've arranged to interview next week for a new assistant.' He beamed at her proudly. 'You've been at me to find one for months. So now you won't be able to badger me any more.'

Alex managed to look pleased. The practice did urgently need another pair of hands.

'That's excellent, Gordon.'

'It's worth it to see that Sassenach smile of yours in place again.'

This time the smile came more easily. 'It shows you're not quite the mean old Scottish skinflint I always thought you were.'

He clapped a hand over the inside pocket of his jacket. 'Don't you believe it, lassie. My wallet is like Dracula.'

'It drinks blood?'

'No, not that. It never wants to see the light of day.'

Alex laughed and saw the worry in Gordon's eyes ease up a notch. To pacify him further, she downed the tea and stood up.

'That was foul, Gordon. Do you really enjoy drinking it?'

'Aye, I do. And you'll thank me for it when it gets to work on you.'

'Talking of getting to work, I'll be off.'

'You're in surgery this afternoon, aren't you?'

'Yes. I'm just going to get ready for theatre.'

'Not too many booked in for today, I seem to remember.'

'No. There's a bitch spay, the inguinal hernia repair on the Tibetan spaniel, and the cat's jaw to be stitched.'

The cat was a tortoiseshell. It had been struck a glancing blow by a car that had sent it skidding along the tarmac so fast that the skin of its jaw and chin had been stripped right back and hung like a furry envelope flap from its throat. There had been a lot of blood and a lot of embedded gravel. The owner, a young man in his early twenties, was so shaken when he drove the cat to the surgery that he had taken a chunk out of a Ford Escort's wing, as he turned into the car park. Trouble did not come alone.

'And the abscess on the guinea pig's cheek,' Alex added. She headed for the door.

'Alex.'

She turned.

Gordon could not let her go without saying at least a mite of what was on his mind. He walked round the desk, Bruno beside him, never more than one possessive inch from the long bony legs.

'Alex, whatever it is that's the matter, let me know if I can help. Or if you need time off.'

For one alarming moment he thought she was going to cry, but instead she brushed her hand over his and said, 'Gordon Tamworth, you're all marshmallow underneath that crinkly shell.'

He watched the familiar figure stride away in her brown cords and beige blouse, hair tied back as usual and noticed that she was thinner. Not a good sign.

'Another pint?'

'Wish I could, Gary, but no thanks.' Rory drained the last of his glass and replaced it on the bar. He and Gary Saunders had donned their architectural partners' hat and gone in unison to pacify the planners with their new design for the car park scheme. It had not gone particularly well and they had stopped off at their local on the way back to drown their misgivings. It was Friday afternoon, hot and sticky, and clients would be too busy clocking off early themselves to pester the office.

'I'm off on my errand to Marlborough,' Rory reminded him.

'Of course, I'd forgotten.' Gary ruffled his shock of blond curls with amusement. 'Sister-in-law to be sorted.' He fingered the carefully trimmed stubble on his chin, a recent sortie that was not proving popular with girlfriends. Great to look at, they agreed, but who wants to kiss a coconut mat? It would have to go. 'No progress with her?'

'Not a scrap. Not yet anyway.'

'So today's the day? Crunch-time.'

'Damn right it is. I've had enough of her stalling antics.'

'Is that why you've been like a bear with a sore arse all week? Growling at everyone.'

Rory grunted but made no comment.

Gary caught the barman's eye and signalled for another pint of ale, but a tiny young blonde who looked no more than sixteen got in first. 'From what you've said, sister-in-law won't give in easily.'

'Neither will I.'

Gary grinned, enjoying the vicarious conflict. 'Go give her hell and take no prisoners!'

'That's exactly my battle-plan.' Rory held up two fingers entwined. 'Genghis Khan and I are like this.' Just then he noticed the blonde further up the bar who was staring at him with open interest. His glance immediately prompted a coy, welcoming smile and the hint of the tip of a tongue.

Gary was miffed. 'You concentrate on your dearly beloved sister-in-law and leave me to handle any other uninvited intrusions. Especially when they're flaunting a bare midriff.'

'You've got yourself a deal, partner.'

'So what's the plan of campaign?'

'Subtlety is not Zena's strong point. I gave her all week to get herself down to the Job Centre, but she refuses to get herself in gear. So I'm doing it for her. An appointment at four o'clock.'

'Sounds like you'll be in for a rough ride.'

Rory coated his determination with an easy grin. 'I'll be taking my flak jacket and riot shield along, just in case.'

A moment later as he left the pub, he saw Gary sidling further up the bar in the direction of the bare midriff.

'Go to hell, Rory Flynn!'

'Zena, I am not taking no for an answer, so don't even bother saying it any more.' Rory stood holding open the front door for her. 'We have exactly sixteen minutes to get to that appointment.'

'No.'

'Zena.'

'No.'

She was standing in the hallway, hands firmly on hips, glaring at him. The blonde hair was neatly groomed to her shoulders, an emerald silk blouse and cream linen slacks hung smooth and soft, no trace of the disruption that was in her face. Anger had clamped her mouth into a hard line and turned her eyes to brittle amber.

'No.' Her voice was strident. 'Go bully your minions at work. Don't try it on me.'

Rory's patience was on the verge of snapping. He took a step forward but she backed off, fast.

'Stay away from me,' she yelled at him.

He heard it. Behind the bluster and display of aggression. Like Hammy yowling her defiance at an intruding stray feline, all raised fur, fury and claws. But behind it, the fear.

'Zena,' he said and kept it calm, 'this will do you no harm. None at all. They are there to help you.' Quietly he moved nearer her, no threatening signals. 'You can come back here afterwards. I promise you I'm not throwing you out.'

'No,' she repeated but this time it was less vociferous.

'Come on, Zena, if you won't do it for me or to help yourself, do it for Alex.'

'Alex? Why Alex?'

'You don't need me to tell you, she's stressed out at the moment. She doesn't need these worries about you as well. Give her some peace of mind. Show her you're making some kind of effort.' He was standing next to her now and could see a tiny pulse twitching at her temple. 'Let's just talk to the Job Centre people and see what they say. You never know, you might even find it interesting.'

'No hope of that.'

'Let's give it a chance, shall we?'

Silence.

'Come on, we'll be late.' He slipped a hand under her elbow and after an initial reluctance, she allowed herself to be steered out of the house and into the car.

As Rory slipped into third gear up the hill, he felt justified in congratulating himself on turning up the trump card. It was curious. He looked forward to telling Alex about his coup. Over her black coffee that morning she had been very negative. 'You haven't a hope in hell of getting her there' had been her exact words.

Hope was something Alex was short of right now.

To take his mind off that thought, Rory concentrated on the

car. The MGF always gave him a punch of pleasure every time
he climbed behind the wheel and on a day like this, with hood
down and sun frying the brain, it was his idea of heaven. He
glanced at his companion and could not resist a raised eyebrow.
It was the first time Zena had been for a run in his car. Obviously
the experience was one she did not disapprove of. She wasn't
clinging to her hair as if it were a wig that threatened to
take flight, nor was she leaning forward to shelter behind the
windscreen like so many women of his acquaintance. She had
forgotten him completely. Her body was pressed right back in
her seat, head tilted up, letting the wind snatch at her face
and hair, whipping fine strands in all directions. Her mouth
was partly open, tasting the air and her eyes half closed. With
her blonde hair fluttering, skin golden in the summer afternoon
light, eyes rimmed with kohl and in her emerald blouse, she
looked like one of the sunflowers in his garden, tall, slender
and very un-English.

He drove at speed. Not to be late, he told himself. When he
slipped neatly into a just vacated parking spot in the High Street,
he turned to her.

'Enjoy that?'

She gave him a cool stare, slid out of the car and said curtly,
'Just because I like fast cars, it doesn't mean I have to like their
owners. Wait for me here.'

He watched her walk unhurriedly along the pavement, turning the occasional head, and into the Job Centre. He was tempted
just to drive away, leaving Zena and all her rudeness behind. But
there was Alex.

Oh Alex, what are you doing to yourself? Doing to us?

He sat and waited.

'So how did it go?'

'No problem.' Zena licked her lips and looked pleased with
herself. No trace of the fear now. She had emerged after half
an hour with a sheaf of papers in her hand, a satisfied smile on
her lips and a swagger in her walk.

Rory caught a tantalising glimpse of the light at the end of the
tunnel. Patience. Just a little more patience. He had driven her

home, letting her enjoy the ride once more, but as soon as she
had flopped into a deckchair on the lawn, he decided her mute
act had gone on long enough.

'Anything positive?'

'No, nothing yet. Just lots of forms. Applications.'

'Sounds good.'

From her reclining position Zena stared up at him, squinting
into the sun, then let her lids close and kicked off her sandals.
'Good for whom?'

'For you.'

'And you, of course.'

'Yes. And me.' He watched a butterfly stagger past, change
course and alight expectantly on to Zena's green shoulder. 'And
for Alex.'

The eyes opened. 'Is that what she says?'

'No. It's what I say.'

'Why are you so sure it would be good for her if I land
one of these?' She flicked a hand towards the pristine pile of
application forms lying on the grass, making the red admiral
take fright. 'Why would she be happy if I beat a retreat from
here? Or is it just that you want the field of battle to yourself?'

Rory pulled up another deckchair and sat down into its
candy-striped hammock. 'It's a home, Zena. Not a battlefield.'

'Gettysburg had nothing on you two last Sunday night, I
assure you.'

'I've already told you, it wasn't a quarrel. Alex was upset.
Emotions from the past all churned up and exploded.'

'What emotions?'

'Can't you guess?'

'No. Tell me.'

'It was after the birthday party.'

'Oh, that old dirge. The childless sob-stuff. I assumed she was
over that.'

'You assumed wrong.'

'So you got caught in the shrapnel?'

'No, not really. The damage was to herself.' He leant forward,
intent on getting through his sister-in-law's veneer of indifference. 'That, Zena, is what worries me and why I want you to

get on with your own life and let her get on with hers. She can't carry you, as well as her own problems.'

There was no response from Zena. Her eyes followed the movements of a white periscope above the begonias and antirrhinums, the tip of Horatio's tail as he wove a covert path towards the bird table. A magpie reared up out of the old apple tree on the edge of the lawn with a machine gun alarm call.

Finally, without taking her eyes off the cat's meanderings, she said, 'She's my sister.'

'She always has been and always will be. She cares for you. But in the last eight years, that didn't seem to count for much with you, did it? Why now?'

The faintest shrug.

'It's because it's all gone wrong for you, isn't it, Zena? I am genuinely sorry about that and over these last few weeks that you've been with us, Alex and I have both tried to help. Even though you don't make it easy. When push comes to shove, it's family that counts.'

Slowly she turned her smooth, perfected face towards him, eyes half veiled behind long protective lashes. 'You're not family.'

Damn the woman, she was impossible.

'No, Zena, I'm not your family. But I am Alex's. And she's the one who matters to me. Your being here, mooning around like an abandoned calf, is raking up too much from the past that is upsetting her.'

'It's not my fault, if she's got problems of that sort.'

Rory had heard enough. He stood up. 'Zena, you are a callous bitch. She offers you affection with open arms and you just abuse it. The point is, her problems are my problems. That's why I want you to . . .'

'I couldn't give a damn about your problems, Rory.'

'And Alex's?'

'Alex is my sister.'

'Alex is my wife.'

They stared at each other. There was nothing more to say. Rory turned and walked into the house.

*   *   *

Zena continued to watch the cat's tail, her fingers tapping out a tattoo of irritation on the wooden arm of her deckchair. Two white ears were just visible in the flowerbed behind the salmon pinks and scarlets of the storm-bruised geraniums.

Not like the prize-winning pelargonium in her mother's conservatory. Her mother had been so proud of it. It had won first prize at the local show and beaten Mrs Hooper's into second place. Huge heads of fleshy flowers, pale violet laced round the edge with dainty white frills and blushing to deeper indigo at the heart. As a child Zena had thought the heavy leaves were lily pads that had been nibbled by tadpoles. Why she should think that, Zena could not now recall, but it may have had something to do with the little artificial pond that gurgled in the corner. Her mother had nurtured and coddled that plant as if it were her third and favourite child. The devotion on her face as she patted and preened and talked to it had been inexplicable to her eight-year-old daughter.

'It's just a mouldy old plant,' she had jeered and Ali had laughed.

Her mother had walked away in a huff. Just like Rory.

It was hot then, just like today. The conservatory had been her jungle, full of tall leafy creepers and the strange, alien passion flowers. Some days she would don her bathing costume, the shocking pink one her mother had finally succumbed to through attrition, and become a naiad of the forest. A naiad. A lovely word she had discovered in her father's crossword. The humidifying spray gave her the power to seek out enemy bugs lurking under shiny leaves and soak them with its rainbow shower. Only the spiders seemed to object. Ladybirds she left alone. Too useful in her mother's eternal war against greenfly.

That was how the mistake happened.

Her cheeks still flared red at the memory. Eighteen years had not managed to assuage it. She had rescued a three-spot ladybird from the pond and decided to place it on the prize pelargonium to guard it from attack. But the insect had been half drowned. When she popped it on the leaf, it just slid off. Instinctively she thrust out her hand to catch it and knocked off a whole branch, bushy with leaves and buds.

The instant it happened, she knew the magnitude of what she had done.

'Shit!'

'Zena, what was that you said?'

Zena had whirled round to find her father in the doorway. Tall and ominous. Incongruous in neat navy shorts. She had burst into tears and held out her hands to reveal the amputated branch.

'Look, Daddy, look. It was an accident.'

The horror in her voice turned his frown to alarm and then to relieved amusement. 'Oh, it's only a geranium, Zena. Nothing major. Don't you cry about that, my Titania.' He sat down on the bamboo stool by the pond and scooped her on to his lap. 'It's all right, sweetheart. It's only a plant.'

'It's Mummy's special one,' Zena had sobbed.

'Is it? Well, don't worry, I'll have a word with her.'

'She'll be ever so cross.' Zena snuggled deep against her father's protective shoulder.

'I'll be ever so cross if she's cross and my cross is worse than hers.' He kissed her tears. 'She won't hurt you, she loves you, my fairy.'

'She loves the silly plant best.'

'Rubbish.'

'Does.'

'No she doesn't.'

'Does.'

'I've never heard such nonsense. I tell you what.' He stood up still carrying Zena in his arms and went over to the now lopsided pelargonium. Without hesitation, he snapped off another laden branch. 'There, now I've done it. I'll tell her I'm sorry but I broke her plant. It will be the truth but she will think I did both. So I'll be the one in trouble, not you.'

Zena had gazed at her father in awe.

'Happy now?'

She had thrown her arms around his neck and kissed him, and he sat down again, bouncing her on his lap, tickling her, making her happy. She had been laughing hysterically when she suddenly became aware that her father had stopped the fun. His gaze was focused on something outside the tall glass panes. Zena clambered round and her whole body hiccuped with fright when she saw someone standing there in the garden looking in.

'It's only Ali,' she squealed.

'Yes,' her father muttered. 'Only Ali.' But he had turfed her on to the floor and told her to run away and play.

Zena watched Horatio's bullet head emerge from the flower-bed, inspect her without approval from his one green eye and then plonk himself down to roll his white coat in a dusty patch of bare soil.

Her mother had certainly been angry about the wounded plant. And Daddy was odd after that. Withdrawn. Untouchable.

Dimly, Zena had known it was all Ali's fault.

8

The horse looked miserable. As if he knew what was coming. Standing against the wall of his stable, head down, ears flat, he shuffled his hooves uneasily in the clean straw. Alex had treated him before, a handsome grey with a history of point-to-point championships and a glass cabinet gleaming with silver trophies to prove it. Though only eight years old, he was broken-winded, unable even to trot round the exercise yard without his larynx breaking into a wheezing roar.

'Poor chap. And he's still so full of jumping. It breaks my heart to see him like this.' The owner, Dave Jarrett, stood in the doorway of the stable, with a face as long as his horse's. He was a big, square man with close-cropped hair and an outdoor complexion, but jeans and checked shirt as neat and clean as his horse's stall. A fresh, sweet-smelling hay-net hung untouched on the wall, only inviting the attentions of a fat, glossy bluebottle.

'Now you've decided on the tracheostomy, Mr Jarrett, there's no reason why he shouldn't perform well again.'

'He loves to compete, you see. Never happier than when he's out there. Leaping over those fences and racing for the winning line.'

Alex wasn't sure whether Dave Jarrett was talking of himself rather than the horse, but let it pass. He had requested a laryngeal bypass to prolong the animal's point-to-point life and she was not in a position to query whose quality of life it was intended to improve. She walked over to the big horse, chatting reassuringly, patted his hefty shoulder and dusted a fly from the corner of his eye. In response he huffed softly through his wide nostrils and raised his head a fraction.

'Don't worry, Steerforth,' she told him cheerfully, 'we'll soon have you jumping over the moon again.'

The horse rolled an eye at her, as if to say he'd heard that one before.

'May I have my case, Maddy, please?'

The veterinary nurse was standing in the doorway in ancient tweed jacket and mismatched tweed trousers, peering over Dave Jarrett's shoulder.

'Coming right up.' The door frame could not accommodate the breadth of both square figures, so Jarrett stood aside and let Maddy step past, holding out the case in front of her. 'Here.'

It was not usual for Maddy to accompany Alex on house-calls but occasionally, like today, it suited them both. Mr Jarrett had requested Alex to perform the operation on Steerforth out at Hilcott in the late afternoon and as Maddy was due to finish early that day, she had suggested, in her monosyllabic way, that she should come with Alex.

'Might join you.'

Alex, who was packing the kit and anaesthetic into her case, had looked up. Since their disagreement last week, Maddy had made a point of not initiating conversation though, conversely, she had hovered day in, day out at Alex's elbow. Alex suspected her of harbouring serious doubts about her mental state, expecting Alex to disintegrate at any minute into tiny pieces, like a shattered windscreen. So Maddy hovered there, dustpan and brush in hand, ready to sweep them up.

'Might join me where, Maddy?'

'Jarrett's.'

Alex was surprised but hid it behind a busy check of the rest of the contents of her case. It did actually make sense. The afternoon's warmth had been unexpectedly dampened by a series of heavy showers, another one threatening any minute and Maddy had not come equipped with waterproofs on her bike today. Dave Jarrett's place was less than a mile from Maddy's cottage, so she had to pass the front gate anyway. Also Alex knew that the nurse enjoyed an occasional house-call to one of the larger animals, as it gave variation to her usual daily round of dogs and cats, rodents and reptiles.

'Good idea. I'll be leaving in about five minutes.'

'Right.'

Maddy bustled off to repeat last-minute instructions to the duty nurse. It was invariably an effort to drag her away from the surgery, as her opinion of human competence was always terminally low. The joint trip would also give Alex a chance to offer a gesture of conciliation with some bridge-building small-talk. But her good intentions were thwarted by Maddy's resolute silence in the car. At Hilcott Dave Jarrett, not usually known for his way with words, had seemed positively loquacious by comparison.

With Maddy's assistance, Alex slipped a head collar on Steerforth and quieted his nerves. When he was still, she pressed a finger into the groove at the base of his neck to raise the jugular vein and smoothly inserted a needle. A dribble of deep crimson blood trickled back. She attached the syringe and injected the cocktail that would act as a sedative. The effect did not take long. Within minutes the horse's heavy head slid lower and lower, legs splayed, breathing slow and rhythmic. Maddy stood beside him, running her hand along the muscular grey neck and crooning her version of a bedtime story, the rope to the head-collar loose in her hand. The memory of a similar rope tearing out of her own hand in a similar stable flickered for a moment in Alex, but was severely doused. Now was not the time.

With typical efficiency, she clipped an exact four-inch-square patch on the animal's throat below the larynx, and administered a local anaesthetic while Maddy prepped the area with cotton wool, Hibiscrub and warm water. A tracheostomy was not a difficult operation if the horse remained quiet. She remembered watching her father perform it on more than one occasion. She remembered his hands. So deft.

The scalpel blade in her own hand made a skin incision, a muscle incision and then was on the trachea. Maddy, eyes alert, stood close at her elbow holding out the sterile kit in its metal tray while Dave Jarrett kept the head raised. The horse did not even flick an ear. When Alex had removed a section of a couple of rings of cartilage and mucosa, she fitted the short tube into the hole and neatly stitched its holding flaps into place. A quick antibiotic injection, a check on the horse's condition, and the job was done. No more than half an hour in all.

'A few hours and he'll be back to normal, Mr Jarrett. But make sure you keep the bung on the tube when he's feeding.'

'That's just grand.' The owner was beaming from ear to ear. 'Just grand.'

Alex gave Steerforth a farewell scratch, winkled Maddy out of the stable into the rain and left Dave Jarrett to his visions of trophies to come.

The drive to Maddy's cottage took only a few minutes and by the time they arrived, the shower had stopped. Alex expected a gruff grunt of thanks and a speedy departure. She was therefore taken by surprise when Maddy suggested she come in and look at Josephine, the adopted goat.

'Anything wrong with her? Not another infection?' Alex asked.

'No, nothing like that.'

Alex climbed out of the car and followed her ungracious hostess up the front path. Path it may have been once upon a time, but now it was a dandelion, chickweed and buttercup zone with the odd glimpse of a dying slab of concrete underneath. The rest of the half acre of garden followed suit. A riot of knee-length grass, sturdy nettles and deceptively delicate cow-parsley heads was interspersed with exact rectangles of close-cropped lawn. These patches bore witness to the appetites of rabbits, guinea pigs and Josephine, whose enclosures were moved haphazardly around the garden at whim.

At the sound of Maddy's chirruping approach, five cats streamed out of an open rear window, voices and tails raised in salute, while inside the cottage a chorus of low- and high-pitched barks erupted like a deafening Vesuvius. Maddy pushed open the back door, releasing the canine hordes which turned out to be only a gallumping great mongrel, all black and boisterous, and a small three-legged terrier that got itself into an instant tangle trying to snarl at Alex and fawn over Maddy at one and the same time.

Maddy mauled their ears affectionately and asked, 'Where's Josephine, boys?'

Both dogs took off with ecstatic barks in the direction of a ramshackle hut that was just about standing in one corner of the garden, surrounded by a patch of teeth-mown grass and new-looking sheep fencing wire. The cats took advantage of the vacated sphere of devotion and oiled round Maddy's legs, very nearly tripping her up as she strode for the shed. Alex traipsed through the wet grass after the menagerie, as always touched by the abundance of animal affection. No conditions. No demands. No offence taken. Just pure, unadulterated, one hundred per cent proof love.

First a white head with feathery tufts on its chin and then a low-slung body ambled out of the shed and up to the fence to greet them. Alex tugged at a handful of long grass and handed it to Josephine who munched it with relish. Especially the dandelion heads. Alex always thought goats appeared to have been designed by an extremely bad tailor. Their flesh seemed to have slipped down under their skin, exposing a knobbly spine to the brickbats of British weather. No warm padding of fat to protect the angular ridge. Definitely a bad design.

'Hello, Josephine.' Alex patted the coarse white hair on its bony head. 'How are you getting on?'

Maddy's strong hand grabbed the scruff of the big mongrel and yanked him away from pestering the goat through the fencing. 'Shut up, Kennet.' He had been named after the canal that she had fished him out of as a puppy. 'Leave Josephine in peace, you noisy menace.'

To please her, he reduced his barks to a throaty whisper but insisted on keeping his nose pushed through one of the holes in the wire fence. The terrier did the same at ankle level.

'Do you take her out much?' Alex asked.

''Course. Comes for walks with the dogs.'

Alex could just imagine Maddy marching through the lanes with her menagerie in tow. Normally Alex would have passed some teasing remark about such a prospect, but at the moment light-hearted banter was beyond her repertoire.

'But I don't want to walk her too far these days,' Maddy added. 'I think she's pregnant.'

Pregnant.

Alex stared at the goat's fecund stomach.

Pregnant.

Maddy chattered on, excited now by voicing the possibility. 'It must have happened before she was abandoned. I suspect she is because she's been eating more recently and that stomach of hers doesn't feel like it's all fat to me. But give her a once-over, will you, just to be certain?'

'Of course.' But Alex's legs stayed rooted to the spot.

'Go on then, girl, before it rains again.'

Alex crushed her reluctance under the steamroller of professionalism, climbed over the fence and stood behind the goat. She placed one hand on each side of the bulging stomach and gently palpated it from side to side. Something hard brushed against each hand. A head? Spine maybe? She felt again. No doubt about it. New, lumpy life growing inside her.

'Well?'

Alex nodded, not looking at Maddy. 'Yes, definitely.' She couldn't bring herself to voice the word aloud.

Maddy crowed with delight like an overjoyed grandparent-to-be. 'Good for you, Josephine.' The goat gazed up at her amiably. 'How far gone do you think she is?'

Alex gently stroked the rotund belly. 'Probably another four or five weeks. Maybe less.'

'Wonderful. Wonderful. Bloody good job, Josephine. Shut up, Kennet, don't you dare startle her in her condition.' The dogs had picked up on Maddy's excitement and were letting loose again. 'Just think,' she said with a hoot of laughter, 'after all these years, I'll have a kid of my own.'

It was too much.

Alex stood up, climbed quickly back over the rickety fence and promptly left. Maddy's puzzled stare bored with pinpoint accuracy into the back of her head as she hurried to the car, but nothing, absolutely nothing could make her stay a second longer. As she drove the couple of miles home, she was furious with herself for crying every wheel-turn of the way.

When Rory arrived home it was raining again and he outsprinted Hamilton and Horatio down the front path. He found Alex in the kitchen preparing a meal, but Charlie Parker's saxophone was at full volume on CD, blaring out his pain for all to know. So she did not hear him come in. He walked up behind her, where she stood chopping mushrooms beside the spotless sink and wrapped his arms around her without warning.

She jumped like a cat on a hot stove. Jerked her head back against his chin and crunched his teeth together painfully. Inside the circle of his arms, she spun to face him and for one unguarded moment he caught a glimpse in the dark eyes of the torment she was putting herself through. Then the shutters came down.

'Hi,' he said through aching teeth. 'How was your day?'

'Fine. I finished early and gave Maddy a lift home. How was yours?'

'Bearable.'

'Hungry?'

'Ravenous. I missed lunch, dashing down to a briefing in Bath.'

'Bath? Sounds interesting.'

'Some Californian heathen actually paid a cowboy builder to wreak havoc on the interior of his elegant Regency town house. Turned it into an open-plan, ranch-style Southfork. Hideous it is. Without planning permission of course. Fortunately the new and very British owner has the sense to put it all back to the original.' He watched the eyes, but they remained well defended.

'You'll enjoy doing that. Your favourite period of architecture.'

'I'll enjoy doing this, as well.' He kissed her on the mouth and she tasted of strawberries. On a plate behind her, he noticed a summer pudding squatting in glorious technicolour. His stomach rumbled.

Alex laughed, 'Food for thought is what you need.'

She tried to disentangle herself but he tightened his arms around her. That was all it took. Instantly she seemed to melt against him, pressing her face into his shoulder as if she would burrow inside him. He kissed her hair and a faint whiff of antiseptic tickled his nostril. That medical smell reminded him, with a little bump of shock, of the weight of responsibility she carried every day. He rubbed his cheek against the glossy golden mane and held her close.

'Is this a private party or can anyone join in?' Zena stood at the door, watching.

'A private party,' Rory snapped.

But Alex broke loose and returned to the chopping board. She seasoned three chump chops with rosemary and black pepper and placed them under the grill. By the time she turned round, the drawbridge was back up.

'It won't be long,' she said. 'Why don't you two have a glass of wine while I mix the salad?'

Rory had no interest in drinking wine with his sister-in-law. He turned to Zena. 'Why don't you make the salad, Zena, while Alex and I sit down over a glass of something?' Pointedly he added, 'We have both been at the grindstone all day.'

For one moment he thought she was going to refuse. Normally she did not lift a finger for the meal. She stared at him and then at Alex.

'Sure, if that's what you want.'

Rory brushed aside his wife's objections and ushered her, along with two glasses and half a bottle of corner shop Beaujolais, into the sitting-room, before Zena could change her mind. Once installed beside him on the sofa, glass in hand, Alex seemed to make an effort to relax. The conversation ebbed and flowed in comfortable rhythm round the familiar topics of each other's day: Gary Saunders' latest computer generated designs, the ferret that gnawed Gordon Tamworth's thumb to the bone and the state of Maddy's dilapidated garden – though no mention was made of the goat. All came in for comment. Muscle by muscle, Rory watched some of the tension in his wife ease, felt her body heavier against his shoulder.

He could still hear her jazz music filtering through from the kitchen and the plaintive sound conjured up the occasion when he had given that CD to Alex for her birthday. Only a few short months ago and yet so much had changed. She had been so obviously happy then. Life together had been fun. Hard work, always busy, but fun. Even the disasters, like the day the old beech tree blew down and stripped part of the roof, had been fun in retrospect. What the hell had gone wrong?

But he already knew the answer. Zena. Zena had come into their lives and awoken the sleeping demons. Now these demons had to be exorcised. Or soothed back to rest. One or the other. But Alex's control over them was seriously in doubt and the question was, would she be able to regain it? Rory studied his wife's hands, as she elaborated on Gordon's interviews for a new veterinary assistant. So slim and lightly veined, so capable. Knowing Alex, he believed she could face down her demons. But what damage were they doing inside? Eating up the heart of her?

But surely everyone possessed their own demons? Maybe they called them by different names – phobias, obsessions, fears, likes and dislikes – but all stemmed from the same source. Emotional traumas of childhood. We've all heard the pseudo-psychology spouted in the media: for anal retention read suppression; abuse breeds abusers.

And then there's siblings.

Rory thought of his own brother up in York, an engineer with comfortable house and the required two point four children. Second marriage. They saw each other twice, maybe three times a year and that was enough. Good friends, exchanged news on the telephone, but they both had their own lives to lead. The umbilical cord had been snapped. So what was wrong with Alex and Zena?

'Food's ready.' Zena followed her voice into the room, stood looking at the cosy image of her sister leaning with assurance on her husband's shoulder and announced, 'I'm going to bed.'

Alex stood up. 'Don't be silly, Zena. At least eat the meal with us.'

'I'm not hungry any more.' She left the room and they heard her footsteps heavy on the stairs.

'She's just trying to make us feel guilty,' Rory said. 'To manipulate your emotions.'

To his relief, Alex nodded. 'I know. She was always good at that.'

For the next two days, Zena was amenable. Both Alex and Rory remarked on it. She even offered to do the washing up and made them all coffee. A bit weak for Rory's liking, but still coffee. Alex suggested she must be feeling sorry about her churlish behaviour of the night before, but Rory doubted that. For some reason she was soothing their ruffled feathers. But what reason? He had the uneasy feeling that something unpleasant was lying in wait, grinning at them from round the corner. Alex said he was being too sceptical.

On Friday he drove to the office, the smooth surface of his mental preparations for the day ahead pockmarked by little twitches of domestic anxiety. Gary Saunders' opening remark did not exactly improve matters.

'A letter from the town planners. Not good.'

Paula Marshall was standing in the doorway of his office, young forehead creased with apprehension. The budding architect had not yet learnt to take the rough with the smooth.

'Okay.' Rory sat down. 'Give me the worst.'

'Good news first.' Gary Saunders was ever the optimist. 'They've agreed the redesign of the car park plus retail units.'

'That's great. So what's the problem?'

Jan Hodge emerged from reception, bearing a black coffee, a fistful of papers and a maternal smile for him, before retreating back to her desk. Hell, the news must be bad.

'Come on, out with it.'

Gary flopped into a chair and grimaced.

Paula Marshall lost patience. 'The money has gone.'

'What?'

She shook her King Charles curls at him. 'The idiots have upset the financial backers. They've pulled out. The development is off.'

Rory absorbed the shock. 'What about the main chain-store? That's self-financing.'

'Zilch. Apparently they won't go ahead without the others.'

'So the whole deal is dropped?'

Gary nodded and groaned at an alarming volume. 'Lily-livered, sodding bastards, the lot of them.'

It wasn't good. Flynn & Saunders had overspent on the scheme. Both time and money. The company needed this contract. It was their breakthrough into the big-time. Rory resorted to the coffee to get the cogs cranked up again. Paula stood staring at him bleakly with her round spaniel eyes and Gary resumed his agonised groans, as if rehearsing for Lear. But Rory was not ready to roll over so easily.

'First, let me see the letter. That might shed a little more light on the subject. Second, Paula, ask Jan to get me an appointment with Boothroyd at the town planning office. Make it for this morning.'

Gary ceased his groaning. 'There's no point,' he muttered, but sat up straighter and fingered the stubble that still clung to his chin, the way he did when on the track of a new computer programme.

Rory waited.

'I suppose we could . . .' Gary's words trailed away.

'We could what?'

'Well, maybe we could approach each of the retailers direct and try to sort out their difficulties.'

'Why not?' Rory jumped in. 'Too many middlemen fouling things up.'

'We could give it a try,' Paula said.

'If we can get them all together,' Rory continued, 'and find out what the problems are, we might be able to pull it together even now. But first I'll speak to Boothroyd and ask him what's going on.' He smiled encouragement at Paula. 'Get going, then. Ask Jan to . . .'

The telephone on his desk buzzed.

'Hello?'

Jan's voice informed him that a company called Strike Hot was on the line for him.

'Who the hell are they?'

'A PR outfit here in Swindon.'

'What do they want? Can't you deal with them?'

'No, they want to speak to you. Personal, I gather. A Mr Barry Parker.'

'Okay, put him on.'

A click. 'Hello, Mr Parker. Rory Flynn speaking. What can I do for you?'

'I apologise for interrupting you at work, Mr Flynn, but your name and company were given to us by a Mrs Taylor.'

For a moment Rory had to think who on earth Mrs Taylor could be. Then it came to him. Zena. Alias Mrs Chetwyn Taylor. What the hell was this about?

'Why would she give you my name?'

'As a character reference on her job application form.'

Of course, the sheaf of papers from the Job Centre. He had questioned her about them and been assured that she had sent them off. Now this character check. Progress at last.

'Happy to oblige. What would you like to know?'

'Well, I was telephoning you for the reference, but first of all I would like to know where she is.'

'What do you mean?'

'She was supposed to be here for an interview at nine o'clock this morning. It is now quarter to ten.'

Rory shot to his feet and changed a curse into a cough. 'Maybe she has been delayed. Or is unwell,' he suggested.

'In which case, she should have rung in to let us know.'

Rory promised himself he would throttle her. 'I'll see what I can find out and come back to you, Mr Parker.'

'Thank you. To be honest, the only reason I have bothered with following this up, as she didn't show for the interview, is because we liked the sound of her CV. I'd be sorry to let a good applicant slip through my fingers if it's just a case of an innocent mistake.'

'I'm sure that's all it is, Mr Parker,' Rory scowled into the receiver. 'An innocent mistake.'

'I do hope so.'

'I will contact her now and I promise that either she or I will be in touch with you immediately.'

'I'm busy for the rest of the morning but give me a call this afternoon.'

'Without fail.'

'Thank you for your help. Goodbye.'

Rory replaced the receiver with a restrained slam, instead of shattering it into the thousand infuriated pieces he was tempted to. The blasted woman was impossible. Dragging her problems into his office life, where he already had enough of his own. And where the hell was she? What was she playing at? She had said nothing about an interview in Swindon. If he had known, he would have been happy to give her a lift in this morning even though he had been a bit late leaving.

A shuffle of feet made him aware that Paula and Gary were staring at him expectantly.

'Trouble at 'mill?' Gary smirked.

'Get out of here, you pair of vultures. Go pick the planning office's bones clean.'

As they trooped out, broad smiles replacing the anxious frowns with which they had trooped in, Rory dialled his home number.

The MGF roared its silver path back up to sixty the moment it was through the village of Ogbourne St George. Its small steering-wheel twitched responsively in Rory's hands as he took the S-bend on the edge. Time was ticking away, taking part of his life with it, and here he was wasting his energies racing back home for his idle sister-in-law, at a time when he should be concentrating on his business priorities. The meeting with Boothroyd was scheduled for twelve-thirty and he was going to have to motor up the M5 to get there. So this unwanted excursion would have to be brief.

From the wrap-around grey sky, a flock of peewits descended on silver wings to the harvested stubble that flashed past his open window. He had not even stopped to put the hood down, a criminal omission as the soil smelt damp and fragrant from the overnight rain, and the buffeting breeze might have gone some way towards cooling his temper.

He had let the telephone ring. And ring. And ring.

No answer.

He had tried Alex at the surgery but she was out on call. There had been no alternative but to risk this mad dash to Zena's lair. Lord only knew what she was up to, but Rory had no intention of letting her miss out on this opportunity. In theory, the fact that the telephone remained unanswered indicated that she was out. Maybe caught a lift from Alex into Marlborough or even, somewhat improbably, walked the mile or two into Pewsey. But Rory doubted both. Despite the unanswered telephone, he felt in his bones that she was there. Hiding.

A stretch of invitingly straight road opened up ahead and he punched the pedal to the metal.

The house was silent.

'Zena,' Rory called loudly as he stood in the hallway, but only feline paws came pattering across the flagstones in response. He tweaked their tails with automatic affection and after a brief glance in each of the downstairs rooms, he took the stairs two at a time. On the landing he called again.

'Zena.'

Silence.

The door to her room was closed. He approached it and rapped sharply.

'Zena, are you in there?'

No answer.

Another rap. 'Zena.'

Nothing.

He turned the handle and the door opened with its usual creak. One part of his brain registered that he must get round to oiling that hinge. The other part scanned the room. It was empty. Disappointingly empty. Bed unmade, duvet in a heap, clothes on floor and chair, and a jumble of pots and tubes, brushes, tissues and make-up on the windowsill and dressing-table. The room was not large, though long and narrow, but had a good-sized casement window with a glorious view out towards the trees at the back of the house. He noted with surprise that the woodland colours were already changing to the darker greens that presaged the onset of autumn.

Now what?

He glanced at his watch. Nearly quarter to eleven. He could not afford to linger, yet he sat down on the edge of the bed and tried to imagine what was going on in his sister-in-law's perverse mind. What was the point of applying for a job and then not going to the interview? Vaguely he wondered what had been in her CV. The one-eyed Horatio padded into the room and sniffed the carpet delicately, warily.

'Not allowed in here these days, are you, old horror?'

The cat leapt up beside him. As if he had not seen his owner for two years rather than two minutes, he rubbed his ugly head and white hairs all over Rory's sleeve, scenting him thoroughly. With feline disregard, he then walked muddy footprints over the sheet. Rory ignored it. On the bedside table he had noticed a slim book and he picked it up to inspect out of curiosity. A history of Avebury and the ancient circle of stones that marched round the village about ten miles west of Marlborough. Surprised, he flicked through it, noting that she had turned the page down two-thirds the way through it. Alex always flinched if she saw pages bent down. 'What's wrong with bookmarks?' she would complain. Obviously her sister had managed to side-step that particular quirk.

It was when he came to the back of the book that the photographs fell out. Two colour snaps: one somewhat discoloured and ragged round the edges, the other new and shiny. The shiny one was of a big, handsome man running out of the sea that was striped with long white breakers, a surfboard under his arm and a wide smile on his face. Blond, tanned, big tombstone teeth and muscles like Buicks. It was Chet. Chetwyn Taylor. Rory recognised him from the one photograph Zena had, uncharacteristically, sent of him from America when they were married. The fact that she carried his image around with her made Rory wonder if the relationship was quite as dead and buried as she had indicated.

The second photograph made him smile. It was unmistakable. Alex as a child. Laughing brown eyes and big, cheeky grin, hair short in a coppery halo. Around ten or twelve years old, he guessed. She was perched on a wooden fence beside her father and on the other side of him was a younger child. Obviously Zena. Behind them a horse's head loomed with friendly curiosity. The father was smiling into the camera but the rather severe character that Rory recalled from his courtship days was plain to see. Tall and angular, hair grey but still bushy, he had draped an arm around the shoulders of each of his daughters. But his head was tilted towards Zena. Zena in a pretty, flouncy dress. Even then, Alex had opted for jeans and a denim shirt.

After another minute spent studying the eternally young faces and surmising that their mother was probably behind the camera, he tucked the photographs back between the pages and replaced the book. He stood up and with a final glance at the jumble of possessions jostling for space – didn't she know what cupboards were for? – he left the room. Horatio trotted after him, voicing shrill objection, and together they made for the master bedroom, checking the bathroom en route. No sign of Zena.

Rory intended to take the opportunity to change his shirt. A trickle from his morning's coffee had smudged a crescent-shaped stain on its cuff. Not the way to impress a client. Already his thoughts were shifting away from the search for his sister-in-law and heading up the M5. He was half-way across the room when it dawned on him.

Zena was in his bed.

His duvet was snuggled round her. The eyes that stared back at him were totally unabashed.

'Hello, Rory.'

'What the hell are you doing in our bed?'

She stretched cat-like and smiled up at him. 'I prefer a double bed to a single. Always have.' Her blonde hair was loose and tousled, and she wore no make-up. It made her look young. Vulnerable.

'It's not normal to climb into other people's beds, you know,' Rory said, more gently than he intended.

She laughed. 'Normal was never my middle name.'

'Get out of our bed, please.'

'You're not using it at the moment.'

But she swung bare legs to the floor. Rory realised that she was wearing one of Alex's nightdresses, the slinky sleeveless one of flesh-coloured silk that emphasised every curve. His eyes took in Zena's full breasts pressed tightly against the flimsy material, nipples clearly outlined. Perhaps Alex had lent it to her. And perhaps pigs had wings.

'You shouldn't be using it either. For one thing, it isn't yours. And for another, what you should be doing is attending an interview in Swindon. With Strike Hot . . .'

'Oh, that.'

'Yes, that. They rang and asked me where you were.'

'I was here.'

'Then why didn't you answer the telephone?'

'I didn't want to.'

'Zena, what are you trying to do? It's absurd. To apply for a job and then not turn up when they ask to see you. It's as if you're on some self-destruct mission. Crazy!'

The smile slipped off her face. She jumped to her feet and came at him aggressively.

'No, Rory, it's not absurd. Not crazy. I applied for the stupid job just to keep you off my back. I don't want it and never have. You were pressurising me.'

'Zena, it's for your own good. As well as my sanity. Can't you see that? You're still young and attractive. So get out there and do something with your life, for heaven's sake.'

She thrust her face at his, cheeks flushed and eyes spitting defiance. 'You sound exactly like my father,' she shouted at him. 'Exactly like him. No wonder Alex married you.'

A slam of the door and she was gone.

Swearing under his breath, Rory started to strip the bed.

9

'You've got to speak to her, Alex.'

'I know.'

It was Friday evening and they had been out with the Donellis celebrating Joanna's birthday. Marco had treated them all to a sumptuous meal at The Angel in Lacock, smoothing out the crinkles of the day. The drive home in the dark along the wide A4 was pleasantly hypnotic and as Rory changed down to negotiate the somnolent town of Calne, once famous for its sausages, he felt able to discuss the subject of his sister-in-law with admirable calm.

'You realise her docile behaviour of the last few days was just to soften us up, don't you? Preparing the ground for this latest bombshell of hers. A blunt refusal to find a job. It's obvious now.'

'I know.'

'Has she said anything to you, then?'

'No, nothing.'

Rory sighed and briefly pondered on whether murder of a sister-in-law counted as justifiable homicide.

'Feeling sorry for yourself?' Alex asked with a smile he could hear in the dark.

'Hugely.'

'Poor old thing. Boothroyd and Zena too much to handle in one day?'

The meeting with the town planners and borough engineer had not gone as well as Rory had anticipated. It was their constantly changing demands, prey to the town's various pressure groups, that had scared off the financial interest. Expectations of retrieving it in the near future were marginal. Rory had dug his hopes up from somewhere round his bootstraps and spent the rest of the afternoon on the telephone.

'Definitely.'

He said it with a laugh, but Alex was serious.

'Trouble at work and then you come back to more trouble at home. No respite from it. I am sorry, Rory, that my family is causing these problems for you.'

'And for you.'

'Yes, but that's different. She's my sister. Blood ties . . . and all that.'

'Don't forget the emotional ties. Emotional history.'

'Yes, that too. She left home before we had even started to turn over any stones to see what was lurking underneath.'

'So you'll talk to her?'

'I promise. I intend to find out what's going on in that head of hers. A couple of days ago, she expressed an interest in visiting Avebury. As the weather forecast is fine for Sunday, I thought we might drive over there while you and Marco fight it out, *mano a mano*, over the Italian Grand Prix.'

Distracted for a moment by the prospect of two hours of unadulterated Italian partisanship at Monza, Rory unconsciously put his foot down, causing the MGF to leap up the long hill out of Cherhill. Silently, the giant white horse carved into the chalk hills watched its headlights glaring a path through the darkness.

'Sounds a good idea.' He didn't want Zena's snide comments spoiling his afternoon. Or Marco's for that matter. 'I'm afraid, every time I try to talk to her seriously, one or other of us always ends up shouting.'

'I've noticed. So much for your calm-but-firm approach.' But Alex patted his knee forgivingly.

Avebury Circle was impressive. The massive sarsen stones, all forty of them, that towered over the landscape, were carefully aligned by neolithic man in three concentric circles of over half a mile diameter. A monument to man's foolhardy determination to leave his mark. No wave would wash away these footsteps in a hurry.

The gentle village had grown up among them, taking them for

granted, but when in 1935 Alexander Keiller excavated the vast ditch that was enclosed by the stones, a tourist industry was born. Coaches, car parks, souvenir and craft shops now plied their trades each summer to assuage the insatiable curiosity of the seasoned holidaymaker. Thousands flocked to catch a reassuring glimpse of the permanence of man's endeavour and to Alex it sometimes felt as if they all chose to come on the same day she did.

But this time she was lucky. It was the end of the first week in September. The nation's children had donned their blazers and been herded back to school, which meant, obligingly, there were still three spaces in the car park. She tucked the Clio safely in a corner and took Zena on the tour. They started with the arts and crafts, and saved the stones for last.

'Americans must go berserk when they see this lot. I know Chet would.'

They were standing in the Rural Life Museum inside the Great Barn, inspecting a display of ancient farming tools that looked more like fiendish instruments of torture to Alex. It was the first time she had heard Zena volunteer her ex-husband's name and she quickly pushed a foot in the door.

'Do you think he might ever come over here? To see you, perhaps?'

'Good God, no.' Zena looked at her sister in surprise. 'I told you, it's over. He's history.' She waved an arm to encompass the ancient beams that cathedraled above their heads. 'Like this place is. Except this is magnificent and he is a turd. I have no desire to preserve him for future generations.'

Then why carry his photograph around, Alex wanted to ask. But refrained from confessing Rory's snooping. There were problems enough.

A sudden influx of the white-cardigan brigade off the latest coach prompted them to drift over in the direction of a demonstration of spinning and weaving. Two women in long brown smocks gave the impression of a time warp. Skilful fingers that knew their craft.

The sisters watched in silence for several minutes, then Zena remarked, 'This reminds me of Mummy. She took us to see weaving once. Do you remember?'

Alex shook her head. 'No.' A complete blank.

Zena frowned. 'Of course you remember. It was a County Show. Daddy was the horse judge and brought us all along to applaud. We went round the craft stalls while Daddy was busy in the officials' tent.'

Snatches returned. Tethered rows of sheep panting in the hot sun, toffee apples and ice cream, her father presenting the blue rosette for first prize. But no weaving.

'I remember the show, but not the crafts bit.'

'That's because it was only Mummy with us,' Zena snapped and walked off into the sunlight outside.

Alex felt herself sink another few inches into the mire.

An hour later, the moment of frisson was also history. Tucked out of sight. But not forgotten. They had done the gift shops, admired the greedy peacocks that strutted as if they owned the place, and were on a deserted ridge half-way round the outer circle of stones.

'This place has a touch of blood and magic,' Alex remarked. 'Human sacrifices and all that.' She settled down on the grass and looked out past the trees to Silbury Hill. In the last half hour clouds had crept up on the sun and veiled its warmth, but in the mellow light the hill stood out brazenly like a gigantic marshmallow.

Zena joined her on the soft earth. 'That's the biggest man-made mound in Europe,' she announced.

Obviously she had been reading her bedside book.

'It's extraordinary to think what people can achieve when they work together,' Alex commented, thinking of the present discord at home.

'Like the pyramids.'

'Or the NASA space race.'

'Americans don't work together,' Zena laughed. 'They're too busy competing.'

'Zena, tell me about America. What happened over there during all those years?'

'I've already told you that. Various jobs, none very exciting. Various relationships, none very exciting. Then Chet, a short-lived version of domestic bliss. And kapow! Over. So I came home.'

Alex noticed the 'home'.

'Why the kapow? You've never explained.' She stretched out on her back and stared up at the soft grey dome that arched above. A deliberate gesture of relaxation. Of trust. Exposing the underbelly.

'There's nothing to explain,' Zena said with an indifferent shrug. She flopped down alongside her sister, but rolled on to her stomach. Defensive. 'We didn't get on any more. The loss of the money stripped away his charm and I didn't like what was underneath. That's all.'

'That must have been tough.'

'Don't sweat about it. I'm better off without him.'

Alex felt the old protective urge to wrap her younger sister in cotton wool. She leant over and gave her an affectionate hug.

Zena looked round, surprised. Pleased.

'What's that for?'

'To say we're sisters.'

Zena stared at her for a moment and seemed about to say something, but changed her mind. Her attention returned to the daisies she was assembling in a stubby pile in front of her. 'Don't forget, I'm a sister-in-law as well, Ali.'

'No, I can't forget that.'

Zena cocked an eye at her and chuckled wickedly. 'Neither can he.'

A breeze sprang up from the west, making the deformed oak that clung with ancient tenacity to the ridge sway and shiver its leaves at the two women. At its base, roots writhed in and out of the soil like sea serpents. Alex, in just cotton blouse and jeans, tightened the scarf at her neck. Her eyes followed a leaf that fluttered down and settled snuggly into the curve of Zena's back, incongruous on the crisp navy blazer.

She felt a surge of affection. The girl was maddening. Always had been. Almost certainly always would be. But they had shared so much of life. The first eighteen years of it. The recent eight years of virtual silence from her was an irrelevance. They had got into too many scrapes. Laughed and cried together too many times as they scrambled out of them for Alex to want to deny the bond between them. She was convinced deep inside herself that Zena had come to her, the same way she used to come when they were children, for Alex to dig her out of a hole. But how could she help, when Zena would not even give her a spade to dig with?

It was time for both feet.

'Zena, you can't go on like this. No job. No effort. Just hiding away.'

Zena did not look round, engrossed in the daisies. 'I know that, Ali. I know. It's just that I'm not ready for Strike Hot and its companions yet.'

'What's the matter, Zena? What's gone wrong? You're not ill, are you?'

Zena laughed into the grass. 'Of course not. Don't be so melodramatic.'

'Then what is it? What are you hiding from?'

'From myself, I guess.'

Alex rolled on to her back once more and plucked a long strand of grass that had escaped the attentions of the local sheep. She chewed on it as she tried to work that one out.

'What trouble have you caused that scares you so?'

'I should never have gone haring off to America like that. Only eighteen, for Christ's sake. My paint wasn't even dry. I made mistakes.'

'Tell me about them.'

'Chet was the worst one.'

'But your postcards implied you were happy. Having fun.'

'Oh, I was having fun all right. But I wasn't happy.'

'Then why did you marry him?'

'Because I was stupid.'

'Did you love him?'

A long pause. Alex watched a buzzard, far above, carve impossibly slow circles into the translucent clouds and tried to imagine its view of her from such a height.

'I thought I did,' Zena told the daisies. 'Or more precisely, I hoped I did. But the reality was that I was dog-tired. Aching from the bruises I'd taken and permanently bad-tempered. Chet was my pain-killer. Like I said, I was stupid.'

'Probably not the first time a marriage was based on that.'

'Nor the last.'

'How did Chet react to the break-up?'

'Chet is a chicken-brained scumbag. So don't go wasting any sympathy on him.'

But still a raw spot that can't be touched, Alex realised.

'So what now?'

Zena turned and sat up, grass strands hanging from her lapel. In her hands was a circle of daisy chain. She placed it with ceremony on Alex's head. 'A perfect crown for you.'

Alex sat up beside her, touched by the gesture. As a child, Alex had always threaded daisy chain crowns, daisy chain bracelets, daisy chain necklaces and daisy chain anklets for her little sister. Daisy chain bonds to keep them together.

'That takes me back,' she said.

'And me.'

The two women smiled at each together.

'I have a plan,' Zena announced.

Alex attempted to pick up the glass of brandy that sat in front of her, but her hand was still shaking too violently. She gave up on it. Who needed alcohol anyway? The adrenalin was charging through her system faster than Marco's Ferrari round Monza. She tried to slow it down by focusing on the young couple entwining fingers at the next table, but they remained a blur.

She knew she was overreacting. Could not think straight. Let alone see straight.

Zena had led her, with tolerant amusement, down from the ridge and over to one of the courtyard tables outside the Red Lion. She had ordered them each a brandy, paid for them out of Alex's purse and sat munching on a packet of crisps while waiting for her sister to float back down into the earth's atmosphere. She hadn't expected quite such a reaction.

By the time her own brandy was gone and she had started in on Alex's, she was growing impatient. 'Well? Is it a deal?'

'Yes. Yes. A thousand yeses. Yes.'

'I'll take that as an affirmative, then,' Zena laughed.

'A very firm affirmative.'

'Rory might not see it quite that way.'

'Rory will be thrilled,' Alex insisted expansively.

As Zena looked at her sister's excited face, she could not help feeling she was being blinded by optimism. The one thing Rory would not be was thrilled.

'A year?' Rory demanded. 'You expect me to let her live under this roof for a whole year?'

'Yes.'

'And pay her for the privilege?'

'Yes.'

'You're out of your mind! Either she or I would end up in a strait-jacket.' Rory was striding up and down the room, unable to believe what his wife had just suggested. What spell had the witch woven over her? 'Why on earth should we agree to that? Alex, think about it seriously. It would never work.'

'It would if we wanted it to.'

'But Alex, I don't want to. That's my point.'

'I do.'

'What in heaven's name has she said to you to make you change your tune like that? What bribe is she offering?'

'A baby.'

Rory froze mid stride.

In shock, he looked at his wife. 'A baby?'

'Yes. Of our own. A baby.'

'And exactly how is she going to produce this miracle?'

Alex sat down, determined to keep calm. Or at least, the appearance of calm. Her palms were moist and she rubbed them hard against her jeans. Carefully, keeping her elation under wraps, she explained.

'Zena will become pregnant, carry the child and when it's born, she will give it to us.'

Rory stared at her, incredulous. 'Is that what Zena has said?'

'Yes.'

'And you believe her?'

'Of course I do. Why would she say it if she didn't mean it?'

'Why does that woman say half the things she does? Who knows? We have no idea what goes on in that head of hers. She may see it as an amusing way of getting at us, for all I know. Raising our hopes and then dashing them to smithereens.'

Doubt slid like a sliver of glass into her stomach. 'Don't say that, Rory. Of course she means it. Not even she would lie about something like this.'

'If it means a few more weeks free board and comfortable lodging, I wouldn't put it past her.'

'No, don't be absurd. I know she wouldn't.' It sounded vehement enough. As though she believed it.

Rory looked at his wife's flushed cheeks, the intense glitter in her brown eyes, as if the flame of maternal instinct was already kindled there. He did not want to douse it with brute fingers. Gently, he said, 'Alex, we both know what she's like. She is unreliable.'

'Let's at least give it a try.'

'No, Alex, there's no point getting our hopes up. The idea's a non-starter.'

Alex wanted to scream, to howl the importance of trying. She caught a glimpse of her own hands in her lap, shaking. Like someone else's. Quivering with need. But her voice came out quite normal, reasonable in its suggestions.

'Let me tell you what exactly she has proposed. She becomes pregnant and lives here with us until the birth. After the birth, she hands the baby over to us and in exchange we give her half of an agreed lump sum of money. We start adoption proceedings and on the day that is finalised, she gets the other half of the money.'

'And what makes you think she will stick to her word?'

'It will all be drawn up in a legal contract.'

Rory started pacing once more. Patiently he pointed out, 'If she changes her mind at the last moment and decides to keep the child, no court is going to force her to give up her own baby. Anyway, it's illegal to pay someone to have a surrogate child.'

'I know that. But you are allowed to pay their costs. Her costs would include loss of earnings during pregnancy.'

'Earnings! What earnings?'

'She could easily find a job if she really tried.'

'My point exactly. Why doesn't she do that instead of this ridiculous scheme of hers? She has got to have some devious motive behind it that we can't fathom.'

'Rory, you're being too suspicious. The reason she's making this offer is simple. She's my sister. She is helping me.

Blood ties.' She had to make him understand. 'She's doing it for me.'

'No, no, my generous Alex. Zena is not like you. That's not enough of a reason. She has never done anything for anyone.'

'We don't know, do we? She has been away too long. I think she's lonely and frightened. Under that brittle exterior, she's hurting.'

'When she's around, so am I.'

Alex smiled sympathetically. 'I know she can be a pain, but if she feels we're offering her a home and a place in our family, I believe she won't need to be so prickly.'

'Caustic is the word.'

'Okay, caustic, if you prefer. She just wants somewhere to lick her wounds and put herself back together again.'

'An excuse to be idle, you mean.'

'Call it what you will.'

Rory stopped pacing and came to a halt in front of his wife's chair. 'No, Alex, even to be talking seriously about this is madness. That sister of yours is up to something. I don't know what. But I don't trust her.' He swept a hand through his dark hair in a gesture of frustration. How could he make Alex see sense? She was blinded by her own yearnings.

'Anyway, I thought you were against adoption,' he reminded her.

'Oh, Rory, can't you see the difference? Zena and I have the same gene pool. We had the same parents. Biologically the child would be partially mine. And you, of course, would be the father.'

It hit him like an express train.

'For Christ's sake, Alex, I am not sleeping with my wife's sister.'

His expression of horror provoked a laugh from her and he felt increasingly irritated. He could hear the sound of battle in the distance.

'Don't be silly, Rory. Of course you won't have to sleep with her. Artificial insemination is what we'll use. Just imagine the result. You would be a father. A son of your own. Or daughter. Maybe even both, if it turns out to be twins. A child that is ours. Of our own making.'

His gut lurched with the desire. Oh God, no. Not that. Not again. He had slammed the lid shut on that after the night of the storm. Painfully and finally. He dare not let it out again.

'No, Alex. No. She would let us down. I know it. I don't intend to put us through that hell.'

Alex leapt to her feet. 'And what about my choice? I say we go ahead with the idea. Of course there's a risk. But it's a risk I'm willing to take.'

'But I'm not.'

The gap between them became a gulf.

Alex's breath was coming fast. 'You have no right to say no. No right to make the decision condemning our child to no life.'

'Alex, be sensible. It's not that . . .'

'To hell with sensible. I want a child of our own, Rory, a child. Please, please, let's have this child.'

Tears fell on to her cheeks and at that moment Rory hated Zena. He wrapped his arms around his wife and stroked her hair, soothing her. He kissed her forehead and murmured against her moist skin, 'You see, she's putting us through misery before we've even started. Can't you realise, it would never work? What if she went along with the idea, living off us until the baby was born, leading you to think you would be the mother. Then disappeared, taking the baby with her? You just can't trust her. It would be ten times harder to bear than saying no now. I'm sorry, my love, but I'm not willing to go through that. But if you want to adopt, let's do it properly. Through official agencies.'

Alex broke free from him. 'Rory, I don't want somebody else's child. I want this one. Our own child.'

Just those words lifted the lid a fraction and the pain began to seep out. Like acid inside him.

'I'm sorry, Alex, but the answer is still no.'

They stared at each other with unaccustomed hostility. The chasm was widening and neither was looking for a bridge.

Alex did not go to work the next day. She called off sick, which only made her feel worse. Rory left at eight in the morning as usual, without comment. They had not exchanged a word.

Zena, wisely, had retreated to her own room the previous

evening and stayed there. But Alex was under no illusion, aware that she must have heard the raised voices. No prizes for guessing the cause. Zena had been right in her prediction. Rory was not thrilled. Yet how could he be so short-sighted? So self-centred? So frightened of seizing this opportunity? She knew he wanted a child every bit as much as she did, so why couldn't he see that Zena was the answer?

She climbed out of bed, feeling just as sick as she had claimed to be to Lizzie at the surgery.

'Stay in bed,' Lizzie had fussed, 'and drink lots of fluids.' Was that what her mother had always taught her? Before the car crash?

Every day of her working life Alex saw examples of how fragile life was. The hold on it was so slender. A child that was biologically part-reproduction of herself strengthened that hold. Staked her claim to immortality. But most of all, would fill the void inside her. The void that she had draped with camouflage nets, so that no one would notice the gaping hole, but which sent soul-splitting echoes thundering through her whenever something crashed through the net. A pram in the street, a cheeky grin through a car's rear window, a giggle of laughter. Or a birthday party.

She was running out of nets.

It was just as she was walking out of the back door, armed with a clutch of plastic bags for picking apples off the profligate old Bramley tree, that the telephone rang. For a moment she stood poised precariously between action and inaction, tempted to let it ring. There was no one she wished to talk to right now. But it might, just might, be the surgery. Duty triumphed and she picked up the mobile phone in the kitchen.

'*Ciao*, Alex. I'm sorry to hear you are not well.'

'Hello, Marco.'

'I rang your veterinary office and there they told me you are not well. *Che brutta cosa.*'

'It's nothing serious. I just had a splitting headache this morning.' That much at least was true. Eyes grainy from lack of sleep and a war-dance thumping away behind them. She and Rory had argued until the early hours.

'I am sorry to disturb your rest then.'

'Don't worry. What can I do for you?'

'*Ieri*, yesterday when I came over to watch the race, I brought pamphlets to show Rory. On the styling exercise that Toyota have just unveiled. *Bellissima*.'

'Ah, yes, I saw them.'

'Well, Monza wiped out all from my head. *Una corsa stupenda*! I forgot to bring them back with me. I have promised to show them to my colleague here today, so may I come round to pick them up? Would you mind?'

'No, of course not.'

'In about half an hour?'

'I'll have coffee ready.'

'*Grazie. Ciao.*'

Alex hung up, wishing she had stuck to her apple picking.

But she was not kept from it for long. Marco arrived within half an hour, smart in Italian suit and tie and bearing a creamy white rose with a strong musky fragrance that reminded her of a persian cat she had once owned.

'To make you feel better.' He stood back and looked at her with an expression of concern. 'You need some rest, *mia povera Alessandra*. You are getting skinny thin.' He pronounced it 'skeenee theen'. 'I will get Joanna to make you my mama's *tagliatele napoli*. To fatten you up.' He wrapped her in a warm bear-hug that made her want to cry.

'I'm fine, Marco, honestly. Just a bit tired. Come and have some coffee. Brazilian and strong.'

'*Magnifico*. Exactly what I need.'

He followed her into the kitchen and while she poured out two mugs of coffee, he made himself at home at the table. Hamilton immediately flowed on to his lap, uttered a throaty greeting, turned round twice and tucked herself into a ball. They were old friends. Marco ran a hand over her sleek, bony shoulders and set off a steady vibration.

'This elegant lady of yours knows I cannot resist her blue eyes. She takes advantage of me,' he laughed, and looked up to see Zena's amber eyes staring at him. She was standing in the doorway, wearing her garish pink kimono.

'Are you so easy to take advantage of, Marco?'

Alex looked round, surprised. She had not seen hide nor hair of her sister that morning. The kimono hung loosely and the hair and make-up looked almost natural. Discreet, with just a hint of tousled.

'Hello, Zena. Would you like some coffee?'

'Great.' She sat herself down at the table beside Marco, the kimono falling open enough to reveal a generous cleavage and bare legs.

Marco smiled broadly, teeth very white against his olive skin. 'Zena, I am pleased to see you. I want to talk to you.'

'That sounds intriguing, Marco. What would you like to talk to me about? The Grand Prix race, Ferrari's chances of winning the championship, Schumacher's success rate or maybe the colours of this season's liveries?'

He knew she was teasing him, but was not quite sure why. 'No, no, no cars today. Today is for working.'

She raised an eyebrow at the coffee and cat. 'So I see. The picture of industry.'

He laughed. 'Industry is what I want to talk to you about.'

'Oh?' she queried, immediately losing interest.

Alex placed the rose in a slim blue vase in the centre of the table and a mug of coffee in front of Zena, but received no thanks. She remained standing and sipped her own. 'Go on Marco.'

'Rory mentioned to me yesterday that you are looking for a job, so I made a few enquiries in our company. And *subito*! They want an assistant in Personnel. Maybe you are interested?'

Alex waited for the answer.

'Mmm, possibly. Depends on my availability.' She eyed Marco speculatively. 'And on what is required.'

'I asked. A certain amount of computer familiarity, they told me. Do you have that?' His black eyes studied her expectantly.

'Yes, of course. Essential these days. No one in America functions without these blasted machines.'

'*Perfetto*! Then I shall give you a name and telephone number to ring. The Personnel Department is expanding and needs some reorganisation. They want someone to . . .' He poured out the details of what the job entailed, but Alex could see Zena was not listening. She was watching Marco. Watching the way his heavy eyebrows lowered when he was emphasising a point, the glossy black of his hair, the expressive mouth and passionately animated hands.

Zena cut him off short. 'Thank you, Marco. It would be interesting to work with you. I'm glad you thought of me.'

He looked slightly surprised. '*Scusi*, but you would not exactly be working with me. Didn't I make that clear?'

Before he could start explaining the job all over again, Alex stepped in. 'I'm sure Zena understands that, Marco. She can learn more when she telephones.' If she telephones.

'*Si*, that is right.' He pulled his business card from his jacket pocket and scribbled a name and number on the back. 'I will tell my colleague to expect a call from you?'

'Of course.' She smiled at him. Like a crocodile before it bites your leg off, Alex thought.

Marco finished his coffee, again apologised with a kiss on the hand for disturbing Alex's rest, retrieved his pamphlets and with a final '*Ciao*' to Zena and Hamilton, drove off in his Alfa. When Alex walked back into the kitchen, Zena was standing at the old pine dresser fiddling with the china displayed on it. A blue and white fine Spode service that had once belonged to their parents.

'I've always liked this willow pattern stuff,' she commented.

Alex was not sure whether it was an innocent remark or meant as a criticism of her for not sharing it between them. But her mother's will had been quite clear; it specified that the service should go complete to Alex.

'That was thoughtful of Marco, wasn't it, Zena?'

'I suppose so. But I'm not dumb. He and Rory obviously cooked it up together yesterday afternoon.'

'I didn't know you had computer skills.'

Zena smiled at her. 'I haven't. I've never used one in my life. I just said it to keep him happy about his cosy little job offer.' She replaced the porcelain cup on its hook, where it swung erratically for a moment, as if trying to escape from its eggshell thin handle. 'He's very Italian, isn't he?'

'Yes, very. Extremely romantic.'

'And passionate.' It was accompanied by a suggestive pout. 'Lucky Joanna.'

'Yes.' Alex thought about the twins and Angelica. 'Lucky Joanna.'

The morning air was pin-sharp and smelt of autumn. The summer seemed to have sneaked away in the night. Somewhere in the village a bonfire must be brewing because there was the faintest waft of woodsmoke on the breeze. Perched up in the ancient apple tree that lurched at a rather odd angle over the vegetable patch, Alex sought solace in the familiar view across the field to the woods beyond. For a while she abandoned her plastic-bag-filling task and just watched the crows squabbling over the nests that sat like dark hairy spiders in the upper branches on the skyline. They would all be off soon, moving on freely like sore-throated minstrels to wherever their sleek strong wings carried them. Another annual ritual completed. And the merry-go-round would start all over again.

She shifted her position to stop the branch digging into the soles of her trainers, but the bag she had half filled and hooked on to a stub of the trunk dipped sideways. It emptied most of its contents on to the last row of the potato plants below.

'Damn the apples,' she muttered and mentally consigned the bruised load to the windfall sack intended for purée.

'Do you want me to help?'

Alex peered down through the foliage to see Zena's upturned face. After Marco had left, she had disappeared back upstairs to shower, so Alex was surprised to hear her voice and the offer of help. Must have been an all-time speed record for Zena in the bathroom.

'Thanks, yes. There are some more bags by the greenhouse. We can pick up the fallers at the end.'

As Zena went over to retrieve one of the recycled supermarket bags, a blackbird that had been chattering with frustration in the briar hedge, suddenly pumped up its courage and chest, dropped down on to one of the errant apples and drilled six speedy stabs into the green flesh. He was rewarded with a beakful of sour pulp and a beetle grub. Zena flapped him away from the crop and then tossed his defaced booty into the hedge after him, but it caught against a heavy branch, rebounded back on to the vegetable plot and neatly decapitated a carrot plant.

'Gee shucks! Right between the eyes,' she laughed.

Alex looked down on the blonde head retrieving the battered apple and as it leant over the feathery greenery of the carrot, she saw a sudden flash of a ginger head bent over a broken flower stalk. She tugged at the memory. For a moment nothing came. Then in a rush, her mother's tears over some plant, giggles in the conservatory and her father's deep laugh. A chill shadow slithered down her spine and took her by surprise. She pushed it away. But the metallic zing of adrenalin soured her tongue. There were enough of today's shadows to chase away, without digging up more from the past.

Alex resumed her apple picking, fingers gentle but firm. Surgical skills inherent in their touch. The bag began to bulge once more. Zena climbed a cautious few rungs up the ladder and collected half a dozen or so, but when she pulled off two apples joined together and a flurry of earwigs scuttled out from between them, she squealed and dropped the lot.

'Shit. Ali, these goddamn apples have a wildlife all of their own. Don't you spray against bugs?'

Alex let Zena chunter on, knowing earwigs and maggoty apples weren't the real cause of her complaints. She was waiting for an answer.

There was no point in putting it off.

Alex placed a last Bramley in with the others and headed for the ground, thin plastic handles cutting into her fingers. The apples would have to be individually wrapped in newspaper squares and placed in layers in boxes in the garage. It was a dirty, fiddly job that always left her fingers covered in print. Perhaps she could rope Zena into it. On the grass, jeans already streaked with green, she knelt down to pick up the fallen apples and that was when her hands mutinied. They would do no more. Except cover her mouth. To silence the scream.

Zena descended the ladder and studied her sister's quivering back.

'The answer's no, I gather?'

Alex could not reply.

'I had a feeling that blasted husband of yours would let us down.'

Let down? Is that what Rory had done? Let her down? Even in the twisting blaze of her anger at him, she knew that was not true. He believed he was saving her from heartache. But he was creating it. Couldn't he see that? See that even the faintest, slightest, most distant hope made it worth all the risk? She turned round and over her shoulder looked at her sister. Tried to fathom the sort of woman she had grown into. Was she really so untrustworthy? As ruthless and selfish as Rory insisted?

Alex could not believe it. Would not believe it.

She was convinced that if there were any difficulties, she would manage to deal with Zena. She was her little sister, for God's sake. How many times had Alex helped her out of her messes when she was small? Now it was Zena's turn.

Alex abandoned the apples and rose to her feet. 'No, Zena, Rory hasn't let us down. Don't see it that way. To be honest, it's because he doesn't want me to get hurt.'

'Hurt? How hurt? He's the one doing the hurting.' She tossed another apple into the hedge and the blackbird chattered his yellow-beaked appreciation.

'It is very hard for anyone to give up a child, Zena. One they have brought into the world. He thinks you will change your mind at the last moment.'

Zena stared at her for so long that Alex thought she was not going to reply. Then Zena stepped forward and put her arms around Alex. Her light perfume was as incongruous in the vegetable garden as her gesture. 'I would never do that to you, Ali. I know what this child means to you.'

Alex squeezed her sister gratefully and said with affection, 'I know you wouldn't. But Rory doesn't.'

Zena released her and her golden eyes widened with mischief. 'We could always find a different father, you know.'

'What do you mean?'

'Instead of Rory, of course.'

'Don't be ridiculous.'

'Think about it.'

'The child has to be Rory's. As well as yours and mine. That's the whole point.'

Zena shrugged. 'Just a thought. Better than nothing.'

Was it? Better than nothing? At least partly hers via Zena's genes. Alex's head ached.

'What about that nice Italian of yours?'

'Marco? Don't be absurd.'

'With him I could do it without the indignity of artificial insemination.'

'Stop it.'

'You must admit, it would be more fun.'

'Marco's a happily married man. With a wife and family. Just leave him out of this. I don't want any more trouble than . . .' She stopped. Zena was grinning at her.

'Just bullshitting you, sister mine. A tease. To cheer you up.'

'Thanks a lot, Zena. Made me feel a whole heap better.'

'No need to be so touchy. Just trying to lighten the atmosphere. And Marco is a honey, you have to admit.'

'He is Joanna's honey. Don't you forget that.'

'No chance of that.' Zena offered a sweet, submissive smile. 'Do you want me to pick up these apples? Or shall we say bugger them, and you can treat us both to a slap-up lunch in Bath?'

Alex linked an arm through her sister's. 'Let's say bugger them. Bugger the lot of them.'

10

Rory's last job of the day was in Marlborough. Not particularly inspiring, but good bread-and-butter stuff. A men's outfitters in the High Street had recently changed hands and the new owners, an importer of wood-burning stoves, had hopes of pulling down a clutch of rickety sheds at the back of the narrow building and replacing them with an additional smart new warehouse-cum-showroom. Rory had explained about the problems of planning permission, as Marlborough's glories were all carefully listed. But if the designs were an obvious improvement and in keeping with the town's character and charm, he felt they stood a good chance. Access and rights of light were going to be the two main headaches.

As he walked down the High Street, the wind scurrying fitfully between the cars, Rory kept his thoughts strictly focused on those problems. Deliberately skirting the one that rose like Everest in the centre of his mind.

Access he could improve by widening the entry from the back alleyway and by incorporating a covered passageway from the main unit. But rights of light were more of a problem. The present sheds' corrugated roofs were far too low. He would have to apply for raising their level but that would affect the . . . Movement in a shop window caught his eye.

Two wooden creatures were dancing. It was the toy shop. In front of an array of plastic kits, radio-controlled cars and Barbie's latest outfit to wow Ken, were two puppets. Electronically animated on the end of long strings. A black kitten with pink nose and twitching tail, about life size for an eight-week-old, was patting the spiky tail of a ten-inch-tall baby dragon, all green wings, egg-head and flashing white fangs. Cute, as Zena would say.

Rory stood and watched them, mesmerised by their repetitive antics. He had possessed a similar cat puppet when he was a child, except that it had been furry and stuffed with sawdust that slowly seeped out over the years. Reluctant to see his ragged companion dwindling, he had taken drastic measures. Shoved his mother's snipped-up stockings inside it to fatten it out. Unfortunately the stockings had not been old ones and his mother had not been exactly pleased. But Rory had been blissfully happy to have Sooty chubby once more, so had been deaf to his mother's complaint. Where was Sooty now? No doubt, long since on the scrap heap. Or maybe he had gone to a jumble sale and had done the rounds. Stuffed and restuffed through generations of children.

Suddenly Rory felt the need to possess that black kitten in the window, with its marshmallow pink nose and stiff white whiskers. To make amends to Sooty. He strode to the shop door but the notice on the door said a firm 'Closed'. Of course, it was after five-thirty. Initial frustration ebbed into relief and he backed away from the door. What the hell was he doing? What would he do with a puppet?

Give it to a child.

No. Because there was no child. And never would be.

'Hi, Rory. How's tricks?'

A hand fell heavily on Rory's shoulder and he turned to see the smooth, shiny face of Alan Beecroft. His expression was decidedly smug, so the estate agency business must be doing well, despite the doom and gloom in the papers about the housing market. The slicked-back hair and alert brown eyes, always on the look-out for a deal, gave the impression of clean-cut efficiency. Only slightly marred today by the hint of five o'clock shadow.

'Hello, Alan.' It did not come out with any enthusiasm.

'Have you heard? That housing development of yours is going great guns. Deposits coming in on all four styles. I hope you're making a packet out of it, because we certainly aim to.'

'That's great. They're attractive designs, even though I say it myself. I'm not surprised they're doing well.'

'Keen prices too.'

'Yes, we managed to keep the costs very competitive. Keep up the good work.' Rory started to move away.

'Hey, what's the rush? I've just clinched a fantastic deal on a place over at Wilton. Come and celebrate with me. My shout.' He clapped Rory on the back. 'Just a quick one at the Silver Trout.'

The last person Rory needed right now was this egocentric prat. He had no wish to have his ear bent with Alan Beecroft's latest triumphs and disasters or hear yet again his harangue about the depths of duplicity that both buyers and sellers frequently sank to. Anyway, Rory had to get home to talk it out with Alex. He opened his mouth to decline. Alex was waiting for him.

'Sounds like a good idea to me, Alan.'

Together they headed for the pub that was conveniently situated only a few yards down the High Street. They reached it before Rory could change his mind.

'Time, please, gentlemen.' The barman smiled with professional tolerance at the two drunks in the corner cubicle. He had seen the smarmy chap the worse for wear on numerous previous occasions. But the other fellow was not a regular customer. Occasionally came in for a meal with his wife, that pretty vet who worked with the jock, Tamworth. 'Closing time. Your taxi is waiting outside.'

Two pairs of bleary eyes strained to focus on him.

'Your taxi is here,' he repeated slowly and clearly, as if for the deaf.

'Axi,' the vet's husband explained to his companion and lurched up out of his seat. His tall frame swayed precariously, seemed about to topple, then regained its equilibrium. 'C'mon, Al.' He managed to walk with a degree of composure to the door. Unfortunately it was the wrong door.

With the skill of long years of patient practice, the barman steered them both safely out on to the pavement. Though well oiled, neither gent had been rowdy and the vet's husband had been particularly generous with the tips. Just celebrating probably. Or drowning his sorrows. Either way, they were going home happy as newts. He handed them over to the taxi driver's care and returned to attend to the cleaning up of his bar.

In the taxi, Rory leant back against the seat and watched the roof-lining turn cartwheels. He tipped his head sideways to avoid it hitting him and noticed that he couldn't see anything outside. Had somebody pulled down the blinds?

'Put the light on,' Alan Beecroft muttered beside him.

'Wha' light, ol' pal?'

'Outside.'

Rory rolled his eyes towards the window once more. ''S dark ousside. 'Cos it's night.'

Alan stared at the blackness flitting past the window like the inside of a tunnel and then at Rory. 'You're a bloody genius.' He clutched Rory's arm weakly. 'My very best pal is . . .' he swallowed carefully 'a bloody genius.' He raised his voice to impart this knowledge to the driver. 'My friend here,' he pounded Rory's chest with a fist, 'is a bloody genius. And he builds things.'

'Oh yes? That's nice, mate,' the driver replied obligingly.

Rory was not to be outdone. 'An' my buddy here, he sells 'em.'

'Good for him.'

'Good for both of us,' Alan Beecroft insisted and rested his head on his bosom pal's shoulder.

'Get off, you wanker.'

But long, satisfied snores announced that Rory's remonstrances were too late. So he made use of the agent's head as a welcome, if bony, pillow for himself. When a hand shook his shoulder, he woke reluctantly and knew it was time to leave the warmth of the taxi. He rebelled and slid further down into the warmth. Anyway, he wasn't sure his legs had any bones. And his head was swirling and grinding like the inside of a blender. The hand shook him again. With extreme caution he opened one eye. But only a slit.

Mind-jarring light swarmed in. He shut it again.

'Rory.'

It was Alex's voice. She must have come to help him out of the taxi. Kind and considerate as always.

'Wake up, you drunken bastard.'

His eyes crept open a fraction, careful to shield themselves with a fringe of black lashes this time.

'Come on, Rory. Wake up.'

Her face floated close to his and he wanted to kiss her, to tell her how beautiful she was, to . . .

'At last, you're conscious, you stupid sod.'

Suddenly his lumbering mind remembered Alan Beecroft. He glanced sideways, instantly regretted the ice-picks that sank into his eyeballs and realised his drinking companion's head was no longer beside him, propping him up. Unless it had turned into a snowy-white, down-filled pillow, that is.

'I'm off now. To the surgery. I was just checking you were in the land of the living.'

Rory's lids raised just a touch more. He looked around in disbelief. He was in his own bed, under the striped duvet his brother had sent last Christmas, morning sunlight battling its way into his brain and a cup of black coffee puffing caffeine towards his desert-dry mouth. On the floor his suit of yesterday lay in a heap.

'I've rung your office. To say you'll be late. I presume you're okay?'

Rory thought of nodding, but remembered the ice-picks just in time. 'Yes, I'm fine.'

'Oh sure. You look it. Green always did suit you.'

He tried a smile but his facial muscles only twitched and gave up the effort. 'Fine,' he repeated, his tongue getting in the way.

Alex stood beside the bed looking down at him for several moments, then bent and very gently kissed his throbbing forehead. 'Bit of a headache, eh?'

'Just a bit.'

'I've put a couple of aspirin beside your coffee.'

'Thanks.' It came out as a grunt.

'Get some rest and you'll feel better this afternoon.'

Another grunt.

Lightly she touched his arm, that was lying like a dead eel on the cover and tucked it under the duvet. 'Getting pie-eyed solves nothing, Rory.'

He had the feeling she continued talking for some time, but his lids had clamped magnetically shut and the next time he prised them open, she was gone.

*   *   *

For the next two days nothing much was said. Zena lurked in her room, avoiding contact in the evenings. During the day she sat and watched television with the volume high, and raided the ice-cream tub whenever the urge seized her. Which was usually during the news breaks. In contrast, Rory ate almost nothing, not even the soup Alex made for him, and nursed his sledge-hammer headache in stoic silence.

Alex let him have space. She did not hassle him. Or preach at him. She made herself wait. She waited while she stitched the ear of a Great Dane that had put its huge head through a window; she waited while Gordon Tamworth introduced her to would-be new assistants and Maddy grumbled about each one of them. Marco Donelli rang to enquire whether Zena had got in touch with the job contact yet and how it was going. Alex parried that one. He could join her in the waiting queue.

After several days, when the grey pouches under her husband's eyes had retreated, she nudged the lid off the subject they were avoiding. The subject that was filling their minds and silencing their tongues.

'We can't keep pretending it's not there, Rory.'

'Pretending what's not there?'

They were both pushing slivers of trout around their plates, but not much was making it on to the forks. Zena had declined to join them.

'The opportunity to have a baby.'

'To have our hopes torn to shreds, you mean.'

'Rory, for Christ's sake, just give her a chance. Please. Give *us* a chance.'

'Everything I said on Sunday is still true. Nothing has changed. We would be risking our hearts and our money on someone we would be fools to trust. You know as well as I do that, at any point, she could change her mind and walk out on us. Baby and all. Legal document or not. We could do nothing to stop her.' He watched his wife's reaction, but unlike last time, her expression was understanding. He found it disconcerting. He concentrated on extracting a bone from the pink flesh on his plate. 'We would be fools to risk it.'

'Then let's be fools.' She put a smile in her voice and he looked up, surprised.

'It will end in tears, Alex. I don't want that to happen.'

'A year of our lives. That's all. If it goes wrong, that's all we've risked.'

'It's bound to go wrong. Zena will make sure it does.'

Alex put down her fork and gave up all pretence of eating. She leant forward and looked at Rory with an open display of affection that he had missed over the last few days. He became aware that she was particularly attractive this evening. Her hair hung loose for a change and she was wearing a low-cut blouse that he had bought as a present for her in the spring, but which she had never worn. She complained that he was trying to get her into what she called 'girl-clothes' and tossed it into the back of her wardrobe. Now she was wearing it. For him. Against her better judgement.

Asking him to agree to something against his better judgement. For her.

But a blouse hardly tipped the scales. This scheme of hers could wreck their lives if it went wrong. The emotions ran too deep. He tried again. Gently.

'Look, Alex, we both agree we want a child. Right?'

'Right. No conflict there.'

'Good. Then let's adopt from an agency. The only conflict is over Zena. You are willing to trust her. I'm not.'

Alex's cheeks were slightly flushed, but her voice gave no hint of agitation. She was the old, familiar Alex again. 'It's not that I trust her completely. I don't. But even the slightest possibility that we end up with a baby of our own, not someone else's, makes it worth the risk. I expected you to feel the same, Rory. We both want the same thing.' She put her hand out towards him in the middle of the table and he covered it with his own. A bridge of fingers. She smiled a reassuring smile at him and added, 'Together we could make this work. Despite the drawbacks.'

Her eyes were so certain. How could she be so positive about it? Nothing would convince him, he knew that. Nothing. To risk their hopes on a fly-by-night like Zena was madness. It would end in heartache and misery. And cost them money they could ill afford. Of that he was certain. But what was he risking if he continued to refuse? The last few days had given him a glimpse of the chasm that could open up.

He squeezed his wife's hand and knew she had won. He was not willing to let even a crack open up between their fingers again. Damn Zena for descending on them. Interfering in their lives. In their marriage. But he could not change it now. She was here, too close, and she had made the offer. Questions catapulted around inside his head and he grabbed hold of the biggest.

'Why would she do this for us?'

'I told you. Because I'm her sister. I'm all the family she has and she needs some love and cosseting. And money. Don't let's forget that.'

'Yes, of course, the money. Easy pickings.'

Alex stood up, still holding on to his hand and came round the table to him. He noticed the rapid rise and fall of her breasts in the low-necked blouse. As if she had been running. 'Giving up a baby can't be easy for anyone, Rory.'

'No, but I'm sure she doesn't see it that way.' He scooped an arm around her and pulled her on to his lap.

She laughed, a confiding, intimate sound and snuggled close. 'Do you want to hear the rest of the deal?'

'Not really.'

'She's no pushover, you know.'

Rory kissed her mouth, her throat, the smooth soft skin of her breast revealed by the blouse. 'I don't want to hear it.'

But the words no longer mattered. Alex ran fingers through his thick wavy hair and planted a kiss on his high forehead. 'I wonder if the child will have your dark looks or our gingery ones.'

Somewhere inside, something burst. There was no going back. 'Okay, I'm listening.' He nuzzled deeper.

'Don't go off the deep end because the conditions are steep.'

'Do I have any say in the matter?'

She raised his hand to her lips and kissed each finger. 'Of course you do. You will be the father.'

He was all too aware of what she was doing to him. Honey instead of a sledgehammer. The word 'father' wiping out all else.

'All right, all right. Let's hear the worst.'

'First, the money. She wants board and lodging. Plus ten thousand pounds.'

'What!'

'I told you it was steep.'

'We haven't got ten thousand pounds.'

'I know. But we could raise it.'

'Yes, if we had to. Or wanted to. We could increase the mortgage on this place, I suppose.'

'Condition number two.'

'Go ahead. I'm wearing my shock-proof armour this time.'

'Okay. She wants to stay a year. Not just the nine months of pregnancy.'

'What on earth for?'

'The three months after the birth are to get back to normal again. Emotionally and physically. And to be with the baby for a short while.'

'If we've managed to put up with her for nine months, I dare say another three months won't kill us.'

Alex shifted uneasily on his lap. 'I'm not so sure.'

'Why? Aren't you happy with that one?'

'Not really.'

'Why not?'

'She wants to feed the baby.'

'So? That's not a problem, is it?'

'Breast-feed, I mean.'

'I realise that.'

'I'm frightened, Rory. She might bond too strongly with the baby. I've seen again and again in animals how overpowering the maternal instinct is when those bonds are formed. It scares me.'

Rory stroked his cheek against the soft down of her hair. 'It's something we would have to be prepared for throughout the pregnancy. And after. That she may refuse to give up the baby.'

'I know. But at the same time I can't help feeling such suspicions make me disloyal to her. Ungrateful.'

'Not at all. Sensibly cautious, I call it. And perhaps she would understand your point of view and shorten the length of her stay.' No harm in hoping.

'I can try. But I don't hold out much hope. She had her conditions all clearly specified. All thought through.'

'Is that the lot of them?'

'Yes.'

'So it's decision time.'

'Yes. I'm willing to risk it.' She tilted his chin to look into his eyes. 'Are you?'

They both knew the decision was already made.

'Okay, tell her we'll make the deal. If that's what you want.'

Alex threw her arms around his neck and smothered him with kisses. 'Yes, yes, yes.'

Zena sat in Alex's chair, grinning like a Cheshire cat. She held all the cards and she knew it. They had gone off to bed now, probably to screw like rattlesnakes, judging by the way they couldn't keep their hands off each other.

'Don't waste it all, Rory,' she had jibed. 'We don't want you shooting blanks when it's time for the real showdown.'

It was all different now. No more tiptoeing round them as if they were made of crystal. She laughed softly and reached for a pack of cigarettes that lay beside her. Yes, it was all different now.

They had come to her with their demands and conditions. No cigarettes during pregnancy. No alcohol. No late nights. Healthy eating and healthy living. Walks in the fresh air, antenatal classes and folic acid tablets. Their list never seemed to end. Adoption papers, their choice of name and their right to decide when to tell the child that Zena was its real mother. That had surprised her. She had expected to remain Aunt Zena forever. But they had insisted on being honest with the child and one day, revealing the true situation. More fool them! But that was fine by her.

She had agreed to it all, of course. Why not? It kept them happy, up on their Cloud Nine. Plenty of time for disagreements later.

The money had caused some minor haggling, but then money always did. She should have asked for more than ten thousand. They'd have coughed up. Even if it meant putting their beloved cottage in hock for the rest of their lives. What were stone walls and mullioned windows compared to clinging, clutching arms and dimples? Nothing – fortunately for herself. Bed and board had been no problem. But they had baulked at her demand for a weekly allowance on top.

'The ten thousand is to cover costs like that,' Rory had insisted. As politely as he could.

But she had dug her heels in. They had claimed they couldn't afford it, not with the additional mortgage repayments they would be making. But they had come round in the end. They had no choice.

It was settled.

Zena lit her cigarette and took a long satisfying drag. Yes, it was all different now.

When it came to it, it was Alex who worked out the optimum dates and imposed enforced abstinence on Rory for a week beforehand. They had made the decision to try DIY artificial insemination, rather than attend a clinic. Their way was faster, cheaper and altogether more private.

More private maybe, but nonetheless, embarrassing.

When Alex watched Rory hand over to Zena the blunt syringe with its precious cargo, there was definitely a faint but discernible blush on his cheeks. Even Zena was subdued. She put a brash face on it, but her manner was awkward, eyes flitting away from his.

'Keep it coming,' Zena had quipped, which hadn't exactly helped.

'I intend to,' Rory had responded. But between them the knowledge roared and stamped its feet. The knowledge that what had until a moment ago been a part of him was about to go, live and kicking, inside an intimate part of her body. An amiable word might help it on its way. 'Thanks for giving it a good home.'

'Home, in this case, is certainly not where the heart is,' she smart-arsed back. 'But you're welcome,' she added with stomach-curdling American sweetness. Then scuttled upstairs to her room.

It was even worse later in the day when she reappeared. She had lain down for a couple of hours after 'the deed', as she termed it, was done. 'To help the little fuckers on their way.' But eventually she came down to report that everything had gone smoothly. During supper and throughout the evening, all three were acutely aware of the thousands of Rory's sperm inside her.

Wriggling and squirming. Swimming their hearts out to create life. Extinction awaited all but one.

The pattern was repeated daily for a week, the only difference being that the contents of the syringe grew steadily less. Mental stress slowed the production line, so that each day the process took longer and Rory heaved a sigh of relief when the week was finally over. Perversely, the moment he handed over the last syringe, he couldn't wait to get his wife into bed.

How Alex managed to get through surgery that week, she never knew. For once in her life, she found it impossible to concentrate on her work. Even Maddy felt obliged to comment.

'That rabbit's stitches need taking out. You forgot yesterday.'

'I'll do it now.'

The lop-eared doe had been savaged by a dog and had required sixteen stitches to seal its wounds. Fortunately an extra day did them no harm. And Gordon Tamworth had looked at her with mild-eyed rebuke when she turned up half an hour late for an operation she had agreed to help out with. It had slipped her mind.

Unprofessional and inexcusable.

Her control was in shreds and her thoughts refused to budge an inch away from Zena and the daily syringes. Emotions tossed and turned incessantly, fluctuating with alarming ferocity from intense gratitude and excitement to black jealousy, fear and resentment. Worst of all was the feeling of irrelevance. Rory and Zena were the star players.

'It's the uncertainty,' she told herself. Once the pregnancy is established, everything will settle into a normal routine. But nothing would be the same. Not now.

Not ever.

Zena was sick of being watched. Oh, not overtly, of course. Discreet, corner-of-the-eye glances that drove her up the wall. The waiting wasn't exactly a breeze for any of them. And Rory was so polite. Teeth-gratingly polite. Even when she accused him of wasting her time if he didn't produce the goods first time round, she failed to provoke him. He turned the other cheek and just calmly left the room. Nothing seemed able to burst their bubble of determined goodwill. If anything, Alex was the one who stamped down on Zena's games. One evening when bored, Zena started tossing her verbal darts across the room, but her sister would have none of it.

'Zena, it doesn't help at all to have you swiping out at Rory and myself just to amuse your ego. Neither of us needs it at the moment.'

'Ah, but I do,' Zena chuckled. 'This waiting is too dreary for words. I'm just trying to liven it up.'

Then, unexpectedly, Alex had smiled her affectionate smile and offered to take her out for a drink at Sandy Lane. To take advantage of still being able to indulge in alcohol, she had laughed.

Unpredictable, she was becoming. Not like Ali at all. Mood swings were the prerogative of the pregnant. And one thing sure as hell was that Ali could never be pregnant.

Over a gin and tonic at The George, she had asked Alex, 'What will you call her? Or him? When she or he finally decides to materialise.'

'We haven't decided yet. It's too early.' Her voice came out lumpy and she had to swallow hard. 'I just want the baby to be perfect.' The greyhound pup with the deformed leg flitted into her mind. 'Perfect and healthy.'

'No problem. Guaranteed.' Zena sucked the lemon twist in her drink. 'But of course, I can't speak for dear brother-in-law's genes. Might be a load of garbage, for all I know.'

'No, they'll be fine.' She wouldn't let Zena needle her. 'A mass of coppery curls would be nice and dark brown eyes like Rory's.'

Zena nodded thoughtfully. 'Yes, of course. Red hair would silence any queries, wouldn't it? Establish genetic connections.'

Alex leant forward on the table. 'Look, Zena, I don't care whether the child has red, black or even bright blue hair. Just as long as it is mine. You are, and always will be, its natural mother and can always be a part of its life. I do realise how hard it will be for you to give up a baby you have carried around for nine months. As well as having gone through agonies to let him or her see the light of day. But the child will be mine. That's our deal.'

'Who's arguing with that?'

'Rory still thinks you may be stringing us along.'

Zena waved a dismissive hand, glossy talons fluttering like ruby tears. 'Bullshit. Where does he dig up his wacky notions? He's dumber than I thought. What would I want with a kid at my feet all day. A few hormonal tears is the worst you'll get from me.'

'Promise me that?'

'Sure. I promise. Lighten up, will you? We're sisters, for God's sake. I would never harm you, you know that.' She raised her glass. 'To your child.'

They both drank, Alex eyeing her sister with careful scrutiny.

Zena smiled placatingly.

11

The beak opened. A fish was popped in and slid down effortlessly. It opened again and chirruped for more.

'You're a greedy guts,' Georgie informed the young penguin that was squatting in its fluffy grey overcoat in front of the keeper.

'He's building up his body weight,' the keeper explained to the boy, as he popped in another sprat. He noticed the other child, standing shyly behind his brother. Twins obviously. Eyes as big and dark as seal pups.

'C'mon, Louis.' Georgie suddenly tired of penguins and scampered back to his mother, dragging his brother by the hand and tipping in his wake the cup of bird seed he was clutching. 'I want to see the ostrich again,' he announced.

'It's a rhea, not an ostrich,' Joanna corrected.

'You spilt my food,' Louis declared, his chin wobbling.

Alex extricated his scrumpled hand from his brother's grip and replenished the seed level from her own plastic cup. 'There you are, Louis. Plenty left now.'

A flutter of sparrows descended on the scattered trail of food on the ground, old hands at spotting children's carelessness.

'Look,' Alex pointed out. 'It hasn't gone to waste.'

Louis smiled possessively. 'They like my seeds.'

'But I gave it to them. Not you,' Georgie said with crushing superiority.

'It's mine,' Louis insisted. 'Out of my pot.'

Georgie flapped his arms like a stubby windmill and the birds took flight to the nearest bush. 'Now they've gone. So there.'

Louis squatted down by the scattering of wheat, corn and

sunflower seeds and with painstaking precision started to pick each one out of the grass.

Alex and Joanna exchanged glances.

'Don't worry, Joanna, you go on up to the rheas. I'll follow on with Louis.' Alex smiled at the snail-speed at which each seed was being reclaimed. 'We may be some time.'

'Georgie, that wasn't very kind, was it?' Joanna called after her son who was already trotting along the pathway to the higher enclosures. 'Thanks, Alex.' She pushed the pram after him, peacock feather waving like a flagpole from its hood and wondered for the millionth time how twins could be so different from each other.

It was Alex's afternoon off. Restless and unsettled, she had jumped at Joanna's invitation to a trip out with the kids. They had come to Rode Bird Garden, a grassy parkland in which gaily coloured macaws flitted freely through the trees. Wiltshire's version of a jungle on a sunny September afternoon. A wide range of birds of all shapes and sizes peered and pecked at visitors from inside their mesh enclosures, beaks agape for accustomed handouts. The big white cockatoo had been the twins' favourite, as it flounced its crest at them and accepted a peanut with a delicate twist of its neck. The toucan, with its beak out of all sensible proportion, had provoked hoots of laughter and turned its back on them in disgust. Louis had tipped an extra pile of seeds into its enclosure to soothe its ruffled feathers.

'Can I help?' Alex sat down on the grass beside his crouched figure, picked up a few ears of corn and replaced them in his pot. As a child, she had done the same thing herself. Carrying an open bag of old Bluey's seed in from the garden shed where it was stored, she had not seen the skipping rope strung across the path. She and the seeds had gone flying, to the delight of the neighbourhood's sparrow population. Zena's story about making a hurdle with the rope to teach Pumpkin, their golden retriever, to jump and forgetting to dismantle it, had been totally convincing. Only now did Alex wonder if she had been gullible. Too credulous. Was Rory right? Was she still naive where Zena was concerned?

'Look, Louis, up in that tree.' Louis was too engrossed in his occupation to react at first, but eventually looked up to see where

she was pointing. 'That flock of starlings has its beady eye on us.
I think they fancy these seeds for their tea, don't you?'

The dark head nodded and he shuffled backwards on his knees,
creating long green smears on his jeans. Alex sat down on the
grass and together they watched the birds pluck up courage. The
sparrows got there first, squabbled with the incoming starlings
and quickly retreated, but with beaks full. Louis laughed and
after a few more minutes Alex suggested, 'We had better find
Mummy now.'

'And Georgie.'

They scrambled to their feet and ran across the lawns between
the trees, startling a peacock out of its haughty indifference. It
veered away from their path, dragging its gaudy tail carelessly
in the dirt. They found the others without difficulty, homing in
on Georgie's squeaks of delight as he imitated the strut of the
gawky rheas. From there they made their way to the pet corner
enclosure.

'Okay, what's the story?'

Alex stared at Joanna in surprise. 'What do you mean? What
story?'

'Come on, don't try to snow me with that butter-wouldn't-
melt-etc look. Something's going on? I can smell the smoke at
a hundred paces.'

'I don't know what you're getting at.' It was too soon. Too
intimate.

Joanna raised one sceptical eyebrow. 'This is Joanna Donelli
you're talking to. Newshound of the century, remember? You're
radiating enough static to light up the whole of Wiltshire. So
don't bat your eyes at me with an innocent "What story?"'

Alex laughed but felt colour flush into her cheeks. Was she
really that transparent?

'All right, Joanna, I admit it. Something is, as you delicately
put it, going on. But it's early days. When I'm certain it's going
to work, I'll tell you. But not until then.'

'You rotten spoilsport. That has just made it harder for me
to wait.'

'My heart bleeds for you.'

'So it should. You're ruining my day.'

Alex smiled and watched a young rabbit, all fluff and ears,

hop up to Louis's outstretched hand and twitch its grey nose at the chunks of corn on offer. The small hand remained rock solid, hoping so hard.

'You'll have to learn to be patient. Like your son.'

Joanna's eyes took in Louis's performance with maternal pride. 'That child possesses more patience than Georgie, Marco and me put together.'

'But he's so like you, Joanna. Very single-minded.'

'Don't try to change the subject.'

Alex chuckled. 'I think you had better rescue your other son. Poor Georgie is being besieged by greedy goats. They haven't learnt about patience either.'

She pointed to the far side of the enclosure where the other twin was boxed into a corner by a handful of small goats, all clammering for food. One bold pair of hooves had already reached up to his shoulder and Georgie's eyes were saucers of alarm.

'I'm coming,' Joanna called. 'Watch Angelica for me, will you, Alex?' She moved across the grass with the speed that only mothers defending their offspring can produce.

The flurry of activity frightened the rabbit into seizing the corn from Louis and retreating with a flash of white tail to the central hutch. Louis came bounding back to Alex in triumph.

'I fed him,' he chirped. 'From my fingers.'

'It's wonderful, isn't it? To be that close to them.'

'Yes. Better than on TV. Better than The Really Wild Show.'

'Would you like to come to the surgery where I work, one day? To see the animals there. And how we make them better.'

He swung on her hand and bounced up and down on the spot. 'Yippee, yippee, yes please.'

She wondered if he had been watching too many 'Rawhide' reruns. 'Okay, I'll arrange for you to visit with Mummy during half term.'

'And me. And me.' Georgie came hurtling at her legs with water-buffalo force. None the worse for goats.

'And you, Georgie.' She checked that his high-pitched bellow had not disturbed the sleeping beauty in the pram, but need not have been concerned. The fresh air and earlier excitement had waved its wand.

'All okay?' Joanna asked.

'Yes, Angelica's still out for the count. And the boys have agreed to come and visit me at work.'

'What fun!' She rumpled Georgie's hair and taking his hand in hers, started to lead him none too obviously towards the gate. Alex trailed behind, taking pleasure in pushing the pram. Louis hung on to its handle, hopping along two-footed like the rabbit. A young girl passed by with a baby in a sling on her chest and a toddler at her feet and nodded companionably. For a brief moment Alex felt like a member of the club.

'Talking of work,' Joanna had waited for her on the other side of the gate, 'what's this I hear about your sister and a job? Marco mentioned it.'

Alex made a show of concentrating on manoeuvring the pram down the path and past the trees. The weird raucous cry of a distant peacock startled the twins and both stared uneasily into the undergrowth.

'Nothing is settled yet, Joanna. Marco is a sweetheart to think of helping her. I'm grateful to him.'

Joanna looked sideways at her and a suspicious smile twitched at her mouth. 'So what are your sister's plans?'

'Nothing definite, as I said.'

'But a job is a possibility?'

'Yes.'

'She can't go on living off you lot forever, can she?'

'Of course not.'

'Marco says she's very attractive.'

'Yes, she is.'

'So why isn't she out in the big wide world fending for herself? Like normal grown-ups do.'

That question had rattled round Alex's own head too many times already. She halted the pram. 'Joanna, don't forget what curiosity did to the cat.'

'But satisfaction brought it back,' Joanna smirked. 'Come on, don't be such a clam. Tell all.'

Alex laughed unrepentantly. 'No chance. You know what a chatterbox you are. I have enough to worry about without that.'

'So you are worried?'

'And you are incorrigible.'

'Of course. Goes without saying.'

'I shall have it printed for all to see on your forehead.'

'How about printing it on your sister's forehead?'

Alex stared at her. 'What do you mean by that?'

'I don't want to tell tales.'

'Like hell you don't! What tales?'

Joanna resumed walking. 'She keeps ringing Marco.'

'What!'

'She telephones him at the office.' Joanna tried to keep it casual. No big deal.

'Why on earth would she do that?'

'That's what I'm asking you. She's your sister.'

'I have no idea. What does she say when she rings?'

'Oh, it's all above board. She asks him about job requirements, training courses and stuff like that.'

'Is that all?'

A pause. 'No.'

'Tell me, Joanna. Tell me the rest.'

'It's probably nothing. But she asks him to meet her for a drink. Or lunch. To discuss possibilities, she says. Possibilities of what, I dread to think. Marco has declined the invitations. So far.'

'Joanna.'

Joanna halted. She looked across at her friend and let her annoyance show through. 'Yes?'

'I'm sorry. I'll put a stop to it at once. I promise. Even if I have to hog-tie her while I'm out of the house.'

'Thanks,' Joanna smiled, relief softening her small features. 'I knew I could rely on you.'

Georgie grabbed his mother's hand and tugged her towards the ice-cream kiosk. Alex followed in their wake, her stomach like mangled dog-meat. She refused an ice-cream for herself, but helped Georgie unwrap his Cornetto. So that's why Joanna had invited her today. Did everyone always have an ulterior motive? And what the hell was Zena's?

We could always find a different father, you know. Zena's words by the apple tree reverberated in her head.

*   *   *

'What the hell are you playing at, Zena?'

Alex had only just arrived home. She marched straight into the sitting-room, following the sound of canned laughter and switched off the television.

Zena, stretched out on the sofa, looked up from the blank screen in surprise. 'Put the blasted television back on, will you?'

'No, not until we get something straight.'

'What are you talking about, Ali? Why so cranky? I was watching Rosanne. Somehow, I never got round to seeing it when I was in the States. There was always so much else to do. But I love the way she . . .'

'Shut up about Rosanne.'

Zena frowned and sat up. 'Hey, what's eating you? Calm down and tell me what the hell has shaken your rug today.'

'I'll spell it out, nice and clear. What do you think you are up to, pestering Marco Donelli all the time?'

'Oh, that.'

'Yes. That.'

Zena slouched back on to the sofa. 'That's nothing. Just something to do when I'm bored.'

Her casual dismissal of it was like petrol on a fire. Alex wanted to shake her.

'Zena, leave him alone. Completely alone. Don't you even know that chasing other women's husbands is against the rules?'

Zena smiled up at her. 'I make my own rules.'

'If you think behaviour like that is just fun, then it's no wonder your own marriage ended.'

That got through. Zena leapt to her feet and stormed over to her sister. 'Shut up about my marriage. You know nothing about it.'

'I know you. Or thought I did.'

'Well, it's amazing just how wrong you can be, isn't it?'

The two women glared at each other. Their anger rose like a brick wall between them.

The tawny eyes were the first to drop.

'Oh hell, Ali, what are we fighting about? I'm sorry if I got you into trouble. Little wifey been sobbing on your shoulder, has she?'

But the anger would not let go of Alex so easily. It was too tightly entwined with fear. Like snakes in her stomach.

'This has nothing to do with Joanna. It is about you. You and your apparent absence of morality. You honestly don't care about messing up Marco's marriage, do you?'

Zena laughed lightly. 'Don't make it all so big-time dramatic. A few phone calls, that's all it was. You're overreacting. Anyway, you know perfectly well that I'm not interested in any man at the moment. Or any job. I've got this baby to make for you.'

Alex felt as if she were running through a maze. The direction twisting and turning away from her. Constantly hitting into blank walls.

'Zena, Rory and I want this baby. But not at the cost of everything else. And certainly not at any cost to my friends. So, I'm telling you, stay away from Marco. If I hear you have made even one more phone call to him, our deal is off. And you're out of here. Do you understand?'

Zena gave her a long, resentful stare, let it hang there for a beat, then let it go. 'Okay, no problem. No more phone calls. Try trusting me.' She put a conciliatory hand on her sister's arm.

Alex shrugged it off in a quick, hard gesture. 'You don't have the slightest idea what I'm talking about, do you?'

The new assistant in Gordon Tamworth's veterinary practice was working out well. Andrew Marsh was a young fair-haired man with gingery beard and wispy eyebrows that shaded gentle grey eyes. Stick-insect thin and soft spoken, he was the ideal candidate for tucking under Maddy's wing.

'Don't you let her bully you, laddie,' Gordon had advised him. 'She's been here so long, she thinks she runs the place.' He chuckled contentedly into his fourth cup of tea of the morning. 'Between you, me and the gatepost, I think she's right, but never let her know it. You stand up to her or she'll walk all over you.'

'Yes, of course I will,' Andrew Marsh said obligingly and instantly lay down beneath her feet.

'He's a nice boy, that Andrew,' Maddy commented to Alex as she was setting up a drip on a post-operative spaniel, the victim of a hit and run. 'Not too full of himself like most boys that age.' The 'boy' was twenty two.

'He's already been a great help. Yesterday I took him out to Ben Featherton's farm and we got through the herd in half the time. He's certainly no slouch.'

'That's what I like to hear.' Maddy finished adjusting the rate of flow into the catheter and stroked the silky head in the cage. 'Don't hold out much hope for this poor old chap.'

'I've patched him up as best I can but it's going to be a struggle. Don't give up on him yet though. He's a real little fighter.'

Maddy nodded and latched the door. 'Yes, you can never tell. Just when you least expect it, they come through for you.'

'Like some people.'

Maddy scowled. 'Name two.'

'You old misanthrope,' Alex laughed and together they went through to the office. Gordon was perched on the edge of the desk, feeding digestive biscuits to Bruno and information to Lizzie.

'It's important to tell the clients to worm routinely. Ideally every eight to ten weeks for horses. They have to break the cycle you see, lass. Roundworm, threadworm, pinworm, it's all the same. And the wee beggars are getting resistant to the chemicals, so make sure you explain they have to regularly alter the class of wormer they're using. And do all the horses on a pasture at the same time.'

He looked up as Alex entered and angled his long legs out of her path. 'Spaniel still with us?'

'He's hanging in there. On a Haemaccel drip.'

'He'll need a careful watch.'

Maddy grunted a surly 'Hmmph' and snapped, 'What do you think I'm here for?'

'To brighten my every day, lassie,' Gordon beamed at her.

'Don't you lassie me.'

'Here, have a cup of tea to sweeten that tongue of yours.'

'Take the roof of my mouth off, more like!'

'Talking of roofs,' Alex interrupted to sidetrack the conversation, 'did the man turn up to sort out the roof on your shed for you, Maddy?'

The previous weekend, a section of the wormy timbers of

the garden shed had finally collapsed, giving the very pregnant Josephine a nasty fright. She had retaliated by promptly giving birth. Both mother and kid had been immediately upgraded on the housing ladder and were now comfortably ensconced in Maddy's kitchen. Much to the chagrin of the resident menagerie.

'No, the lazy layabout didn't turn up. Don't talk to me about . . .'

The telephone rang and Lizzie picked it up. 'Good morning. Tamworth Veterinary Surgery. How may I help you?'

After a few seconds, she handed the receiver over to Alex. 'It's for you.'

'Who is it?' Alex mouthed.

'Your sister.'

What on earth was Zena ringing here for? Good news? But surely it was too early to know yet.

'Hello, Zena. What's the problem?'

She listened.

All three people in the room watched her with sidelong curiosity. But when she finally hung up, having only uttered an 'I see' and a final 'Goodbye', she left the room. The washroom was empty when she reached it and she snapped the lock shut behind her. With a moan that came from way down inside, she leant back against the door and squeezed her eyes closed to keep back the tears.

Zena had started her monthly. First blood this morning. Alex had of course known this might happen. Had told herself a thousand times to be prepared for it. But the disappointment was still enormous. Overwhelming her carefully constructed defences. Slowly she slid down the door to the floor, sank her head on her knees and started to dig out the bricks again.

That evening was surprisingly companionable. Rory watched Alex being depressingly cheerful, assuring him and Zena that it was only an initial hiccup and nothing to worry about. Next time they would strike lucky. Oddly the setback seemed to draw them all closer, as if even Zena was feeling the need for support and encouragement. Rory wondered if she was blaming herself for the failure. Or him? Or maybe nobody? Either way, the evening was not as unpleasant as he had anticipated, especially when the two sisters started unearthing stories from their childhood. To his considerable amusement, he learnt that his wife had been the skipping champion of Form Three, had suffered a bad case of unrequited love for Clive Eynon, the boy who sat next to her in class, had been a dunce at French and at eleven years old had hacked off her long golden tresses after seeing Mia Farrow in *Rosemary's Baby*. Her mother had cried for a week

It came as an unwanted intrusion when the telephone jangled, demanding Alex's presence at a foaling the other side of Pewsey.

'Just what I need, today of all days,' was her only comment before she packed her medical bag and was gone in a puff of Clio. Her rueful smile lingered in the room like perfume.

'Well, Zena, that leaves just us.'

'Shall we just die of boredom or have you any other suggestions?'

Recalling that the only time he had come half-way close to liking his sister-in-law was when he discovered her delight in sports cars, he asked, 'How about a run in the MG? To blow away the autumn mists. Though we seem a bit low on mellow fruitfulness.'

'Don't go all arty on me. Just concentrate on the motor.' She stood up, long legs accentuated by the shortness of her skirt. 'Come on, let's hit the road and rip up that tarmac.'

Five minutes later they were crawling through the lanes behind a tractor and trailer. Threads of hay billowed over the windscreen and dropped onto their laps and hair.

'Christ, this is real hicksville, isn't it? Hayseed and corn dollies. Why don't you live in a proper town?'

Rory laughed. 'Marlborough is a proper town. But a country town. And we like it here. Just be patient until we get on to the A4. Wide and straight and built to belt.'

She shut up after that, eyes closed and head back against the rest, wind tugging at her hair and blouse. With hood and windows down it was real freedom when they finally reached the open road. Rory kept the speed down as close to the speed limit as he could but the sixteen valve engine begged to be let loose. At

Beckhampton roundabout, he swung north up through Avebury towards Swindon and the motorway. A south-westerly wind was bringing in fat sulky clouds that promised rain later, but the soft grey twilight had an eerie prehistoric feel that transformed the fields into misty swamps and the buzzard swirling over the great sarsen stones into a pterodactyl on long leathery wings.

'Show me something you've built.'

They had not spoken since the lanes. Rory was surprised by the request but quite willing to oblige. At the next junction he doubled back and headed for the housing development that was selling so well.

'Here we are. In all its glory.'

He had parked outside the show-home and immediately noticed the light was on inside it. Curtains drawn. In the gloom, the group of houses had acquired a look of age and permanence that gave him a sense of how they would look in ten or twenty years time.

'Not bad,' Zena commented. 'If you want to live on an estate, that is.'

'Don't be such a snob.'

'Any chance of seeing inside one?'

'I don't have the keys, but it looks as if someone is making themselves at home in the show-house. So let's find out who.'

They walked up the neat front path and rang the bell. No answer. Rory rang again and added a rap on the door for good measure. After several minutes a light popped on in the hall and the door opened a crack.

'Alan! What the hell are you doing here at this hour? It's a well-known fact that estate agents are all lazy bastards. It's too late in the day for you to be working.'

The door opened wider to reveal more of Alan Beecroft. He wasn't at his best. His normally slicked-back hair was rumpled over his forehead, his shirt was buttoned wrongly and he had lipstick skid-marks over his mouth. His face dropped its wary frown with relief. 'Oh, it's only you.' His dark, assessing eyes skipped to Rory's companion with interest.

'Hi, I'm Zena.'

'My sister-in-law,' Rory added to scotch any suspicions.

'Hello, Zena. Come to admire brother-in-law's handiwork, have you?'

'Something like that. I'm a great believer in hand work.'

Alan blinked, took in the innuendo and broke into a grin. 'A girl after my own heart, I see. Come on in.' He stepped back and led them over the immaculate beige carpet to the room he had obviously just left. The door stood open and on the squishy velour sofa in matching beige was curled a small, nervous-looking woman of about thirty. She had short dark hair, huge green eyes and very good legs. Her lipstick was smudged.

'This is Mrs Lorna Blake . . . I was just showing her over the house, as she couldn't make the time during the day. She and her husband are interested in buying. Mrs Blake, let me introduce the genius architect, Mr Flynn, who designed the houses. And his lovely sister-in-law, Zena. Don't let me stop you having a look round, Rory, if that's what you . . .'

Rory put him out of his misery. 'Don't worry, Alan, we're not staying. It was just a whim of the moment.'

'Sure,' Zena cut in with a smile that made no secret of her delight. 'Some other time will do. We'd hate to disturb your . . . work.'

Mrs Blake blushed profusely, managed a polite 'Nice meeting you', but did not stand up. Rory suspected her skirt might fall down if she did. At the door, he could not resist commenting to the estate agent, 'Now I know why you call them "show" homes.'

'Piss off,' Alan Beecroft laughed and shut the door on them.

In the car driving home, Zena was in jubilant mood, delighted by both the wind in her tail and the sexual frisson from discovering Alan Beecroft's illicit little escapade. At her request, they stopped for a drink at the Red Lion in Avebury.

'I'm going to make the most of my ten days of debauchery before I'm back on the wagon and those damn syringes.'

Over a pint and a gin the conversation became more stilted than it had been in the car. Something to do with the loss of the sense of freedom and motion. But she was making an effort, there was no doubt about it. Rory began to think that, at this rate, they could manage to stumble along together for the required twelve months without too much bloodshed. A few bruises perhaps and the odd cut. But nothing fatal. He might never actually get to like his sister-in-law, but maybe he could get used to her. For the first time since he had agreed to the surrogate scheme, he allowed himself to hope. A chink of genuine light.

'What are you grinning at?' Zena demanded.

'At you. And your sister. And your weird ideas.'

'You can be such a prick sometimes, Rory Flynn. But I have to admit, you do have a cute car.'

'Thanks for the vote of confidence.'

12

Rory had his nose deep in bills of lading when Jan Hodge popped her head round his office door and announced with her usual sunny smile, 'Your wife rang. She says she will be dropping in to see you about one o'clock.'

Rory grunted an acknowledgement and went back to working out how the contractor had been able to cut costs so sharply on the new garage extension. Something not quite right there.

Jan studied the bushy curls bent over the spread of papers and decided she had better make the message clearer. 'That means, don't disappear for lunch.'

Rory looked up, surprised to find her still there. 'What's that?'

'I'm just pointing out that as your wife is coming in, don't disappear at lunchtime.' Even now she knew she only had half his attention. If that.

'No chance of that. Not with all this to plough through.' He waved a hand over the stack of paperwork. 'Half the bloody rain forest is right here on my desk.'

'I'll bring you another coffee,' Jan offered to soothe his frayed temper. He had been like a bear with a sore head all morning. Snapped at poor Paula when she forgot to let him have her latest ideas and even growled at Gary Saunders, but received a typical 'Bugger off' in reply. Jan presumed it was the loss of the town centre redevelopment that was eating at him. Over the past few weeks he had fought tooth and nail to salvage something out of it, but it was too late. Coffin-lid was down. Memorial hymns over. The money men had taken fright, zipped up their wallets and gone shopping elsewhere. It was a bitter blow to the company. Gary gave a good impression of water off a duck's back, but she knew Rory had taken it hard. He had been counting on that business to balance the books for next year. But she had faith in him. He would root out another honeypot from somewhere for them to stick their fingers in, she was certain.

'Coffee, Jan.'

With a forgiving smile that at fifty years old she had down to perfection, she returned to reception, produced a coffee and a chocolate Hobnob and left him to his figures. Allowing herself a brief respite, she watered the two potted palms, picked out a cigarette butt from one of their tubs, poured herself a glass of milk and then settled back at her desk. She had a report to type by tomorrow. The reception was not to her personal taste, all black and chrome, but the furniture was well designed and surprisingly comfortable. She swivelled smoothly in her chair and set about the keyboard. It was at exactly five to one that Alex Flynn walked up to her desk, wearing a broad smile, a stylish navy skirt and blazer and her hair loose and shining. Under her arm was tucked what looked like a bottle of something interesting in green off-licence paper.

'How's Boy Wonder this morning?'

'Growling, I'm afraid.'

Alex laughed and Jan was struck by how young she looked. And how attractive. Suddenly she felt depressingly aware of her own sagging jawline and slumped waistline. The crows had done a good job around her eyes as well, but at least her hair was still her crowning glory, even if the colour was no longer quite all her own.

'He's snowed under today, Alex, and has a meeting at two o'clock.'

'Don't worry. Half an hour is all I need.'

At that moment Gary Saunders drifted through on his way to the local pub for his usual pint, pie and chips.

'Hello, gorgeous.' He gave her a tight hug, a kiss on the mouth and ran a hand down her spine.

'Hello, Gary. You're looking well.' His long hair was combed and his shirt collar clean.

'Not as well as you are.' He lightly brushed a coppery wave from her cheek. 'Very tasty.'

Jan shook her head in despair. 'Ignore him, Alex. He's suffering withdrawal symptoms because he has been forced to forgo any carousing for the last few days.'

Gary groaned. 'Don't remind me. Another two days of monastic existence.'

'That doesn't sound like you. Someone died or something?'

'As good as. It's my elderly aunt. She comes to stay for a week every year and won't let me out of her sight. That's why I'm off to sneak in a pint while I can.'

'Tucks you up with a hot chocolate and teddy bear, does she?'

'Every night.'

Alex laughed unsympathetically. 'Good for her. Treat 'em mean is what I say.'

'So that's why the genius is so touchy today, is it? I hope you've brought your whip and chair for entering the lion's den.'

'Been that bad, has he?'

'Worse.'

'Then watch me wave a magic wand. Two minutes and he'll be all purrs.'

'Really? Would you care to try some of that magic on me first?'

'Go cuddle your teddy bear. And drink your cocoa like a good boy.' Alex grinned and walked over to Rory's office. She entered quietly and shut the door behind her.

He was at his desk still engrossed in the figures. Without raising his nose, he muttered, 'More coffee, Jan.'

'How about champagne instead?'

He looked up, startled. Instantly he took in his wife's wide smile and dressy outfit. The celebration bottle. The undisguised happiness.

He stood up. 'It's yes?'

'Yes.'

'Positive?'

'Absolutely and utterly. The doctor says it is definite.'

Rory came very close to Alex and wrapped his arms around her as gently as if she were carrying the child herself. 'That's wonderful. World-shatteringly wonderful.' Words didn't even come close. The idiotic grin on his face was stuck there.

Alex draped her arms around his neck and gave him a long, soft kiss that aroused more than just his interest. 'Congratulations, father-to-be,' she whispered against his lips.

'Thank you, mother-to-be.'

The two of them couldn't stop smiling at each other like toothpaste adverts, but eventually got round to opening the champagne and toasting each other in Rory's discarded coffee cups.

'I've been on tenterhooks all morning,' he explained over the bubbles. It wasn't what he wanted to say. But how many times could you keep repeating the words 'father-to-be'? 'Happy now?'

'Ecstatic.'

'That makes two of us.'

'Three of us, actually.'

Rory raised his champagne. 'To the three of us.'

'And Zena.'

'I never thought I'd say it, but thank God for Zena.' He chinked his cup against his wife's. 'To Zena.'

Her smile grew another inch. 'To Zena.'

At first Zena accepted her promoted role with all the grace of a newly crowned queen. As long as she was pampered, petted and waited on hand and foot, she was sweetness itself. She became picky about her meals, expressing a need for smoked salmon, prawns, melons and Cambozola to tempt her taste buds. She made the most of her sister's euphoria to exploit her position – an electric blanket now the nights were turning chilly, a television in her room and a weekly selection of magazines to while away the hours she must spend resting. Alex knew she was being taken for a ride but was too grateful to quibble.

It was when Zena started being sick that her sweetness evaporated.

'Goddamn it, if I'd known I was going to nearly die every morning, I'd never have agreed to this. It's bloody purgatory.'

It was seven-fifteen on a Sunday morning and she was shouting.

'But it was all your idea in the first place,' Rory took pleasure in reminding her and received a hefty kick on the shin from his wife.

'It's horrible for you, but it won't last long,' Alex soothed. 'Morning sickness usually disappears after three months.'

'Three shitty months,' Zena wailed and staggered, pale and bedraggled, back to her bed.

Alex was patient. She provided sympathy, warm drinks, hot water bottles for her stomach and a supply of fresh nightwear. But insisted that Zena clean up the bathroom after herself. That caused a few days' friction.

'It's your bloody baby that's doing it,' Zena complained but she recognised a brick wall when it hit her. Reluctantly, she agreed.

The legal formalities were gone through and a contract was drawn up. Alex made one last-ditch attempt to persuade her sister to agree to a rented flat in Marlborough, but Zena was adamant. She wanted a cosy, ready-made nest. With all the trimmings. Neither would she shift from the twelve-month clause. Nine months was a non-starter as far as she was concerned. Alex knew she was in no position to haggle, so put a brave face on it. It was the cigarettes that caused the biggest dust-up. Zena readily agreed to give them up the moment she found out she was pregnant, but within a fortnight was renegotiating.

'Just a couple at the weekends,' she insisted. 'Only at first. To make it easier. I'll cut them out altogether eventually, I promise.'

Patiently Alex went over the arguments again. The dangers to the baby, the significance of the first three months, the loss of birth bodyweight.

'Please, Zena. This is important. For the child's sake.'

Zena had sulked and grumbled, but eventually had given in. She took to chewing gum instead and though Alex hated the spearmint smell and the endless ruminant chomping that went on all evening, it was better than nicotine. Much better. But she was no fool. What went on when she and Rory were at work, only Zena knew. But as Alex never caught even a whiff of stale cigarette odour on her clothes, she decided Zena was being straight with her.

Alex was pleased when Zena took to going for occasional

walks. The winter was turning out crisp and cold, with the odd flurry of snow to remind them what might lie in store. The bare skeletons of the trees looked fragile as they bowed to the northerly winds that swept down from Scandinavia. But bright, clear days when the sky was as blue as a coral sea came to tempt Zena out of the house.

'A dose of healthy living,' Zena explained. 'To get the old muscles into action again and the lungs pumping pure oxygen into this kid of ours.'

'Keep it gentle though. No American over-the-top workouts.'

Zena had chuckled, 'Done that, been there. All in moderation now, I assure you.'

The fresh air and exercise did in fact seem to be doing her good. Her skin glowed and she lost the air of lethargy that had hung round her like smog. Pregnancy suited her. After a tramp across the fields together one day, as Alex watched her breeze into the house, fingers and nose tingling from the frost, it suddenly dawned on her that Zena was happy. Really happy. This relaxed, family life was exactly what she had wanted. She was enjoying every moment of it.

This revelation turned a tap inside Alex, a tap that released a flood of affection for her sister that carried them all contentedly through to Christmas in a glow of mutual harmony. The festive season came and went with suitable good cheer, office parties that included Zena and no note of discord even when on Christmas Day she indulged in a couple of glasses of wine and curled up in a sleepy ball on the rug in front of the log fire. Alex draped a blanket over her, led her husband under the mistletoe and kissed him with a passion now usually reserved for the bedroom.

'Mmm, and Happy Christmas to you too,' Rory had murmured, his lips not leaving hers. 'What was that for?'

'For giving me the best Christmas present ever.'

He kissed her again and they crept upstairs.

Snow lay like icing on the windowsills and was smudged carelessly over the panes so that they looked like chattering teeth. January had come in with a whiplash that had taken the breath away. Plumbers were doing a roaring trade and plastic sledges were at a premium.

Alex carried the tray upstairs. A steaming bowl of carrot and coriander soup, her sister's latest passion, and a good chunk of Cambozola and granary bread neatly arranged beside it. Apple juice in a glass. Zena had been tired this afternoon. And had looked it. Purple smudges had flowered under her eyes and she complained that her legs ached.

Alex had panicked quietly, packed her upstairs for a bath and bed. Promised her a light supper on a tray. Zena had declined anything to eat but Alex was hoping that a more relaxed mother-to-be might now be a hungry mother-to-be. The tiredness had been her own fault. After months of doing next to nothing most of the time, Zena had taken it into her head to spend the day at the January sales in Bath. On a Saturday, for heaven's sake. On the coldest day of the winter. She had arrived home looking grey and exhausted, but pleased with herself. In her hand she was clutching carrier bags laden with maternity-wear that she had purchased with her new-found income.

Alex knocked on the door.

'I'm decent,' Zena called out.

Alex walked in and found her sister parading in front of the wardrobe mirror in one of her new, loose dresses. It was a deep French blue, soft wool with pearl buttons and Peter Pan white collar. Alex stared at it and felt her stomach flip with a stab of jealousy.

'That's pretty.' She put the tray down on the bedside table and sat on the bed.

Zena twirled in the dress and it billowed pregnantly. 'Not quite this size yet, thank God.'

In fact, she was nowhere near needing maternity-wear and her still slim body looked faintly absurd in its loose folds.

'Unfortunately,' Zena said with a grimace that gave her premature wrinkles, 'the time will soon come and I'll be mooning around like a beached whale.'

Alex was surprised that, despite the complaint, the prospect did not seem to depress Zena unduly. 'You'll look lovely.' She was relieved to see the bath had brought colour back to

Zena's cheeks and the bruised smudges had retreated to faint shadows.

'Bullshit. But I don't mind you saying it.'

They both laughed and Zena pulled the dress over her head. She was wearing nothing underneath. Unselfconsciously, she stood sideways to the mirror and patted the slight bulge on her stomach.

'Gross,' she moaned, but the expression in her eyes said otherwise.

Alex could not help but stare. It was many years since she had seen her sister completely naked, except for that brief glimpse of her in the bath before Christmas. The beautiful new breasts were high and surgeon-assisted firm. Alex had hoped the implants might prevent breast-feeding, but no such luck apparently. The lightly freckled limbs were slender and surprisingly fit looking for a couch potato. The recent walks had done them good. And years of keeping up with the American Joneses had obviously left their mark. Only around the upper thighs and bottom was there a slight loosening that hinted at the months of inactivity. And the gingery pubic bush reminded all those privileged to see it that she was not a natural blonde. But it was the swelling at the stomach that drew her eyes. Still small, like a little cushion of fat under the skin. A baby in there. Growing, developing, listening.

Her baby.

It was still too incredible to be true.

'Can I touch?'

'Sure.' Zena walked over to the bed and stood in front of her sister, an amused smile banishing the last of the tiredness. 'Feel away.'

Very delicately Alex laid her fingertips on the smooth skin. It felt soft. Nothing more. No lumps or bulges. Not like Maddy's Josephine. Not yet.

'Satisfied?'

'Yes,' Alex nodded. 'Thanks.'

Zena picked up her kimono from the bed, slipped it over her shoulders, tied the sash and sat down beside Alex. Alex felt exactly as she had when, as a child, her best friend, Judith, had let her hold and handle her new tortoise and then had taken it away again before Alex had sated her fascination with the wrinkled, prehistoric face. But how do you ask your sister if you can continue to stare at her stomach?

'Zena, you know how grateful I am for what you're doing for me, don't you?' She had said it before, but felt the need to say it again. Now that she had seen the baby.

'This incubation act, you mean? Don't fret. It suits us both this way.'

'Why did you and Chet never have a child?'

Zena shrugged and with a bare foot stirred a bundle of underwear that was lying in an untidy heap on the carpet. 'Not our scene, I guess.'

Alex thought about the irony of it. One sister wanted a child but couldn't, the other didn't but could. Fertility was so casual. So indiscriminate. So profligate. Teenage mothers kept the conveyor belt supplied for infertile thirty-year-olds. And then there were the scientists. Pushing back the barriers. Yet fertility was still falling. Slowly wiping out the western world. What then?

'Why did Daddy back off from me like that, Ali?'

The question took Alex by surprise. Zena was quietly eating her soup and had spoken without looking up.

'I mean, why so suddenly?'

'Oh Zena, who knows? He never let on what was going on inside his head. All those hours he and I spent driving round the streets and farms on calls, we never talked anything but animals. He never opened up. Not once. In all those years. However hard I tried.'

'But why do you think? You were older. Knew more what was going on.'

'I honestly have no idea.' Shadows, like wisps of ash, floated into her mind but Alex slipped an arm round her younger sister's shoulders, wiping them out. 'But Zena, he never backed off from you, as you put it. He didn't parade his feelings for you so much, that's all.'

'Bullshit. He avoided me throughout my teens. Like the bloody plague. Didn't want to come near me, the bastard.'

Alex heard the hurt that no amount of smart-aleck bluster could hide. Knife sharp. It came as a shock. Zena and her father had quarrelled so much throughout those years that Alex had not realised, until now, that the rebellion had been a fight not to escape, but for his attention. She must have been blind. Too preoccupied with her own ambitions to see her younger sister's confusion.

Maybe too eager for his attention herself.

'Zena, he adored you. Always did. Right until the end. After you'd gone, every letter on the mat, every phone call, he hoped they were from you. Not that he said much, but it was obvious.'

'Like Mummy was with you?'

'What?'

'When you went away to university. She always hoped you'd ring. You never did.'

'That's not true. I did telephone sometimes.'

'Only if you had some good test or exam results you wanted to tell Daddy. To impress him.'

The sisters stared at each other, uneasy emotions bubbling too close to the surface.

Alex shrugged and smiled bleakly. 'Who'd have kids, for heaven's sake?'

The laughter papered over the crack and Zena returned to her carrot and coriander. She dipped a piece of granary in it and popped it into her mouth. When she had swallowed, she said, 'Daddy didn't deserve you, you know.'

'What on earth do you mean by that?'

Zena dipped another strip of granary. 'You know perfectly well what I mean. After what he did to you. We wouldn't be sitting here with you leering jealously at my stomach if it wasn't for his selfish stupidity.'

'Don't you start that. You sound like Mummy.'

'She was right.'

'No. No, you're both wrong.' Alex stood up. Angry with herself for getting rattled so easily. 'You're wrong. It was my own fault.'

'Bullshit.'

'It was. I shouldn't have . . .'

'I know, I know. You shouldn't have let go the rope. I've heard it all before. But it's bullshit. You shouldn't have been inside that stable. Who are you trying to kid? Yourself?' Her eyes were suddenly tired and she pushed the soup away. 'He was no angel, dear sister. No god that you have to placate and please. He was a bloody good vet who had no idea how to bring up kids.'

Alex refused to listen to any more.

'You're wrong, Zena. Wrong.'

'Don't be so damn stupid, Ali. Look around you. You have everything you could possibly want. Your life is gift-wrapped, chocolate-box perfection. Why hang on to your guilt fantasies? Be careful or you won't have any bloody chocolates left.'

Alex walked out of the room.

Rory had his feet up, a beer in his hand and sheer magic on the screen. Saturday evening and he was watching a video of Mansell's magnificent triumph at Silverstone in 1992. It was one of his favourites. A brilliant drive. And the fans invading the track, risking life and limb to get a touch of their hero. Mansell had been forced to abandon his Williams after taking the chequered flag to escape being torn apart by adoring hands, all wanting a piece of him. The sight still gave him a tingle every time. Sadly, the Formula One season was long since over and Rory still had three months to suffer before the new one started.

When the withdrawal symptoms proved too much, he soothed the pangs by a couple of hours in front of one of the races from his video library, no matter that he knew by heart every twitch of the wheels and every corner taken too wide. It never failed to give him a shot in the arm that sent the emotions soaring, heartbeat hammering and kept him whistling the catchy theme music under his breath for the next five days. Something which drove Gary Saunders round the bend. He even tried doing Murray Walker's job as commentator by watching with the sound turned down, but it wasn't as easy as it looked. Hats off to Murray.

As he watched Mansell's blue and yellow streak take Copse Corner right on the limit, wheels riding the black and white kerb, front end fighting to break loose, another noise penetrated through the roar of the engines charging up the hill towards Becketts. A metallic noise. Nearer home. He blipped the sound control down a notch and listened again. It was there all right. Coming from the kitchen. Rory recognised it instantly. Pots and pans doing a war-dance. Alex was at it again. The kitchen cupboard cleaning routine. For two and a half seconds he considered turning up the volume on the race and telling himself the noise had been merely a figment of his imagination. But his conscience jabbed an elbow in his ribs and reminded him that the race was, after all, on video and he had actually seen it at least fifteen times before. So perhaps freeze frame and a head round the kitchen door might be the wise move. It took another fifteen seconds to convince his finger to press the button. Senna froze into two hundred m.p.h. immobility down Hangar Straight.

'What's up?'

Alex did not miss a beat, Jif and J-cloth scrubbing relentlessly. 'Nothing.'

'Good. Just spring cleaning in the middle of winter, are we?'

No reply. Rory stared round the kitchen and wondered how on earth they had managed to accumulate so much stuff in such a short time. Every cupboard door stood open to reveal empty shelves, like toothless mouths asking for more. On every work surface, table and chair were heaps of crockery, cutlery, pans, cake tins, electric whisks and blenders, food in every shape tin and packet, neatly stacked tea towels and recipe books. On the floor beside an EC mountain of cat food stood a pile of plastic tubs bulging with discarded pencils, blunt sharpeners, stray pegs, lengths of string, free coupons, as well as screws and plastic bits that appear from nowhere and defy you to find where they belong.

Christ, it would take all night to put this lot back.

He wandered over and perched on top of a stack of table-mats plonked on one of the chairs.

'Zena say something, did she?'

Alex was on her knees, head inside the old three-cornered pine cupboard that Rory had spent months of his life restoring to its present sheen. She said nothing but the yellow Marigolds continued to work overtime.

'Didn't she fancy the soup, then?'

'Don't be facetious.'

'It's better than fat-headed. Come on, Alex, let's put all this stuff back. You can tell me what she's done over a quiet drink in front of the fire. Much more sensible.'

'Like the man says, I've started so I'll finish.'

'Wouldn't it have been better to do one cupboard at a time? Instead of all at once?'

'No.' She moved along the floor on her knees and dived into the next open mouth. As she scrubbed, Rory watched her bottom in its snug black ski pants twitch from right to left with the effort. Maybe racing cars weren't the only moving objects worth viewing.

'So what's the trouble?'

'I told you.' Another squirt of Jif. 'Nothing.'

'So I see. What did she say? Whatever it was, it's not worth getting yourself into a knot over.'

The black pants wriggled as Alex backed out of the cupboard. She swivelled round to look at him and sat back on her heels, Marigolds still very business-like. 'It's nothing, Rory. Honestly she's not to blame.' She offered an apologetic wince that was meant to be a smile. 'You know what I'm like. Just overreacting. By the time I've finished up here, I'll have scrubbed it out of my system and be sweetness and light once more.'

He grinned at her. 'Promises.'

This time her responding smile was less effort. 'You hope!'

He rummaged in one of the pots of bits and pieces at his feet and was rewarded with a stab from a drawing pin. 'By the way, on Monday can I borrow your car?' He sucked the red teardrop from his thumb.

'What's the matter with yours?'

'Nothing.' He watched the black pants wave at him once more as she resumed the scrubbing. 'Just that I have to take a 3D model of the library scheme we're working on up to Birmingham and it won't fit on my back seat. I need your hatchback.'

'Okay. I've got the morning off but I'm due in at midday, so I'll use the MG. It'll make a change.'

'Don't go carting any of your muddy, bleeding or vomiting patients around in it, will you?'

She chuckled inside her cupboard. 'I was thinking of taking Old Macdonald's sow and piglets to market in it.'

'They'd be bacon before you could say eggs, if they laid even a trotter inside it.'

'I thought you liked bacon.'

'Not in my car.'

'I'll scrub them with Jif before they get in.'

He laughed and over her shoulder the smile she gave him was more relaxed. She immediately noticed where his gaze was focused and wiggled it at him like a cat about to pounce.

'Go and watch Mansell's rear end instead of mine. When I'm through here, I'll join you for that drink.'

He stood up, patted the article in question as he passed and returned to 1992 with a clear conscience.

13

Monday morning dawned dull and frosty. An English winter's day like a lifetime of others, when the damp creeps into the bones and the cold makes them ache. As it was Alex's morning off, there was no rush to get up, so she enjoyed the indulgence of coffee and Marmite toast in bed and a kiss from Rory before he left at eight.

'Mmm, I could get used to this,' she murmured as she snuggled further down among the pillows, careful not to disturb one cat at her feet, the other on her stomach.

'I'll pop home at lunchtime to give you a blanket-bath, if you like?'

'No thanks. I've got Pierce Brosnan coming over to play doctors and nurses.'

'Well, be careful where he puts his Walther PPK.' He blew her a kiss and left.

Alex contemplated the day ahead, decided to do something about the cat scratches on the utility room windowsill before going to work, shut her eyes for two seconds and fell fast asleep. When she awoke an hour later to the soft whisper of drizzle on the window panes, she realised how much she had needed the extra rest. The headache was gone and there was a lightness to her limbs that she had missed. Maybe the talk with Zena at the weekend had done her good. It was stupid to let herself get uptight. Everything was going so well. Zena was behaving herself. No trace of nicotine, and the trip to Bath on Saturday had been a perfectly understandable desire for a change of routine. Alex had offered to take her by car, but she had insisted on going for a day out on her own and travelled by bus. But everything was fine. Just fine.

Then why did she feel as if she were hanging over a cliff, clinging on by her fingernails? For heaven's sake, get a grip on yourself. Of course Zena evokes all kinds of childhood recollections. We haven't seen each other for nearly ten years. That meant her sister's present materialisation out of the transatlantic blue skipped all the events that cluttered up Alex's immediate present and took a nose-dive straight into the past. That's normal. All families experience that. They lug around the weight of emotional baggage from childhood, but that doesn't mean they have to go weak at the knees when confronted with it.

But then they didn't all have a door so tightly shut that they had very nearly forgotten its existence. Or a sister whose arrival was the slim and insidious key that flicked open the lock so abruptly that it let all the demons loose. To tear around with their pitchforks inside her head. A perfectionist, Zena had called her. How perfect could a woman be if she couldn't even perform the basic function of producing a child?

She watched a lone raindrop slither out of control down a pane of glass. When it hit the lead ridge that, like a flattened silver snake, divided the window into rectangles, it lost all shape and momentum.

Lack of control.

That's what was frightening her. Stealing the breath from her lungs and thumping her right in the solar plexus. She had learned at her father's knee the importance of control. Of trusting yourself to deliver the goods. But this time she couldn't. The goods were beyond her ability. She had to trust Zena instead. Was forced into it. And that went against the grain.

She had not told Rory everything. Not about the times that Zena had let her down. Let down her father, her mother. And herself. Not bothering to turn up at agreed times, leaving Alex stamping her feet in the cold. Telling secrets she had sworn never to reveal; not feeding Alex's white mice for a week when Alex went to stay with a friend in Norfolk and returned to find them both dead. Giving her word and breaking it. Again and again.

Deep down, Alex knew that the Zena she had grown up

with cared for no one but Zena. Now Alex was working hard
at believing Zena had matured, grown into an adult in America,
had learnt that there were others in the universe as well as
herself. Not for one minute did she doubt that to carry someone
else's child was a gesture of enormous generosity. And Alex was
grateful beyond words.

Then why the tensions? Why the headaches?

Trust. Faith. Such abstract intangibles. Could she trust Zena?
Have faith in her promises? The words were chasing round
in tighter and tighter circles in her head. It all came back to
control.

She kicked off the duvet, disturbing the two sleeping beauties,
jumped into a hot shower and viciously rubbed at her hair as if
trying to scrub the thoughts out from underneath it. She put
on an old pair of jeans, pulled a faithful sweater that had seen
shapelier days over her head, grabbed sandpaper and brushes,
and set about the offending windowsill. An hour later, it was a
gleaming virgin white, all trace of the hieroglyphics of cat-claw
marks removed. It was one of the widest and sunniest sills in
the house and both cats had adopted it as a cosy vantage point
from which to observe the comings and goings in the garden.
It gave them a front stalls view of the bird-table that was far too
high for even their interior-sprung hind legs. Sometimes when
they were mewling round her ankles because they were bored
and it was too wet outside for feline frolics, Alex would scatter
handfuls of bread on to the bird-table. Horatio and Hamilton
would crouch on the utility windowsill, chattering their teeth
harmlessly at the influx of fluttering wings the other side of
the glass. Pussy-television, Alex called it.

She rinsed her brush in white spirit, shut the utility room door
to keep out the culprits until the new paint was ready to fend
off any renewed assault, and checked her watch. Eleven-fifteen.
Plenty of time to make herself a coffee and change before leaving
for surgery. Better put a head in on Zena too, to say goodbye. She
had heard no sound from her room all morning, so assumed she
was still asleep. It was nothing unusual for Zena to sleep until
lunchtime.

Bearing a tray of coffee, toast and sliced pear, she knocked and
opened the door. The curtains were still closed, the light gloomy

and uncertain. An empty feel to the room. At first Alex thought she must be mistaken. That Zena must be somewhere under the jumble of duvet on her bed. She put down the tray, realised the bed was empty but was only mildly surprised. She must be in the bathroom. Automatically Alex shook and straightened the duvet and the surprise turned to unease.

The bedding was stone cold.

Quickly she checked the bathroom. Empty. A flicker of relief surfaced. Visions of her sister slumped over the bowl in a pool of blood backed off. Please God, don't let her miscarry. Alex was alarmed at the speed of her own panic. Was it that close to the surface? A tiny scratch and out it seeped, red and gory.

She checked the rest of the house, then returned to Zena's room. What clues? She opened the curtains and let in the grey light of winter. The rain had eased up but the sodden trees and bushes dripped as if the garden were crying. The room was the usual mess. Alex had at first tried to persuade Zena to tidy it up a bit, maybe hang up the occasional blouse or skirt, but when she received a blank wall response, she had taken to blitzing the room herself. Until the day she had arrived home and found the neat, orderly drawers and hangers of her own cupboards strewn all over the bedroom floor. Tit for tat, Zena had termed it. Alex had stopped after that. It may be her house, but for the moment it was Zena's room. Back to control again.

And now she had lost that control. Zena had slipped from her grasp and was gone. Rory had been right all along.

Use your head, for Christ's sake. Look around you. Is this the room of someone who has moved out? Hardly. Clothes, make-up, radio, all lay around like permanent residents. Her pink hairdrier was still plugged in and her new maternity dresses hung untouched in the wardrobe.

So what was missing?

The camel coat was gone. Fawn ankle boots as well. That was as far as Alex could get. Her mind was wading in tar and could come up with no other clothes. So all it meant was that Zena had gone out. Where was the harm in that? Probably while Alex was painting. She'd had a Satchmo CD playing and wouldn't have heard anything from the utility room.

Then why didn't she say goodbye?

Faint stirrings kicked into life. What if it had been early? While she slept. Suddenly Alex left the room at a run, down the stairs and burst out through the front door. A startled wood pigeon clattered its wings in the yew tree by the garage as Alex raced up to it. The up-and-over door stood open.

The MG was gone.

It was one o'clock. In the morning. A freezing sleet was turning the roads to sheet ice and reducing visibility to a few yards. Rory let the curtain drop back into place, shutting out the sight that was sounding alarm sirens in his head. He threw two more logs on the fire, as much for something to do as for their heat, and resumed his furious pacing round the room.

He would wring her neck. If ever he got his hands on it, that is. If ever she came back.

He glanced across at Alex, sitting so still and taut in her chair, eyes on the fire, ears tuned to the faintest growl of an engine. Zena was putting her sister through hell. As thoughtlessly as she dumped her week's dirty washing in a heap on Alex's washing machine. The whine of the wind and the crackling of logs were the only sounds in the room. No words. Everything had been said. Questions asked. And asked again. Where was she? Why hadn't she said she was going? Had she had an accident? Would she shelter somewhere overnight until the weather eased? Should they telephone the police? The hospitals? Over and over.

He knew the police would take no notice. Zena was a young, unattached adult with a car at her fingertips and money in her pocket, a free agent who had every right to go out and enjoy herself. And Rory was sure that's exactly what she was doing. A night on the tiles. But where? With whom? Doing what? For God's sake, doing what?

Then there was the car. Rory could not pretend to himself that some of his concern was not for his beloved silver sports. More than likely his sister-in-law would eventually turn up in one piece, but what about the MG? How many pieces would that be in? He wished to hell he had never taken the woman out in it. He should have seen this coming, especially when he had been fool enough to announce that he was using the Clio instead today. He had bumped into her outside the bathroom last night and suggested she ask Alex to take her for a blast in it this morning if Alex had time before surgery.

He had served it to Zena on a plate.

He strode over to the window again and peered out into the darkness. No let up at all. Hell, she would have to drive with Senna's flair for the wet if she was going to avoid any damage. To herself. Or to the car. He looked again at his wife. No change there, except for Hamilton in a ball on her feet. She was wearing an old paint-splattered sweater and her fingers had wound themselves into coiled spirals inside it. The lamp behind her painted soft shadows on her face but it was the shadows in the eyes that disturbed him. Bleak and desolate.

What was she seeing in the flames? Tyres skidding on ice? A silver bullet piercing seventy m.p.h. wings of steel? Mangled metal, bones and blood? A baby's blood? A sister's blood?

Rory stroked her head and she leant against him for a moment, as if sheltering from her thoughts.

'Don't make such a big deal out of it. I've said I'm sorry. What more do you want?'

She didn't look sorry. Anything but.

Zena had eventually crept in at nearly half past four in the morning. Oblivious to their concerns, she had looked surprised to see such a stern reception committee and immediately sulked when asked to explain her behaviour.

'I'm too tired for this. Bed is all I want now.'

She did in fact look exhausted but still on the tail end of a high, eyes bright and jumpy. Her blonde hair was pinned up in an elaborate plait and she was wearing heavy make-up and perfume, a strappy silver dress Alex had never seen before that showed plenty of cleavage but gave no warmth, and droopy hand-crafted silver earrings. She looked stunning. No hint of a stomach.

Alex looked sick.

'Where have you been?' Alex's voice was serious. Even Zena took note.

'Out.'

'Zena, where did you go?'

Zena chucked her camel coat on to the sofa. 'To London, if you must know. Is that a crime?'

'No. But you should have told us you were going and would not be back till late.'

'And asked to borrow the car, I suppose.' She smiled mischievously at Rory. 'Would you have let me use it, dear brother-in-law?'

'No.'

'Exactly.' Zena obviously felt she had proved her point and headed for the door.

'Zena, you could have telephoned. I've been worried sick about you.'

'More fool you, Ali. You know I can look after myself.'

'But can you look after the baby?'

Zena actually laughed. Laughed and patted her flat stomach. 'Don't worry, I'm wearing a girdle. Baby is just hunkydory in there.'

Slowly Alex walked up to her and stood very close. 'Take it off. Right now.'

Zena glanced at Rory. 'Here?'

'Right here. Right now,' Alex repeated.

'Don't be stupid. I will . . .'

'Take that girdle off the baby.'

'Okay, okay. No need to get uptight. Off it comes.' She lifted the slinky dress above her hips, hooked her fingers into the elasticated strait-jacket and yanked it down. 'Wow, that feels better,' she sighed and straightened her dress with a wink at Rory. 'Getting a good look at what you missed?'

So far Rory had left the talking to Alex. Afraid he would say too much. But the jibe cut loose his tongue. 'Don't you give a damn about how much you've upset Alex? Or me? Are you such a selfish bitch that you will take everything you can get from us, including stealing my car? You could have been dead in a ditch for all we knew.'

Zena laughed, a nasty, bitter sound. 'Don't give me that caring what happened to me crap. All you two care about is the baby.'

'That's not true and you know it.' Alex's voice was still low, controlled. Rory had heard her like this before. When they had come across a drunk in a Swindon car park one night, beating his dog with a wooden railing. A rusty nail had protruded from the business end. Alex had spoken in that same low voice then, just before she floored him with a knee to the groin.

Rory cut in quickly, 'Make it simple for us, will you, Zena? Just tell us what you did in London.'

'And why should I do that?'

Alex laid a hand, very lightly, on Zena's arm. 'Because it's our baby as well as yours.'

Zena tried to pull her arm free, but it was suddenly trapped. She looked at her sister and visibly decided not to push it. 'All right, if it will shut you up. I went shopping in Knightsbridge, bought myself this cute dress and so had to wear it somewhere. I met a guy in a bar, we had dinner, then went clubbing. I drove home. That's it. Like I said, no big deal.'

'Did you smoke?'

'Two puffs. That's all, I swear.'

'Drink?'

'A couple of glasses of wine. The rest of the night was Perrier water all the way. I'm not stupid, Ali, I know what I'm doing. Anyway I was driving.'

'The man. Who was he?'

'Nobody. Just some guy. Nothing happened, so don't get so dramatic.'

'It had better not have.'

Without warning Zena exploded. 'Leave me alone, will you? I'll do what the hell I like. When I like and with whatever bum takes my fancy. You have no control over me, Ali. None at all.' She yanked her arm away but Alex blocked her escape.

'Of course I have no control over you. And it seems to me, neither do you.'

'Now where have I heard that before? That's what Daddy used to say to me, isn't it?'

Suddenly Alex's eyes were full of tears but Zena wouldn't stop. 'You'll never be him, Ali. Never. You can be a vet, wear men's clothes and spout his words.' She was shouting now.

'But you'll always just be Alex. So don't play father with me.' She pushed past Alex and slammed the door.

Rory put his arms around his wife and held her close, absorbing her shock. Now was the moment to strangle his sister-in-law. Before she did any more damage.

Zena kicked off her shoes, decided to leave her make-up and teeth till the morning, stripped off the dress and collapsed into bed.

God, she was tired. So bone-weary tired. Driving home she had found her eyes shut on the motorway and nearly lost it in front of a lorry. She would tell Rory about the little dent in the rear wing tomorrow. No need tonight. He'd shout and scream, of course, but he'd get over it. Her eyes closed and music started up in her head. She smiled as she drifted round the dance floor. It had been a red-hot evening all right. One thing she was certainly not going to tell them about was the two hours in a hotel room between dinner and the club. That was something they might not get over so quickly. Nor the roll-your-own that had kept her up on the ceiling all night.

Rory dialled the number at exactly eight o'clock that morning. Despite only a couple of hours' sleep, he was not tired. Just angry. He had gone out early to inspect the car.

Come on, Doug. Turn off your Jimmy Hendrix and pick it up.

'Hello?' The voice the other end sounded surly and preoccupied.

'A little job for you, Doug.'

A chuckle cackled down the line. 'Pranged your precious baby, have you, lad?'

'Not me. Men aren't that stupid.'

'A woman? God forbid!'

'Who else would be so incompetent, insensitive and just plain deceitful?'

The chuckle became a roar of laughter. 'Should be kept off the roads, they should.'

'Can you fit it in today?'

'Sorry, mate, I'm up to my balls in it. It's all this ice about.'

'Doug, we are talking life and death here. My life and your death.'

'Look, I wish I could help today, but . . .'

'I'll bring it over in half an hour. Plus a case of scotch.'

A satisfied snort. 'Got yourself a deal there, Rory.'

It was the day for the antenatal clinic. Alex did not even feel like talking to her sister, let alone taking her to the hospital. But she had promised. Anyway, it was just as well for Zena to have a check-up today. God only knew what she had or had not got up to last night. Also Alex had agreed to pick up Rory at six, as his MG would not be back from its repair until tomorrow. Poor old Rory. It was his baby.

In the car driving to Swindon, the conversation was stilted. Zena had slept until three in the afternoon and breezed into the Clio looking fresh and rested. Having spent the morning in surgery, Alex had reached the stage when she felt she had fur growing in her mouth, so did not feel inclined to talk. There was nothing left to say anyway. At Princess Margaret's Hospital there was the usual waiting and magazine thumbing and Alex's patience was rewarded when, in the cubicle, she was allowed to observe. Zena stretched out on the couch while a very cheerful young doctor with vivid blue eyes and a cold stethoscope examined her and chatted away informatively with a string of students he had in tow. He pronounced that all was well, blood pressure and urine tests fine, so keep up the good work and get plenty of rest. A cheery smile and he was off to his next stomach.

Alex was relieved.

By the look of her, so was Zena.

After a plastic coffee to kill time, the atmosphere had not warmed up noticeably but Alex did make an effort.

'Come on, let's get out of this morgue and I'll buy you a Coke in the pub while we wait for Rory.'

'Oh great! Don't get too carried away will you?'

'No. I won't.'

As they walked out to the car park, Zena asked, 'Don't

you ever want to kick up your heels and make a run for it, Ali?'

'Run to what?'

'Freedom.'

'No, I don't. Freedom is all very well, but you have to fill it with something. You're forgetting, I enjoy the work I do. Every day of it.' She inserted the key in the lock and opened the passenger door. 'It may seem strange to you, but I do like my life. And my marriage.'

Zena gave her a long look. 'Nothing ever stands still, Ali. Things change.'

Alex obliged with a smile. 'That's why we're here at the hospital.'

She drove to the Duck & Feather near Rory's office, where they had arranged to meet. He wasn't there when they arrived, so she ordered a Coke and a Perrier, and settled at a corner table. The bar was just beginning to fill up as shops and offices closed. After the icy fog outside, it was warm and welcoming, all beams, horse brasses and red lamp shades. A magnificent stuffed mallard in a glass case glared, forever angry, across the room. Rory arrived only ten minutes late with Paula and Gary on his coattails. They had already met his sister-in-law at their Christmas party and greeted her with smiles.

Rory kissed his wife, nodded at Zena and persuaded Gary to buy the round. The chat was of library designs and Birmingham. Zena did not even pretend to listen. When Gary returned with the drinks, he sat down beside her and immediately included her in a separate conversation.

'I hear you've clonked Rory's MG? Not a pretty sight, I would imagine.'

She turned her amber eyes on him with headlights full on and said softly, 'He's throwing a tantrum because I took away his toy.'

The Birmingham conversation stopped in mid-flow. Rory looked at Zena, then at Alex and his dark eyes ached with tiredness. He'd had enough of it all. Enough of Zena. He wanted his house free of her, his wife free of her and his own head free of her. But like it or not, he knew she was here to stay. He must have been out of his mind to agree to it, to think it could possibly work.

Alex's eyes caught his across the table, brown and bright and still so full of hope. She winked at him and suddenly his doubts seemed irrelevant.

14

Maddy's stout legs pumped away at the pedals but the incline seemed steeper today. Gritting her teeth, which was difficult as she was chewing on a toffee bonbon, she leant over the handlebars, put her back into it and just scraped over the brow of the hill. The freewheeling ride down the other side gave her muscles a chance to catch their breath and nearly rattled the old bicycle out of its frame. It was what she called her district-nurse-bike, black, upright and with a wicker basket attached perkily to the handlebars. Except that it was now less of a basket and more a series of holes. At the bottom of the hill, the legs started up again at a sturdy pace and home drew nearer.

Not that Maddy was in any kind of hurry. It was actually her obligatory day off, but she had just ridden into Marlborough to check on a patient whose kidneys, like her own, had seen better days. It was midday and midweek. And already mid March, she realised. She may not be in a hurry herself, but the year certainly was. In the grassy banks that skirted the lane, creamy primroses were starting to sniff the air, and today's sun and southerly breezes had tempted out a rash of wild daffodils. Ahead of her where the stubby shadow of a budding horse chestnut tree had lain across the road, she saw a dark shape, like a sack, slumped on the side of the tarmac. A black-and-white striped sack that only last night had still been a badger. She knew it was too late but nevertheless dismounted, checked that he was stiff and cold, lifted him on to the grass verge away from the grinding wheels and sprinkled a shroud of twigs and leaves over him. She would notify the local badger people.

'Damn cars. Think they own the bloody roads,' she snorted as she clambered back on to her boneshaker.

As she swung round the curve that brought her to her front gate, she was astonished to see a figure in her garden. It was sitting on what would be her front lawn if she ever cut it and feeding dandelion leaves through the wire mesh enclosure to the surprised rabbits. The blonde head turned as Maddy yanked open the gate on its drooping hinges and wheeled the bicycle up to the front door. She disentangled the Waitrose carrier bag from the basket and walked up to the intruder. It was that flighty sister. The one having the baby.

'What are you doing here?' The frown was meant as a deterrent.

Zena remained seated on the patch of warm grass and stuck a finger through the wire to scratch a furry head. 'Just resting. I got carried away by all this spring energy. Walked a bit far. I remembered Alex saying that this' she paused '. . . house . . .' a pointed smile, 'is yours. So here I am. Resting.'

Maddy looked down on the smooth young face and objected to it. Could she tell it to go? Or was it really in need of help?

'I take in sick animals. Not sick people.'

Zena laughed. 'Don't worry, I'm only tired. Not sick.'

'Can't you go and be tired somewhere else?'

'Too late. I'm already here. You're stuck with me.'

Maddy knew when she was being laughed at. She turned and stomped indoors, pushed her bicycle into the hall and released the dogs. They hared off into the garden sounding suitably fearsome and Maddy hoped they would be a more effective deterrent than a frown. Perhaps madam out there would take herself off now.

'Any chance of a glass of water?'

Maddy was in the kitchen dumping her shopping on the table. She looked round and found Zena leaning in the doorway. She was wearing a floaty flowered summer smock, much too flimsy for spring temperatures, that clung in soft folds to the bulge at her stomach. Maddy stared at it, unabashed, and then at the face. It was very pink.

'What's up with you, then?'

'Just hot. Like I said, I overdid the walking and have a bit of a headache.'

'Blood pressure more like.'

'Better not be.'

'Sit down.'

Maddy swept a ginger cat off a bentwood chair. The curved backrest was tied together with string that had turned grey but Zena decided to risk it. A glass of water was plonked on the table for her. It didn't look too clean.

Maddy watched her sip the drink as if it were poisoned and decided to ignore her. The dogs had trooped back in to inspect the stranger and were avidly sniffing every available inch of legs and clothes. Probably reeked of Alex's cats. Unfortunately the sister seemed indifferent to their attentions. Maddy dumped a load of butcher's bones and off cuts into a preserving pan, ran water over them and set it down on the ancient and very grimy stove. Within minutes the room stank of boiled meat.

'You don't believe in overdoing the housework, do you?'

Maddy looked around her kitchen trying to see it through these unwanted lioness eyes. It was a good-sized square room, plenty of space for animals as well as herself. Admittedly the ceiling was yellow with age and speckled with grease spots, the formica cupboards maybe a mite grubby and one of them had lost its door. Tins of dog and cat food jostled with bags of rabbit pellets, dust and muddy pawprints on every surface. Well, there was no point in putting it all away in cupboards if you were only going to pull it all out again. She noticed a bucket of dirty water standing by the back door. How long had that been there? And Rocky, the black-and-white tom with only half a tail, was as usual in the sink licking water from the dripping tap.

'No one invited you in. If you don't like it, clear off.'

'Don't get me wrong. I'm not a great believer in it myself either. The cleanliness is next to godliness brigade leaves me cold.'

'Not like your sister, then.'

Zena shook her head. 'No, not like my sister.'

Maddy sat down on another bandaged bentwood and rummaged through the shopping on the table for a packet of digestives. The cycling had made her hungry. It always did. 'Why are you having the baby?' She opened the biscuits, tossed the broken top ones to the dogs and munched on one herself.

Zena smiled. 'Don't beat around the bush, do you?'

'No point.'

'I'm having this baby for Alex.'

'So she says.'

'Then why ask?'

'Seems strange to me, that's all. You're not exactly the maternal type.'

'Of course I'm not. That's why it's not a problem for me. I just felt like a year of the easy life. Isn't that what women do all the time? Opt for the easy life, the easy security of home, child and happy husband. What's the difference, except that I can walk away from it at the end of the year? With a nice useful cheque in my pocket.'

Maddy studied the face, eyes so brash and arrogant. What was behind them? They reminded her of a vixen she had once nursed, that made a fine show of fangs and ferocity, but was terrified if you came too close. Shades of Alex wove in and out of the expressive mouth and the lift of the eyebrow, like a haze that seeped under Maddy's dislike.

'Alex will be happy. But thank God, she's still going to work part-time for us. Not give up the practice completely.'

'No, not Alex. She wouldn't give up her beloved surgery. Not even for a child. She wants to have her cake and eat it. Best of both worlds.'

'And why not? She's a bloody good vet.'

'Is she?'

'One of the best.'

'I'm not surprised.' Zena reached out and took a digestive, uninvited. 'So was our father.'

'So I hear.'

'Does she talk about him, then?'

'Sometimes.'

Zena leant forward, elbows on the table, pushing a path through the groceries. 'And does she tell you what a slave-driver he was?'

'No.'

'That whatever she did, however hard she worked, it was never enough?'

'No.'

'Or that he never fussed over her, laughed with her or loved her the way he did with me. Is that what she forgets to mention? And does she also forget to tell you that she hated me for it? That somehow she managed to destroy it for me. For both of us.'

Maddy stared at the flushed cheeks and the eyes darting too brightly. Hormones getting out of hand. 'You're not well. I'll ring Alex.'

'No.' Zena put out a hand. 'Don't.'

It was like looking at the pathetic little vixen again. 'All right. Better rest though.'

She helped Zena up to her own room, tucked her between sheets that bore traces of cats creeping in for warmth when wet and cold at night, and left her to sleep. In the kitchen she scooped up a handful of pellets and went up the garden to seek solace in Josephine and Miranda.

Zena spent several days in bed. Alex collected her from Maddy's that evening in the car, called the doctor and pretended not to panic.

'Blood pressure's up,' he told her when he came downstairs after what seemed an age. 'Plenty of bed-rest and she'll be fine.' He handed her a prescription. 'This will help bring it down.'

'And the baby?'

'Sounds full of energy. Heartbeat like an elephant's.'

That evening Alex rang Gordon Tamworth and begged part of her annual leave, starting immediately. Gordon had been his usual generous self and told her to take whatever time she needed. 'We'll cope. Anyway, we will soon have to get used to managing without you some of the time. Good practice for us.' She wasn't sure if that made her feel better or worse.

She spent the days keeping Zena amused. Together they filled in the crosswords in the magazines, played Scrabble and Cluedo with blatant rivalry and watched afternoon panel games on Zena's television. Lazy days that drew them closer, tied the knots tighter. Easy laughter and light-hearted teasing that scrupulously observed any 'Do not walk on the grass' signs and quietened Alex's tremors. It was foolish to be fearful when everything was so obviously going well and Zena doing her version of sweetness and light.

It was on the third day of eating lunch perched on the end of her sister's bed watching with suspended irritation as Annalise dithered over Sam, when Alex suddenly felt Zena give a little jerk in the bed.

'Anything the matter?' The forkful of carrots hung in front of her mouth.

'He's at it again.'

'At what?' Assuming the reference was to the Sam on the screen.

'Wriggling. Like a whirling dervish in there.' She patted her stomach under the bedcover. Her face was free of make-up and her hair needed a wash, but to Alex she had never looked prettier.

The carrots returned to the plate. Since the day she bought the maternity dresses, Zena had not invited Alex to see or feel her stomach again. Alex had watched its growing curve from an unspoken distance.

'What does it feel like?'

'Weird.' Zena thought for a moment. 'Like bongo drums inside me.'

'It doesn't hurt?'

'No, not at all. When you get used to the weirdness of it, it's cute. Tickly. As if someone has released a balloon inside me without tying up the end first. It's scooting all over the place.'

'Wait till it really gets going. I've seen it in pregnant mares. Like a football team.'

Zena pushed back the bedcover. 'Have a feel.'

'I'd love to.'

The stampede in Alex's emotions was kept well out of sight. Without rush, she placed her tray on the floor but did not even notice when Horatio made a dash for the unexpected offering. She slid further up the bed until she was beside Zena. Beside her baby. Zena was wearing a baggy Minnie Mouse nightshirt that came to her knees. 'Sweet Dreams' it had printed down the side. Sweet dreams are made of this.

'Go ahead.'

Alex reached out and rested a hand on the bulge at Minnie's skinny waist. It felt different. No longer soft and pliable like last time. It was firm and protective now. A definite person in there.

Rory's baby.

Their baby. Sealed off from the world, untouched and untouchable.

Softly she stroked the mound, feeling, exploring, getting to know the tiny life inside. A minuscule flutter under the nightshirt exploded into her mind.

'What on earth are you crying for, you dumb dope?' Zena was laughing at her. Watching her.

Alex had not realised that tears were pouring down her cheeks and quickly wiped them away with her hand. 'Bit emotional, I suppose. You know what pregnancy does to a woman's hormones.'

This time they both laughed and Alex bent over and kissed her sister's cheek. 'Thanks.'

'Exciting, huh?'

'It's the most exciting thing that's happened in the whole world. Ever.'

'In the universe, I would say.'

'Definitely.'

'What about the discovery of Black Holes?'

'Doesn't come close.'

'I think I have to agree there.'

'Great minds think alike.'

'Exactly.'

By the end of the week the doctor pronounced the danger over, blood pressure almost back to normal, but with dire warnings about the consequences of overdoing it. 'Pre-eclampsia is something to steer clear of. So you take it easy,' he chivied.

'I'll be good,' Zena smiled sweetly at him and he left with an extra bounce in his step.

Another couple of weeks passed during which Alex managed to stop expecting every phone call at the surgery to be one from Zena. Or the hospital. Saying the blood pressure was back up. She calmed down and began to enjoy the pregnancy with her sister. Together they attended antenatal relaxation classes, practised breathing and panting on a cushioned floor, until Zena would rebel with a 'Panting's for dogs', roll over on the cushions and fall straight to sleep. Obviously the relaxation was working anyway.

Rory watched their antics with thankfulness that he did not have to go through it all. A front-row seat at the birth was his allotted role and he viewed even that with a mixture of eagerness and dread. Especially after Alex made him sit through a video of a birth. All that blood may be second nature to vets, but bricks and mortar were more in his line.

But as he watched the sisters together day after day, he noticed a change. Slight at first, but definitely there. A kind of indefinable blurring of the edges. It started with Zena's make-up. Or rather, lack of it. Whereas before, the only times he ever saw her without full warpaint was if their paths crossed outside the bathroom last thing at night, now she took to going days without any trace of it. Before going to the hospital or for a shopping trip to Marlborough with Alex, she would brush something on her lashes and lips, but small beer by her standards. Rory found it unsettling at first to be living with a different face and when he queried it with Alex, she smiled at him with irritating superiority. 'I told you so. It was just a shell. The care and attention she's getting now make her feel safe, so that she doesn't need the mask. She can be herself.'

'That's what worries me.'

'You old grouch. You just can't bear to admit you were wrong.'

Maybe that was true. But it wasn't just Zena who was changing. It was Alex as well. Only in little ways, but they took Rory by surprise. Empty cups were no longer instantly whisked away into the dishwasher, newspapers sat around in re-readable piles and the vacuum cleaner stayed under the stairs for days at a time. No matter how well you thought you knew your partner, you occasionally ran into newly constructed walls. Rory trod round them lightly.

Then there were the photographs. Alex had always been one for carefully posed smiles into the lens that inevitably looked stilted and formal. But now she took to snapping away freely to catch the moment as it really existed. Rory wondered if she was aware of the change, of the loosening of the reins. Was it just that the ball of pain that was childlessness had been cut loose from her ankle? That she could move about with a hop and a skip without the constant effort she'd had to exert previously? Or was it Zena? A sibling symbiosis that was bonded by the past.

But what of the future?

'Rory, may I have a word?'

It was Paula's voice, scattering his thoughts. Rory had just left the office and walked to his MG, silver paintwork pristine once more. His head was juggling questions about balancing the company's accounts with the more intricate feat of balancing on the tightrope at home, when he looked up and saw his trainee architect's plump figure waiting for him at the car.

'Hello, Paula, can't keep away from your desk?'

She had been working hard recently on the new library scheme, taking more of the responsibility off his shoulders, but had left early today for a dentist's appointment. He was surprised to see her back.

'I just wanted a word in private.' Her speech was faintly slurred and for a moment he thought she had been drinking. Then he remembered the root canal filling.

'How's the tooth?'

'Can't feel a thing yet. Half my jaw is numb.' She touched her cheek experimentally and wrapped a handful of dark curls over it for protection. 'But I have to talk to you.' The big spaniel eyes were worried.

Certain that it was something to do with her private life, or maybe a tiff with another member of staff, Rory was happy to offer a shoulder to cry on. 'Come on, cheer up. It's not the end of the world yet. I'll buy you a drink at the Duck & Feather and you can tell me what the problem is.'

The day was bright but breezy and she pulled her jacket more tightly round her, nodded and bustled along beside him without speaking. Once seated at a table in the lounge bar, with a straw sticking out of Paula's lager to bypass the numb lip, her eyes were, if anything, even more apprehensive.

'Okay,' Rory said with an encouraging smile, 'what's the matter? It must be pretty urgent to bring your wounded molar back here to speak to me.'

'It is.'

Rory waited while she worked out how to start.

'It's Gary.'

Oh hell, what had his partner been up to now? Surely Paula had more sense than to get involved with him. Rory had told him time and again to keep his fingers out of the office pies.

'Making trouble, is he?'

'More like tidal waves.'

'Who has he upset this time? You?'

'No.' Her big brown eyes lowered to her drink and she fiddled with the straw. 'Not me.'

'Then who? Not Jan, I hope. The office would collapse into a black hole without her to keep it functioning.'

'No, not Jan.' Still she did not look up.

Rory glanced at his watch. 'Come on, Paula, don't keep me in suspense. Who has Gary messed up this time?'

At last she raised her eyes to his. 'You.'

Rory's shoulder-to-cry-on smile slipped and he frowned uneasily. 'What do you mean?'

Paula took a deep breath and finally came out with it. 'After work yesterday, you know we all had a drink in here. To celebrate the baby.'

Rory had kept the pregnancy quiet until now, not wanting to tempt fate. But as everything was looking good, he had yesterday imparted the news of his impending fatherhood. The congratulations had been boisterous and liquid.

'Yes. We wet the baby's head somewhat prematurely.'

'We were all really happy for you, Rory. And for Alex. It was great news. Everyone had a good time.'

'Especially Gary. He was pouring it down like he'd sprung a leak somewhere.'

'That's what I'm coming to. Gary and I were the last ones to leave. After everyone else had gone, he bought us both a double brandy and it just spilled out.'

'What? The brandy?'

'No, no. The secret.'

'What secret?'

Paula's eyes took to the straw again. 'About him and your sister-in-law.'

'Zena?'

'Yes.'

Rory felt his breath stop and curdle in his lungs. 'What about them? Tell me, Paula.'

'I hate dumping him in the shit like this.'

'To hell with the shit. What did he tell you?'

She was losing her nerve, eyes everywhere but on him.

'You've gone this far, Paula. No way of backing out now.'

She flicked her soulful spaniel gaze up to his and blurted it out. 'He thinks he is the father of Zena's child.'

Rory blinked. Stunned like a calf in the abattoir.

'I'm sorry, Rory. Really sorry. But I had to tell you. Maybe it's not true. He was as drunk as a skunk and perhaps got his brain scrambled. But I did believe him, Rory. He was terribly upset about it. But he wasn't going to say anything to you because he didn't want to hurt you.'

Rory stood up. 'The feeling is not mutual. I am going to break his bloody neck.'

'It's the truth, I swear.'

Gary Saunders was in his chair, keeping the desk securely between Rory and himself. He could feel the sweat trickling inside his shirt.

'I had no idea what you were planning to do, Rory. How could I know you were intending a surrogate baby? You didn't warn me. And neither did she. At the Christmas party, we'd got on like a house on fire, so when I bumped into her in Bath, of course I took her to lunch. Why shouldn't I?'

Rory was leaning forward, hands firmly on the desk. Gary's neck within reach. 'And after that?'

'I've told you. It was two days later. She rang me from London. Said come on up for the evening. For fuck's sake, Rory, it was innocent fun. For both of us. Both adults, both out for a good time. That was all.'

'So you screwed her?'

Gary cringed a little lower in his chair. 'Yes. A hotel room. Then off to the club. Christ, Rory, how was I to know?'

'Did you ever touch her before then?'

'Never, I swear.'

'Not before Bath?'

'No, I had only met her once. At the Christmas party with you and Alex. And nothing happened in Bath. Only London.'

'If you're lying to me, Gary, I will cut your prick off personally. With a blunt knife.'

Gary's voice rose. 'Ask Zena. She will tell you it's the truth.'

Rory believed him. Sick relief swamped all else.

'You are lucky, Gary. Your neck and your prick are reprieved.'

Gary looked at him, amazed to see the danger ebb. 'Bloody hell, mate, about time you got your head on straight. But what has made you see sense?'

'Because she was already several months pregnant when she went up to London.'

Gary heaved an enormous sigh of relief. 'So you are the father. Not me.'

'Yes. I am the father.' Rory walked out of the office. A few words with Zena would not be out of order.

All the way home his head was drumming with the pictures of Gary with Zena. Gary in her arms, Gary in her bed, Gary in her body. And the baby in there already. At risk. Hammered and humped to hell and back. He knew Alex would be furious. So much for sisterly trust and devotion.

He parked the MG in the garage and stormed into the house. Inform Alex first. Then together they would confront Zena. He heard the honkytonk of Scott Joplin drifting down from upstairs, so strode up to their bedroom. When he reached it, the door was slightly ajar. He pushed it open further but stopped in his tracks and stared.

Alex was standing with her back towards him in front of the full-length mirror. She was humming loudly to herself to the bouncy chords of 'The Entertainer'. It was one of her favourites, played by the composer himself and had drowned out the sound of Rory's approach. She did not see that she was no longer alone.

Rory could only catch a sliver of her face as she turned her head slightly at an angle to the reflection, but even from that glimpse it was obvious she was smiling broadly. Her hair was loose and swinging like a soft veil around her, and her long legs were encased in jeans with a man's tartan shirt on top.

It was the shirt that had riveted his gaze.

Whereas her arms and legs were their usual slim selves, her stomach bulged under the cotton shirt, a lumpy imitation of her sister's. A pillow instead of a placenta. She was turning from side to side, assessing and admiring the sight of her suddenly swollen belly, unable to take her attention from the mirror for even a moment. Absorbed in her own fantasy. She stroked the bulge with gentle, caressing hands and rested them on its ledge in the gesture so beloved of the pregnant.

Very quietly, Rory backed out of the room. He felt a sense of invading her privacy more intimately than in even the most private act of love-making.

Downstairs, Zena was as usual in front of the television. She greeted Rory with a smile that spoke of a contented day and uncurled her legs from the sofa.

'Hi, father-to-be. Have a good day at the grindstone?' She indicated the cushion beside her. 'Come and have a look at this footballer of yours. He's scoring goals faster than Maradona ever did.' She patted her stomach affectionately.

With the Gary affair on the tip of his tongue, Rory took the offered seat beside her reclining figure and studied the spot where her hand had lain. She was wearing only a navy tee-shirt and leggings, and he could clearly see what looked like a distinct pulse in the bulge that had replaced her previously slender waist and ironing board stomach. The thin cotton material was shifting like a drumskin in a marching band. Rory thought of Alex with her pillow, inert and feather-filled.

'Weird, isn't it?' Zena smiled. 'Cut it out, buster, or you'll pop out of your pod like a champagne cork.' She chuckled delightedly and tickled her stomach once more.

Rory could not take his eyes from the drumbeat inside her body. Never before had she invited him to look.

'Want to feel?' Without waiting for a reply, she took his

hand, lifted the tee-shirt and placed his fingers on the bare skin underneath. 'Lively little bugger, isn't he?'

Her skin was warm. Taut and stretched. With a thin brown snake of pigment tracing a line from the flattened belly-button down into the elastic of the leggings. Rory's fingers suddenly jumped as an internal kick took exception to the added weight of his hand. A kick from a real flesh and blood foot.

His own flesh and blood.

He stroked the round, warm bulge as if it were part of himself and held it possessively between both hands. Dimly he was aware of something in the back of his mind that he had been meaning to say to Zena, but whatever it was it wasn't important now. The drumroll started up again. She didn't hurry him. Let him take his time. Fingers lingering, touching, stroking, learning about the world his child was inhabiting. He imagined the throb of Zena's heartbeat vibrating through the cradling fluid, the sound of his own voice reaching newly formed ears.

'Pregnancy suits you, Zena.'

'I know,' she purred and stretched like a cat in front of a fire.

Rory pulled the tee-shirt down and smoothed it back into place. 'Make sure you keep looking after him. Or her. And yourself.'

'Of course. I do.'

Rory looked at her face. Smooth and untroubled, pupils puffed wide with pride, so natural now, just like the process her body was going through. The brittle lines of stress had been ironed away, but for how long? Pain, tiredness and sleepless nights loomed in the not far distant future.

Suddenly he remembered Gary.

'Any chance of a cup of tea?' Zena wriggled her feet back up on to the sofa. 'Your offspring is leeching me dry.'

Rory smiled with resignation and stood up. 'Certainly, m'lady. On a silver platter, I presume.'

'Why not? I deserve it, don't you think?'

'Zena, a cup of tea is the least you deserve.'

'And a biscuit with it.'

'Don't push your luck.'

She laughed softly, Alex's laugh, and snuggled down into the cushions. Contented and relaxed. No stress. For her or the baby. So why bring up the Gary affair? It was ancient history now and the baby had survived the encounter with no ill effects judging by the strength of its kicks. Why rake over dead ashes and risk burning the house down?

'One cup of tea on its way.' As he left the room, he heard Alex coming down the stairs, still humming happily to herself.

15

March crept with pleasure into the longer days of April and spring declared itself open for business. Magnolias and wisterias brought a blaze of the exotic to gardens and Zena took to sleeping with three pillows propped under her feet at night to stop her ankles aching. Alex began to stockpile disposable nappies, zinc ointment and musical mobiles, and couldn't walk past a rack of baby clothes without adding to her shopping list. Meanwhile Rory played his part as expectant father and redecorated the third bedroom as a nursery. He transformed its sedate regency stripes into colourful sunflower yellow, enlived further by huge hand-painted murals of Bambi and Thumper with big smiley eyes.

Zena watched and nodded her approval of the preparations around her. Her walks grew shorter and the visits to the hospital more frequent. To Alex's surprise, Maddy took to dropping in occasionally for a milky tea as she cycled past on her way home. Checking out the cub's progress, she called it. Oddly, Zena did not seem to mind and they traded insults as readily as others traded knitting patterns. When Alex returned home at seven o'clock one evening after a particularly long and disappointing day – she had lost a feline favourite to old age and a young setter with a weak heart on the operating table – she found her husband in the garden digging a large hole in the lawn at the side of the house.

'What on earth are you doing? Trying to escape to Australia?'

It was almost dark, mist hanging like grey smoke over the hills and judging by the size of the hole, he had been at it for some time.

Rory turned and smiled at her. His hands and jeans were grimed with soil but he looked pleased with himself. 'I'm making a sandpit.'

Alex burst out laughing. 'You're mad. Absolutely round the twist.'

'I thought you'd be pleased. Look,' he waved a hand over the dark rectangle that opened like a grave in the grass, 'it's a good size.'

'It's a splendid size, Rory. It's just that it's way too premature. But I'm sure the cats will thank you for it.'

Rory looked at the mountain of earth he had disinterred and had still to cart away, and sank his spade into it with an energy Alex envied. He started to fill the wheelbarrow. 'Never mind if it's a little early for a sandpit. Best to do it while I have the time. It might get a bit hectic when the baby's here. And anyway, you and I can play sandcastles in it in the meantime.'

Alex laughed and sat down on the grass on the edge of his handiwork, stretching out her tired feet inside the hole. 'It'll be an electric train track next.'

'I was actually thinking of a doll's house.'

'Rory, what a wonderful idea! A unique, Flynn-designed residence in all its miniature glory.' She kicked off a shoe and wriggled bare toes in the moist earth. 'What if it's a boy?'

'A den-house in the garden instead?'

'Brilliant! He'd love it. Hiding away with his friends.'

'And his dog.'

'Like the Famous Five?'

'Talk about rose-coloured spectacles!' Rory abandoned his spade with a laugh. 'Ours are every colour of the rainbow.' He sat down beside her on the damp grass and slipped an arm around her waist. 'Nervous?'

She leant against him. 'Of course. Aren't you?'

'Why do you think I'm out here digging holes in the ground at this time of night?'

'Because you're mad?'

'Could be. Or maybe because I was wrong.'

She turned and studied his face, shadows carving Heathcliff hollows in his cheeks.

'You were right, Alex. All along. I should never have been so mistrusting.'

'About Zena?'

'Yes. You only have to look at her to realise that what she claimed was true. She just wanted somewhere to rest her idle bones for a year. A pain in the arse she is without doubt at times, but despite everything, it has worked. I didn't think it would.'

'It was a risk, Rory. You were right about that.'

'But thanks for knocking some sense into my thick skull.'

She kissed him forgivingly and for a moment they sat in silence together in the gathering gloom, heads both dark as the night crept into the garden and robbed it of its colour.

'We're not out of the woods yet,' Alex murmured.

'Which particular trees did you have in mind as cause for concern?'

'First tree, she could still leave with the baby. After it's born.'

'No, I really don't think she would.'

'You've changed your tune, haven't you?'

'I know. But having lived with her all these months, I cannot see her ever letting a kid take over her life. Not her style at all. She's just enjoying playing mother-bountiful but will be off to a new role when this is over.'

'I hope you're right.'

'And the second tree?'

'Money.'

'Oh, for heaven's sake, don't lose any sleep about that. We've been over the figures. It'll be tight, but we'll manage.'

'With my income cut in half after the birth and the extra repayments on the mortgage, it puts a heavy load on you.'

Rory hugged her to him. 'Atlas is my middle name.' With his free hand he picked up a small dry stick that his spadework had knocked off a shrub on to the lawn and demonstrated his muscular prowess by lifting it above his head.

Alex laughed, just as Zena materialised out of the shadows.

'Christ, you two look as if you've dug yourselves an early grave.'

'More like a second childhood. Rory is making us all a sand-pit.'

'Why do a dumb-arse thing like that? You really should tie

that white jacket tighter at the back, Alex, before he frightens the neighbours. But sitting in the almost dark studying a black hole in the ground qualifies you both for the funny farm.'

'We're just building castles in the sky,' Rory laughed and tossed the stick up in the air as if to join them. It was meant to fall harmlessly, but just at that moment Zena stepped forward and it caught her on the shoulder.

She gasped, though the blow had been no more than a graze, and froze.

Rory jumped to his feet at once. 'I'm sorry, Zena, it was an accident. Are you okay?' He moved towards her but she pulled back sharply.

'Stay away from me. Like hell it was an accident.'

'Zena, I'm sorry. It was stupid, but I didn't mean it to hit you.'

'You meant it, Rory. Whether you know it or not.' She turned and stalked away, her slight waddle making her look vulnerable.

'Hell, Alex, I'm sorry. Just when things were going well.'

Alex stood up and offered a small, pacifying shrug. 'One step forward, two steps back. It's the best she can manage.'

The shriek scooped Alex from her deep nest of sleep. She clung on to its warmth for a brief selfish second, burrowing deeper into its soft folds, but another sharp moan of distress tore them from her. She opened her eyes, heart working overtime.

It was dark. Beside her in bed, Rory was sitting upright, alert and listening.

'It's Zena,' he said.

Alex listened. The moaning had started again. Oh God, not the baby. Not yet. Please God, not the baby. She leapt out of bed and raced in the dark along the landing to Zena's room.

'Zena, what's the matter?' She pushed open the door and was met with darkness. Her stumbling fingers found the light-switch. She expected blood. A bed in turmoil. But the bed was empty.

'Zena.'

A high-pitched whimper came from a corner of the room. A bundle of duvet shivered there on the floor.

'Zena?'

With a shock, Alex realised her sister was under the duvet. Very gently, she lifted a fold of it. 'Zena, it's me, Alex. Are you all right?'

What a bloody stupid question to ask. The wide, frightened eyes staring up at her were anything but all right. Alex crouched down, wrapped an arm around her sister and stroked the tangled hair from her face.

'What is it, Zena? Are you ill? Is it the baby?'

The amber eyes slowly started to focus, coming back from a long way away. They stared at Alex as if struggling to put the pieces together in her head. Her face was drained of any colour and her mouth tried to work, but nothing came out except short harsh gasps. Then, as if the brain had suddenly snatched into gear, she let out a deep, shuddering sigh and leant her head on Alex's shoulder. Alex rocked her gently.

'It was a nightmare, wasn't it?'

She had forgotten the nightmares. Zena the teenager with the brash eyes and unrelenting tongue, quivering in the dark in Alex's arms.

Alex had forgotten.

The spasms were subsiding into steadier, smoother breaths and Alex tried to quell the overwhelming sense of relief that it was not the baby, just a nightmare. Just a nightmare. Simple words to dismiss the terror that reduced a rational adult to a mindless, quaking imbecile. She felt the crumpled figure detach itself from her arms.

'Like old times, huh?' Zena's voice was weak but the shakes had gone. She leant back against the wall, ran a hand through her blonde hair to drag it into some kind of order and took a deep, steadying breath. The smart-arse smile crept back into place. 'Gave you a fright, I bet.'

'My heart's turning cartwheels.'

'Join the club.'

'And the baby?'

'Don't fuss. He's still fast asleep, lucky little bastard.'

'Let's get you both back into bed.'

She helped Zena to her feet and as she put an arm around her waist to lead her back to bed, she felt the electric shock of a sudden kick under her hand. The baby was objecting to all this nocturnal disruption of its rest. Zena did not even seem to notice the sudden activity inside her body and collapsed on to the bed with ungainly haste. Alex tucked the duvet around her and for a moment held her hand.

'All right now?'

'On top of the world.'

'Would you like me to stay? Or a drink of water maybe?'

'No, push off and let me sleep.' But her fingers still held on to Alex's.

'What was it about, Zena? The nightmare.'

The fingers dug into Alex's palm and a shudder ripped a hole in the veneer of Zena's composure. 'Suppressed anxieties, isn't that what they're supposed to be about? Well, obviously mine are about the baby.'

'That's normal in pregnancy,' Alex soothed her. 'It's a big responsibility.'

'It was some bastard throwing bricks at me.' She laughed self-consciously. 'Really dumb. I was pinned on one of those spinning wheels they have in knife-throwing acts in the circus. Naked and massively pregnant. The macho brick-heaving bastard had a black bag over his head and was hurling huge bricks at . . .' She broke off, snatched her hand away and curled up on her side. 'At my stomach.'

Alex recalled the stick in the garden. Bouncing off Zena's shoulder. 'Sounds horrific.'

'Just a dumb dream.'

'It's over now and you're safe. You and the baby. We won't let either of you come to any harm.' She tried the childhood magic wand. 'Doc Ali is here, so never fear.'

'Old Mother Hen, more like it.' But the voice was smiling. 'Go flap your wings elsewhere.'

'Are you sure you wouldn't like a warm drink or . . . ?'

'Nothing, thanks.'

'Will you be all right on your own?'

'I'm not on my own, am I? That's the whole point.'

That was exactly the point.

'Get some sleep then. Sweet dreams this time. Try something along the whiskers-on-kittens line instead.'

Zena yawned. 'Kittens make me throw up.'

'Don't let the shell crack or I might think there's a soft, squishy centre in there somewhere.'

'Push off.'

Alex smiled and switched off the light. 'Sleep well.'

But Zena did not sleep. Well or otherwise. She lay curled in a lumpy curve, foetal ball wrapped around foetal ball. She stared into the darkness and watched the shapes slowly emerge within it, as her eyes accustomed themselves to its black shadows. Black shapes. Nightmare sharp. Black bricks hurtling at her, crunching into her flesh. Black bag for a mask. Her dream threaded together with skeins of black. The only flare of colour coming from the pumped-up muscles of his body, naked in the spotlight and glistening with sweat. No number of masks could disguise that body from her. As he raised each brick, the broad shoulders flexed, pectorals like Buicks and biceps as thick as her waist – when she'd had a waist. The white scar on the ribs where he had burnt himself on a branding iron. It was Chet Taylor. Her husband. Tracking her even into her dreams.

She rolled clumsily on to her back and spread her hands like a protective shield over her swollen stomach. The baby kicked contentedly.

God, she had been stupid to marry that dumb prick. Not that he'd been without his attractions. A cute tight butt and rock hard everywhere. But everywhere! Prick, brains and fists, all eighteen-carat iron. The prick and brains had suited her just fine. She'd done with clever. All her childhood clever had been rammed down her throat. Clever and hardworking. Well, cut her loose and she'd opted for dumb and lazy. Inherited business and no need for brains. Just that wide, wonderful grin to bait the hook and blue eyes you wanted to swim in.

And the letters from Alex describing her happily-ever-after life. Marriage had seemed a piece of cake. It had worked at first. The fun and games had carried them on a wave of sickly delight that eventually rotted the gut. And then the real fun had started. The fun Chet had been waiting for.

A connoisseur of front-door slams, Zena had learnt to be.

Each nuance a hint of the reaction needed. There was the big, bold slam, confident and full of 'Honey, I'm home.' Fly into his arms and ravish him in the hallway. The short, sharp slam that lingered in the air like depression and demanded cutesy girlishness to tempt out the grin. And then there was the whisky slam. Aggressive and bull-headed. Not much to do then except hide the Southern Comfort and sit very still, hoping he would fall flat on his face. Get it wrong and trouble cranked up on all cylinders.

She shut her eyes to blank him out, but they insisted on popping open again and he was still there. Swaying slightly with that lop-sided grin of his. The moment his kick bounced open the door to whatever room she had chosen for retreat, she had always looked steadily at him. She had learnt that. Painfully. He did not like her to hide her eyes behind a veil of lowered lids. What he did like when he was drunk were mind-games. Mind-games and sex.

He would come weaving unsteadily towards her and stand very close. Invading her space. He was a good-looking man. Even through the fog of her fear she could still recognise that. Sun-bleached hair, laughing eyes, wide Nordic cheekbones. So decent looking, so all-American boy. But his eyes were not laughing now.

'You didn't tell me.' His voice did not betray the depth of the alcohol.

'What didn't I tell you, Chet?'

It was a mistake. Never question him. His pelvis thrust forward in anticipation, aggression feeding the erection crouched behind the Levis.

The blow snapped her head to one side.

'You didn't tell me what day it is.'

'Try looking on the calendar.'

Mistake number two. Never smart-arse him drunk. The second blow rocked her head the other way.

'Don't give me none of that goddamn English lip of yours.'

She dragged her eyes like lead weights back up to his. His pupils were gaping holes. He was waiting for another answer. 'No need to hassle me, Chet honey. Just buy yourself a talking clock.'

'I was supposed to meet Buck Haddon tonight. You didn't remind me.'

'I didn't know.'

This time the blow was harder. She tasted blood.

'Don't lie to me, you bitch.'

Fear was turning her innards to liquid. Like that deadly virus in Zaïre. Is that what fear is? A deadly virus?

His fists started in on her. Her own hands spread in wafer-thin protection, but she remembered not to cry out. He didn't like her to cry out.

'Zena.' His voice was shockingly soft.

Her eyes were shut tight. She opened them quickly.

'Zena, what day is it today?'

'Tuesday.'

The fist shot out. 'No. Try again.'

Her mind was jelly. 'It is Tuesday.'

Again the fist. 'No.'

'Wednesday?'

This time the blow was open-handed, first one cheek, then the other.

'Wrong again.'

What did he want? For Christ's sake, what did he want her to say?

'Any day you want it to be, Chet.'

He smiled. Pleased. 'Good, Zena.'

His hand came towards her again and she flinched in readiness. But he laughed loosely and patted her head with indulgence, like a favourite but misbehaved puppy. 'Good girl.' Then he pulled her to the floor, ripped off her panties and within three minutes had screwed her and fallen into an alcoholic cavern of sleep.

It had taken her another six months to leave him. How could she have been so dumb? The apologies next day were always as abundant as the flowers that arrived by the armload. Along with the promises that it would never happen again. Cheap, easy, blue-eyed promises. She should have packed her bags the first time the bastard laid a hand on her. What was it that kept her there? From the dark safety of her bed, she looked back and asked herself what was the real reason she had stayed. At the time she had called it love. Ever-optimistic, rose-tinted love.

But now three thousand miles of Atlantic had enabled her to see through that smokescreen. So what had it been? Self-flagellation for disobeying Daddy all those years? Dumb-arse determination to show she could make a success of her marriage just as well as her oh-so-perfect sister could? Or was it simply the money while it lasted?

To hell with it all. They were both well rid of each other. She had left and that's all that mattered. One blow too many, a miscarriage and she was out of there. Straight from the hospital to the airport.

She wrapped her arms around the new life inside her and chuckled to herself. This Wiltshire featherbed fitted just fine. In all the right places, soft and supportive. She smiled, shut her eyes and slept.

It was Maddy who brought the state of Zena's fingernails to Rory's attention. He walked out of the house one morning and found her waiting for him, bicycle to hand, at the garage. It was raining and he thought she was after a lift into Marlborough. He swung open the up-and-over door and invited her under its shelter.

'You can leave your bike in here but don't go dripping all over my upholstery.'

'You can keep your upholstery. It's for weaklings who are frightened of a few drops of rain.'

He looked at her fiercely yellow oilskins and eyes stern behind the speckled lenses and decided it was the rain that should be frightened.

'So what can I do for you, Maddy? Why are you lying in wait for me? Like a spider disguised as a daffodil.'

A sniff of satisfaction greeted that. 'Because you're too bone-headed to see what's under your nose.'

'You always have been one for flattery, haven't you?'

'That flighty sister-in-law of yours is scared.'

'Zena? Scared? I've known water-buffalo more scared than she is.'

Maddy scowled and wiped a drip from her nose. 'Don't be such a man.'

Rory laughed. 'It may have escaped your keen notice, but I am in fact a man.'

'Exactly,' Maddy huffed and turned her bicycle round so that it was pointing out towards the drive. Narrowly Rory watched it swing its mudguard half an inch from his off-side wing.

'Okay, tell me what makes you think she's scared.'

'Don't you see anything for yourself? Haven't you noticed her nails?'

'Fingernails?'

'She's bitten them to nothing. They used to be long and painted.'

Rory unlocked the car with a smile. 'And that's your evidence? Bitten fingernails. Maybe she just cut them because they'd get in the way with a baby. Or perhaps they broke because she's short of calcium. Who knows?'

'I'm telling you, that kid's scared.'

'Of what, for heaven's sake.' He remembered the nightmare a couple of weeks ago.

'How should I know? You're the one who's living with her. Of pain maybe. Or the birth. Or of being chucked out on her ear when you've got hold of the baby.'

'Maddy, we're helping her in every way we can. Not treating her like Cinderella. Anyway, why are you telling this to me, instead of to Alex?'

Maddy treated him to another scowl. 'Alex has enough on her plate.'

'And I haven't?'

'No. Men are expert at shifting the emotional load on to their wives. Talk to Zena, Rory.'

Rory slid in behind the MG's steering wheel and rolled down the window. 'You know you're an interfering old bat, don't you?'

She glared at him with ill-concealed amusement. 'And you are a rat-eared piece of male ego with one too many women in your house.'

'They're sisters, for heaven's sake.'

'They'll scratch each other's eyes out, if you're not careful.'

'You're even madder than your name, Maddy. That eye of newt and toe of frog diet of yours is rotting the brain.'

'It's a warning.'
'We've already passed the Ides of March, thank you.'
'Talk sense and maybe you'll see sense.'
Rory climbed out of the car again, came over to the bulky figure and studied her face with serious concern. 'Why are you stirring things up, Maddy? Waving your wooden spoon around. I thought you liked them both.'
Her green eyes glared at him without amusement this time. 'That's why I'm warning you, you dolt.' She lumbered her bicycle back out of the garage and the rain immediately began to ski down her oilskins with enthusiasm.
'Anyway, who says I like them?' Without a backward glance, she pedalled off down the drive.

'Worried? Of course I'm not worried.' Zena looked at her brother-in-law curiously. 'No more than any healthily pregnant woman would be, that is.'
'Apprehensive about the birth, perhaps?'
'What is this? Twenty Questions? Your milk-of-human-kindness costume doesn't quite hang straight on you. I'm too used to the gloves off, knuckle-duster at the ready brother-in-law to fall for this load of claptrap.'
They were walking in the woods at the back of the house. Just a gentle stroll, with Rory adjusting his stride to her heavier pace. The leaves and the birds were out in force and enough gentle sunlight squeezed through to dry out the muddy path from the previous day's rain. It was a Saturday morning and Alex was on call. A cat with a dislocated leg had summoned her to the surgery and Rory had taken advantage of her absence to suggest a dose of fresh air. It was easier to talk to his sister-in-law when they were walking side by side instead of when confined by four walls, face to face in fixed formality.
Rory turned and smiled at her. 'I'm all marshmallow underneath these prickly spines, you know. Mrs Tiggywinkle in disguise.'
She laughed an easy, relaxed sound. No ghouls and ghosties hiding there, surely. Maddy must have got her wires crossed.
'What happened to your nails?'

Zena lifted a hand to study its uneven tips with distaste. 'Not a pretty sight, I have to admit.' She raised a fair eyebrow at him. 'But no big deal to masculine sensitivities, I would have thought.'

Maddy had at least been right there, he had to admit. When he returned home that evening he had taken a good look at Zena's fingernails and they were indeed nearly all short and rough. One or two had escaped the blitz but the sophisticated array of neatly painted ovals was a thing of the past. Why would she be biting them now? It had to be nerves. And who could blame her? Rory wouldn't fancy going through the rigours of labour and childbirth either.

'It's probably being with Alex again that has made me revert to childhood habits,' Zena continued, as she sat down on the mossy stump of an old beech tree that had long since warmed someone's hearth.

Rory found a dryish patch beside her. 'Nail nibbling?'

She nodded, staring out through the trees. 'No significance in it.'

'Just a bit tense.'

'For heaven's sake, Rory, of course I am. I just want the baby to be okay. Healthy and normal. Ten fingers, ten toes and everything else in the right place.' She kicked out at a stone among the dead leaves and it rolled over on to its back, sending a frantic clutch of woodlice into panic stations.

Rory did not even notice. He had heard the anxiety. Quietly he asked, 'Is there any reason why you think the baby might not be perfect?'

'Of course not.' It was too quick.

'Something you've done?'

'I said no.'

'In London, perhaps?'

A hesitation. 'No.'

'With Gary.'

She glanced at him quickly, then looked away again with a faint smile. 'How long has Mrs Tiggywinkle known about him?'

'A while.'

'He was fun. A real mover.' Her smile grew into a deliberate thorn in Rory's side. 'But no, I don't think a humping session would do our baby any harm. He was only a tiny scrap of a thing then.' She looked down at herself and grinned. 'Not the bloody great whale he's turned into now. There was room for all of us.'

'Then what is it? What else?'

A scurrying in the branches overhead made them look up in time to see a grey squirrel launch itself with kamikaze grace into thin air and land with impossible ease on the slender bough of a silver birch on the other side of the path. Rory waited for an answer but she continued in silence to follow the animal's darting progress down the trunk.

'Zena, if there's any risk to the child, I have a right to know.'

She shrugged but still did not look at him. 'I don't really think there's any risk. I'm just being jumpy.'

'Jumpy about what?'

She plucked at the lichen on the flaking bark beside her knee and her face set into uneasy lines. 'I was out to have a good time. The baby wasn't real to me then. Not like now.'

'So what was it? Drinking? Smoking?'

'Drugs.'

Rory felt as if a trapdoor had just opened at his feet and he was hurtling down to the bottom of a dark well.

'What drugs?'

'I don't know.'

The black waters closed over his head.

'Did you inject anything?' A baby born addicted.

'Christ, no. Nothing like that.' She turned to face him for the first time. 'I'm not out of my mind, pregnant or unpregnant.'

'So what was it? Pills?'

'No. Gary offered me a cigarette. A roll-your-own.'

'Marijuana?'

Zena shrugged again, offhand once more. 'May have been. I have no idea. Ask Gary.'

'I intend to. How many?'

'What?'

'How many cigarettes did you smoke?'

'Just one. That's all I needed.'

Rory breathed clean air into his lungs. Even one joint was not good, but sure as hell it was not as bad as it could have been. There should be no ill-effects at all on the baby. He looked at her and wondered how she managed to look so relaxed while harbouring such fears. Or maybe she knew the risk of damage was negligible and just wanted to be reassured. Even took pleasure in frightening him. With Zena, you just never knew.

She raised her gaze to his and the tawny eyes with their long gold lashes were so full of remorse that Rory decided to believe her fears were real.

'We'll speak to your doctor. And I'll find out from Gary exactly what was in the cigarette. As long as there were never any more.'

'Only that one, I swear. And I haven't smoked even nicotine or had a single sip of alcohol since. I reckoned enough was enough for the poor little sod.'

'We'll get you checked out.' He stood up.

'And Ali?'

Oh Christ, Alex.

'There's no need to upset her. Especially if everything is fine.' He held out a helping hand.

Zena took it and eased herself to her feet. 'Thanks, Rory. Maybe there's more to you than just a cute car, after all.'

16

'Rory.'

'Mmm?' Rory was already in bed, *Autocar* magazine in his hand, gleaming steel curves in his head.

Alex came out of the bathroom wearing a flimsy nightdress and traces of toothpaste. 'What about Edward?'

'Edward who?' His eyes did not stray from the sensual flanks of the Jaguar's sleek body and he wondered if the National Lottery had any plans for dropping one into his lap.

'Just Edward. As a name.'

'Okay.'

Alex could see she was not getting far. She sat down on his side of the bed and closed the magazine for him. That gained his attention. 'For the baby if it's a boy.'

'Edward?'

'Yes.'

'I don't think so.'

'Why not?'

'It was your father's name.'

'Exactly. That's why it would be special.' The idea had come to her a couple of days earlier and she had been mulling it over, trying it for size, fitting it to the baby. 'It would be a reminder.'

'I'm not sure I want that kind of reminder of him. Especially as he was the one who caused your hysterectomy. Not exactly appropriate, is it?' He saw her frown and hurried on with, 'I'd prefer William, after William Lyons of Jaguar. Or Nigel, after good old Mansell. Maybe even Ayrton, after . . .'

'No, Rory,' Alex laughed. 'Not everything need be connected with cars.'

'Anyway, I thought we had settled on James. James Scott Flynn. Formula One World Champion of the future. I can see him up there on the podium with the champagne and applause and the . . .'

'Dream on, you dope.'

She left it for now. Let him get used to the idea. Maybe James Edward Flynn. Yes, she liked that. So would her father. She stood up, allowing Rory to dive back into the glossy pages and went over to the dressing-table to brush her hair. In the mirror she watched the bristles carve paths through the copper mane, raising static and flyaway ends like golden gossamer in the wind. The moment merged with other similar moments, the same motion, the same hair. But belonging to Zena. She used to stand behind her little sister, brushing, combing, plaiting, the object of her attention jiggling and complaining impatiently. Her mother would beam at the finished result and plant a kiss on her elder daughter's forehead. So freely given. Why could one parent shower praise so readily, while the other could only squeeze out a considered, 'Not bad. But . . . ?' There was always the 'But . . .'

Except for Zena, of course. No 'Buts' for Zena. Zena when she was button-bright and only had to turn her laser smile on him to gain her every whim. That was before. Before the shutters came down blocking her out. Before the resentment, the teenage rows and rebellion. Before . . .

Before the conservatory.

Alex put down the brush with a heavier hand than was necessary and shook her head hard, undoing much of her work. Was she shaking memories into her head? Or out of it? She didn't know and didn't want to know. With a quick step, she slipped into bed and snuggled up close to Rory's side, toasting her feet on his warm ones.

'Iceberg,' he moaned.

'How about some fire to melt me?'

Rory smiled and dropped his magazine to the floor.

Alex was in a stuffy barn with her arm up to the elbow inside a pregnant Fresian cow, when her mobile phone rang. It was nearby in her jacket pocket hanging on a nail, but she was not exactly in a position to answer it.

'Get that for me, will you, Andrew?'

Andrew Marsh, the assistant who would be taking over much of Alex's workload when she cut her hours, rummaged in the jacket. He had come out to the farm with her to examine a cow that 'weren't quite right', as the farmer had put it. Off her feed and unwilling to get about much.

'It's Gordon,' Andrew relayed the information with surprise. 'It sounds urgent. He wants to speak to you.'

Alex extracted her arm and peeled off the arm-length glove. What on earth was her boss flapping about now? Not like him to ring her when she was busy. She accepted the phone Andrew was holding out to her.

'Hello, Gordon, what's the problem?'

'Alex, a wee bit of news for you.' His accent had grown thicker with excitement. 'It's that bonnie sister of yours. She rang to say the wee bairn is on its way oot.'

'Gordon, please, please, talk English. You mean the baby's coming?'

'Aye, that's what I said. It's on its way.'

'Ring her for me. Call her back, Gordon. Tell her I'm coming. Right now. Tell her to hang on. I'll be there as fast as I can. To take her to hospital. Have her waters broken? Is she all right? Tell her to keep calm and . . .'

A boisterous, delighted Scottish laugh broke into her tumble of words. 'You're the one to calm down, lass. She sounded fine, in no great hurry. I'll call her and tell her you're on your way.'

'Yes. Please.'

'What about the cow?'

For an absurd second, Alex thought Gordon was insulting her sister and then remembered where her arm had been until two minutes ago. 'Andrew, can you take over from me here?'

'Happy to oblige. Another emergency?'

'Yes, yes, an emergency. A baby.' She grabbed her jacket and bag, and raced for the Clio in the yard. 'My baby.' As she climbed behind the wheel, she realised she was still clutching the telephone. 'Gordon, can you pick up Andrew for me? Or he'll have to walk home from here.'

'Aye, 'course I will. Get off to your bairn and good luck to both you lassies.'

'Thanks.' She snapped the car into gear with an audible crunch.

'And drive sensibly, mind you. Take care.'

'I will. I'll take great care.'

The hospital was hot. Alex dabbed with a flannel at her sister's damp forehead and got ready for the next push. She could recognise in Zena's face when the next contraction was coming and was all prepared to make the effort with her.

'Pant this time,' the midwife instructed. 'No pushing. Baby's not ready yet.'

'I'll push this baby out if it kills me,' Zena shouted but the words came out as a hoarse croak and as the contraction tightened, she panted obediently along with her sister.

Alex was holding her hand tight, riding the pain with her, using the moments of respite to offer a cool flannel or an encouraging smile. It had been going on for what seemed like days, but was in fact only seven hours. Only! Only seven hours of having your body usurped by an earthquake on a Richter scale of at least one hundred. Torn apart, split in two and shredded through a mincer, all under the bright lights and critical gaze of green-coated strangers who had seen it all a thousand times before.

'You're doing great, just great, Zena.'

It was Rory. On the other side of the bed and almost a stranger himself in green cap and gown. Alex realised she must look equally weird in her hospital get-up. Just the idiotic grin on his face and the concern in his dark brown eyes indicated his total involvement in the turmoil of emotions.

Alex had reached home in world record time and found Zena quite casually having a bath and a cup of tea. The contractions had been going for two or three hours.

'Two or three hours! Why didn't you ring the surgery earlier? Come on, let's get to the hospital.'

'Don't be silly. It'll be ages yet. It's more comfortable at home than having blue starched nurses peering at my insides on a hard

NHS bed.' She balanced her saucer on the mound and sipped the tea. 'No rush.'

Alex had contained her impatience and taken her timing from Zena. It was only when the waters broke that she put her foot down, both with Zena and the car. She had rung Rory to warn him they were leaving and he met them at Princess Margaret's Hospital to begin the helpless wait, while Zena's body was put through the grinder.

'Okay, push this time.' The midwife offered a cheery smile of encouragement. 'Push hard.'

Alex took a deep breath with Zena and together they went through the practised routine. Zena's moans and groans increased in volume and Rory held her other hand between his to give her something to crunch down on. It went on and on. Longer than Alex thought possible. How could the baby survive such a battering? Or Zena? Her sister's face was drained beyond exhaustion, her eyes stupefied with pain and her bottom lip cracked and swollen where she had bitten into it with the effort.

How could she put her own sister through this hell?

'Pant, Zena, pant,' she urged.

'Just a little nick now, so that you won't tear,' the midwife explained.

Zena shrieked in agony and thrust forward, groping to protect herself and earning herself a mild rebuke. 'Don't, dear, it's sterile conditions down here.'

'Bugger the sterile conditions,' Zena bellowed and collapsed back on the pillows as the next contraction took hold.

Alex looked at the hand squeezing her own so fiercely. The veins stood out like snakes under the skin and it was damp and hot to touch. She stroked it gently. Whatever we're paying you, Zena, it's not enough. Not by a long way. For this you deserve . . . what? A medal? A sun-bleached holiday? No, nowhere near enough.

For this you deserve a baby.

The thought shocked Alex and for a moment she lost her concentration on the breathing. Don't be foolish, she doesn't even want the baby. She held on to that certainty with a vice-like grip and relief trickled like sweat down her spine.

But what Zena did deserve were the three months with the

baby. No question of that. This torture needed at least that to wipe it from the brain cells. Three months, that's all. Not much to ask. For the first time Alex was genuinely happy to be able to hand over that tiny gift to her sister in return for her breath-taking generosity. The hand in hers seemed to die as the contraction ebbed and Zena wilted on to the pillow once more, face streaked with sweat and tears. Alex watched Rory chivy her with a laugh and a joke, and receive a flicker of a smile in response. Thank God he was here.

The last stage passed quickly, as if Alex's mind had jumbled up its clock and only skidded to a halt when Rory yelled like a five-year-old waiting for a train, 'It's coming, it's coming. I can see it.'

'It's too bloody big,' Zena shrieked.

Alex panted through the last contractions with her sister and suddenly the baby was there. Airways cleared, squeaks of protest uttered and then at Zena's breast. A boy. Greasy, snuffling perfection. Through tears, hugs and kisses, congratulations were bestowed and emotions allowed to break loose.

When Alex held the baby in her arms, she wanted the world to stop. Right there. Trailing its clouds of glory.

'He's gorgeous, Alex. Absolutely gorgeous.' Joanna Donelli scooped the tiny bundle out of the Moses basket with a casual ease that Alex admired. 'He's a stunner, isn't he? Your hair, Rory's eyes and skin like ice-cream.' She danced the baby in front of her, cooed maternally at him and received a froth of bubbles in response. 'Look at him kick. A footballer, if ever I saw one.'

'I know. I've told Rory to put his name down for Spurs.'

Joanna laughed. 'Jamie Edward Flynn, you'll be a heart-breaker. Already your mother can't take her greedy eyes off you.'

She handed him over to Alex, who cradled him effortlessly in the crook of her arm and leaned a smiling face over him. The brown eyes latched on to her mouth and slowly edged up until they reached her eyes. Another puff of bubbles escaped and was accompanied by a small snort of pleasure. They were in the garden, seated lazily on loungers under the shade of the old apple tree on the front lawn. Hamilton was curled up at Alex's feet, keeping a wary blue eye on the intrusive bundle that made the strange noises and smelt enticingly of milk. The day was warm with a scattering of half-hearted clouds that made Alex think of the pack of cottonwool balls in Jamie's cupboard. But then, these days everything made her think of something connected with Jamie.

From the newly finished sandpit came a shriek of laughter as Georgie and Louis endeavoured to carve a tunnel through their carefully constructed castle, only to find gravity had other ideas. Georgie flicked a spadeful at Horatio who had been tempted in by the expanse of soft sand and was just digging himself a neat hole. Ears flat back, he fled into the shrubbery.

Joanna smiled and shook her head indulgently. 'Monsters the pair of them. Just you wait, Alex. Enjoy the peace while it lasts.'

'Angelica seems no trouble.'

Joanna's scepticism melted. She beamed blissfully at her daughter who was merrily chortling to herself on a rug as she played with the variety of rattles and cuddly toys that had been showered on Jamie. 'Just goes to show the superiority of the female gender exists right from birth.'

'Or maybe that the second round of offspring is more contented because the mother is more relaxed? A happy mother makes a happy child.'

Joanna laughed and rolled a squishy chiming ball back on to the rug. 'Maybe so. You've been reading your Penelope Leach again.'

'Of course. I used to be a good boy scout.'

'Always prepared?'

'You should have seen my granny knots.'

'Talking of being prepared, what are you going to do when your sister leaves? About looking after Jamie, I mean.'

Alex watched the miniature lashes slowly droop, shudder awake and then subside into instant sleep. She felt the flimsy chest sigh and settle closer into the curve of her body.

'That's all arranged.'

'Oh yes? Who's going to be there when you're out vetting all over the place?'

'There's a girl who works in our office. Lizzie Baker. She's absolutely marvellous at caring for animals and when I was moaning about what I was going to do, she offered her services.'

'As nanny?'

'Yes, part-time. I intend to keep it to a minimum, as I can shift my duty rota around to fit in as much as possible with Jamie. Gordon is being typically helpful about it. He's an angel disguised as a daddy-long-legs.'

'Alex, I know animals are your bag, so to speak, but are you really going to use someone who is trained to stick thermometers up poodles' arses as the carer of your child?'

Alex looked up from Jamie's sleeping face with surprise. 'Yes, of course. She's very good.'

Joanna shook her head in exasperation. 'Good with wounded animals does not necessarily mean good with kids.'

Alex smiled at her friend's scandalised expression. 'Of course it does. She gives them so much love.'

'You're crazy. Why not get a trained nanny?'

'Joanna, I know this girl. She's good. Not some stranger off an agency list. We work well together at the surgery and I know we will get on easily together with Jamie. So stop fretting that she'll feed him dog-biscuits.'

'And Zena? What does she say about it?'

'Nothing. She has passed no comment. Lizzie has been up to the house a number of times already to get used to Jamie and how we do things. She's even got her own car. But no, Zena hasn't said anything.'

'But you think you have her blessing?'

'Yes.' It was just a beat too slow in coming.

Joanna pounced on it. 'Problems?'

'Not exactly.'

'Too many cooks in the kitchen?'

'Something like that.'

'Two mothers and only one child, I'm not surprised. You'd need a Solomon to keep the peace.'

Alex shook her head. 'No, don't go putting words in my mouth. Typical journalist, as always.'

Joanna laughed and shouted to the boys to stop rubbing sand in each other's hair. The sun sneaked out from behind a cloud and a butterfly mistook the scarlet ladybird on Jamie's outfit for a flower. It landed on his chest, rustled its wings in disappointment, reeled its tongue back in and took off for more promising fare where the asters waved their heads on the other side of the lawn.

'Where's your dear sister now?'

'She's in bed. Catching up on lack of sleep. You must remember the bone-shaking exhaustion of the early days all too clearly yourself.' Alex added sweetly, 'But of course you didn't have me doing all the dogsbody stuff for you.'

Joanna sat up, delighted. 'Lazy old milch cow, is she? Feeds the child and leaves the rest to you? You should remind her you're a busy vet with other demands on your time and attention. That would sort her out.'

'I have no intention of "sorting her out".' Alex stroked the gingery velvet on the downy head. 'She's very good with Jamie and that's what matters.'

That was in fact the only thing that mattered, Alex reminded herself. The rest was minor irritation, nothing more. If she was the one doing the washing, ironing, nappy changing and bedmaking, then that was fair. As it should be. Zena was performing her agreed role. Pregnancy, birth and three months' breast milk, antibodies and all. That was the deal. No mention of nappies. And when Zena was asleep like now, Alex could assume the role of sole mother, besotted and milk-stained. No sharing with her younger sister. Like she had been forced to do with her roller skates.

That thought jumped in from nowhere and Alex squashed it abruptly, stamped on it. Unconsciously her bare foot descended on Hamilton's skinny tail and the cat leapt off the lounger with a squawk of protest.

'Sorry, Hammy.'

Sharing with her sister. Was it so hard? There had been no problems of that sort during the pregnancy. So why now?

Because Jamie was here. Soft and snug in their arms.

Shared.

Like the blue and yellow roller skates. They had been Alex's, but she had almost grown out of them. Almost, but not quite. Daddy had ordered that Zena should be allowed to use them as

she had almost grown into them. Almost, but not quite. They
had been Alex's pride and joy. Until Zena scuffed the toe caps
and spilt glue all down one side, that is.

Alex was cross with herself for still minding. Abruptly she
stood up and placed the sleeping infant into his basket in the
shade. She pulled the hood up against the slight breeze and
turned away from him. What the hell was she doing? Some
kind of penance?

She found her sharp-eyed friend watching her closely, so
gave a smokescreen smile and offered her another iced drink.
'I could do with a spot of cooling down myself. How about you,
Joanna?'

Alex was not sleeping well. Each night she was woken by hungry
cries for the two o'clock feed and more often than not, she was
still counting Old Macdonald's sheep when it was time for the
six o'clock encore. She waited until she heard Zena pad along
to the nursery and then would roll out of bed and brew up a pot
of coffee for Zena and herself, careful to keep her sister's weak.
While Zena crawled back into bed, Alex would go through the
nappy routine and croon childhood lullabies until Jamie was
contentedly asleep in his cot once more. She then collapsed
either into bed or a hot bath, depending on whether she was due
at the surgery or not. She knew only too well how tetchy she was
at times becoming and how it took all Rory's good-humoured
patience to winkle her out of it. But she was just too tense to
break the spiral.

It was Maddy who brought her to her senses.

'Going to miss that sister of yours when she goes, aren't
you?'

They were attending to a duck that had been brought in from
the River Kennet, fishing line entwined so tightly round one of
its legs that it had embedded into the flesh. Alex was snipping
gently at the nylon while Maddy held the bird quiet on the
examination table.

'Miss her?'

'Yes. She tells me she will be leaving in a couple of months.'

'Yes, that's right.'

She eased the cutters behind another strand of nylon and snipped it free. The wide rubbery foot wriggled in protest and the bill tried to pluck at her hand but was restrained by Maddy's firm grip around the bird's neck.

Yes. Of course she would miss Zena. Oddly, it had not occurred to her before. So obsessed had she been with anticipation of becoming the one and only mother to her son that she had forgotten how much Zena had come to mean to her. Not only was Zena her sister, but she had given her the most precious gift on earth.

'Yes, you're right, Maddy. I will miss her. And so will Jamie. And he's bound to create when he has to change over to formula milk.'

'He'll survive.'

'I'm sure he will,' Alex laughed and managed to snip at another couple of strands. The flesh was inflamed over the fishing line and would need a few days of antibiotics before the bird could be released. He hissed at her ungratefully and tried to stamp his wounded foot.

Yes, they'd all survive. Even though a guilty, selfish part of Alex did not want Zena coming anywhere near Jamie in the future, she knew that it was unreasonable. She was just being over-defensive. Self-protective. But at the same time she did not wish to lose her younger sister. Not now they had got to know each other after all those years apart. Become friends again.

'Have you got a sister, Maddy?'

'Used to. Up in Birmingham. Dead now.' She tucked her arm more firmly around the duck's wings, as if to tuck in the memories.

'I'm sorry. Were you close?'

'No. Hardly ever saw each other. Birthday and Christmas cards was about the lot. Never got on, not even as kids. We had different aims in life.' The regret was not quite hidden beneath the indifference and she ran her thumb down the throat of soft white feathers, smoothing away pain. Both hers and the duck's.

'That's a bit like Zena and myself. We had some good times together when we were young, but from the beginning we were headed in different directions. Wanted different things.' One last cut and the leg was free.

'Bloody fishermen,' Maddy scowled. 'Should have their lines wound round their own necks. Soon buck up their ideas about leaving it around, that would.' She relaxed her hold on the irritated white neck and he rewarded her with a nip that drew blood. 'Soon be over, old chap. Calm down now.'

While Alex drew up the antibiotic injection, Maddy said as if there had been no change of topic, 'It seems to me you and that sister of yours wanted exactly the same thing. Not different at all.'

Alex looked up sharply. 'What do you mean by that?'

'Nothing you don't know already.'

'What has Zena been saying to you?'

'Nothing.'

'One day, I swear, you'll be burnt at the stake, Maddy and I'll be the first to light the touch-paper.'

Maddy gave a satisfied chuckle. 'It's like acid.'

'What is?'

'Jealousy.'

'I'll be coming for you with torches and the wood in a minute. All sisters experience some jealousy. It's perfectly natural. They're always compared with each other. Aunts, uncles, friends, teachers and even parents, all compare and contrast. But sisters also have a deep bond. It's indestructible. They may bury it, stamp on it and ignore it, but they can't break it.'

Maddy shook her head, green eyes stern. 'You have too much faith in people.'

'Better too much than too little.'

Over the increasingly vociferous white head, the two women exchanged smiles that agreed to differ.

It was later that afternoon that Alex went in search of Lizzie. She found her sitting in a chair in the office, bottle-feeding a young fox cub. An anti-hunt protestor had brought in a litter of four cubs after the parents were shredded by hounds and Lizzie had volunteered to become surrogate vixen. Unfortunately, one by one most of them had died, unable to adapt to life without their mother. All except one. Bright-eyed Rufus had shaken off any initial doubts and was getting stuck in to the new milk supply.

'Lizzie, how do you feel about coming over to the house again tomorrow afternoon? To get to know Jamie better. Maddy has reminded me it's only another eight weeks and then it'll just be you and me.'

Lizzie looked quickly back to the contented ball of fluff on her lap. 'I don't think it's a good idea. Not while your sister is there.'

'Why not? What has she said to you?'

'Not much.' She glanced up at Alex's face and immediately felt guilty at the alarm she had put there. 'Honestly, nothing very much. That's the trouble, she hardly speaks to me at all. But she makes it plain she doesn't want me there. Won't let me hold Jamie at all and just gives me jobs to do that keep me out of the room.'

Alex sat down. 'I'm sorry, Lizzie. That must have been extremely unpleasant for you. I had no idea.'

'But I could drive over when you are at home. Zena couldn't object if you gave me Jamie to hold, could she?' The young face was so eager to become involved.

Alex thought about Zena. Zena and Jamie. Quietly she said, 'I'll have a word with my sister. And sort out what the problem is. She's very possessive about him, I know. But that is probably because she'll be leaving him soon. It's not going to be easy for her, so maybe we'll have to cut down on the visits for now.'

Lizzie's disappointment was obvious. Alex gave her a reassuring smile. 'It's only for a few weeks. Anyway, I'll speak to Zena and maybe find it's just a misunderstanding.'

But as Alex left the office to prepare for a tooth extraction on an elderly pekinese, the young girl's hopeful, 'Yes, just a misunderstanding', found no answering echo in her own mind.

17

As Alex drove home, she welcomed the warm breeze that carried the scent of new-mown hay in through the open window. The summer had wrapped itself in its customary bright costume of vivid greens, cobalt skies and the flashy scarlets of roses, geraniums and poppies. She was floating along on the sound of Coleman Hawkins' tenor sax in 'Stella by Starlight' and had released her hair from the scarf so that it ruffled like an unruly copper halo in the breeze.

The discovery that she was going to miss Zena had altered her mood. The minor irritants and tensions had dissolved like salt in water and she was aware only of affection. Even the business with Lizzie was excusable when viewed through this rosy hue. She laughed at herself, at the emotional Big Dipper she was riding and wondered if Zena was going through the same. Adults were supposed to be able to build safety breakwaters to ward off childhood emotions but at the moment hers had definitely been pounded flat by the waves.

She found Zena in the kitchen, making herself a tuna sandwich and Jamie asleep in his carrycot on the table. She was wearing her kimono, though it was five-thirty in the afternoon, and her hair was wet from a shower. Alex could not help noticing the gingery roots creeping through. Genes making themselves felt.

'You're back earlier than I expected.' Zena's greeting was not exactly welcoming.

'Gordon helped out, so I got through my shift quicker. How's your day been?' She leant over the carrycot and kissed the delicately smooth forehead. Like a warm, firm peach but a few milk spots on one cheek. His eyelids did not even flutter. She had wanted them to open so that she could pick him up.

'Don't wake him, for God's sake. He's been grizzly all afternoon and has only just gone off.' Zena was obviously not in the best of moods.

'You go and rest. I'll keep an eye on him.'

'His cot bedding needs changing. It's wet.'

'Don't worry, I'll do it.' Better get the Lizzie discussion over with now. 'By the way, how do you feel about Lizzie coming over to help? She seems to think you don't like her being here.'

Zena shrugged. 'I don't.' She cut herself another slice of bread.

'Why not?'

'I don't need her.'

'No, not while I'm here to do everything for you. But when you're gone, you know perfectly well I will need her, so it's better if she and Jamie get to know each other now. We've been over this.'

Zena slapped butter on to the bread. 'What you do after I'm gone is your business. While I'm here, I don't want her around.' Suddenly she turned round and fixed Alex with the big, pleading eyes that turned the clock back twenty years at a jump. Please Ali, get Tinker down from the tree; please Ali, lift me up on to the high wall; please Ali, tie my laces.

'Please, Ali.'

Alex was quite willing to give the old, comforting smile. 'Okay, if it means that much to you.'

'It does.' Zena waved the butter-knife in the air to emphasise her point. 'Jamie and I haven't got long and we can manage easily without her. Anyway, he's happiest with just us. Just you and me.'

'And Rory.'

'Yes, of course. And his father.'

'I'll go and change, and then take over from you.'

'Don't forget the cot.'

'I won't.' Or the machine load of washing. Or the dishes in the sink. Or the meal to cook. 'Go and watch *Neighbours* or something and you'll feel in a better mood.' A dose of fantasy-reality always cheered her sister up.

'Good idea. I'll take my sandwiches in with me.'

'Better take the carrycot as well or Hamilton will be curled up in there like a hot-water bottle with him.'

'Blasted cats.'

Alex laughed, stole a bite of one of Zena's sandwiches and went upstairs humming Coleman Hawkins' 'You'd be so nice to come home to'.

It was Sunday afternoon and Rory had suggested a walk as there was no Grand Prix until next week. Despite the high cloud cover that made the day feel as if it were wrapped in silver foil, the air was warm and still, perfect for pram pushing. Zena opted to stay behind watching the omnibus EastEnders, as she had missed one of the episodes during the week.

'Sure you won't join us?' Alex encouraged and received a nudge in the ribs from her husband.

'No, you can have my share of the fresh air. Anyway, I don't fancy all those gnats divebombing around out there. It's the Square for me.'

Out in the village lanes, Alex was amused by Rory's antics. He insisted on being in charge of pushing the pram and the moment he spotted anyone else out on a walk or at work in their gardens, he performed manoeuvres that would have done credit to Silverstone so that he could proudly strut his parental stuff under their noses. When the local milkman's wife took a breather from trimming her hedge and admired the son and heir with appropriate expressions of delight, she put the cherry on top of the icing for him.

'He's the spitting image of you, Mr Flynn, the spitting image. Got your lady wife's gorgeous hair of course, but look at those eyes. Yours all over. Bright as two buttons, aren't they?'

She dangled a dirty finger, with more earth under its nail than Rory had in his vegetable patch, in front of the eyes under discussion. A chubby star of a hand grasped it and hauled it towards an open mouth, sucking motion already underway.

'Thank you, Mrs Pilcher, but we can't stay longer,' Alex interrupted, elbowing her husband into motion, so that the finger drifted out of reach.

Two lawn mowers, a dog walker and a cyclist later, Rory was

positively preening with pleasure and wondering if anyone had ever fitted an electric motor to a pram.

'You old show-off,' Alex teased. 'Kenneth Branagh has nothing on you when it comes to milking an audience.'

'Why hide your light under a bushel when it is – how did old Jim Farne put it just now? – "shiny as a silver sixpence"?'

'I preferred Mrs Lowell's "cuddlier than a koala" myself.'

'That's only to remind you she's just come back from visiting her daughter in Ozzieland.'

'Parents can't resist basking in their offspring's reflected glory, I suppose.'

'Quite right too. I certainly intend to when Jamie is World Champion racing driver.' He grinned at the earnest little face looking up at him so attentively. 'You'll share the champagne with your old dad, won't you, Jamie?'

Alex laughed. 'Dream on. But talking of champagne, we should be celebrating today.'

'Celebrating what?' Rory pulled into the side of the road to allow a car to pass.

'Jamie's birthday. He's exactly a month old today.'

'One whole month! Wow, almost old enough to sign with Williams Team.'

'Might have a spot of trouble reaching the accelerator pedal though.'

'You're right.'

'That he'll need a shorter car?'

'No. That we should celebrate. We haven't been out for ages, so let's go into town for a meal and live it up a little. After all, only once in his life is a fellow just one month old. Better make the most of it.'

'Sounds like a great idea.'

'A table for two and champagne on ice.'

'Three.'

'Three bottles of champers? Isn't that a bit over the top?'

Alex smiled. 'Don't pretend you don't know what I mean. That ostrich act gets you nothing but a beakful of dirt.'

Rory manoeuvred the pram round an elderly labrador that had emerged on arthritic limbs from a front gate. 'I suppose we have to?'

'Yes.' Alex gave the old dog a pat. 'Hello, Jasper. Bones a bit creaky today?' A pink tongue whispered over the back of her hand. 'We must include Zena, as it is her son's birthday we are celebrating.'

'Do you think she'll want to come?'

'Ask her and find out.'

'What about a babysitter?'

'I'll see whether Lizzie is free. If she is, she'd be happy to oblige, I know. We needn't be out for long, so that it would fit in between feeds. It would make a nice change. For all of us.'

Rory performed a neat handbrake turn, spinning the pram on its rear wheels to face in the reverse direction. 'Let's go and ask your dear sister then.' As they ambled back the way they had come, he admitted, 'It wouldn't really be fair to leave her out of it. She has stuck faithfully to her side of the bargain.'

'So far.'

Another car squeezed past with a wave of the driver's hand.

'Alex, you're putting yourself through the wringer about that for nothing. She's not the baby-rearing type, I'm certain.'

'But look at her with Jamie. She loves him, Rory. How can she give him up?'

'Yes, she loves him. But she loves herself more.' He took hold of his wife's hand and placed it on the pram's chrome handle, warm in the afternoon heat. 'Don't think you can wriggle out of it so easily. We're stuck with this little monster for another twenty years at least.' He smiled contentedly. 'Can you see Zena agreeing to that kind of commitment?'

'No. No, I can't. You're right, Rory, it's not her style at all.'

'She'll take the money and run.'

'Are you so sure?'

'One hundred per cent sure. Anyway, even Zena would not do something like that to her own sister.'

'My, my. Gone up in your estimation, hasn't she?'

'To be honest, yes, she has. She has stuck to our bargain and I have to admit, she looks after Jamie well. Maybe this whole experience has helped her grow up.'

Alex looked at their child and could not resist the tug of gratitude towards her sister. 'Mmm, maybe.'

The dinner was at the Silver Trout in Marlborough. It was conveniently nearby, not too pricey and served up an excellent range of fresh seafood. Both sisters turned heads as they entered the bar and Rory was amused by the effort they had both made to outdo each other. Alex was wearing make-up tonight to emphasise her attractions, larger eyes and higher cheekbones than her sister, and her hair hung in a glossy flame-coloured curtain around her bare shoulders. She was wearing a silky summer frock, emerald green and sleeveless, cut straight and short to show up her boyish hips and full breasts. He had only seen her in it once before at a friend's wedding and had forgotten its existence until now. At her throat was her mother's locket, red gold to match her hair. When, in the bedroom, she had stood before him and asked how she looked, he had wanted to peel the dress off, silky inch by silky inch and make love to her in just the locket. Later tonight, he promised himself.

There had been too many nights recently when she had been too dog-weary to do anything except sleep, but tonight she was looking bright-eyed and bushy-tailed. For now he had to be content with a tantalising touch with fingertips and an inadequate 'Stunning'.

'When you've picked up your jaw and stopped drooling, shall we go downstairs? Lizzie will be here any minute.' She kissed him with deliberate provocation, disentangled herself from his clutches and hurried down to answer the doorbell.

Zena, of course, was late.

While Alex took Lizzie up to Jamie's room, Rory poured himself a good belt of whisky and sat down to enjoy it. Alex had offered to do the driving this evening so that he could indulge in a few over the balloon limit. At least she wasn't on call tonight, so there was no risk of her disappearing from under his nose. Especially in that dress. He was half way through his scotch, looking out the window at the sun sliding gracefully behind the tops of the old beech wood, when he heard her come into the room, smelt her perfume, the Chanel No 5 he bought her one

Christmas and which she almost never wore. Except sometimes in bed.

He turned and for a split second was confused. Alex had changed into a black dress and had blonde hair. Then his brain unscrambled the signals and it was Zena standing before him. Zena in a black, clinging dress with neckline low enough to display her costly assets, black high heels and a choker necklace of glossy jet. Her blonde hair was freshly washed and full of bounce, cut to just below jawline now. Heavily kohled eyes, bright red lips and the perfume wafting around her in waves completed the picture of sophisticated, seductive elegance.

She was waiting for his comment.

'You look lovely, Zena.'

'Lovely? Is that all? What happened to absolutely knock-out or just plain drop-dead gorgeous?'

'English understatement has a lot to be said for it. You do look lovely.' He stood up. 'Can I pour you a drink?'

For a moment she was tempted. 'No, better not. I'll stick to Perrier now and save my one glass of wine for the meal. Don't want Jamie singing "Roll out the Barrel" all night, do we?'

'Definitely not.' Rory poured her a tall glass of Perrier and added ice and lemon to spice it up.

'Cheers,' she said, raising her glass to him. 'Here's to playing Happy Families.'

'To happy families.'

They smiled at each other over their glasses, both aware of the world of difference between their two toasts.

In the restaurant, which was as always fairly full on a Sunday evening, the sisters were sitting side by side opposite Rory, their faces a disconcerting mixture of similarity and sharp contrasts. The same high forehead, straight nose and long slender neck, creamy skin lightly freckled now by the summer sun. Zena's hair was honey blonde and her lips fuller than Alex's, courtesy of USA clinic collogen, but the main difference was in the eyes. Rory loved his wife's eyes. Deep chocolate brown, clear and full of warmth, with a mischievous humour in them that always kept him guessing. Whereas her sister's had never lost their tawny lioness challenge. Dangerous eyes. Attractive in their promise of excitement. But he knew which ones he was happy to be married to.

'So the library scheme is going along faster than you expected?' Alex was asking, but Rory was having difficulty concentrating. The two faces kept getting in the way of his thoughts. Probably the couple of large whiskies in the bar had not exactly helped.

'Yes, they like what we're doing so much that they're pushing the finance through quickly. Paula has worked hard on it. I'm impressed by how well she's coping.'

'What about Gary?' Zena enquired almost innocently.

'His work is always good.' Rory did not want to talk about Gary in front of Zena.

'I haven't seen him for months,' Alex commented. 'Not since that time at the Duck & Feather. Why don't you invite him over with his latest conquest for supper one evening? He's always good company.'

'Yes, Rory, why don't you?' Zena echoed with a smile.

It still rankled. Rory drained his wine glass. 'Not just now. We often have Jamie bouncing around in the evening and I prefer my son's company to yet more architect chatter. I get enough of that at the office.'

Alex stared at Rory with surprise. 'Trouble brewing? Gary been putting his foot in it?'

'It's not his foot that I worry about.'

Zena burst out laughing and Alex looked from one face to the other. After studying her husband for a moment, she let the subject drop.

'Maybe later then,' she said and turned easily to her sister. 'Talking of later, have you decided where you intend to settle down eventually?'

'Not really. But it won't be in the middle of fields and cow pats like this, that's for sure.'

'How about London? Or is that too expensive?'

'I was thinking of Bath as a possibility. Nice shops.'

Rory refilled his glass. 'No plans to return to America then?'

Zena laughed again. 'No, not a chance of packing me off across the water again, dear brother-in-law. Certainly not on what you've paid me so far. You will just have to get used to the fact that you're stuck with me. Like a wasp to fly-paper.'

'Bath isn't far away,' Alex remarked. 'It means you could see plenty of Jamie.'

Zena smiled at her. 'Exactly.'

Alex concentrated on her trout for a moment, but when she looked up her sister was still watching her.

'Don't mind, do you, Ali? If I visit Jamie.'

'It's natural that you should want to see him. He's your son. Bound together by the undeniable bond of blood. But he's also mine. Bound by love. And it's natural that I should want that bond between Jamie and myself to be allowed to develop strongly. So yes, of course you must visit him. But not too often at first.'

To her surprise, Zena nodded understandingly. 'No problem.' She leant over and kissed Alex's cheek. 'Don't worry, I won't make trouble for you, I promise.'

Rory and Alex exchanged glances of relief and the conversation flowed more freely after that. Rory ordered another bottle of champagne with which they toasted each other, then their son and the future.

'What will you do, Zena? Rory and I have a future mapped out with Jamie, but what about you?'

Rory looked at his wife's brown eyes, so full of concern for her sister, and felt like leaning across the table and kissing her, but thought better of it. He picked up his glass, then placed it down again carefully. Perhaps he'd had enough just for the moment. His gaze moved from his wife to the copycat face beside her and he heard his wife's laugh come from the other, fuller lips. Zena had been saying something about a cat having nine lives and that she still had plenty to spare. She licked her lips and looked exactly like a fluffy tortoiseshell that had just finished the cream. Rory was surprised to find himself feeling distinctly maudlin about what his sister-in-law had done for them. Despite the fact that he knew she had made use of them to cushion and finance her life for over a year, the payment she had given in return more than balanced the debt.

'Zena, you're a brick,' he announced.

The two women looked at him askance.

'A prick?' Zena asked.

'No, no. A brick. You're a real brick.'

'And you're a real drunk,' Alex chuckled and took his hand in hers. Hers felt soft and warm, and Rory liked it wrapped round his own.

'Mrs Flynn?'

The restaurant manager hovered in his funeral suit at Alex's elbow.

'Yes?'

'There is a telephone call for you.'

Alarm leapt at Alex's throat. The only person who knew where they were was Lizzie. Lizzie with Jamie. She stood up and almost ran to the reception desk.

'Hello?'

'Alex, thank the Lord I've found you.'

Relief kicked loose the muscles in her knees and she held on to the counter for support. It was Gordon Tamworth.

'What is it, Gordon? You sound upset.'

'Aye, lass. I got this telephone number from Lizzie. I need you in surgery right now. Thank God you're here in Marlborough already.'

'What's happened?'

'A car crash. An estate car with four dogs in the back, a horse-box trailing a mare and foal. And another two dogs. They were running loose on the A4 and caused the whole accident. I know you're not on call but . . .'

'I'll be right there.'

'Thanks, lassie. Be quick, mind.'

Alex returned to the table and explained the emergency that meant she had to leave. They had in fact all finished their meal except for dessert, which Zena and Rory were more than willing to forgo. Rory settled the bill at speed, gathered up jackets and they made a dash for the car. It was nearly nine-fifteen and just beginning to grow dark enough for headlights. Zena drove the Clio to the surgery at the end of the High Street and even in the rush Rory was surprised to note how well she handled the car. As Alex jumped out, she called to Rory, 'Send Lizzie over here as soon as you get home. I'll need her help.'

'Give us a call when you need to be picked up.'

'Don't worry about that. I'm sure Gordon will drop me home when it's all over.'

Rory watched his wife run up the path to the door, her green dress unsuited to such activity, riding up her hips. The door swung open the moment she reached it and swallowed her into its world of blood and bones. Rory felt bereft.

'Stupid bloody dogs,' Zena grumbled as she slipped the engine smoothly into gear and headed for the Pewsey road.

Rory told Lizzie the tale of horror and passed on his wife's plea for help.

'Okay, I'll go straight there. Not a murmur out of Jamie all evening.' As she hurried out to her elderly Fiesta, it was not just the approaching gloom in the sky that robbed her cheeks of their colour. Alex had told Rory of her reaction to the sight of blood. Poor Lizzie. No wonder she preferred nannying. Not a pleasant prospect in store for her. Not a pleasant prospect for any of them at the surgery. Rory waved her car out of the drive and stood for a moment looking out at the garden. Slowly it was hiding its boisterous summer colours behind the veil of darkness that seemed to creep up from the ground and spread its tentacles up into the trees. It appeared mildly odd to him that the garden was swaying fractionally in front of his eyes, a gentle rocking motion that made him think of a hammock.

'You need a coffee, Rory. Black and strong.'

Zena was standing behind him. The hall light was on and had painted a golden halo around her head. A more unlikely angel he could not imagine. The thought made him smile broadly.

'Premature dementia has obviously set in. I always knew you were teetering on the brink and tonight you've dived off the cliff.'

'You're the one talking nonsense, Zena, not me,' but the smile had somehow got stuck on his face.

'Go and sit down and I'll make some coffee to wash out all that crap inside you, you piss-artist.' She laughed, Alex's laugh, and added, 'You're not exactly the aggressive type after you've had a few, are you? More in the lost lamb line.'

Rory walked as near steadily as damn it into the sitting-room and found himself in Alex's chair. Zena had been babbling rubbish. He would take no notice. His eyes closed and immediately he discovered that a picture of his wife was printed on the inside of his eyelids, breasts and hips shifting invitingly under the green silk dress. The dress would be covered now. By a stiff androgenous overall that denied the existence of any curves or soft crannies that smelt of Chanel No 5. Antiseptic and anaesthetic would be her perfume now. And the musky scent of blood.

He admired her ability to deal with death. To snatch life from its jaws and present it like a casual gift to its owner. But he knew the toll on her was sometimes high. Tonight would be one of those times, he was certain. She would nail down the lid on her emotions while she got on with the job, efficient and skilled, but eventually, like Pandora's box, they must fly out and do who knew what damage? Rory felt an overwhelming urge to protect her from herself.

'Coffee.'

His eyes opened unwillingly and registered that Zena was placing a cup on the table beside him. It smelt black and very Brazilian.

'Thanks.' Then he noticed the snifter of brandy beside it.

Zena let her gaze wander over him assessingly, but passed no comment. She moved over to the oak shelving to the right of the fireplace and rummaged among the stack of CDs. Rory watched her skip over Alex's jazz pile and concentrate on his classical collection. As she bent slightly over to find what she was hunting for, her dress rose, giving Rory a full view of the backs of her thighs. They were smooth and slender and went on forever. The black dress clung to the curve of her bottom and it could as easily have been Alex's rear. Except it wasn't green.

Rory distracted himself with a few sips of the brandy but was still watching the hypnotic movements of the black dress when the music started. It was Debussy. *La Mer*. His favourite.

'Dance?'

She was standing before him holding out a hand and a smile.

'To this? It's sacrilege.'

'Don't be so crabby.' She reached forward, took his hand and hauled him to his feet. For an instant, he swayed as his head reeled with the sudden movement, but immediately her arms were around him.

'A gentle swim in the waves,' she murmured against his cheek and guided him unnoticeably into the middle of the room.

She felt soft in his arms and smelt good. How long was it since he had danced? He couldn't remember the last time. And certainly never at home. The roar of the sea rose and crashed around him, giving him the electric shiver down the spine that Debussy never failed to trigger.

'Good, huh?' she whispered, her head nestled against his shoulder and arms linked behind his neck as they slowly circled the room.

'Mmm.' Her hair smelt of honey and feathered his cheek with its silkiness. Her bare arms looked fragile. He turned his head and let his lips touch very briefly the golden skin of her shoulder. It was warm and infinitely soft. She responded with a purr and a faint arching of her back that moulded her body closer against his. He was immediately aware of his own body reacting without heed for the lack of intention inside his head. He had no doubt that she was equally aware. She was humming under her breath, following the piano's ebb and flow and moving with easy grace very slowly against him. Her back under his hands felt hot, as if an internal combustion started up an engine inside her and its heat was flooding over them like the waves of Debussy. He knew it was time to release her. Before he got burnt.

He closed his eyes. Immediately Alex came dancing in her green dress into his arms and he could feel her soft breath on his cheek . . .

'Waaah.'

The cry came from upstairs. It was Jamie.

Zena froze.

Rory instantly took his arms from around her. The veil of dove-grey mist in his head tore apart with a shriek that rocketed into his brain. He took two steps back from Zena and a deep breath that was like cold water. He could feel the sweat on his scalp.

'It's Jamie.'

The cry came again and this time Zena moved. 'Feed time.' She looked up at Rory from under long lashes. 'How about a raincheck?'

'No, I think not.' He offered her a polite smile. 'But thanks for the dance.'

'Any time. All you have to do is whistle.' She walked over to the door, swinging her hips at him, then looked back over her shoulder. 'Just put your lips together and blow.' With a chuckle, she disappeared.

Rory felt sick.

He turned off the music, carried the brandy and the coffee to the kitchen and threw them both down the sink. He drank a long glass of water, turned the lights off except the one in the hall which he left on for Alex, and steered himself upstairs. He dumped his clothes on a chair, collapsed into bed and was instantly asleep.

It seemed like hours later that he felt Alex come to bed. He had not heard her arrive home and did not wake until she slipped under the duvet beside him. He recognised her cold feet and faint hint of Chanel.

The brandy fumes still breathed a fog in his mind and all he could muster was a grunt in greeting. Even then he wasn't certain it hadn't stayed in his head. Her body curled up to his like a close-fitting glove and her hand at his groin reminded him of the green dress and his earlier promise to himself about later. With little coaxing, he rolled on top of her, his lips seeking her mouth, hand securing a breast. Her hips rose to his, legs wrapped round him, fingers touching, caressing and in the dim fog of fumes, tiny sparks of warning began to flash.

It was Alex. But it wasn't Alex.

It wasn't her mouth.

It wasn't her breast.

He jerked back from her but the legs held him tight.

'Alex?'

'Mmmm.' The perfume wrapped itself round his brain. Her fingers soothed and guided, and as he entered her and felt her hips buck under him, he knew it wasn't Alex.

It wasn't his wife.

Rory lay awake, listening to the hall clock chime the hours. Just after midnight he heard the front door close and Alex's footsteps on the stairs. She spent a long time in the bathroom and he thought about the red stain of pain she was trying to wash out of her mind. When she finally emerged, she came in quietly and in the dark so as not to wake him and slid into bed with a soft sigh of pleasure.

It was like the sigh of a branding-iron on his forehead. 'A' for adulterer.

He turned towards her as if roused from sleep and curled an arm around her. She nestled tight against him, her breath coming warm on his neck and her icy feet burrowed under his calf. She smelt strongly of her apricot shower gel and he was grateful for that. The Chanel was gone. Its perfume washed down into the sewers. He would empty the whole bottle down there in the morning.

The morning. The cold harsh light of day. No soft shadows to cloak the sins of the soul. Nothing he could do would prevent it arriving with its clear, pin-sharp reality. Nothing would stop the clock. Or turn back its filigree hands. Tomorrow would come. Tomorrow and all the tomorrows.

Rory enfolded his wife in his arms and kissed her smooth, apricot forehead. She murmured something indecipherable and eased herself silkily into sleep, seeking its dark comforting folds to blank out the nightmare at the Marlborough surgery. His own nightmare was not to be tamed so readily and the clock continued to chime the wakeful hours towards dawn. His arms remained wrapped around his wife, keeping her close, as if they could hold together their marriage by physical force alone.

18 ∫

Smooth blue skies that looked as if they had just been swept clear of all debris announced that Monday morning had made its entrance with the promise of another glorious week of summer. When the bedside alarm yanked Rory from the fitful doze that he had managed to find for the last couple of hours, his eyes felt as if they had been polished with sandpaper and his right arm ached from its possessive position around his wife.

Alex was immediately fully awake, gave him a quick kiss on his morning stubble and nipped out of bed.

'I want to get over to the surgery as early as possible to see how last night's injured are doing. I'm frightened we may have lost one of the dogs during the night. A bearded collie. She was hanging on by no more than a thread when I left. Maddy was spending the night there.'

She disappeared into the bathroom, so Rory was spared the need for a response. He closed his eyes and listened to the incessant drumming inside his head in the hope that there wouldn't be room in there for him to think. But the thoughts squeezed through the cracks. The thoughts and the memory. He pulled the duvet right up to his chin but it provided no protection from them, so he threw it aside and went downstairs. Mewling whiskers besieged his every move until he had fed Hamilton and Horatio, then he made coffee, peeled a pear for Alex and buttered her some toast.

When she walked into the kitchen looking bright and fresh in white tee-shirt and jeans, she was surprised to see him nursing a mug of coffee at the table with no indication of movement towards getting ready for the office.

'You're going to be late, aren't you, Rory?'

'Probably.'

'Oh, like that, is it? Feeling a bit the worse for wear?' As she passed him to sit down to her breakfast, she stroked his head with cool fingers. 'Poor old thing. That's rotten for you.' Despite the words of sympathy, her eyes were speckled with amusement and she tweaked his chin, but only gently. 'Bad boy,' she chuckled and he looked at her closely, but saw nothing more behind her words.

'No problems with Jamie or Zena, I hope, after I deserted you both last night?'

'No, of course not. Why should there be?' It came out sharper than he intended.

'Okay, old grouch, just checking. Stick your head under a cold shower and that will wash away the glue from between your ears.' She concentrated on demolishing her breakfast at speed, dropped a kiss on the nape of his neck, patted his cheek and took off in the Clio.

Now it was just Zena and himself.

Rory remained a long time over his coffee. When it was cold and his headache worse, he went back upstairs, showered, dressed, then sat and waited for the sound of his son demanding a morning feed.

Zena was yawning when she walked into the kitchen expecting everyone to have left for work. Her hair was tousled like wind-blown wheat and her kimono hung open, unbelted, indifferently revealing the inner curves of her breasts, her stomach still soft from childbirth and a bright bush of ginger curls above her slender thighs. She stopped in her barefooted tracks when she saw Rory sitting at the table, but made no attempt to close the kimono.

'Well, hello there. Waiting for a rerun?'

'No, Zena. But I am waiting to have a talk with you.'

'Just a talk?'

'Yes. Just a talk. About last night.'

'No regrets, surely?' She laughed with languid amusement and went over to pour herself a coffee from the pot bubbling quietly on its electric hob.

'Yes, Zena, I do have deep regrets.' So deep he could drown in them. 'But I can't alter what happened. All I can do is make clear that it won't happen ever again.'

Zena gave him a smile over her shoulder. 'Are you telling me you didn't enjoy it?'

'What I'm telling you is that it was a big mistake.'

She carried her mug of black coffee over to the table and sat down opposite Rory. The kimono still swung open loosely but Rory kept his eyes on her face, avoiding even a glimpse of the body that had betrayed his senses so effortlessly. She sipped the coffee, her eyes alert, watching him over its rim. Her lips blew a gentle puff of breath at the spiral of steam rising from the mug and she smiled conspiratorially at him. 'It takes two to tango, you know.'

'I know. I was out of my mind.'

The eyes still watched. 'What is that supposed to mean?'

'I love Alex. I would never do anything to hurt her.'

'Didn't look that way from where I was lying.'

'I was drunk, as you well know.'

'Thanks for the insult.'

But he was not prepared to let her wrong-foot him. Not this morning. 'I was drunk. And you had no business in my bed.'

'Drink lowers the barriers, Rory. Melts the resistance. It doesn't create desires that don't already exist. Let me remind you that you had no problem performing, so the drink had not . . .'

'Zena, I have no intention of going over the details of last night. Both of us were in the wrong. I don't mean it as an insult to you, because of course you are desirable. Attractive and tempting. But not for me. I am happily married to your sister and want to stay that way.'

She raised an eyebrow at him. 'So I noticed.'

Nothing she said could make him feel worse than he already did. The next step was to hang on to his marriage.

'Zena, if Alex learns about last night she will be desperately hurt. By both of us. A knife in the guts from her husband. And from her sister. I don't want that.'

She smiled, catlike. 'A bit late for remorse, isn't it?'

'Much too late.'

'Want wifey kept in the dark, do you? Like all the other

unfaithful husbands – have your cake and eat it.' The smile stayed but the eyes became hard. It made Rory wonder about her American Chet Taylor's track record.

'Then why did you come into my bed last night? What possessed you to do such a destructive act? It's not even as if we get on all that well. You couldn't call us exactly soul mates.'

Zena laughed. 'Ah, but that's where you're wrong. You are in fact my sole – as in s-o-l-e – mate, because sure as hell, there's no one else around here for me to hump. So what's a girl supposed to do when she feels the itch?'

Rory stared at her suggestive pout and his teeth grated with disbelief that he could have succumbed so easily.

'Maybe, Zena, it had more to do with where I was, rather than who I was.'

'What do you mean?'

'In bed. In Alex's bed.'

Her eyes narrowed and the seductive silk slipped away. 'What the hell is that about?'

'I mean not just any man would do for you. No, it had to be Alex's husband.'

'Don't talk crap.'

'Do you feel any regret at all, Zena? Any sorrow for what you deliberately did to Alex. To your own sister, for Christ's sake. When you weren't even drunk.'

'Don't hide behind "drunk", Rory. You're not so virgin white yourself.'

'I am only too well aware of that.'

'Then don't start throwing stones.'

'Stop pretending it was all a casual whim. You came into my bed, uninvited, with the deliberate intention of seducing – without any resistance, I admit – your sister's husband. Why did you want to hurt her so badly?'

The amber eyes were fixed on his and he could see the undercurrents rising to the surface like whirlpools in the sea. He watched her struggle to hang on to the glib, sophisticated sheen that she wrapped around herself as casually as the kimono, but it was swept away by the force of the waves that raced up the beach. Her hands pushed the coffee away from her with a vehemence that made it spill a black oil slick on to the table.

'Because she has everything.'

Maddy's words crashed into Rory's mind. 'They'll scratch each other's eyes out, if you're not careful,' she had warned and he had been too blind to see it.

'Zena, Alex has worked hard to earn what you call her "everything". Damned hard. She . . .'

'Don't tell me how good she is, how clever she is, how conscientious she is. How all-round bloody walk-on-water perfect she is! I grew up hearing that catechism every single day until it was branded into my brain.'

Rory looked at his sister-in-law and for the first time with his eyes open. He saw the gaping wound, red and raw, that all the smart talking was supposed to hide. How could he have been so totally blind, even after he had been warned? So unable to smell what was festering under his nose? Or even hear the cries? The anger that he had been trying to dump on her, but which he knew underneath the layers was really at himself, evaporated as invisibly as the steam of her coffee. Into its place rushed an understanding and a desire to befriend that he had never felt for his sister-in-law before. Not even in those mind-searing moments in bed.

A heavy silence settled in the kitchen like cement dust, while Zena struggled to brick up the hole. As if to hide the internal effort from his view she pulled the silky kimono round her and belted it tightly, then concentrated on swirling her coffee, round and round. She made no attempt to drink it.

When she seemed more in control, Rory tried to reach her. 'Zena, I'm sorry. Sorry that I didn't have more sense than to hurt you this morning. Just plain old-fashioned male panic, I'm afraid. Trigger-finger flailing and found you as a target. It should have been my own head that got the bullet, of course. I apologise.'

She lifted her head and smiled at him, the hole all securely bricked up and neatly repainted. 'You men all think with your pricks, so what's new?'

'You were right when you said that alcohol was no excuse. The decision was mine and so must the consequences be. Whatever they are.'

'Certainly you had no excuse, but you must have had a reason. Every action has a reason, Rory.'

'And you have obviously worked out mine?'

'Yes, I have. The green-eyed monster at work with his pitch-fork.'

'Jealousy? Who do I have to be jealous of? Not Gary Saunders, if that's what you mean.'

'No, I wasn't thinking of Gary.'

'Then who?'

'Jamie.'

'My own son?'

'Yes. I know you love him, that's obvious. But he takes a lot of my dear sister's time. From where I'm sitting, your nose looks knocked out of joint and you haven't even noticed.'

'No, that's absurd.'

'A bit short of nookie, maybe? Wife not giving you the attention you were used to? So you strike out at her, way below the belt. It's an old, old story.'

'Rubbish.'

But was it? Alex was juggling her job and the baby, working flat out at both. Of course she was tired. Not just physically, but emotionally drained each day. Any smiles tended to be reserved for Jamie and she fell instantly asleep the moment her head hit the pillow at night. So maybe Zena was not so far off the mark.

Or maybe she was talking through her proverbial and he had just been drunk and plain horny.

Either way, his marriage was still at stake. 'Zena, whatever the reasons on your side or mine, last night should not have happened. I hope you agree that the best course of action now is to put it behind us. We can each deal with our conscience as we see fit. But for Jamie's sake and for all our sakes, during these last few weeks let's carry on as we were.'

'As if it never happened?'

'No. You and I will both always know it did happen.'

'But not Alex?'

Rory leaned forward. 'Would you prefer her to know? Is that what you want?'

The amber eyes stared uneasily into his for a long moment and finally she gave the slightest shake of her head. 'No.'

'Then let's keep it that way. I don't want her hurt.'

'And when I'm gone, you can play happy families and pretend I don't exist.'

Rory stood up, walked round the table and put an arm around the slender shoulders in the pink kimono. 'I have a lot to thank you for, Zena. For Jamie. And for your silence now. There's no way I would want to pretend you weren't a part of our lives.' He kissed her cheek, felt it flush under his lips, and gave her a warm, brother-in-law smile.

Oddly, there was no awkwardness between them when Alex came home. She seemed unaware of any seismic disturbance and only commented to Rory that he looked tired. Her mind was still on the canine carnage from the road accident and she was depressed by the loss of another of the dogs during the day. She and Gordon had worked all afternoon to try to save the collie but in the end its splintered body had had enough. Maddy had reminded them both briskly that the three remaining dogs were doing well, but it was still a blow. Especially as the mare in the trailer had already been destroyed. With the resilience of youth, the foal survived physically unscathed but was traumatised by the loss of its mother and by her distress before she died.

Rory listened to the stress behind Alex's words, all so carefully calm and controlled, and gave thanks for his own afternoon of tedious client meetings that had gone on interminably. Zena said she didn't want to hear and retreated upstairs to her room. That night in bed, Rory made love to his wife and gave thanks a second time. Nothing could obliterate the guilt. Nothing. But, as Alex snuggled against him with a contented yawn, he still did not know how he had come to betray her. He wanted no other woman. Would never risk losing her. Yet he had accepted Zena into his bed. Her sister. He rolled on his side, draped an arm round his wife and inhaled with familiar pleasure the antiseptic aroma that clung to her hair.

The days continued to pass and only in the evening when Jamie was at last in bed was there time to draw breath and check that everything was still standing. After supper one evening when Zena was soaking in one of her baths and Rory was sitting with Jamie draped asleep on his shoulder ready for his cot, Alex commented, 'You and Zena seem to have sheathed your claws recently. Fatherhood robbed you of your aggression, has it?'

Rory laughed, but felt his stomach curl. 'No, but it has certainly united us more. She and I are now too busy disagreeing over eye focusing distances and feeding patterns to have time to remember to get the real knuckle-dusters out.'

Alex came over, rumpled his hair and leant over with a kiss for the gingery down that was nestled against his chin. 'Thanks anyway. It makes life distinctly more peaceful. I'm even beginning to think we should invite her to stay longer.'

Rory jumped so quickly he tipped the small head off its perch but automatically steadied it with his hand instead. 'What? For heaven's sake, Alex, don't even suggest that she . . .' And then he saw his wife's teasing eyes laughing down at him.

'Rory Flynn, you are a real sucker.'

He whispered softly into his son's sleepy ear, 'Just remember, my boy, you can never believe women.'

'Sexist.'

'How about believing this instead?' He pulled Alex towards him, her hair loose and tumbling on his face, each kiss denying his guilt.

It was some weeks later that Rory found the cache.

It was a Saturday morning, damp and drizzling with mist settled for the day on the hill tops, and Alex had driven off to Swindon with Zena and Jamie to buy something or other for the nursery. Though what more one small child could possibly need that he did not already have, Rory could not imagine. Rory had been comfortably entrenched in coffee and the newspaper run-down on the next day's Grand Prix race at Spa in Belgium when the telephone rang.

'Hi, Rory, it's Joanna. Wet enough for sea lions this morning, isn't it? Is Alex there?'

'Sorry, no. She's out emptying the Swindon shops.'

'Damn. The girl has no sense of timing.'

'What's the problem?'

'I need some information from her.'

'Can it wait?'

Grumbling noises rattled the line and ended with an irritated, 'Not really.'

From past experience Rory had learned not to get involved in female exchanges of information, so he offered a bland, 'Well, I'll tell her you called and get her to ring you back the moment she's home.'

'When will that be?'

Rory hedged. 'Lunchtime-ish. Maybe later.'

'That's no good at all.'

'Sorry, best I can offer.'

'I suppose you'll have to do instead.'

'Joanna, you overwhelm me with your vote of confidence.'

'I need a telephone number.'

'Can't you just look it up in the directory?'

'Don't be so simple-minded. If I could do that I would already have done so. I want you to be an angel and find it for me.'

'What's the rush?'

Joanna took a deep breath to contain her impatience and explained, 'I'm writing an article for a magazine on children's clothing styles. Not exactly earth-shattering stuff but it's a start back into freelance.'

'So where does Alex come into this?' Rory eyed his coffee growing cold on the table out of his reach. He put down the receiver, retrieved his mug and returned to the telephone. Joanna was still talking.

'. . . so the woman gave me the catalogue with her home number scribbled on the top of the front page. I lent it to Alex to see in case she was interested in something for Jamie.' The flow ceased.

'So you want me to find this catalogue.'

'That's right. I need that number. Urgently.'

'Can't it wait until this afternoon when Alex will be back?' He did not relish wasting his morning hunting high and low for a booklet on children's clothing.

'Are you deaf, Rory? I just told you. The woman is flying to Greece for a week this afternoon and I need to speak to her before she leaves.'

'Joanna, it could be anywhere. You know Alex. Everything is tidied away.'

'Please, Rory. Please.'

'It's above the call of duty.'

'I know. I'll be grateful for life. Name your price.'

'A dish of your *tagliatele napoli*.'

'Done. Now start looking.'

'And . . .'

'What else?'

'A guaranteed win for Williams over Ferrari tomorrow.'

'I'll put sugar in their petrol tanks myself, I promise.'

'It's a deal then,' he laughed and hung up.

The search took as long as he had expected. He started with the obvious places like the magazine pile, the correspondence drawer and the cupboards downstairs. He drew a blank where the catalogue was concerned, but was rewarded for his efforts by coming across his file of cuttings on last season's races that he had lost a month ago. It was on a shelf under the stairs. He had made the mistake of leaving it lying around too long and it had been tidied away. Admittedly the find did delay him somewhat, as he could not resist browsing through it to refresh his memory.

The clock striking its Westminster chimes reminded his stomach that it was almost chop-grilling time, so he dutifully put the file to one side for later and continued the search upstairs. The dressing-table, chest of drawers and bedside cabinet all produced nothing of interest except a card he had given to Alex for her last birthday and which she had kept. He smiled to himself. She was getting sentimental in her old age.

It then occurred to him to try Jamie's room, as presumably the clothes in the catalogue were for him, but no luck. A cuddly profusion of teddy bears, rabbits and elephants with fur still new and fluffy and a tall black and white spaniel with big round eyes that were the spitting image of Paula's at the office, but no catalogue. He sat in the chintz nursing chair for a while pulling the cord on a fat yellow chicken to make it play the tune 'You are my Sunshine', as well as flapping its stubby wings in time to the tinkling notes and rolling its eyes like a demented custard. It had a strangely hypnotic effect.

But he knew he was just delaying the inevitable. A search of Zena's room. He did not like going in there. It was too personal, too intimate, far too redolent of her. The last thing he wanted was a reminder of details that brought that night charging into his head with the force of a rampaging bull. He and Zena had learned to jog along amicably on a daily basis, but he wasn't kidding himself. He had long ago acknowledged that his eyes were well and truly focused on that moment when the door would shut behind her. The final brush of cheeks and wave of hands. Not long now. Ten days and the year would be over. Give or take a day or two because who, except himself, was counting?

Determined to get it over with quickly, he opened the door to her room and took a cursory look round. Everything was in its usual jumble but at least that meant if the catalogue were there, it should be fairly visible. He started with the dressing-table, rummaging around greasy piles of cotton wool, pots of make-up, old television papers and the occasional flimsy piece of underwear. Accelerating, he checked through unruly heaps on the beside table, tallboy, windowsill, chair and floor but failed to turn up any catalogues. That left the wardrobe. Unlikely that she would put it in there, but with Zena you never knew. He opened the doors.

No catalogue. But propped in the corner was a tall, nylon rucksack and judging by its bulging cheeks, it was full. Curiosity easily got the better of any scruples. Rory lifted it out and opened its drawstring neck. Disappointingly, it seemed to contain just clothes. He recognised Zena's white jeans on the top and almost put it back where he'd found it without burrowing any deeper, but something made him investigate further. It was the oddity of the situation. Why on earth would Zena neatly pack a bagful of her clothes? Getting ready for departure in a couple of weeks?

Maybe.

As he tipped the bag slightly on to its corner to push an arm deeper inside, he heard a muffled but unmistakable tinkle. A musical chime that he instantly recognised. It was one of Jamie's rattles. The one with the happy sunflower face.

That settled it. Carefully he started to remove the clothes. The jeans, a couple of tee-shirts, a pair of shorts and a sweatshirt. And a pair of sandals. Then the clothes stopped but the bag was still over half full. Rory stared down into its dark mouth at a white, lacy shawl. It had been a present for Jamie from his brother's wife. He lifted the soft material out and underneath was packed another layer of clothes. But this time they were Jamie's; brightly coloured miniature garments that announced all too clearly the reason for the bag.

Without hesitation, Rory picked up the rucksack and tipped it upside down on the carpet. Out tumbled clothes, followed by a soft squeezy ball and the sunflower rattle, an assortment of baby creams and shampoo, and finally a handful of disposable nappies. No doubt the side pockets held nursing bras, make-up and cheque book. Don't forget the cheque book.

Zena was going to make a run for it, taking their son with her.

Rory threw the bag across the room and it thumped against the wall before collapsing on to the unmade bed. Ironically, where it fell, he noticed a children's clothes catalogue sticking out of the duvet's folds. He snatched it up and walked out of the room.

Zena breezed in first as Alex was still extracting Jamie, pram and parcels from the car. One look at Rory's face and her cheery, 'I'm exhausted from all that sh . . .' trailed away. 'What's up with you? Found a dead body or something?'

'No, not a dead body. A rucksack.'

Zena turned her back on him, tossed her shoulder-bag on to a chair, flopped on to the sofa and closed her eyes. 'God, my feet ache.'

Rory didn't give a damn about her feet. 'Zena, it's quite obvious what the rucksack is for. I want an explanation.'

She opened her eyes a tawny slit and said casually, 'You shouldn't go snooping in other people's cupboards.'

'When were you planning on leaving with that bag?'

She smiled at him. 'I wasn't.'

'That's not what it looks like.'

'Sit down and I'll explain.'

He remained standing. 'Explain away.'

'After Jamie was born, I wasn't sure how things would work out here. I thought perhaps Ali might get really possessive and not want me around. But I was determined to have the agreed three months with my son, so not long after I came home from the hospital, I packed the rucksack.'

'So that you could walk out whenever you pleased. With Jamie.'

Zena kicked off her shoes and massaged the sole of one foot with her fingers. 'Sure. If necessary. Until the three months were up.'

It sounded so plausible. And she was so convincing in her casual indifference to being found out that Rory was tempted to believe her. But only tempted.

'You're lying, Zena. I don't believe that rucksack has sat there, packed and ready, for nearly three months.'

She smiled at him with genuine amusement. 'Believe what you like. It's the truth.'

At that moment, Alex walked into the room chattering to the baby in her arms. She was showing him a new toy, a tubby panda that looked as if it had had no trouble finding bamboo shoots recently. Jamie's gaze was transfixed by its huge black eyes.

'Look, Rory, it was irresistible. Jamie couldn't take his eyes off it in the shop, so I just had to . . .' Belatedly she sensed the tension that threatened to burn a hole through the ceiling and looked from her husband's face to her sister's. 'What's going on?'

'Ask Rory.' Zena started on the other foot. 'He seems to have got himself twisted in knots over nothing while we were out stuffing ourselves with pizza in Swindon.'

Alex studied him with concern. 'What's happened, Rory?' She came closer and Jamie instantly held out a grasping hand to him.

Rory took his son in his arms and gave his wife a brief reassuring kiss. 'Nothing has happened. Zena's right. I misunderstood something, that's all. Put your feet up and I'll make you a cup of tea.' He walked into the kitchen, keeping his arm tucked tightly round his son.

19

'Have you set a date with her yet?'

Alex looked up from her Penelope Leach tome and glanced across at her husband beside her. They had come to bed early but he still seemed restless and alert, almost as if listening for something. He was supposedly engrossed in a wartime evacuee's autobiography but she had noticed that no pages had turned for some time and his fixed gaze seemed preoccupied. She wondered again what had happened today to unsettle him while she was in Swindon with Zena.

'A date for Zena to leave, you mean?'

'Yes.' He closed his book. 'It's time for her to go.'

'She's still arranging things. I know she has the names of several estate agents in Bath and is intending to look at some flats for rent, but nothing is settled yet.'

'Then get her to settle it.'

Alex looked at his tense profile, the high forehead creased in a frown. 'What is it, Rory? Why the sudden rush?'

'The year is almost up, that's all. It's time for her to leave. That's what was agreed in our deal.'

'No other reason?'

He turned to face her and she was disturbed by the tip of fear she saw in his dark eyes. 'No other reason.'

'Rory, what on earth has got into you to make you so uptight suddenly?' She put a hand to his face and soothed the frown away with a soft movement of her thumb. 'Tell me.'

'Nothing. It's just that I'm worried that now it's come to the crunch, your sister will not want to give up Jamie. She'll decide to take him with her.'

Alex stroked his stubbled chin. 'Oh Rory, of course she won't. She and I have talked about it all, how she'll come and visit often so that she doesn't lose touch with him. Don't forget, he's been the centre of her life for the last few months, so of course it'll be a wrench for her. But when she gets herself a flat and a job in Bath, she'll start to build a new life for herself.'

'You hope.'

'I'm sure.' She smiled at him confidently and he envied her such certainty. But then she hadn't seen the rucksack.

'How come you're so convinced of her good intentions now?'

Alex thought for a moment and surprised him with her answer. 'Because I was blind before.'

Blind. Blind like he had been.

She continued, 'I understand her so much better now, Rory. We've become close. All the bravado is just for show. Underneath it all, she is very loving. Just look at her with Jamie. And very lonely. I let her down badly when we were children by not giving her the friendship she needed. I won't let her down this time. Look at what she's had to give me to make me realise how much she wants a sister, not just a few lines twice a year on a sheet of letter paper.'

'I hope you're right.'

'I know I am.'

He wanted to believe, to take the step of faith that would bring peace of mind. But the bulging rucksack kept blocking his path and there was no way he could tell Alex about it. He had his back to the wall where upsetting Zena was concerned because he could never be certain she would not retaliate. And he had not only given her a gun, but had loaded it for her.

Maybe Alex was right and he was just being blind to her sister's real needs and intentions. But every time he tried to slip past the rucksack unnoticed, Zena's own words, so crippled with pain and anger, rattled like hailstones inside his head. 'How all-round bloody walk-on-water perfect she is.' She believed Alex had everything. So she had taken her husband. Why not her child?

Abruptly he said, 'Okay, maybe you're right, but let's play it safe. From now on, one of us should always remain at home with her.'

'What?'

'I know it will mess up my work and your surgery hours, but we can take it in turns. If business suffers, let it suffer. I am not willing to risk losing Jamie. It would only be for a week or so and that way we can always keep an eye on his whereabouts.'

Alex looked at him as if he had taken leave of his senses. 'For heaven's sake, Rory, that smacks of advanced paranoia. I wouldn't dream of taking such ludicrous action. Especially not now, when she and I are both beginning to trust each other. An idea like that would be a slap in the face for her. No, Rory, definitely not.'

'What if you're wrong?'

'I'm not.' She took his clenched hand in hers and said gently, 'I know I'm not. Just trust her.'

'Perhaps we should have Jamie's cot in here with us at night anyway. Just in case.'

Alex burst out laughing and then regretted it, as she realised that was what he had been listening for earlier. Stealthy footsteps on the stairs. 'She's hardly likely to creep away with him in the middle of the night. Honestly, Rory, you really are getting paranoid. Come on, we've trusted her this far and she's not let us down. You're jumpy only because of your own fears, not because she has given you reason to be.'

Alex waited, wanting Rory to say yes, of course his fears were unreasonable. Instead he shook his head and suggested, 'What about one of us spiriting Jamie away? To keep him safe until she's gone.'

Alarm stabbed at Alex's stomach. She tightened her grip on his fist. 'For God's sake, don't try that. All hell would break loose and she would never sign those final adoption papers. No, you're being unfair to her, Rory. You just have to trust her.'

'Do I?'

He sounded anything but convinced.

Neither slept well, tossing and turning so interminably that both cats abandoned the churning duvet for the more predictable, if harder, bottom step of the stairs. At six o'clock in the morning Alex finally gave up all pretence of sleep and went downstairs to make a pot of coffee. She fed the mewing pink mouths and then heard Jamie add his voice to theirs. Animals and babies showed no respect for Sunday morning lie-ins.

The morning passed in an oddly subdued atmosphere with Rory taking refuge behind the Sunday papers and coffee pot in the kitchen, while Zena watched a video of the film *Point Break* that had been on television late the night before. She had a soft spot for Patrick Swayze. That left Alex to take advantage of having Jamie all to herself and she wallowed in the intense pleasure with shameless abandon. In his sunshine yellow room she cuddled him, sang nursery rhymes, blew kisses on his tight little drum of a stomach, played silly games with brightly coloured bricks and finally, when his eyes started to droop, read him to sleep with 'The Three Little Pigs'.

After an early lunch, Rory swapped the helter-skelter of sister-in-law uncertainties for the easier hairpin dangers of the track and took himself over to Marco Donelli's to watch the Belgian Grand Prix. The afternoon was warm but unpleasantly sultry, as if it was storing up a thunderstorm for the evening. When Alex pushed Jamie in his pram out for a walk along the village lanes, she found her lungs objecting on the inclines to the lack of clean oxygen and her throat demanding a long, cool drink. A cocktail of fruit juice and Perrier was sitting in the fridge at home and just the thought of it quickened her step.

By the time she reached her front gate, Jamie was asleep again, so she tucked the pram into a shady corner of the garden where the honeysuckle could waft its scent into his dreams, stretched the cat-net over the top in case either of the moggies came in search of a convenient nook for an afternoon doze, and went looking for that drink. In the kitchen she found Zena fiddling with a necklace that had come unstrung, vivid blue lapis lazuli that was one of her favourites.

'Had an accident?' Alex headed straight for the fridge and poured herself a glass of the cool fruit cocktail.

Zena nodded, concentrating on the rethreading. 'Yes. Darn thing caught on my jewellery box handle when I was taking it out. How was your walk?'

'Sticky. Jamie is zonked out for the next hour but he loved the excitement.'

'Excitement? On a walk in these might-as-well-be-dead lanes?'

Alex laughed, 'All a matter of what you're used to. A tractor roaring past, dogs barking, new faces cooing over the pram and a particularly noisy magpie make it the Piccadilly Circus of his life.'

'And of yours, I suppose.'

'Of course. I get my fix from seeing a mallard chaperoning her six ducklings across the road to the stream like we did just now and Mrs Tucker's garden ablaze with roses that knock the Chelsea Flower Show's winner into a cocked hat. High as a kite I get.'

'God, you're boring.'

'And you're lazy.'

Both sisters laughed and Alex finished her drink. 'I'm going to do some gardening now. It looks as if it might rain later, so I want to get the back hedge cut while it's dry.'

'You're a glutton for punishment.'

'How about giving me a hand? A bit of healthy exercise.'

'No thanks. I'll look after Jamie.'

'But he's asleep.'

'Exactly, I'll sit and wait for him to wake up.'

'Don't strain yourself,' Alex grinned and let herself out the back door.

In fact she was quite content to work away on her own, clipping with the shears and trundling the barrow, allowing her head to dwell uninterrupted on Rory's comments of last night, while her hands inflicted neatness on the over-boisterous hedge. Rory was wrong but she just couldn't make him see straight. It distressed her to see him gutting himself with that rusty old knife of unfounded fears just because he failed to recognise how much Zena had come to rely on them. They had become her life-line back to normality and there was no way she would cut herself adrift from them once more. Of that Alex was certain.

What she was less certain about was how Zena would cope with leaving her son. But frequent contact with him should soften the blow. And knowing Zena, she would quickly be on to something new. In a few months she would probably be content to play the traditional doting aunt, affectionate but thankful to hand him back to his mother at the end of the day. If only she could make Rory see that fact, it would make these last days so much easier. A relaxed, happy family.

Her own childhood family had been dismally short on both those qualities. Neither relaxed, nor happy, she could see in retrospect. At the time she knew nothing else, so thought that was what happiness was, like the blind man feeling the elephant's tail. But there had been too many tensions twanging the wires taut. She was acutely aware that having Jamie around had released some of those tensions in herself, altered her priorities. Perspectives had changed. And it wasn't just Jamie. Zena as well. Living with Zena this last year had given her the chance to dig around in those childhood emotions and root out so many that had been buried too deep.

Like the guilt.

How could she have been so insensitive to a little sister's needs? So full of her own aims and ambitions. And was Zena right? That Alex's only purpose in life had been to please her father. To the exclusion of her sister and of her mother. Well, she was trying to make up for it now and would keep trying even after Zena had moved out. Would keep her involved.

She raked up another stretch of twigs and leaves and dumped them into the barrow. The oppressive heat was making her feel uncomfortable and she promised herself a shower as soon as she was finished. Her arms were beginning to ache from the repetitive movement with the shears and she wondered, as always when clipping the hedge, about investing in an electric hedge-cutter. Though finances would be tighter from now on. She found herself humming nursery rhymes under her breath and it made her smile. So much for Bird and Ellington.

'Ali, Ali.'

It was Zena. Her voice shrieking in panic.

Alex dropped the shears and started to race towards the house.

'Ali, come quickly, Ali. For God's sake, Ali, help me.'

Zena was running down the back path, her movements oddly jerky. There was a dark stain down the front of her white blouse.

Alex reached her and seized her arm to stop her flight. The skin was icy cold.

'Ali, help me.' The eyes were huge, pupils caves of fear. 'Help me.' Her lips stumbled over the words, drained of all colour.

'What is it, Zena? Are you hurt?'

No answer.

Alex fought to control her own rising panic. She checked the stain on her sister's blouse. Not blood, thank God. Looked like black coffee. Gently she took Zena's face between her hands to focus the darting eyes.

'Calm down, Zena, and tell me what has happened. Are you hurt?'

'No.' The blonde head was shaking too much and the cheeks were white and clammy. She was sliding into shock.

'Zena, what . . . ?'

Suddenly realisation hit Alex like a hammer blow. She abandoned her sister and raced into the house, bands of terror clamping down tight on her lungs so that she had to fight to draw breath.

Jamie. Where was Jamie? She tried to call his name. Only a dry whisper emerged. Jamie. Oh God, let it not be Jamie. Please not Jamie.

The kitchen was empty. She wasted no time. She ran towards the sitting-room, her ears straining for the sound of his cry. Or even a whimper.

Nothing. Except her own rasping breath and the drumbeat battering her ears.

For a split second she almost made for the stairs to hurry to the nursery, then changed her mind. It would only take one moment to check the sitting-room. The door was wide open and she rushed in, eyes everywhere.

He was there. Lying on his side on the sofa. Hamilton sat at his feet, sniffing his bare toes and purring gently, blue eyes startled and reproachful at Alex's sudden arrival. She rushed to her son's side and at first felt relief blunt the edge of her fear when, for a brief wishful second, she thought he might just be asleep. But then she saw his colour.

He was blue.

Alex scooped him up and his body lay lifeless and inert in her arms. Something inside her seemed to tear apart.

'Ali, it's my fault. All my fault.' Zena had stumbled into the room, tears streaking her cheeks and voice several octaves too high. 'I've killed him.'

Alex did not take her eyes off the silent face of her child. His eyes were closed, as in death, and his skin had lost all trace of its peaches and cream. It was blue and growing more so every moment. His rosy lips were a dull purple.

No, he couldn't be dead. Not Jamie. No, no, no.

The tiniest shudder of the body kicked her mind into action. Not dead, but dying in her arms. Desperately she clawed at the tatters of her knowledge. He was blue. That meant oxygen starvation. He couldn't breathe. Oh God, he couldn't breathe. Four minutes was the time limit. How long had it been already?

Beside her Zena was sobbing over and over again, 'I've killed him.'

'Zena, listen to me. What happened? Has he swallowed something?'

More incoherent sobbing was the only response. And then Alex saw them. All over the floor. The beads. Bright blue spheres of lapis lazuli, smooth, round and absolutely perfect for blocking airways.

'Zena, did he swallow a bead?'

Zena managed to nod her head and screamed, 'Ali, save him. Ali, please save him. The necklace broke again and he got hold of one. It happened so quickly, I . . .' Tears drowned out the words.

Alex was already peering into Jamie's mouth but there was no sign of the blockage. Her hands were shaking so badly she hardly trusted herself, but in an instant she had tipped him upside down and was rapping his back.

Nothing happened.

The tiny lungs gave another faint convulsion as if making one last effort. Time was running out.

Zena was kneeling on the floor, moaning quietly now. The tears had stopped.

Alex stood in the middle of the room with her child dying of asphyxiation in her arms and her sister descending into shock at her feet. She made the only decision left to her. She laid the boneless body on the coffee table and flew to fetch her veterinary case from the study. Time started to slow down, as if she were in a video being run on freeze-frame, and each scene flickered on to the screen in her head with pinpoint clarity. Her case standing black as death against the wall in the study, the Siamese fleeing from her running feet, ears flat as a rat's against the narrow head, and then Jamie, like a doll abandoned by its fickle owner on the table. A beautiful fragile doll.

She snapped open the case and forced her brain to think clearly. Scalpel. But what could she use as an airway. Think. For God's sake, think. A wide-bore needle would have to do. No time for more. A deep breath. Could she do it?

Could she cut her own child's throat?

Performing a tracheostomy on a horse was one thing. She had been trained and prepared for it, but carrying out the same operation on a human being was quite another. Especially when that human being was your own son. She was a vet. A vet. Not a doctor. But she did not hesitate. Before the thoughts and fears had time to paralyse her hands, she lifted the scalpel, felt with the tips of her fingers for the rings of the trachea in Jamie's stubby throat and sliced through the skin.

Blood trickled in a thin Ribena line down his neck.

She refused to let her mind dwell on it. The blade slid through the thin tissue and exposed the cartilage of the trachea. Instantly she slid the point of the hollow needle into the mucosa between the rings of the windpipe. It was soft. Much softer than the horse's had been.

Nothing happened.

The chest lay as still as a tomb. Alex leant over and blew down the needle. Immediately the lungs expanded a little and the small body reacted as if to a deep internal earth-tremor. A shudder that vibrated right through every vein and echoed all the way down to a spasm of fingers and toes. Oxygen started to pump in, restoring life with casual ease. The flimsy ribs heaved rapidly up and down as if rushing to make up for lost time, limbs began to flail, cheeks blossomed a healthy pink and finally the silent lashes lifted. Dark, bewildered eyes looked out from under them and at the sight of her started to crinkle into Jamie's familiar heart-lurching smile of recognition. But half-way through, pain triggered panic. He opened his mouth to cry but no sound emerged. Just the moist bubbling of escaped air in the blood and mucus at the point where the needle entered the hole in the windpipe.

Alex lifted him, pinning his arms and body close to her own. She told herself it was to prevent him dislodging the needle, but she did not fall for it. She needed to hold him tight, needed to feel him kick and struggle against her. Needed to feel his life.

'Zena, go and telephone for an ambulance. Quickly, Zena, dial 999.'

Her sister was still kneeling on the floor, eyes riveted to Jamie's scrumpled face as if he were Lazarus himself. Her jaw hung open in disbelief. 'He was dead,' she murmured. 'I saw him. He was dead.'

Alex felt her hands start to shake. Oh God, hang on, just hang on until the ambulance. 'Zena, he's alive now. But he needs help immediately. Go and telephone.'

Zena continued to stare blankly, as if she had not heard.

'Zena, please help.'

Nothing. The words were not getting through.

Alex abandoned hope of assistance from her sister and clutching Jamie, she ran to the telephone. Holding Jamie tight, it took her three attempts to dial correctly, but when the voice asked, 'Which service do you require?', she managed to give the necessary information in a voice so steady that it astonished her shell-shocked brain.

She dropped the receiver and returned to the sitting-room to await the blue wail of the ambulance. Kneeling on the floor in front of Zena, she thrust Jamie's arms inside his tee-shirt, pinning them to his sides and this enabled her to restrain his frantic head-twisting with both hands. The tube of the needle stayed firmly in place, growing out of his neck like a bloodless artery that had lost its way. His mouth was open wide in a soundless circle of distress and pain.

'It's all right now, Jamie,' she soothed. 'Don't cry, don't cry, you're fine now. Fine now.' Her words seemed to tumble into ruts and get stuck in them. 'Zena look, he's fine now.'

Zena continued to stare out of huge black pupils and shake her head from side to side, again and again.

'It's okay now, Zena. Help is on its way and Jamie is fine. Aren't you, Jamie?' She even dredged up a smile for him, as she fought back against the destructive wave of shock that threatened to engulf them all. 'And who said our life was boring? Sunday afternoons in Bath won't be a patch on this, will they, Zena? Enough excitement to last a lifetime.'

She kept up the chatter, the words immaterial, just the flow of her voice, shaky and unsteady. And all the time she prayed the ambulance would arrive any minute.

The nurse was tired. Her face was as crumpled as her blue uniform, but nevertheless she offered a ready smile along with the cup of tea for Alex and Rory. They were sitting on stiff chairs either side of the small cot in which Jamie lay sleeping peacefully. Around them were other cots and other anxious parents hovering with tense, tired eyes. Jamie's long lashes curled softly on his cheeks and he looked relaxed and contented, the pink picture of health and innocence. None the worse for wear. Except for the small dressing on his neck that covered the two stitches.

Alex watched the butterfly rise and fall of his chest, unable yet to dismiss totally the fear that it might stop once more. Irrational, she knew. She sipped the unwanted tea, glanced across at Rory, exchanged thankful smiles for the thousandth time and returned to the chest-watching. The hospital had been magnificent. They had lifted the crushing weight of responsibility from her own chest, whisked Jamie away to a specialist who had performed the flexible bronchoscopy to remove the blockage. The blue bead was at this moment burning a guilty hole in her pocket. A couple of stitches and chest x-rays had followed to make sure nothing had collapsed, and Jamie had come round quickly from the whiff of anaesthetic.

That was the moment she and Rory had been on the edge of the cliff waiting for. To watch his eyes flicker open, to see recognition rather than the blankness of the damage that so easily could have been. He had woken cross and crochety, fists beating the air like angry little pistons and mouth open in a wail of hunger.

To Rory's ears the sound was sweeter than all the Williams, Ferrari and McClaren engines rolled into one. He had watched

fascinated while Alex lifted him from the cot and for the very
first time fed him herself with the bottle supplied by a nurse.
Jamie's initial disgust at the unfamiliar object had soon been
overcome when he discovered its contents and he had taken
to the task with the lusty enthusiasm of Schumacher for the
accelerator pedal. Despite his sore throat.

Alex had been entranced. A blissful smile of Cloud Nine
proportions had wiped out the fine lines that stress had drawn
round her eyes and mouth. Rory had been shocked by his wife's
appearance when he arrived at the hospital, the MG driving like
a turbo-charged bat out of hell to get him there. She had looked
pale, frail and paper-thin, as if all her strength had drained
into keeping Jamie alive. He knew that it would pass, but he
could not prevent himself wrapping his arms around her to
stop any careless breeze from fluttering her away from him.
As Jamie recovered, so did she, and Rory was delighted when
she placed his contented son on his lap along with the last half
of the bottle.

'Let's see you get in some practice,' she smiled.

As the level of milk dropped at a speed he could hardly have
bettered himself, Rory had to drag himself down off Alex's cloud
and point out to his drooling brain that this would be the first of
many. That this was what it had all been about. Jamie, himself
and Alex. A family. A child, a father and a mother.

But this child had two mothers.

Zena.

Rory wanted her gone. Out of his house. Out of his mind.
Taking his guilt away with her. Nothing could ever diminish
the gratitude he felt towards her for carrying his child, but he
also knew nothing could equal the relief he would feel when
she was no longer there. A daily reminder. A daily threat. As
he handed the sleepy Jamie back to Alex, suitably winded and
petted, he made the decision to take his sister-in-law to Bath
in the morning. He would drive her there in the MG and do a
tour of the agents and flats, make a choice and pay the deposit.
Enough was enough. The year was over.

'I think I'll go home and get a few things for staying here
overnight.'

Rory looked up, surprised. 'You want to stay all night?'

'Yes. It's not really necessary, I know, but I'd feel better if I did.' She cocked her head at him in the gesture that always made him smile, because it meant she knew she was being irrational. After what she had done, she had the right to be as irrational as she pleased.

'Okay. And while you're gone, I'll speak to the nurse and see if there's a spare one of these cots you can squeeze into.'

Alex laughed. 'Anyway, I'm a bit worried about Zena. She sounded so quiet on the telephone. I wish she hadn't refused to come to the hospital with us.'

'But you said she's okay now. Over the shock.'

'Yes. But she was very quiet.'

'That's natural. So would you be if you had nearly killed your own child.'

'Don't, Rory.'

'That's how she must be seeing it.'

'I know. That's why I think I should go and speak to her, while Jamie's asleep.'

'Do you want me to drive you home? Or shall I stay and do my best rottweiler act while you're gone?'

'Rottweil away, please. But I'll be back before his next feed.'

'No rush. I can always give him his bottle myself if you're delayed.'

'Bastard,' she grinned and stood up. Leaning over the cot, she murmured a goodbye to Jamie, brushed her lips on his cheek, soft as breath, and inhaled his baby smell that now seemed more essential to her life than oxygen itself. She walked round to Rory, who rose from his chair and took her in his arms. For a long moment she clung there, head on his shoulder.

'How could I have been so stupid, Rory?' The words were mumbled into his shirt. 'I didn't need to cut his skin. Just stick the needle through it into his windpipe. That was all. I should have known better.'

Rory kissed her cheek. 'My darling Alex, you saved Jamie's life. It wouldn't have mattered a damn if you had cut a complete circle right round his neck, as long as you got that needle in. That's all that counted.'

Her coppery head nodded against him, as if to convince herself. She raised her face to his. 'Some vet, huh?'

Rory smiled at the clear brown eyes. 'A bloody good vet and a bloody good mother.'

'I'd better go off and be a bloody good sister now.'

Reluctantly Rory let her go.

20

It was almost dark as Alex drove home. The MG swept tunnels of light through the gloom that was settling like a veil of dust over the brooding ancient stones at Avebury. Earlier she had travelled to the hospital in the ambulance with Jamie, so was using Rory's car now to return home, but found she had to keep its speed right down as her concentration was all over the place. A rabbit played chicken in the middle of the road which didn't exactly help.

She did not bother to back the car into the garage, as she would be using it to return to the hospital soon. Anyway, the way her co-ordination was jumping around, she'd be lucky to get it inside in one piece. The lights were on downstairs and as she opened the front door, it was like stepping into a welcoming cradle, safe and enclosing. After the harsh edges and alien sterility of the hospital, the hall looked soft and mellow, its lights lending a gentle sheen to the battle scars of the old oak chest and grandfather clock. The familiar tick of the pendulum followed her across the hall and she could feel the tension start to ooze out of her with each step.

A momentary stab of guilt that Rory was still stuck inside that chrome and glass cage in Swindon ruffled her sense of relief, but not for long. She would soon relieve him of his vigil. And tomorrow Jamie would come home. Jamie in her arms. Laughing, kicking and crying. Alive. Breathing so effortlessly, pink and mobile. The lifeless blue doll on the table jumped into her head uninvited and she pushed it away. She wasn't ready for that yet. Later, maybe. When her scorched emotions had grown a fresh, protective skin.

Right now it was Zena she had to sort out. Something was

not right, she was certain. The words on the telephone, when she had rung from the hospital to say Jamie was recovering, had been quiet and subdued. Deliberately unrevealing. Zena said she was fine, just fine and was sorry she had been so little help. Her voice tight and unfamiliar. She must be feeling terrible. Hideously responsible.

'Zena,' Alex called.

No reply, but there was a crease of light escaping under the sitting-room door, so Alex headed in that direction. A sudden fear that the vivid beads would still be rolling in erratic blue circles on the carpet when she entered the room took an irrational hold. She shook her head to clear it and felt the tiredness rattle around. No point getting jumpy. Everything was under control now, so no fanciful might-have-beens, please.

Zena was waiting for her. She was standing by the window, obviously keeping a watch for Alex's return and looked well armoured in her beige linen suit and gold jewellery. On her face was the expression of a stranger. Cool, distant, polite. At her feet lay a suitcase and rucksack.

'Zena, what's this? You're not leaving now, surely?'

'Yes.'

Alex wanted to go over and hug her, to break the brittle shell. But you don't hug strangers. Instead she dropped into her chair and rubbed at the knots behind the lines of tension on her forehead. 'But why tonight?'

'I've booked myself into a hotel in Chippenham. I'll catch a bus from there to Bath in the morning.'

Alex's befuddled brain fought to make sense of it. Why was Zena so hell-bent on leaving all of a sudden? 'That's silly, Zena. At least stay here tonight anyway. There's no reason to dash off.'

The amber eyes stared at her as if they had never shared more than half their lives together. 'Yes, there is.'

'But why? Jamie is better now. He'll be home in the morning. I would have thought you would want to be with him tomorrow to see for yourself how chirpy he is.'

'I'll take your word for it.'

The indifference came as a shock. 'What reason do you have for leaving so abruptly, Zena?'

A slight shrug, nothing more. 'Let's just say he's well and

truly your child now. Not mine. You're the one who has given him a life.'

'He will always be yours as well. Nothing can alter that.'

'Everything is altered now.'

'No, Zena, you're wrong. Jamie is still your son. Don't let an accident with your necklace make you walk out on him. That's not the way to end it.'

Zena was still standing with her back to the window, a wall light casting a golden glow over her blonde hair, so that it gleamed like a lioness's pelt in the sun. But now she took a step forward.

'Alex, don't tell me what I can and can't do.'

'Of course not. It's just that I don't understand how you . . .'

Another step forward. 'That's exactly the trouble. You've never understood. Never been able to see what was right under your nose, because your eyes were always looking only in one direction. It used to be at Daddy, then at your career as a Daddy-replacement. And now it's the baby. You see only what you choose to see.'

Alex stared at her sister and felt the glass bubble of sisterhood, that she had constructed so cosily around them, crack and crumble about her. The falling shards were sharp.

'Zena, I know I hurt you as a child and, for what it's worth, I've said I'm sorry. But I thought we were forming a stronger relationship now. As adults. Not just children competing for Daddy's attention.'

'You can't see it even now, can you? That it's the same thing all over again, except this time it's Jamie we're competing for. And once again you've proved how bloody brilliant you are. Saint Alexandra Flynn, the life-giver!' She laughed, a harsh mocking sound.

'So you're running away again. Like last time. Repeating the pattern. If you can't have things your own way, just chicken out and head for the hills. Is that it? Is that what you want?'

A long, spiky silence stretched between them, until Zena said quietly, 'No, it's not what I want. Not what I planned.'

'Planned? Was this all a plan?'

Zena's mouth widened in a smile, but the eyes remained flat and wary. 'Of course it was a plan. Only you would believe I was doing all this out of sisterly devotion. Even after Rory warned you. You took no notice of him because your eyes were on that baby and on nothing else.'

A sheer and shadowy chasm suddenly yawned at Alex's feet and she quickly tucked them under her on the chair.

'Of course I realise there was self-interest on your side, Zena. We gave you a home and an income. And you took every advantage of us, I am aware of that. You needed us and we needed you, but I don't believe that the bond of our being sisters didn't influence you.'

The laugh this time caught Alex unawares. 'Of course it influenced me. Are you blind? It was the reason for everything. And it's the reason I'm leaving.'

Alex was weary. Too weary for this. The afternoon had left her feeling emotionally battered and bruised, and she knew she might say something now that she would regret. She stood up.

'Zena, please stay tonight. I have to get back to the hospital now, but we can finish this discussion in the morning.'

'I won't be here in the morning.'

'For heaven's sake, why not? Stop talking round and round in circles and just spit out the truth.'

Her words seemed to snap a fragile chain in Zena, letting loose her anger. 'The truth? You want the truth? You want to hear the reason I'm here?'

'Yes. Tell me.'

'To have your child. And to walk away with him. To show you what it's like to have someone you love taken away from you.'

The words were out.

Immediately, Zena turned aside and sat down, eyes catlike, watching her sister. The faintest of smiles gentled her mouth, as if she had just spat out an aching tooth and was enjoying the release.

Alex remained standing, staring down at the neat blonde figure on the sofa. 'Why, Zena?' Her words were soft, incredulous.

'Oh, Ali, don't look so nuked. It's fairly predictable really. You had everything – a degree, a career, a home and husband. When I left home – or as you pointed out just now, ran away – I was a mess. I thought I could start afresh in a new country, but how could I build a better life when I was still carrying round all that junk from childhood?'

Alex sat down on a chair. 'Go on.'

'Nothing much to go on with. I screwed up again, marrying a guy I knew Daddy would have hated. Someone dumb and physical to flush out all that intellectual crap he and you were always forcing down my throat.'

'We tried to encourage you to do well at school, that's all.'

'Encourage or force? What's the difference?'

'So you planned a revenge?' It was said quietly, as if asking the time of day.

'Of a kind.'

For the first time Alex looked away. At the darkening shadows creeping in the window, at the white cat blissfully asleep on the embroidered footstool, at her own hands so still on her lap. Anywhere but at those tawny eyes. The room seemed to shudder with the sound of the silence. Alex had no idea how long it went on, but when she forced her gaze back to her sister, Zena was still watching her. Waiting for a reaction.

'I think you ought to leave now, Zena.'

Zena gave a curt laugh and leaned back against the cushions. 'Come on, Ali, you can do better than that. No shouts and screams? Or recriminations and tears? No accusations of deceit? That tight-arsed control rigidly in place even now.'

'Zena, just leave. Take your bags and go.'

Zena smiled softly and shook her head, setting the honey-blonde hair swaying. 'You ruined my plan for me, Doc. Jamie was my child. I love him. I was going to take him with me. Then you went and saved his life and made him yours.'

'I've told you before, he will always be yours as well.'

But it was as if Zena had not heard. 'Like you took Daddy away. And Mummy.'

'That's absurd. I . . .'

'You didn't even notice, did you, the way she fussed over you all those years? Always warming your gloves before you went out with Daddy in the freezing rain to some god-forsaken farm. Waiting up till all hours for you with steaming mugs of cocoa and hot-water bottles. Devotedly sticking plasters over all your nips and scratches.'

'Of course I noticed and was grateful.'

'Like hell you did.' Zena tried another laugh but it came out wrong, tight and choked. 'Ironic, isn't it? There she was, wanting you; there you were, wanting to be Daddy. And there he was, wanting me – at first anyway.'

Alex leant forward. 'And you? Who did you want?'

'Don't you know? Even now?'

'Daddy?'

'Yes. But most of all I wanted to be you.'

Alex stared at her sister, watched a tear trickle down her cheek and get swept aside. Zena having Rory's baby, living in Alex's house, using Alex's money, sitting in Alex's chair. Suddenly it all made sense. Such screaming, obvious, blatant sense that she was appalled at her own blindness. Zena was right. She had only seen what she chose to see. She rose from her chair, went over to the sofa and sat down next to her sister.

'Zena, be yourself. Not me.'

'I tried that in America. It didn't work.'

Alex wrapped her arms around the trembling shoulders and held her sister close. There was nothing to say. For a long while they stayed like that, the warmth of their bodies merging together, until Zena asked the question she had voiced once before.

'Why did Daddy back off from me so suddenly?'

Alex pulled away gently, releasing her sister. 'I told you, Zena. I don't know.'

Zena's eyes were insistent, would not let her off so easily. 'I don't believe you, Ali. You were old enough to understand. You must know really, but you're refusing to tell me.'

'No, honestly, I . . .'

A broken branch full of buds in the conservatory.

'I don't know.'

Zena laughing up at Daddy. His smile so enthralled he did not notice his elder daughter outside in the garden.

'Zena, he never stopped loving you, I do know that.'

Loving her. The glass cold against her nose as she peered in through the jungle of pinks and greens. Daddy's shirt a crisp white, sleeves rolled up, and shorts neat and navy.

Abruptly Alex stood up, strode over to the window and

drew the curtains. Shutting out the darkness. Shutting out the memory.

'Ali, tell me. Remember.'

Alex did not hear. She remained standing by the window, her hand still holding a fold of the curtain, her eyes tracing the outlines of its flowered pattern. Soft pinks and deep lavender, the colours in her mother's conservatory, the stems fleshy and twisting. Twisting into her mind. Green and leafy. The glass cold as death on her skin. Daddy laughing, eyes wide with pleasure, the strong skilled hands lifting Zena off his lap.

His lap. Shorts navy and neat. But not so neat suddenly. The light material bulged now, no longer flat and loose. Although only eleven, Alex had been around enough animals to know what an erection was. And to know what it was for. She could not make her eyes move away from the navy mound, studying the way the cotton material rose in unaccustomed folds, shading almost to black in the valleys.

The conservatory glass started to mist over from her breath and she wiped a hand across its chill surface. The movement broke the spell and it was then that she looked up. Into eyes as cold as the glass that separated them. Her father was staring back at her, the knowledge of her awareness turning his cheeks the flame colour of one of her mother's geraniums, but he did not rise from the stool. He placed his hands over his lap, large capable hands that covered the treacherous shorts.

Alex ducked away and raced down to the far end of the garden, desperate to outrun the knowledge that was scorching her brain. She threw herself into the hideaway hole deep inside the buddleia bush where it was damp and cool, and was horrified to find she was crying. Eleven-year-olds didn't cry. Maybe Daddy would forget. Maybe he didn't even see her behind all those leaves.

But that cold glass barrier was always there between them after that, so transparent no one else could see it. But Alex could feel it, always there.

Everything changed. Daddy became moody and withdrawn, working longer and longer hours, pushing himself to exhaustion. And pushing her along with him. She remembered it now, all of it. Her mother increasingly short-tempered with him, Zena

baffled at first by the change in him and then angry and difficult.
And all the time Alex had known the breakdown of the family
was her fault. An eleven-year-old's crime. She had locked that
knowledge into a cellar and thrown away the key, but out of
the blue Zena had returned into her life bearing its duplicate.

And Daddy? Was it just a one-off moment of weakness for
which he never forgave himself? It explained why he avoided
Zena like the plague when she was a teenager, so careful not to
allow a repetition.

'Ali.'

Alex realised that she was still holding on to the curtain. She
turned and looked at her sister's expectant face, a face that had
intended to hurt her so badly.

Just as she had hurt Zena. Full circle.

'Ali, what is it?'

Alex returned to the sofa and sat down. 'I've remembered
something that happened years ago. Something that explains
why Daddy changed towards you.'

'What? Tell me.' The words were quick and eager.

So Alex told her.

They were sitting at the kitchen table, drinking coffee. Neither of
them really wanted it, but it gave their hands something to do.

'Poor Daddy,' Zena said for the tenth time and pushed her hair
back from her face, as if to push the thoughts from her mind. She
had fixed her make-up and telephoned for a taxi, despite Alex's
remonstrances, so that they were just killing time until it arrived.
'He never touched me, you know. Not ever in any way that was
improper.'

'No, he wouldn't. He was always big on decency and morals.'
Alex had Hamilton curled on her lap and was stroking the soft
fur over and over, as if to soothe the memories back to sleep.
'But it explains so much.'

'Yes. It explains everything.'

Alex studied her sister's face and behind the shock that was
registered there, she could see the blue sky of relief. Of understanding.

Zena raised her eyes from her coffee. 'His rejection of me

wasn't real. He was trying to protect me. And himself.' Her gaze anchored on the shadows in Alex's dark eyes. 'But what about you? Who was there to protect you?'

'I was.'

Slowly, Zena nodded. 'Yes, that's true. There was only you. Is that what all your need for control is about? All that neatness and order and tidying things away? Everything on a tight rein in case, if you ever let go, all those emotions and memories would stampede through your head, and to hell with your neat and tidy drawers.'

Alex stared in surprise. Was Zena right? Was it so obvious?

And now the cellar door stood wide open. No more secrets to hide away in the dark. Maybe now it would be safe to loosen the reins.

Alex finished her coffee. 'Stay tonight, Zena. If you must go, leave it until the morning. Please.'

'No. It's better if I go immediately.' She gave a low laugh. 'Before you and Rory come after me with hatchets.'

'With muzzle and lead, more like!'

The sisters smiled at each other, wanting more. The sound of the doorbell startled them both.

'My taxi,' Zena said but made no move.

Alex put out a hand. 'Come and see us?'

Zena smiled. 'All right, if I must.'

'And Jamie?'

'You can be damn sure of that. Give him a big kiss from me tomorrow and tell him I'm sorry about the bead.' She blew a kiss, as if it could be popped in the fridge and kept until tomorrow. 'And Ali, love the little blighter for me.'

'Come and love him yourself.'

The doorbell rang again.

Zena stood up. 'You can tell Rory he's got his house and family all to himself again. That'll put a smile on his face, almost as big as when Hill is in pole position.'

'You've already put one there by giving him Jamie.'

'I almost kept him, Ali.'

'Almost. But not quite.'

'No.'

'Maybe you don't need revenge any more?'

Zena smiled so broadly that for a brief moment Alex felt a twinge of unease.

'Maybe I don't,' Zena said and went to answer the door.

When the taxi driver had taken the case and rucksack to stow in the boot, Alex stood with Zena in the hallway.

'Here, take this to smooth the edges.' She handed Zena a cheque. 'I know we've already given you half the agreed money, but save that for when you find a flat.'

Zena glanced at the figures on the cheque, two hundred pounds, and shrugged. 'Thanks.'

There was a silence, as they both sought for words, the rumble of the taxi's engine in the drive reminding them that their time was up.

Alex reached out and hugged Zena. 'Daddy wanted us to be the alpha and omega of his life. The A and the Z. Let's start our own lives now. Thank you for telling me the truth. It's a beginning.'

'If it's truth you want, dear sister, there's more where that came from.'

'What do you mean? Truth about what?'

Zena smiled her cat-smile. 'About Rory. About your husband.'

The taxi rumbled louder as the driver revved the engine impatiently in the darkness. Alex ignored the hint.

'What is it, Zena? What truth about Rory?'

'Sure you want to know?'

'Don't play games. Not now. Just tell me the truth.'

Zena took a long breath and the words came out in a rush. 'Rory is not Jamie's father.'

Alex gasped in disbelief. 'What? Of course he is. The syringes were . . .'

Zena shook her head. 'No, I'm afraid not. After the first failure with those blasted syringes, I thought he might be a dud in the sperm stakes, so I didn't use his dicey donations during the second month. I junked the blasted syringes.'

'You're lying to me, Zena.'

'No. It's the truth, Ali. You asked for it, so here it is. I went looking elsewhere for my stud and found a great one in Rory's friend.'

'Who?' Alex shook her sister's arm. 'Not Marco.'

'No, not after you warned me off him. It was Alan Beecroft.'

'The estate agent?'

'Got it in one.'

'But Jamie looks so like Rory with his dark eyes and . . .'

'Exactly. Have you had a good look at Alan recently? Dark eyes, nice forehead. I called in at his office in Marlborough, we had a drink and he seemed a reasonable choice. So we got it together on several afternoons in one of his empty houses.'

'Does he know?'

'No, of course not. As soon as I was certain I was pregnant, I dumped him.' She leant forward and kissed her sister's flushed cheek. 'Don't look so shell-shocked, Ali. He's still the Jamie you know and love. Still your son.'

The door was open, the taxi waiting. Zena saw Alex shiver, but it was not from the chill night breeze that rustled through the hall as if seeking a hearth to curl up on. Suddenly Zena seized hold of her sister's hand.

'Ali, I'm sorry.' She stared at the damage in the shadowy brown eyes. 'I'm so sorry. I would change it if I could, but I can't. Don't love him any the less for it.'

Slowly Alex shook her head. 'No chance of that. Whatever else may have happened between us, I will always be grateful for Jamie.'

Zena put her arms around Alex, held her close for so long and so tightly that it seemed she had forgotten the taxi, then just as abruptly released her and offered a bright smile instead. 'I guess we can let Daddy rest in peace now, poor bastard. Time to get on with our own lives.'

Alex nodded.

The taxi's engine revved more insistently.

'So that's it, then, Ali.'

'Yes. That's it. It's over.'

'When I'm settled, I'll give you a call.'

'Do that.'

Both sisters looked at each other and both knew the gulf would take time to bridge. A quick embrace, then Zena was gone, out into the darkness. Alex watched her disappear into the taxi with a final wave and wondered if that last bombshell was really the truth, or whether it was Zena's parting shot at disrupting her life. She knew she would never know for certain. But of one thing she was absolutely sure – she would never breathe a word of it to Rory. Never rob him of his fatherhood.

Zena had given them a child. Nothing could alter that and as she watched the red tail-lights of the taxi slide away down the drive, she knew she was the lucky one. Like Zena said, she had everything.

Zena leant back in the taxi and watched the dark silhouettes of the trees flit past like shadowy sentries of the night guarding her secret. She rested her hand lightly on her stomach, stroking it with her fingertips, enjoying the knowledge of the life it contained. Rory's sperm had proved to be spunky little swimmers after all. She wasn't feeling sick at the moment, like she had this morning and yesterday morning. Like she would tomorrow. But this time she did not mind the nausea. She had got what she came for. And more.